Books by Fran Stewart

<u>The Biscuit McKee Mystery Series</u>:

Orange as Marmalade
Yellow as Legal Pads
Green as a Garden Hose
Blue as Blue Jeans
Indigo as an Iris
Violet as an Amethyst

Poetry:

Resolution

For Children:

As Orange As Marmalade/
Tan naranja como Mermelada
(a bilingual book)

Non-Fiction:

From The Tip of My Pen: a workbook for writers

Violet as an Amethyst

Fran Stewart

Violet as an Amethyst
the 6th Biscuit McKee Mystery
Fran Stewart
© 2011

1st edition: © 2011 Fran Stewart

All rights reserved. No part of this book may be used or reproduced in any manner whatsoever without written permission from the author, except by a reviewer who may quote brief passages in a review.

ISBN (Softcover): 978-0-9839777-2-8
ISBN (Hardcover): 9780-9839777-8-0

This is a work of fiction. Any resemblance to any person living or dead is purely coincidental.

This book was printed in the United States of America.

Journey of a Dream Press
PO Box 1565
Duluth GA 30096
www.JourneyofaDream.com

To Polly Hunt Neal
with deep gratitude
for her hospitality and her friendship

"I hold my face in my hands
To keep my loneliness warm."
-- Thich Naht Hahn

The People of Martinsville

Biscuit McKee, librarian in Martinsville, Georgia
    her husband **Bob Sheffield**, the town cop
    her sister **Glaze McKee**
    her cat **Marmalade**
        Excuse me? Widelap is my human

The three "Petunias" (library volunteers)
    Esther Anderson
    Sadie Masters
    Rebecca Jo Sheffield, Bob's mother

Connie Cartwright, glass blower
Cornelia Przybylski and her great-grandson **Hugh**
Dee Sheffield, one of the car pool with Glaze and Maddy
Easton Hastings, a red-haired woman
Father John Ames, priest at St. Theresa's and Maddy's brother
Hank Celer, owner of CelerInc.
Henry Pursey, minister
    his wife **Irene** and daughter **Holly**
Ida Peterson, grocery store owner
Madeleine "Maddy" Ames, Glaze's roommate
Margaret Casperson, wealthy town benefactress
    her husband **Sam**
Melissa Tarkington, newly-engaged owner of Azalea House Bed & Breakfast
Miss Mary, dance instructor
Nathan Young, family physician
Polly Lattimore, nurse
Pumpkin, proprietor of Healthy Self Herb Shop
Red Butler, architect
Reebok Garner, Bob's deputy

Roger Johnson, owner of Mville Garbage
Sharon Armitage, hairdresser
    her husband **Carl**, kenaf farmer and gas station owner
Susan, a visitor to the town
Tom Parkman, owner of restaurant and vocational cooking school
Mrs. Zapota, mother of a missing son, **Charles**

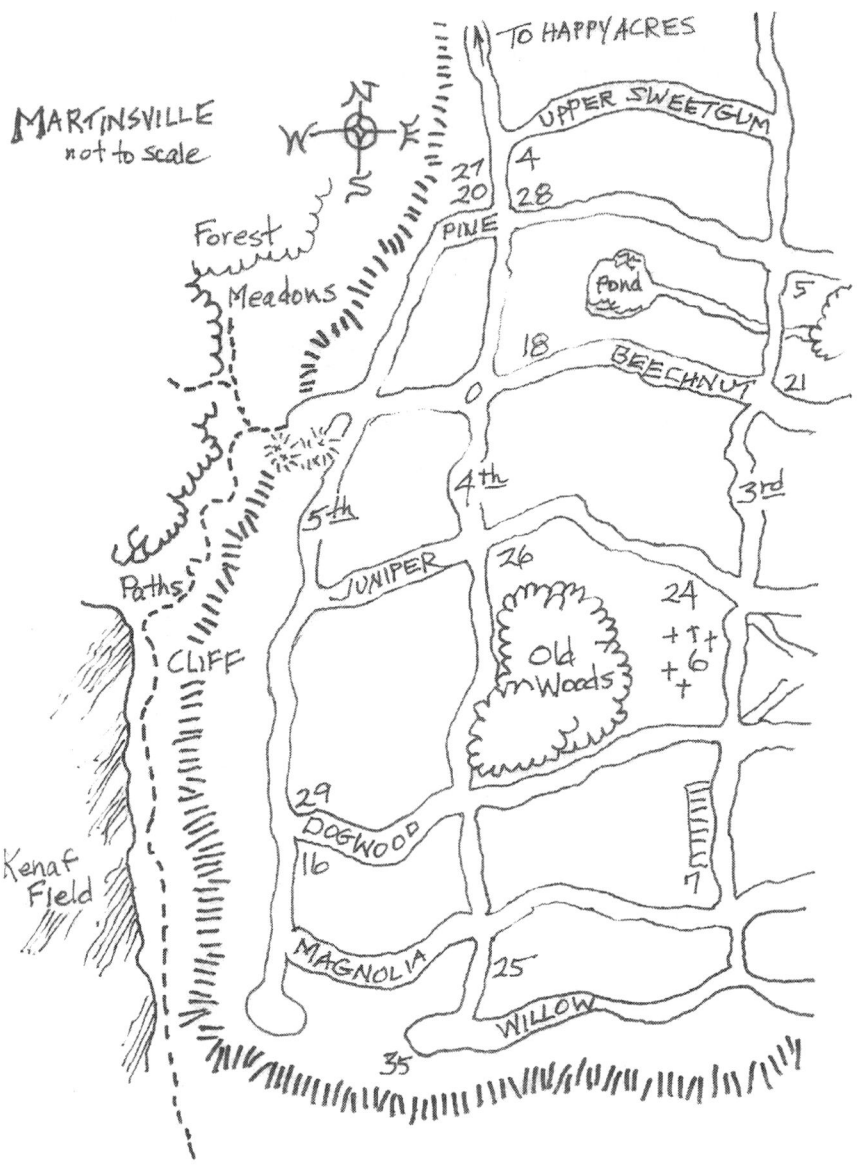

1	Healthy Self Herb Shop	10	DeliSchuss / "The Delicious"
2	Beauty Shop	11	Dr. Nathan Young's office
3	Biscuit & Bob's house	12	Father John Ames / the Rectory
4	Glaze & Maddy	13	Gas Station
5	Brighton & Ellen Montgomery	14	Gazebo in the town park
6	Cemetery	15	Grocery Store
7	Tom's Restaurant / Vocational School	16	Ida & Ralph Peterson's house
8	Chief Movie Theater	17	Library
9	City Hall / Police Station	18	Maggie & Norm Pontiac

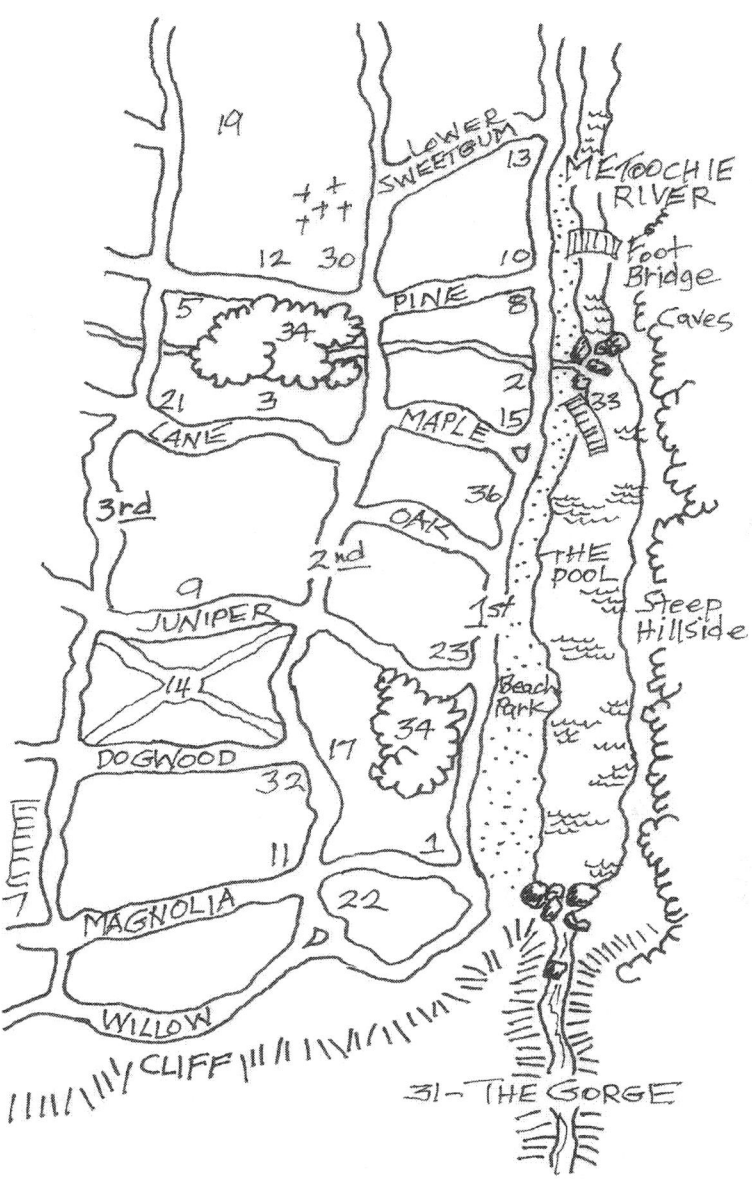

19	Marvin Axelrod's Funeral Home	28	Sadie Masters
20	Mary & R.W. Johnson III	29	Sharon & Carl Armitage
21	Matthew & Buddy Olsen	30	St. Theresa's Catholic Church
22	Melissa Tarkington's Azalea House	31	the Gorge
23	Miss Mary's School of Dance	32	Tom Parkman
24	Old Church	33	Town Dock
25	Rebecca Jo Sheffield & Dee	34	the Old Woods
26	Rev. Henry & Irene Pursey	35	Margaret & Sam Casperson
27	Roger Johnson IV	36	Frank Snellings' Frame Shop

Keagan County
not to scale

- Surreytown
- The Cliff
- County Rd.
- Russell Gap
- Garner Creek
- Hastings
- Metoochie River
- Braetonburg
- Martinsville
- The Pool
- The Gorge
- Enders
- The Lake
- The Cliff

DAY ONE
THURSDAY

CHAPTER 1
2:00 a.m. to 4:00 a.m.

~BISCUIT McKEE~

IT *WAS* A DARK AND STORMY NIGHT, DAMMIT, and I was stuck, gasping for air, desperate for warmth, wedged between two branches of a drowning pine tree as the rain-swollen Metoochie River tried its best to uproot the almost completely submerged tree and drown me. If it didn't freeze me first.

I had no idea who had pushed me from the dock, but I knew I hadn't simply slipped. A moment after I'd sensed I wasn't the only one standing there watching the surge of the storm water, two big hands hit the middle of my back.

What on earth had I been thinking to take a walk at 2 a.m. when I could have stayed curled up next to Bob? Obviously I'd lost my mind, and now I was paying for it.

I prayed for a convenient lightning bolt to strike the man who'd pushed me, whoever he was. I prayed for dawn. I prayed for a friendly boater or a sudden river-drying drought. My only chance was to hang on and hope for rescue. I screamed for help again and again, but heard no answer above the roar of the river. Visions of Snoopy, pounding away at his typewriter on top of his red-roofed cartoon doghouse, careened around inside my muddled head. It was a dark and stormy night; it was a dark and stormy night. I couldn't get beyond that first stupid sentence.

I'd been sound asleep, in the middle of a very satisfying dream, when Marmalade had padded up my leg, over the curve of my hip, and wiggled her way under my arm. Breathing is difficult with a cat against one's nose, so I'd shifted onto my back. She shifted with me and placed her paw over my eyelid. It's hard not to wake up when that happens.

Look outside the window.

I swear, in the middle of the night her purr sounds like a dump truck.

Someone is in the backyard beyond the fence.

I pushed her out of the way—gently, but firmly. "Let me sleep, Marmy," I mumbled. Bob stirred, muttered something but didn't seem to wake up, and settled back down. "Go 'way," I said again as she balanced on my hip like Snoopy on his doghouse roof, and continued to nudge me with her paws and her head.

Come to the window. Come to the window now.

"Shh! Don't wake up Bob."

Now!

When she let out one of her gurgly yarps I gave in. "Awright, Marms." I considered pulling the blanket over my head, but knew she'd never let me get away with it. "What's going on? Did you find a mouse?" I slipped into my robe and stretched as she jumped down and bounded to the big window. Our beautiful private backyard is bordered by woods and precious little else. Everything looked peaceful, the vegetable garden, the shed, and what I could see of the compost pile tucked behind it. The moon, behind a pattern of intermittent clouds, was bright enough to cast shadows from the trees that lean over the chain link fence.

Look!

Marmalade squawked again. I scanned the dark outline of trees against the moon-bright sky. Maybe there was an owl or some other kind of night bird out there.

Mouse droppings!

She snorted and I climbed back into bed. Before I settled in, though, I took one more look out the window. Maybe she'd seen a raccoon, or a possum. If only the creek back in the woods were closer, I'd be able to see it burbling along. I did a bit of my own burbling, and tried to get back to sleep, but after a year or two of tossing—why does everything seem longer in the middle of the night?—I gave up. I slipped out of bed, debated the merits of a cup of chamomile tea versus a long walk. Decided on a short walk and grabbed my sweat pants and a balled-up tee-shirt from the top of the overloaded laundry basket. Something fell on the floor, but I ignored it. I could always pick it up tomorrow.

Bob mumbled and rolled to the middle of the bed. "I'm taking a walk," I whispered. "Want to go with me?

"Why?"

He hadn't answered my question.

"I can't sleep."

"What time is it?"

"About two." I prodded his arm. "Come on. We'll just take a short walk."

He did open one eye—I'll give him that much credit—but only long enough to say, "I'd rather sleep, Woman," and he closed his eye.

I know a lost cause when I see one. "Okay, spoilsport. You'll be sorry you missed it. I'll just walk around the block. Be back soon." I leaned forward to kiss him, but he heaved one of those I'm-almost-asleep sighs and wrapped his arm around my pillow. I settled for laying my hand briefly on his shoulder.

I detoured to the bathroom. I considered flushing, just to wake him up again—our toilet was pretty loud—but decided that would be childish of me, and eased my way down the stairs. Let him sleep if that was what he wanted.

The night air wasn't cold, but it wasn't particularly warm, either. It was a typical mid-summer night in the mountains of northeast Georgia, the foothills of the Appalachians. Our valley tended to stay cooler in the summer and warmer in the winter than the surrounding areas. I heard a distant roll of thunder as I opened the front door, even though it wasn't stormy outside, so I ducked back in and threw on Bob's favorite sweatshirt hanging on the coat rack. He wouldn't mind if I borrowed it. Otherwise I'd have to go back upstairs for one of mine, and that might wake him up. I grabbed my raincoat too, just in case. I debated an umbrella. No. The raincoat had a hood. Anyway, if it rained, who cared? I figured I was drip-dry.

I looked around for Marmalade, who had preceded me down the stairs. She stood in the doorway to the kitchen, outlined against the nightlight we kept on beside the pantry.

"Want to come with me?" I talk to my cat all the time, and she almost always purrs right back at me.

Come out to the backyard, now!

Her purr was more peremptory than usual. "It's not time for breakfast yet; you'll just have to wait—at least till the sun comes up."

Mouse droppings! I am going back to bed.

I eased out the door and closed it gently to the sound of her funny sneezes. Dust in her little nose? She sounded surprisingly like Bob, whose nose had been stuffy lately. Maybe that was why neither one of them wanted to go with me. Well, phooey on them. I'd have a wonderful walk all by myself. Now, which way to head? Uphill, I decided, and turned right at the end of the walkway, power-walking to tire myself out. I used to take slow strolls if I couldn't sleep, but walking fast worked better. I'd get home too tired to think.

Bob had been stewing about something lately. I could tell he had, but each time I asked him if anything was wrong, he'd put me off. "Nothing to worry yourself about," or "I can't talk about it yet," or he'd just change the subject. Doggone, stubborn male. It would be a lot easier if he'd talk it over with me. I thought of all the times I'd talked things over with Melissa, or with Glaze. But then I remembered a book I'd read about how men look at problems differently than women do. He couldn't talk it out with me, not the way I confided in my women friends. What a ridiculous way to go about life. Of course, it might have been police business that had him simmering. Still, I knew how to keep a confidence. Didn't he trust me?

If I'd been smart, I would have headed straight back home right then, to my warm bed, but I was too steamed about that husband of mine. I crossed 3rd Street and chugged my way up to 4th, where I tossed a mental coin—which way?—and turned right toward Pine Street.

This whole block was Maggie and Norm's spread, a mini-farm within the town limits. I listened as I walked along their sturdy fence—heavy-duty because goats are regular Houdini's, or so Maggie had told me—but the barnyard crew were all pretty silent. Fergus, their Great Pyrenees watchdog appeared quietly on my right, probably just checking to be sure I didn't have any predators along with me. "Humans are the worst predators," I whispered to him, "but you wouldn't know that, would you, big guy?" He made a low snort and accompanied me until I turned the corner onto Pine Street, at which point he snuffled again and ambled back to the goats he would spend his whole life protecting.

Someone issued from the street ahead of me, and my heart did a little skippy dance. Bob, I thought. He'd decided to join me. But before I could call out, he turned to his right and walked quickly down Pine Street. He didn't walk with the same rhythm Bob had. It looked like a man, but in the dark I couldn't be sure. Who'd be out on a night like this? Although I didn't like the idea of adding streetlights to our quiet roads, there were times, like this, when they'd be convenient. I looked up at the sky. The moon, which had been shining so steadily a few minutes ago, tossed fitfully among the incoming clouds. I could never see such a sight without thinking of that poem *The Highwayman*. I'd memorized the whole thing when I was in seventh grade. *The moon was a ghostly galleon, tossed upon cloudy seas.* Made shivers run up my spine.

Whoever was walking ahead of me was too far away for me to recognize even if there had been a street light. He crossed Pine Street at an angle. Halfway down that block he turned left into St. Theresa's. Of course! Henry, our minister. He and the Catholic priest, Maddy's brother, were good friends, and it was common knowledge around town that Henry was a member of Father John's prayer team, or whatever they called it. Nobody—no Catholic, that is—had wanted the 2 a.m. to 4 a.m. prayer shift, so Henry had been "filling in." I was willing to bet that tonight he was praying for his wife to hurry home. They were both such dear people.

Way ahead of me I saw headlights turn to their left onto Second Street. Probably Reebok taking his usual turn around town. Bob and I had joked about Reebok's fresh-faced enthusiasm, his rookie determination to protect this town. "It's not a bad idea," Bob had said, "driving around town once or twice each night." In a town with only two police officers, Reebok seemed to want to fill the role of three cops all by himself. But then Bob had spoiled the picture by telling me that he had repeatedly caught Reebok polishing his badge.

At the corner of Pine and Third I had another chance to go home, to head back past Ellen's house, past Matthew's house, and down the remaining half block to home. I was tiring, but wasn't worn out enough yet to get to sleep. And I definitely needed to sleep, because Melissa was probably bringing her fiancé to dinner tomorrow night, or rather, tonight, although Chad had warned Melissa that he might be gone for a few days. Some sort of meeting in Atlanta, but she was pretty vague about its nature.

It was hard to believe I hadn't met him yet, but he wasn't from Martinsville. I thought back to what few conversations I'd had with Melissa recently. I couldn't recall her having mentioned where he was from. In fact, I don't think she'd even told me how they'd met. I'd have to ask her the next time I saw her, whenever that would be. Maybe they'd tell us over dinner.

She and I had grown so close that year I'd rented a room from her, and we'd remained good friends even after I married Bob. The past few months, though, she'd been hard to reach. Other than taking care of her B&B guests at Azalea House, she'd spent most of her evening hours—I wasn't sure about her nighttime ones—with the wonderful, the amazing, the talented Chad. She'd even missed a couple of tap dance lessons, forcing our group to disperse after class rather than heading up the hill for our usual Tuesday night gabfest at Azalea House. And then two Tuesdays ago, she'd waltzed into class with a ring the size of a small boat, an exquisite amethyst surrounded by a circle of small diamonds. Ida thought it looked fake, but for once she'd held her tongue about it and only told me of her suspicions the next day.

I will admit I was a bit miffed that Melissa had made her engagement announcement to the whole class first instead of confiding in me beforehand, but I felt better when she announced, "Of course, Biscuit's going to be my matron of honor." In fact, I already had a dress picked out. I'd chosen it for my sister's wedding, but Glaze had shown no inclination whatsoever toward accepting Tom's frequent proposals, even though we all expected her to cave in eventually.

I walked on down Pine past St. Theresa's, planning what to serve for dinner on the offhand chance that Chad got back from Atlanta in time. All I ever cooked was homemade soup and homemade bread. And ice cream for dessert. Simplicity was best. That way I didn't have to think about convoluted menus. There were plenty of fresh veggies in the garden. That would do it. A thick, rich vegetable soup, with dill bread. I yawned.

The night sounds from various critters in the Old Woods, a stand of original trees that filled most of the block our house was on, had lulled my brain, if not my body, into droopy-eyed somnolence. I almost missed seeing the car parked back underneath the edge of the trees, tucked into a place where no car should be. The weight of a car could damage the roots, compacting the soil and making it harder for the trees to live. The locusts and katydids got quiet all of a sudden, in that eerie way that insects do. I must have disturbed them. "Sorry," I said quietly. It was probably just a couple of kids fooling around in the back seat—something I did not want to confront. In the sudden illumination of a bolt of sheet lightning, I made note of the license plate. Luckily, the plate was an easy number to remember. I'd tell Bob. He loved these trees as much as I did. He'd issue a citation or something. Surely there was an ordinance against parking under such ancient trees. Of course, I'd have to wait to talk with him until he woke up tomorrow morning, even though I'd rather shake him and make him listen to me. I listened to the tone of my thoughts. Picky, picky, picky, Biscuit, I told myself. Let him sleep. So what if he didn't feel like walking in the middle of the night?

I turned downhill to resume my walk. The rains from upriver had been so severe, the Metoochie was swollen well beyond its usual limits, almost as much as during the floods of two years ago. I'd just go take a peek at it from the dock. For no reason whatsoever, I felt like running—it was downhill, and the wind was at my back—and run I did, all the way to the dock, the hood of my raincoat fluttering behind me and my footsteps echoing off the buildings once I crossed 2nd Street. I was in no shape to be doing this, but it felt good, although my legs would probably give out on the uphill climb back home.

I'd barely made it to the end of the dock, when I felt the vibration of someone running up behind me. Before I could turn, I was in the water, gasping from the shock of it.

I struggled against the current, but it was far too strong, so I concentrated on keeping my face above water. Surely the boulders would stop me, the ones at the bottom end of the Pool, the wide section of the Metoochie that formed a favorite swimming place for the town children, although swimming had been forbidden for now with the river this high. Those boulders, piled at the point where the current flowed into a narrow straightaway between towering cliffs, normally served as a barricade to power boats. But now those boulders were far enough under water that I didn't encounter them. Just as well, I might have been dashed to death.

I was pretty sure I was going to drown. Paddling like crazy, with nothing to slow me down, I was swept by the current into the mile-long Gorge. The moonlight was blotted out by the looming cliffs bordering both sides. It was nothing but sheer, bloody luck that I ran right into the pine tree that stood atop what we all called Lone Tree Island, an outcropping of rock three-fourths of the way down the Gorge. Every summer, Lone Tree played host to countless canoes and kayaks whose paddlers picnicked on its meager shore. Small shrubs had taken root, and that one tall sturdy pine. Nobody knew how it managed to hang on, or where it got the nutrients it needed, but the tree had thrived.

When I rammed into the tree, it knocked the

breath out of me—what little breath was left. Gratefully, because I'm not much of a swimmer under the best of circumstances, and these were not good circumstances at all, I pulled myself up onto that branch, and then higher. I had to get out of the water. All those Red Cross lessons about water safety came back. There was no way I could survive much longer in the water. I couldn't, could not, let myself be pulled back into that raging river. My legs felt like watermelons and my arms were even worse. At that point, I could still think relatively straight. Hypothermia. That was my greatest danger. When I didn't come home, Bob would send out search parties. They'd find me. But I had to be alive when they did. I couldn't die.

Marmalade! Who would take care of Marmy? Bob would. He loved her as much as I did. This was ridiculous. He'd find me. He had to. Of course, if he'd come on the walk with me, this never would have happened. A tiny hot spot of rage tightened my throat. Or maybe we both would be here. The tree wouldn't hold us both. He was a better swimmer than I was.

My thoughts kept revolving, like one of those doors going around and around, pulling fragments in and spewing them out and not getting anywhere.

I couldn't die. My laundry wasn't done, and I hadn't flushed the toilet. Glaze would come to help Bob pack up my things and she'd find dirty clothes and a toilet full of stale—I didn't want to think about it.

I hoped the tree could hang on until the water receded. It had made it through the floods two years ago. Surely it would stay firm through this one.

I clambered, screaming for help, up one more branch, high enough to be completely out of the water but not so high as to worry about whether the branches would support my weight. My teeth were chattering. Not a good sign. I zipped up the raincoat the rest of the way—not an easy task curled against the scratchy trunk of a pine tree. I reached behind me to dump excess water out of the hood and pulled it up over my head. The danger would be falling off the branch, but I had to get curled into a ball to conserve as much body heat as I could. With hands that were losing feeling, I groped around the trunk. On the other side of it, what I thought was the downriver side, the branches were thicker, and closer together. I pulled my way around there, unable to see where I was going, wishing I had gloves on, and getting a face full of sharp pine needles.

I wedged myself as best I could between three branches, two big interlocked ones that held most of my weight, and a smaller one above them that pushed against my hip, reminding me of Marmalade perching on that very spot of my anatomy. That should hold me. I curled into the smallest ball I could possibly make, pulled the hood down as far as it would go, and breathed on my frozen fingers. I sure could have used that cup of chamomile tea. It was then I remembered to scream again. "Lone Tree Island!" That way they'd know where I was. "Lone Tree!" But I finally gave up. It took too much energy. Nobody would be listening at this time of night anyway. I settled down to wait for dawn. I'll probably be dead by then, I thought, but my bright purple raincoat will be easy to spot. They'll find my body. If the water doesn't rise any higher.

Then I thought about my un-flushed toilet again. I will not die. I stuffed my frozen fingers in my mouth two at a time to warm them. I tasted blood and pine sap. I will not die. I need to kiss Bob. I will not die. I need to hold Marmalade again. It was a dark and stormy night. It was a dark—

CHAPTER 2
Thursday 2:00 a.m. to 5:00 a.m.

~HENRY PURSEY~

THE REVEREND HENRY PURSEY SETTLED HIS REAR END into one of the short pews in St. Theresa's prayer chapel, but he couldn't settle his mind. He'd heard from Irene. She said she'd be home this weekend, but he wasn't sure things were settled between them. She'd told him she needed some time, and she'd taken off to visit her sister in Ohio. A month ago.

Didn't twenty-three years of marriage count for something? What did she need to think about?

Henry rearranged his back end on the hard wooden pew and took a very deep breath. He knew what she had to think about. She had a husband who was a durn fool; that was what she had to think about.

He usually had no problem waking at 1:50 and getting here by 2:00. When Irene was there beside him, he felt like life just rolled along the way it was supposed to. But this morning he'd been late getting up from that half-empty bed, late getting here to the prayer chapel. Usually he never saw a soul on his way here. Tonight he'd seen one car and before that, he thought he might have heard some footsteps up the block behind him. Ordinarily he would have turned to greet the fellow night-time traveler, but tonight he simply didn't feel very companionable.

The statue on the little altar in front of him didn't move, but Henry got the idea that maybe she thought he was worrying too much. He'd stay till a bit after 4:00 so he could give his full two hours of prayer. That wouldn't make Irene any happier, but it felt like the right thing to do. Of course he hadn't prayed once since he walked in the door. He leaned forward, put his elbows on his knees, and rested his face in his cupped palms. And tried to pray.

FRAN STEWART

~REEBOK GARNER~

Deputy Reebok Garner, named for an African antelope by parents who were unaware of high-priced running shoes, always polished his badge before he took his usual turn around the town. Every evening before work, and at least once around midnight, he drove up and down every street in Martinsville. He enjoyed the night shift. The dark was friendly. He was a night owl anyway. He never could understand people who were bright and alert at sunrise. Their cheery early morning smiles always intimidated him. Luckily he'd found this job, where he could work when he wanted to.

He put one final finishing flourish on his badge and checked his watch. Two a.m. A lot later than usual. He'd gotten busy cleaning out the filing cabinet and answering what few calls came in, mostly lonely people wanting to talk to someone who would listen. Maybe he'd cut his regular route a little short and only drive the south end of town. Maybe he'd just forget it this once. It wasn't like it was on his job description. Nothing ever happened, anyway. He'd make a fresh pot of coffee and put his feet up on the desk, like the Chief did sometimes. No, he needed to stick to his routine. Drive every street. Then he could come back and put his feet up.

The trouble was, he thought as he slid into his car, there wasn't anyone else to answer calls at night. But he still felt he needed to drive along each street, checking the houses and businesses. Nestled at the bottom end of a dead-end valley, dead-end except for the outlet of the Metoochie River that passed through the Gorge, Martinsville was an incredibly sleepy little village. Burglary was unheard of. There'd been only one car accident in all the time since he'd taken the job, when Mr. Harper had a minor stroke and sideswiped Ida Peterson's car. He'd bumped up over a curb, taking out four of her prize rose bushes in the process. And that fatal crash up the valley awhile back, when little Willie's mother was killed, but the Braetonburg force had handled that one.

He took a quick turn around town. Up 1st Street, left onto Pine, another left and down 2nd Street, back and forth through the dark, quiet village. Nothing moved except the wind. Just before he'd turned left onto Second Street he'd seen Henry crossing Pine Street to go pray. Everybody knew he did that, even though Henry thought he was anonymous. The couple who had the midnight to 1 a.m. shift had stayed an hour late one night, and they'd seen him come in. Nobody could keep a secret in a small place like Martinsville.

This cruising around town was a waste of time, really, but he'd done what he considered his duty. Now it was time for that coffee.

The office was quiet, as usual. Reebok wondered briefly what it would be like to have another police officer to talk to during the long stretches of the night shift. Every other town in the valley had at least five officers—some had even more than that. So what if those towns had more than twice the population of Martinsville? Martinsville was growing. Look at all those new houses north of town. Happy Acres. He loved the friendly sound of that name. When he'd driven through there Wednesday evening before beginning his shift, the whole subdivision had been just that—happy.

He'd cruised through the numerous cul-de-sacs of the new neighborhood, his open window inviting in the sounds of the summer evening. Birds on the final feeding frenzy of the day fluttered around front yard bird-feeders, rising with a clearly audible whoosh of feathers as Reebok's car neared. Music drifted from the piano teacher's house as the professor pounded the keys. That Mozart guy, Reebok thought, or maybe Bach. He wasn't really up on that sort of music. He noted license plates as he went. Not that he wrote down the numbers. He mostly just checked to be sure they had a current registration. Those little stickers in the lower right-hand corner were easy to spot. Farther along the street a different sort of music had poured from a corner house where a would-be high school band practiced every chance they could get. Reebok was young enough to appreciate their musical style, but even to his untrained ears, the emanations from the dark brown house needed work, a lot of work.

Reebok paused in his reminiscences to pour another cup of coffee. He loved the smell of coffee. In fact, he liked all kinds of smells. In Happy Acres, wonderful dinnertime odors wafted out of the houses. One house smelled like his dad's grilled chicken. How long did smells linger? How long did the memory of a smell last? His dad had been dead three years, and all it took was a breeze in the right direction over an outdoor barbeque, and Reebok was home again.

He shook himself and went back to recalling his drive. Right after the grilled chicken smell, he'd passed two young couples out for an evening stroll. Then he stopped short as a tiny white Chihuahua ran out in front of his car, followed almost immediately by a medium-sized brown dog. Both dogs bounded across a lawn toward a man wearing a Hawaiian shirt, and Reebok had waved when the man shouted a quick apology. That Chihuahua sure was cute. When Reebok was a little kid, the people who lived next door had a white Chihuahua named Seven, because it had the perfect shape of a seven in black hairs right in the middle of its back. Reebok wondered what had happened to that little dog. Still reminiscing about his childhood, he'd turned right into the next side street, driven to the cul-de-sac at the end of it, and circled back around. When he turned back onto the main street through Happy Acres, he paused as a car in front of his slowed to a stop to pick up a man waiting at the curb. Current license. Vanity plate, nothing but letters. Two teenagers crossed the street in front of him, holding hands. Young love. I'll get a girlfriend someday, Reebok thought. There must be someone around like Miss... He squelched that thought. There was nobody like her. He circled the block, nodding to passersby. Another vanity plate, this one nothing but numbers, probably the owner's birthday or anniversary. This section of town was full of vanity plates. Reebok briefly wondered why and then forgot about it.

All the usual goings on of a sleepy village. Even so, Reebok had straightened his back and gripped the wheel more firmly as he drove back to the station. Things could go wrong. And he couldn't be on duty all the time. He felt bad about that, but at least they had the 911 center up in Russell Gap. It serviced the whole valley.

He wished he had a real police car instead of just using his own wheels. He had one of those flashing lights he could slap onto the roof if he needed to. Trouble was, he'd never needed it. So why did he need a real police vehicle?

There had been so much talk recently about all the money Margaret Casperson plowed into the town. He was going to ask her—well, he supposed he'd have to go through channels and propose his idea to the Chief first. He pulled a yellow legal pad from the desk drawer and started listing the reasons why the department could do with a full-time dispatch staff. First of all, someone was needed to handle the phone calls 24/7. He wrote that down. Only there weren't that many calls. The town hall secretary answered the phone during the day if the Chief was out, and the Chief had a pager so she could contact him. But she left at five, and the Chief usually left before six, and then it was just Reebok. Maybe there wasn't such a need. He started to cross out number 1.

Instead, he added a number 2. If something went really wrong, two people weren't enough. They needed a dispatcher, but they needed another officer even more. The Chief kept telling Reebok he couldn't work such long hours, but Reebok had argued that there wasn't any reason he couldn't hang out at the station. Just in case. They didn't even have to pay him for all those extra hours. His mother told him repeatedly he needed to get a life. But he *had* a life, one he loved.

Number 3. Two cruisers, one for him and one for the new officer, the *junior* officer. Reebok liked the sound of that.

The phone rang. "Yes, Sir?... No, I haven't seen her... I can't hear you, Sir. What's that noise?... Are you sure, Sir?... Right away, Sir." Not even pausing to shine his badge, he grabbed his car keys and ran.

~~~~~

~SHARON ARMITAGE~

Sharon Armitage was only vaguely aware of her husband heaving his bulk up to a sitting position. She yawned and turned on her side. "What's wrong, Carl?" She didn't really want to know. She'd rather sleep.

"I feel kind of funny. I need a drink of water." He waited.

She was almost sound asleep and Carl needed water? He wouldn't drink it right out of the tap. Oh no, it had to have ice in it. It was... she took a quick look at the lighted clock dial... three ridiculous minutes after two. She absolutely refused to get up and walk into the kitchen to get him ice water. Let him get his own. Yep. She had to open the hair salon earlier than usual in the morning and she needed her sleep. She waited him out.

Finally, with a martyred sigh, he got to his feet. "I'm gonna go outside for awhile. It's too hot in here."

Sharon mumbled something, turned over, and was back asleep within seconds.

At 2:45 Carl fell beside the bed, moaning and clutching his left arm. Sharon dialed 911 in a panic. *I should have fetched him the water.*

~~~~~

~CORNELIA PRZYBYLSKI~

Cornelia Przybylski, long-time resident of Enders, Georgia, couldn't sleep. Her oldest great-grandson, who was staying with her over the summer, had gone out right after dinner, and he wasn't back yet. This was ridiculous. She'd had plenty of sleepless nights when her children were little and even more so when they were in their teens. Now, with Hugh a responsible young man almost through college, only one more year to go, she still felt obliged to remain awake until she knew he was inside safe and sound. She hadn't even put on her pajamas yet. Silly to sit around the house in pajamas.

Cornelia knew her friends called her a tough old bird. Well, that she was. Tough. As tough as they came, even now in her eighties. A little slower than before, maybe, but tough. She'd had some problems that had slowed her way down a couple of years ago, but she'd bounced back. She was better than ever now.

Just an hour or so ago she'd listened to the late-night radio station, and it said they'd found the body of a woman floating face down in Enders Lake. Asked if anybody knew of a missing woman. Poor thing. What a way to die. Cornelia had always respected the water. She'd never been afraid of it, but by golly, she respected it. She'd lived here in Enders all her life, and that lake had killed five people that she could remember. Now here was a sixth one. Come to think of it, the lake wasn't the culprit. Stupidity was the problem. She'd be willing to bet that woman hadn't worn a life vest. She'd probably never learned to swim either.

All of Cornelia's children and grandchildren and great-grandchildren—how could she have lived long enough to have those?—could swim like little dolphins.

She heard the front door creak open. There was a reason she'd never had those hinges oiled. "Hugh," she called. He was the biggest of her dolphins, and she loved him dearly. "Is that you?"

"Of course it is, Grana. Who else would it be? Why are you still up?"

She ignored his question and raised her cheek for a peck; that was about all she ever got from Hugh, who was shy to the point of... No. He wasn't shy exactly. He was more self-effacing. Not like Hugh's seventeen-year-old sister, who always had a big hug for her great-grandmother, but who also had to be the center of attention. "Why've you been out so late?"

She heard a sharp intake of breath, but he'd schooled his face by the time she glanced up at him. "I've been trying to get the Susie Q's radio working."

"Well, did you?"

"Sorry, Grana. I couldn't figure out what was wrong."

She looked up at the grandfather clock. "You worked on that radio till almost three in the morning?"

Hugh looked a bit sheepish. "Oh Grana, with the river flowing so fast and high, I was worried about Susie, so I decided to keep her company for awhile."

Cornelia chuckled. Boats never had a problem with

rising water. They just floated on top unless some durn fool tied them up with no slack in the bow line. "That boat," she said with real affection in her voice. "I think my old runabout is the reason you agreed to stay here with me this summer."

"Not fair, Grana. I'm repairing your roof."

"And doing a lovely job of it." He was built like a Greek god. Strong as a horse. I'm being trite, she thought. But he *was* strong. How she and that scrawny husband of hers—rest his soul—could have come up with the genes to contribute to such a specimen, she'd never know. She smiled up at him and patted his hand. "I enjoy listening to you singing while you're up there hammering."

Hugh got one of those funny looks, one Cornelia couldn't decipher. "What?" she asked. "What's wrong."

"Nothing." He rolled his shoulders back and swiveled his head around. "It's just that I... Talk about singing, when I was down at the landing just now, I thought I heard somebody singing from up in the Gorge. Maybe not singing exactly, but it had words."

Hugh wasn't the sort to be taken with fancy. "What kind of words?" she asked him.

He shuffled his feet. "Kind of high-pitched and... kind of like a ..." He shook his head. "It sounded like 'Lone Tree.' It went on for a minute or two, and then it stopped."

Cornelia held her hand out for some support. The old bones didn't shift as well as they used to, but she'd have to be doggone near death before she'd let somebody drown. She'd worked water rescue years ago, when she was younger. And she could still steer circles around anybody when she was at the wheel of the Susie Q.

"Come on, don't just stand there. Get me my slicker, and let's get out of here."

"Grana, what—"

"Close your mouth, boy, get your rear in gear, and

grab your wetsuit. I'll drive, but you're the one who's going to have to jump in the water."

    Cornelia always kept the Susie Q stocked with survival gear. Life vests and life rings aplenty and warm blankets stowed in a waterproof unit. She'd checked the batteries on the heavy-duty searchlight only last week. "You topped off the fuel tanks?" she hollered back across her shoulder as she stepped gingerly over the hull.
    "Yes, Grana. But I don't see why we're—"
    "You heard a voice, Hugh." She fumbled with her key. Darned arthritis. "Where there's a voice, there's a person. And a wet person won't last long on a night like this. Hurry now. We need to cast off!" She eased the Susie Q out of the slip and headed for the gaping mouth of the Metoochie River.

~~~~~

~PUMPKIN~

Shouting and loud thumps blended with Pumpkin's dream. She had no idea how long she'd sat there in her robe and pajamas, slumped in her easy chair. What time was it anyway? Her book had fallen from her lap and lay splay-paged over the base of her floor lamp. She rubbed her hand over her face and felt a trail of drool down her chin. Disgusting.
    More shouts and pounding, like a fist against her front door. They'll break those old glass panes, she thought. She stepped into her cow slippers, the ones with MOO stitched on the insteps and a pink nose where her toes went. She'd inherited those—sort of—from Annie McGill, the woman who used to live here.
    More shouts—the words were indistinguishable. Tying

her robe, she hurried downstairs, flipping on lights as she went.

She began to make out words as she opened the door at the bottom of the staircase, flipped on the lights, and entered her shop. Beyond the shelves of organic, all-natural, environmentally-conscious products, she saw a man outside the door. He wore a black wetsuit. He waved his hands at her and yelled again. "Help! Call 911!"

~~~~~

~REEBOK GARNER~

Reebok and the Chief met up back at the station. "I've been up and down all the numbered streets," the Chief told him.

"Yes, Sir. And I've driven all the east-west ones." This town was laid out on a grid, made possible by the topography. The streets running parallel to the river, all five of them, stretched the length of the town north to south. Those streets were numbered; First Street ran next to the river; Fifth Street hugged the cliff. The streets that ran up the steep incline away from the river were the east-west ones.

"We start waking people up." The Chief grabbed the phone on his desk. "I'll start with Glaze. You call Melissa. And get Tom."

Reebok stepped over to his desk and dialed Azalea House. Melissa Tarkington was one of Miss Biscuit's best friends. "Miss Melissa," he said as soon as she picked up, "Miss Biscuit's missing, have you seen her?" He looked at a yellow sticky note the Chief handed him. "We're meeting at the station as soon as you can get here."

Tom was next. "We're going to plot out a map, and assign blocks for everyone to search so we don't miss anywhere."

"Be right—" Tom hung up before he finished his sentence.

Before Reebok could call Dr. Nathan, the phone rang. "Martinsville Police, Deputy Garner here."

"This is the 911 operator in Russell Gap. We received a call for an ambulance at the Martinsville town dock. A woman suffering severe hypothermia was reported."

"Chief! Ambulance to the dock!"

"Your town ambulance," the operator continued, unflappingly, "is on its way back from an earlier run carrying a heart attack to Russell Gap."

"Who had a heart attack?"

"I don't have that information. But your ambulance should be at the dock within minutes."

"Uh, thank you. We'll get right on it."

Reebok couldn't catch up to the Chief, who'd peeled his car in a loud screeching u-turn from in front of the station. He saw Melissa and Tom running across the town green. "She's at the dock. Hypothermia. Get in!" They both scrambled into the back seat and Reebok sped down Juniper.

One of the ambulance crew bent over a gurney, pressing some sort of instrument against Miss Biscuit's head. It had to be her. Had to be. Two people Reebok didn't recognize moved away from the Chief and walked to one side to join—was that Pumpkin? He couldn't tell for sure. The tall one, the one in a wet suit, blocked Reebok's view of her.

Reebok turned when a car zoomed to a stop. Glaze and her roommate Madeleine tumbled out of it. "We saw the lights. Is it Biscuit? Is she okay?" Glaze ran toward the stretcher but was restrained by the ambulance driver.

She's dead, Reebok thought. She looks dead. The flashing red lights from the ambulance made her face look gray. And she wasn't moving, hardly even shivering. That, he knew from what he'd read, was a bad sign.

One of the medics spoke to the Chief, although he never took his eyes off Biscuit as the other medic checked to be sure the straps were secure. Everyone leaned closer to hear what he said. "We're taking her to the Montrose Clinic, Bob. I don't think she can make it all the way to the hospital. We'll do our best, but, her temp is below 90 degrees." He gestured to the implement in his hand. "This is just a quick reading. Her core temp could be higher than that, but we don't dare take the chance."

The Chief didn't even answer the man, just clambered into the ambulance and settled down next to Biscuit, leaving Reebok behind. *That was the way it had to be,* Reebok thought, *but I'd give anything if I could help her.* He ground the toe of his shoe into the sand that littered First Street.

"Will she be all right?" The small voice next to him quivered on the last two words.

Two slippers with MOO written on them appeared beside his boot. The moonlight was bright enough to show the black and white pattern on the slippers. Cows. *Miss Biscuit is dying, and I'm here looking at cow slippers.* "I don't know, Miss Pumpkin. We'll just have to hope."

"She needs to be at the hospital in Russell Gap," Glaze said, with steadily increasing panic evident in her voice.

"The Montrose Clinic is good." Tom laid a hand on Glaze's shoulder. "They don't have an emergency room, but their staff is top-rate. They'll take good care of her."

"I'm headed to the Clinic. Anyone want to ride along with me?" Glaze spun around, not waiting for an answer, and sprinted toward her car.

Maddy and Melissa piled in the back and Tom up front with Glaze.

Reebok turned to Pumpkin. "Do you have any idea what happened?"

She motioned to the two people waiting off to one side. A tall young man, the one in the wet suit, with a blanket wrapped around his shoulders, held his arm out to one of the wrinkliest women Reebok had ever seen and escorted her up to the street. "Cornelia Przybylski," the woman said. "And this is my great-grandson, Hugh. He needs a place to change out of his wetsuit so we don't have a second hypothermia case on our hands."

"I thought wetsuits kept you warm," Reebok said.

The old woman chuckled. "Spoken like somebody who's never been in one."

Reebok started to speak, but she kept right on talking. "Wet suits keep you relatively warm while you're in the water, but once you're out in the air, they act like any sort of wet clothing." Her head swiveled around like a bird dog searching for a scent. "And in a breeze like this, they're downright cold."

"Come down to Healthy Self." Pumpkin motioned down the street. "That's my herb shop. I live above it." She nodded to the young man. "You can take a hot shower. Will that help?"

"Thank you, ma'am." His teeth were chattering. "It sure will."

Reebok thought Pumpkin seemed a bit surprised at being called "ma'am." She looked about the same age as the young man. The fact that Reebok was that same age himself didn't matter at the moment. "Why don't all of you come on down to the shop?" Pumpkin said. "I'll make us a nice pot of hot tea."

"You hurry on, Hugh," Mrs. Whatever-her-name-was said. "I'll walk along more slowly with the Sheriff here."

"Deputy, ma'am. Deputy Garner."

"So who was this wet young woman, Deputy?"

"The Chief's wife, ma'am. Her name is Biscuit McKee."

"Was that Chief McKee who went with her in the ambulance? He looked mighty worried."

"Sheffield is his name. She kept her old name when they got married."

"Humph. Young people do that nowadays."

"She's not exactly young, ma'am. I think she's in her fifties." Way too old to be interested in him. Anyway, she loved the Chief. That was pretty obvious.

Cornelia skewered him with her glance. "Like I said, she's young. When you're as old as I am, you'll think fifty is spring-chicken years." She humphed a bit more. "Sheffield. Sheffield, you say?"

"Yes, ma'am."

"Name sounds familiar. I think I met him a few years ago."

~~~~~

~HENRY PURSEY~

Henry closed the door of St. Theresa's prayer chapel quietly. He always felt bad leaving the place empty when nobody showed up on time for the 4 a.m. shift. Ordinarily he would have considered staying an extra hour, but he had an early morning counseling session, and it wouldn't do to spend the whole time yawning.

He'd come to look forward to these two quiet hours every night. He'd heard that 2 a.m. was the dark night of the soul, the time when people were most likely to lose hope, to be awash in fear. Tonight, he could truly believe that. This had been his own dark night; he was so afraid of what was coming.

He paused next to John's community garden. It was growing well, what Henry could see of it, especially those tomato plants. A siren, coming from down around First

Street, interrupted his thoughts. "There's someone other than myself I can pray for," he muttered and headed for home.

~~~~~

~REEBOK GARNER~

Reebok felt himself relax in the cozy atmosphere of Healthy Self. When Pumpkin had taken over the store after Annie's death, she'd changed the name. It used to be *Heal Thyself,* but Pumpkin had told Reebok she thought that sounded stuffy. So she'd just moved the space over three letters. Reebok liked it better this way.

Pumpkin settled everyone in her office, a pleasant room behind the shop with several couches and a tiny kitchen. Hugh, warm now, with his chest swaddled in a spare robe of Pumpkin's and a blanket wrapped around the rest of him like a kilt, sat beside his grandmother. He'd left his dry clothes in the boat.

"Let me finish my tea first, boy," his grandmother told him, "and then I'll run down and get them for you."

"I can do it, ma'am," Reebok offered, "if you'll tell me where to look." He wasn't much of a boat person, but he couldn't let a frail old lady go walking around in the dark.

He found the clothes tucked inside a waterproof bin right near the front of the boat, just like Cornelia said they would be. She'd said *the bow,* of course, and had laughed at him when he asked if that was the front or the back. *It's the pointy end,* she'd told him.

Just as he got back to Pumpkin's, the clouds moved in and a downpour began.

"Thank you," Hugh said as he took the clothes. "I didn't think about them while I was trying to get help. Grana's radio isn't working, and we had to find a phone quick." He turned toward Pumpkin. "Your light was the only one we could see on the whole street."

"I'm sure that's true. All of the other places along here are businesses. I'm the only one who lives above my shop."

"It's a good thing you were still awake," Reebok said.

She got a funny look on her face, but he couldn't tell what it meant.

"Yes." She wiped her hand over her chin. "Yes, I'm glad I was… awake."

Hugh left to get dressed, and silence settled over the rest of them. Cornelia's bright yellow slicker and Hugh's wet suit, both draped over chairs, dripped onto the braided rag rug.

"Tell me what happened," Reebok said when Hugh came back downstairs. They recounted as much as they knew. It was anybody's guess why Biscuit had been in the water to begin with. "She's not a swimmer," Reebok told them. "She told me once that she could do a dog paddle and that was about it."

"Then she's luckier than I'd have expected, finding her way to the Lone Tree." Cornelia raised her mug as if to toast Biscuit. "Susie and I had a hard time holding against the current."

"Susie?" Reebok jumped to his feet. "Is she still with the boat?" He hadn't seen anyone when he went for the clothes, but maybe she was in that cabin sort of place. "I didn't see her there. I'll go invite her in."

Cornelia gave him a quizzical look, turned to Hugh, and the two of them exploded in laughter. "You'd have a hard time getting her here," she said.

"She's awfully heavy," Hugh added between guffaws.

Cornelia practically spluttered. "She never could walk very well, either."

"And I don't think she likes tea." The two of them were

almost doubled over.

Reebok was indignant. Was she disabled, this Susie they were making fun of? How dare they?

Cornelia held up her hand. "You see, Deputy, this Susie you want to invite for tea ..." She chuckled a bit longer. "She's the Susie Q. My runabout."

When Reebok looked blank she spread her hands and added, "My boat?"

It took him about five seconds before his belly started to quiver and he joined in the laughter.

Pumpkin called the clinic at 5:15. Biscuit was still unconscious, listed as critical. She spoke with Bob and relayed what Cornelia and Hugh had told her.

"He said he'd call me when she regains consciousness," she said as she hung up, "but I'd be surprised if he does."

Reebok was incensed. He squared his shoulders. "The Chief always does what he says he's going to do."

Pumpkin frowned slightly. She sat back down and looked at the cows on her feet, turning her slim ankles one way and then another. "I'm sure he does, but he's awfully worried right now. I wouldn't expect him to remember." Turning to Cornelia, she said, "I sure hope you're going to wait for the rain to stop before you leave. These couches both make out into beds. You can get some sleep before you try to take... Susie... back downriver to Enders." Was it his imagination? Reebok thought she might have looked up at him and suppressed a smile when she said "Susie."

Cornelia and Hugh held one of those conversations carried on only with looks, eyebrows, shrugs, and nods. Reebok gathered the general gist of it. He was right. "We'd be happy to rest a little," Cornelia said, "but we'll have to get an early start. The weather forecast said the storms upriver are ending. The level's going to drop soon. We've got to get the Susie Q past those boulders before that happens, or she'll be stuck here until the next flood."

"It'll be light in another hour, Grana." The clock over Pumpkin's desk said 5:23. "It wouldn't do to face those rocks in the dark. Let's rest until then and we'll leave right at dawn."

Before he left, Reebok took down their names and phone number. Cornelia had to spell her last name two extra times before he got it right. He couldn't see how a name that sounded like Shuh-bill-ski could possibly start off with a P and an R and a Z, but she'd told him it was a good old Polish name. He drove his own car back up to the station. He'd grab his raincoat and walk back down to retrieve the Chief's car.

"Miss Biscuit, please don't die."

The only thing that answered him was the unrelenting downpour.

CHAPTER 3
Thursday 8 a.m. to 10 p.m.

~BISCUIT McKEE~

THE ROOM I WOKE IN WASN'T MY OWN. This room was beige and boring. But it was warm. Something tickled the back of my hand. "Bisque?" said a soft voice.

The voice and the tickle both reminded me of lamb's ears, that fuzzy gray-green plant that lined one of the garden paths at the library. The library. The place I worked. I knew that much. But that name. Nobody called me Bisque. I was Biscuit. Biscuit McKee. The voice seemed familiar though. I turned my head far enough to the left to see him, and my ear connected with fabric, something billowy and warm.

"Bisque," he said again.

"Bob." My croaking voice felt like it was dragging a salt-hardened rope up through my scream-roughened throat.

"She's awake." It was a voice I didn't know. That voice picked up my other hand and took my pulse. "Good." It tucked the blankets—there were a lot of them—more firmly around me. "I'll get Dr. Prescott in here." She looked like a nurse. A stethoscope around her neck.

My parents stood at the foot of the bed, between my son and my Auntie Blue. All four looked worried and relieved at the same time.

I tightened my grip on Bob's fingers. "You... found me."

"Not me, Bisque." He shifted his rear end closer to me on the narrow hospital bed and feathered my hair away from my eyes with his free hand.

Over his shoulder I could see my sister, hovering. Her eyes were red. She was a good swimmer, unlike me. "Come here, you," I said. I inhaled her sweet vanilla-scented perfume as she leaned down to kiss my forehead. "Are you the one who found me?"

Glaze shook her head and pushed back her prematurely white hair. Our grandmother's hair. She was younger than I was, but she'd been white-haired for two decades, ever since her mid-twenties. She shook her head again, as if she were unwilling to speak, and adjusted the warm pillow thing closer to my neck.

"Neither one of us," Bob said. "Do you remember Cornelia Przybylski?"

"Shuh-BILL-ski?" I could barely get the name out, much less remember who it was.

"That old, old woman I met down in Enders a couple of years ago."

It was beginning to come back. "The next-door neighbor," I said. "The one with all the Ps and Zs in her name? The bird-watcher?"

"Right. Her grandson apparently heard you calling, only he thought it was a ghost or something. When he told his grandmother, she insisted on driving her boat up to Lone Tree. He jumped in the water and got you out of the tree somehow or other. Said you were wedged in there just above water level."

"Wedged in." Yes. That sounded right. "I remember. I was afraid I'd fall off the branch. I was so, so cold."

Bob cradled my chin in his big, comforting, warm hand, the other hand, the one I wasn't holding onto. "He almost couldn't get you loose. You were ..." His palm Braille-read the map of my jawline. "You were completely unconscious. Mrs. Przybylski forced that boat of hers the rest of the way up the Gorge against the current to our town dock, and the ambulance brought you here."

"Where am I?"

"The Montrose Clinic. Garner Creek. The ambulance crew said you'd lost so much body heat they didn't think you'd make it all the way up the valley to the big hospital."

"Montrose. The place ..." My mind was so fuzzy. "The place where Glaze got the cast on her finger?"

"That's a good sign," a voice interrupted from the doorway. "If you're remembering things like that, you must be getting better." I'd never met Dr. Prescott, but Glaze had told me about her. I couldn't imagine they had two female doctors here with such thick glasses.

Glaze stepped to the foot of the bed, out of the doctor's way, and Bob started to stand, but the doctor waved him back down. "You stay right there. I imagine your wife needs something to hang onto other than a cold tree." She took one of those little light things out of her pocket and shone it in my eyes. "Next time you go walking at night, how about you stay away from the river?"

I considered that for longer than it should have taken me to make sense of it. "I didn't do it on purpose," I said. "Somebody, somebody ..." I yawned. My eyes wouldn't stay open. "Pushed me," I managed to say.

My mom gasped, and Bob went all still, except for one hand which tightened painfully on mine. A good painful. I tried to hang onto it, but I felt myself slipping away.

"Who pushed you? Off the dock, you mean?"

I nodded. I wanted to answer him, but the words wouldn't come.

~~~~~

~REEBOK GARNER~

Reebok answered the phone, hoping the Chief had an update on Miss Biscuit, but it was Dee Sheffield in a panic.

"I stopped by Glaze and Maddy's to pick them up for work. We always car pool, and there's nobody here. Glaze's car is gone, and there's no note or anything."

"It's all right, Miss Dee." He explained what had happened, trying to stem her increasing agitation.

"Guess I'll forget about work today," she said. "I'm heading to the clinic right now."

"That's good, because some of those folks are going to need a ride home."

"Will do!" and she was gone.

When he still hadn't heard from the Chief, or anybody else, by 8:45, he drove up the valley to Garner Creek. All the way there, he berated himself. Could he have prevented her from falling in the water if he had been on time starting his route? That's what I get, he thought, for starting out late. Never again.

~~~~~

~BISCUIT McKEE~

As we waited for the doctor to sign my discharge papers, Bob used the delay to further his investigation. "Before you walked out onto the dock, did you see anything?"

All I could do was yawn. And shiver. I still felt cold.

Glaze tightened her hold on my hand.

"No," I said. A muscle twitched just below Bob's ear.

"Anything at all," he persisted.

I wanted to hit him. "I already told you. All I saw was what I always see when I walk there." I covered my mouth. Why do I always close my eyes when I yawn? I'd have to think about that. Had I ever seen anyone yawn with open eyes? "Except for Henry. I saw him going into the church, but he does that every night. I saw the swollen river," I added. "That was the only thing different."

"Let's go over your route, then."

"My root? It wasn't a root; it was a branch." I thought

back to the way I'd fought my way to what felt like the safe side of the tree. "Actually, there were three of them."

"Route, Woman. Where you walked when you left our house." Bob was using his patient voice. I couldn't see why. I was being cooperative. Answering his questions.

"When you left, which way did you head, uphill or straight down to the dock?"

"I power-walked up to the barrel." Everybody knew where that was. Sometime back in the 1940s an enterprising soul, tired of fender-benders across from her corner house, painted a 55-gallon drum bright red with the word STOP stenciled four times in white—one STOP facing each oncoming street where Beechnut Lane intersected Fourth Street. That particular crossroad was large enough that drivers often forgot to look both ways, almost as if they were in a parking lot. According to Bob, the town police records hadn't shown a single accident there once the barrel was in place, smack dab in the middle of the intersection. It was so successful, they'd added another one where Willow and Magnolia merged into Second Street. If you wanted to indicate *that* intersection, you said, "*down* at the barrel." The one I'd been talking about was "*up* at the barrel."

"From there I turned right on 4th Street, over to Pine ..." Reebok Garner, Bob's ever-vigilant deputy, took notes as if this were actually interesting. Good grief. "... and all the way down to 1st Street." My mind was still fuzzy, but I did remember that much.

"You wouldn't have gotten hurt if you'd come to visit me," Glaze said. I bridled a bit at her reproachful tone. "From the barrel," she said, "you were only two blocks away. I would have made you some tea."

Before I could argue that I wouldn't have wanted to wake her and Maddy at two in the morning, Bob interrupted. "Why in the name of all that's holy would you go out on that dock in the middle of the night, Woman?"

He couldn't be too angry with me. He was calling me Woman. It was usually a term of endearment, but I thought that maybe right now it meant he was exasperated. When he was frightened for me, he called me Bisque, the name my mother, a potter, gave me at birth. He almost never called me by my nickname, Biscuit. I'd always wondered about that, ever since I met him, but I'd never thought to ask him why not. Mostly he just called me Woman.

"Don't you remember what happened the last time the river flooded?"

I remembered all too well how the town dock had been swept away during the torrential rains two years ago. But the town had "rebuilt the dock," I argued, "longer, sturdier, heavier, built to last. I was perfectly safe."

"You were not! You ended up halfway down the Gorge, stranded, almost—"

Reebok interrupted, something he almost never did, especially not with Bob, whom he idolized. "Did you see anyone on your walk, ma'am?" He flashed an apologetic but strangely steely glance at Bob. I think he felt he was protecting me.

"Of course I didn't see anyone," I said. "It was the middle of the night." His earnest face peered at me over his notepad. "I saw Fergus." Bob shook his head, but I ignored him. "And I'm pretty sure I saw you, at least I assumed it was you, turning from Pine onto Second."

Reebok's face went completely blank for a moment. "Me? You were there?"

"Yes. I was maybe halfway down Maggie's block. And then I saw Henry." Something niggled at my memory. "Wait. I did see a car."

"You just told us that," Bob said. "Reebok's car."

"No. This was a different one."

"Could you describe it?" Reebok held his pen at the ready, like one of those bird dogs with its front leg raised in a point.

"No, Reebok. It was dark."

"Where was it?" He was certainly bird-dog persistent.

I thought about it. "I remember being angry about it," I said. "I know what it was! They'd parked right underneath the old trees. On Pine Street."

"Did you see anyone in the car?"

"I didn't want to get too close to look," I said with some acerbity. "That's not the sort of thing I care to witness."

It took Reebok about three seconds to figure out what I meant. His blush, when it came, suffused not only his face but his neck as well. I daresay he must have been pink down to his toes. I exchanged one of those woman-to-woman glances with Glaze, and she put a hand over her mouth, but I could see the crinkle lines of her merriment.

He cleared his throat. "Of course not, ma'am." Another throat-clearing. "Do you remember anything else?"

"No, not really."

Reebok's arm dropped lower in disappointment. The nurse interrupted before he could ask more questions. There was a phone call for one of the officers. Reebok left to take it.

I searched my memories of that walk. The heavy texture of the air the way it feels before a storm. Stepping out onto my front porch and deciding to go uphill rather than down toward the river. Halfway up to 4th Street I'd almost turned around. But the crickets were singing. I'm not usually a lyrical person, but I did recall that, once I'd quit grumping about Bob, I'd been particularly happy as I tromped along in the fitful moonlight. So I'd gone on up Beechnut and circled around.

Something tickled my fuzzy brain, like a mosquito in the middle of the night. "Something about the car," I said.

Bob squeezed my hand in encouragement. "Was it an unusual make or model?"

"Robert Sheffield, you know I can't tell one car from another."

His jaw muscle twitched again.

"It was white," I said helpfully. But there was something else that wouldn't come clear.

Bob reached out and traced a little X on the end of my nose. It was something he did occasionally, usually when he didn't know what else to do with me.

That was it. The X. "The license," I said.

"What was it?"

"Something funny. Something with an X. ML ..." The logjam in my brain cleared. "That's it! Ten-sixty-six."

"Ten-sixty-six. You're sure?"

"Of course I'm sure. That was the year of that horrible Norman invasion. William the Conqueror. My history teacher called him William the Illiterate. He said he was referred to as William the Bastard. Once he had some of his enemies skinned alive. A horrible role-model for a vanity plate."

"And those first three letters were what again?" Bob pulled a pad of yellow sticky notes from his shirt pocket. Bob and his sticky notes.

"First three? I told you. MLX."

"I thought you said XML."

"No I didn't. They're—" But I was interrupted once again as Reebok burst back into the room.

"I need to get back to the station, Sir. Some evening joggers found the body of a woman floating in Enders Lake last night. No identification. They've put it on the radio, but they want us to spread the word through town."

"Why didn't they call sooner?"

Reebok drooped like a dog that's been reprimanded. "They did, Sir, but I wasn't at the station to take the call. We were both out... out looking."

Bob nodded absentmindedly and peeled off the top

note. "Here. Take this and run the plate before you start calling people. And keep asking about ..." he lifted my hand to his lips, "about our unknown assailant."

"Yes, Sir!" He didn't salute, but the back went even straighter as he gave me a discreet thumbs-up. "I'll get on that right away, Sir. And, Sir? Your car's back up at the station."

"Thanks."

Bob turned back to me. "Is there anything at all you remember? Any little detail you haven't told me, even if you don't think it's important."

"I've told you every single... nothing much happened... it was a normal walk until the very end. Except for the car. That was the only thing different."

"Tell me again. Try to think of yourself as being there. Describe it to me, what you're seeing, what you're thinking ..."

Ha! I thought. Fat chance of that. Not when I was thinking about what a stubborn guy *you've* been lately.

"... what you're hearing, what you're smelling. Let it roll through your mind like a movie, and—"

"Wait! Smell. There was a smell, just as he knocked me off the dock. The wind, there was a pretty stiff breeze. It was... it was ..." I was spluttering, but the words wouldn't come fast enough. "It smelled like ..." No. It couldn't be. "It smelled like Carl."

"Carl? Carl Armitage?"

"You know, that obnoxious musky aftershave he wears? How it always precedes him like a suit of armor? Maybe that's how I knew it was a man. I smelled the aftershave just as he hit me. I think I did. It happened so fast."

"Carl." Bob's voice had a tone I'd never heard before.

"It couldn't be Carl," I said. "He wouldn't."

"I think I'll have a little talk with him, just to be sure."

Glaze drove us home, finally. Bob couldn't question me anymore because I fell asleep on the back seat.

I woke to hear them discussing me as if I were so much raw meat.

"I hate to wake her." Glaze's voice drifted over the seat. "You go on. When she wakes up, I'll get her all tucked into bed."

"She shouldn't be left alone."

"Don't worry. I already called in to tell them I wouldn't be at work, maybe for a couple of days. I'll stay with her."

"If you're sure. I really do need to talk to somebody about something."

"Ah!" There was laughter in my sister's tone. I knew she'd heard our whole conversation. She knew Bob suspected Carl. "The mysterious cop at work," she added.

"Glaze!" I'd never heard him sound so sharp with her. "Somebody tried to kill my wife."

She made some soothing sounds. "I know. I was trying to lighten the mood a little. You go do your job and I'll take care of Biscuit."

~~~~~

~BOB SHEFFIELD~

Carl wasn't at his gas station. Bob drove on up to Fifth Street and knocked on Carl and Sharon's front door.

"Oh Bob," Sharon said, "thank you for stopping by. I just talked to the hospital. Yep. Carl's in the ICU, but they said he's stable now. Oh, what am I thinking?" She stepped back and motioned him in. "Come on in. I shouldn't leave you standing on the porch."

Bob settled onto an overstuffed chair. "Tell me what happened." He really didn't want to sound like he had no clue what she was talking about.

"Well, Carl woke me up middle of the night. It was three minutes past two. Yep. I know because I looked at the clock. He said he was going to step outside and I, I'm so sorry about this, I went back to sleep. The next thing I knew it was quarter to three and Carl was having a heart attack right beside the bed. I dialed 911 so fast I thought the phone was gonna catch fire. Yep. They got to him real fast, but they told me he might have died if I hadn't taken that CPR course. It's so nice having our own ambulance right here in town. Yep. They had him up to the hospital in Russell Gap in no time at all. I had to stay here with the girls, there was no time to call anybody to come watch them, so I couldn't go with him in the ambulance, but they told me they'd keep me informed." She paused for a quick breath. "I'm just so glad you came to ask about him. Yep. That's the nice thing about a small town. We all care about each other. How did you hear about it?"

Should he lie? Or should he tell her he thought perhaps *her* husband had tried to kill *his* wife? No, probably not a good idea. Better just to be vague. "Word gets around," he said. "Keep me informed, will you? I'll want to talk with Carl once he's up to it."

"Of course, of course. Yep. You are such a good friend to him."

~~~~~

FRAN STEWART

My Gratitude List for Thursday
Five Things for which I am Grateful:
    1. Mrs. Przzlybzybzzlski (How on earth is that name spelled?)
    2. Her grandson – I wish I knew his name
    3. The simple fact that I'm alive
    4. That blessed tree
    5. My husband
    <u>I need to list more than five for tonight</u>
    6. My sister, who did my laundry this afternoon while I was sleeping—did I remember to thank her or was I still too fuzzy-minded?
    7. The Montrose Clinic
    8. The ambulance crew who kept me alive. I'm going to take them a loaf or two of my homemade rosemary bread.
    9. Dr. Prescott. She needs bread, too.
    10. And, of course, Marmalade who is purring so raucously against my leg as I write

I am grateful for
Widelap who is home now
Softfoot, even though he wasn't here this morning
    to feed me
Smellsweet
my cat door
this soft bed
I will add
    Curlup, who fed me when I walked to her house

DAY TWO
FRIDAY

CHAPTER 4
6:30 a.m. to noon

~BOB SHEFFIELD~

AT FIRST LIGHT, BOB DROVE AROUND THE BLOCK to where Biscuit had seen the white car. He hoped to get tire prints, but the rain had effectively eradicated any trace of a vehicle. He should have sent Reebok yesterday before he tried to run the plate.

Bob and Reebok had both interrogated Biscuit, hoping to jog her memory. She might have seen something or heard something, but she was as clueless as they were. The license plate was a bust. She'd obviously mistaken the letters or the numbers. Or both. Probably not the numbers. She was sure of that date, 1066. Maybe hypnosis would help her remember it correctly. He didn't know of any hypnotists in the valley, though. Maybe Atlanta.

And that white car. He mulled over the possibilities. It could have belonged to the man who'd tried to kill Biscuit. She must have seen something she wasn't even aware of.

Then again, the car might have held a couple of kids fooling around, the way Biscuit had first suspected. If that was the case, he needed to find them. They might have seen someone before or after they got busy doing whatever they were doing. There were an awful lot of white cars in this town, but he supposed he and Reebok would have to talk to all the owners.

And he'd have to talk to Henry, too. See if Henry had seen anything.

He discounted the third possibility, that the car had been stolen. No reports of a missing car had come in. He'd have Reebok check with the other towns up the valley. Best to cover all the bases, though he doubted anything would come of it.

There had to be a reason she was pushed. Nobody did that just for fun.

The smell, too. Carl and his aftershave was something of a joke around town. How on earth did Sharon put up with it? Bob didn't know of any other man who smelled as much as Carl did. Couldn't the guy tell he was overdoing it? Maybe his nose was so deadened by years of using the stuff, he couldn't sense how much he splashed on.

But Carl had been in the hospital. No. That wasn't true. Sharon said he'd woken her at 2:03. Biscuit had no idea when she'd been attacked, but she'd left the house at two. She was sure of that. And Carl was back home having his heart attack—serve him right if he was the one who'd pushed Biscuit in the water—at a quarter to three. He would have had time to push her in. With his weight, running up the hill to get home would be enough to bring on a heart attack. But why? What the hell could Carl Armitage have against the town librarian? He'd always been kind of flaky. But he was industrious. Between the gas station, the movie theater, and the kenaf farming, Carl stayed busy. Still, he wasn't from around here. He and Sharon had moved here from New Jersey. Bob wasn't the sort to believe in stereotypes—New Jersey mobsters and such—and Martinsville was more accepting of outsiders than some southern towns. Still, Bob didn't know Carl as well as he knew people he'd grown up with.

Of course, Reebok was even newer to town, but Bob trusted him implicitly. Young, yes. Naïve, definitely. But honest as they came. Bob was fairly sure Reebok had a crush on Biscuit, but Biscuit treated him like she would an enthusiastic puppy.

Usually, when there *was* a crime, he and Reebok solved it fairly quickly. But this unknown attacker hadn't done anything—anything they knew about—since Wednesday night. If it was Carl, well, he was in the hospital. If it was somebody else, then he was still around; Bob was sure of that. Afraid of that. The question was *where*. Who was he? What would he do next?

Bob drove toward the station slowly, listening to the news, not quite ready to begin the daily routine. He'd come to rely on Reebok Garner's efficiency and unfailing cheerfulness. Quite a deputy. Worked more hours than he was paid for. Martinsville's gain, I guess, Bob thought. Too bad he hadn't been cruising down by the dock Thursday morning when Biscuit was shoved into the water.

They needed a bigger force. Bob had handled the job for years by himself, as his father had before him. Martinsville was just a sleepy village, but the town charter specified, for some unknown reason, that the town had to maintain *an officer of the peace*. Good for the residents. Good for the children growing up here. One officer of the peace—or even two. That wasn't enough when something went wrong. Like what had happened to Biscuit.

Before Bob had left the house this morning, Biscuit had gone back to bed, wrapped in her flannel pajamas. She couldn't seem to get over feeling cold. Why'd she have to take a walk that late at night? And who the hell had pushed her in the water? She could have died. This was no prank, like painting somebody's mailbox or messing up the letters on the church signboard. This could have killed his wife. He'd have the head of the man who did this to her.

If only Reebok had driven—no. He couldn't blame Reebok. The fellow had combed the town looking for her as soon as Bob asked for his help. And he'd kept up all the next day, after he left the clinic, questioning everyone about what they might have seen or heard. Nothing. Absolutely nothing had come up.

Bob parked in front of town hall. The police station was really just an annex on one end of the gracious old building. It had its own entrance, with "Police" stenciled on the door, but Bob liked to go in through the town hall's main entrance. That way he could check his mailbox and connect with the other people at work.

He knew Reebok would have prepared yet another tidy report sitting precisely in the middle of Bob's desk. It wasn't that Bob didn't appreciate knowing what phone calls had come in. It used to be nobody ever called in the middle of the night unless something was really wrong, because they knew they'd be waking up Bob. Now that the town had a night deputy, and one who thoroughly enjoyed talking to people, the call list got longer all the time.

He turned off the radio as Ralph started another one of his announcements and trudged up the front stairs.

~~~~~

> This is Radio Ralph, the voice of Keagan County
> with an update on your early morning news,
> all the news worth listening to. The body of a
> woman thought to be between the ages of 30 and
> 50, found floating in Enders Lake, has still not
> been identified. Enders police spokesperson C.P.
> Maguire stated that there were no identifying
> papers or driver's license on the woman. The cause
> of death was believed to be drowning. Anyone
> with information about a missing woman, should
> contact ...

One particular man in the valley turned off the radio, tapped his thumb against the edge of the table, and smiled. She was dead. He had nothing to worry about.

~~~~~

~BOB SHEFFIELD~

Bob lifted the multi-page report. Miss Stokes had heard a noise, he read, but while she was reporting it, she saw that it was only a possum in the garbage can on the curb. Old Mr. Harper remembered that he'd seen somebody who looked like he might be the brother of one of the felons pictured in the post office—not exactly like him, but close enough that he could have been related, maybe. Carl and Sharon's youngest daughter called because she'd woken up at midnight and her mother wasn't in the house. Yes, she'd checked the kitchen, the bedroom, everywhere. Then she'd found her mom sitting on the front porch swing, just breathing in the night air. Reebok had assured her that she could call any time she was worried. That was what he was here for. "Poor thing," he said as Bob's finger reached the relevant item. "With her father in the hospital, she's really scared."

It was all written up. Time of call, who called, what was said, what Reebok replied, ad infinitum. Still, Bob had had a good night's sleep, other than Marmalade waking him up, which seemed to be a nightly event now. Instead of resenting this needlessly detailed report, he should be glad he wasn't the one who'd had to answer those calls. "Thanks, Garner." He finished glancing through the report and turned aside to blow his nose. "Good job."

"Sir? There's something else you should know about."

"Yeah?"

Reebok held out a few sheets of paper. "Somebody reported a missing person."

"Garner."

"Yes, Sir?"

"A missing person is more important than a possum in a garbage can."

"Yes, Sir. Of course."

"So, don't you think this report should have been on top of the other one?"

"Oh. Yessir." His crisp *Yes, Sir* had turned into a garbled single word. Under other circumstances, Bob might have been amused.

Reebok handed the report to Bob. "Sorry, Sir."

"Keep it in mind for the future. Is this the dead body in the lake?"

"No, Sir." Two distinct words. "A male," Reebok added. He stood respectfully while Bob skimmed over the report.

"He's been gone since ..." Bob looked back at the top of the page, "since Wednesday morning?"

"On the next page, Sir. He said he was going out that evening, not to expect him back."

Bob turned the page. "So his... wife ...?"

"Mother, Sir."

"So his mother went about her business yesterday and never noticed he wasn't home?"

"Yes, Sir." Reebok motioned to the report, as if to emphasize that he'd written it all down. "Apparently that's not an unusual occurrence. She said she thought she heard the back door open and close once on Wednesday evening before dinner time, but she wasn't sure about that. Charles had his own separate entrance at the back of the house."

"And yesterday?"

"The father got up before the mother. By the time she came downstairs, her husband had left for work, and she assumed the boy had hitched a ride from his father. Sometimes they did that. Carpooled."

Bob looked back at the age of the missing person. Hardly a *boy*. As if he'd read Bob's mind, Reebok said, "That's what his mother called him, Sir."

Bob had given up on trying to make Reebok relax a bit. This *Sir* business got old real fast, but it was hard to be upset with Reebok, who had taken all the preliminary information, filled in all the forms he needed to. A damn fine deputy if only he'd put the person before the possum.

"You know we won't officially treat this as a missing person until he's been gone 72 hours."

"I know that, Sir, but his mother was quite concerned. She said it wasn't like him at all."

"He most likely took off with his buddies, or maybe he's found himself a girlfriend."

"Yes, Sir. I suggested as much to his mother. That is, the *first* part, about going off with friends. She said he'd never stay away all night without at least calling her."

"Garner." Bob's tone combined world weary with Psychology 101. "How many grown men do you know who call home every day?"

Reebok's normally eager countenance took on an affronted air. "I do, Sir. My mother would worry if I didn't call her when I got home from work."

Bob didn't know what to say. He waved his hand in dismissal, and Reebok left, reminding Bob as usual that he was "available if you need me, Sir. I don't need much sleep."

"Thanks, Garner. I'll call if necessary." Bob turned back to the missing person report, only half listening to the quiet tip-tap-tip-tap of footsteps. Reebok always walked with a slightly off-kilter gait, as if one leg were minutely shorter than the other. Before the deputy reached the front door, Bob was immersed in the details of the story. Charles Zapota lived in the new development north of town. His parents had been one of the first couples to buy a house there. Bob was amazed that Garner managed to get so many irrelevant details so quickly. People, particularly older people, loved talking to him. Given that Reebok called home every day, he'd have had lots of practice. The narrative he'd written filled in all the info that wouldn't fit in the check boxes and short lines of the report form.

Charles Zapota had grown up in Surreytown, the village at the top end of the Metoochie River Valley. Ten years ago, he'd left home with very little notice and travelled around the country, calling home religiously once a week. He'd come back to the valley a year ago to help his parents after they bought the house in Happy Acres. His father, the mother had explained, wasn't as spry as he used to be and the house, even though it was new, needed quite a bit of work.

Bob rubbed the back of his neck. Cheapskate builders, he thought. Throw up houses and never care about the quality. Rather like his brother Barkley had done in Atlanta, cutting corners so he could spend more money on his girlfriend. It didn't sit right. No wonder Dee had divorced him. It was good that Dee had moved in with Ma. Ma loved her like a daughter.

He picked up the phone. "Ma? Are you okay?"

"Well, of course I am." She sounded startled. "Is anything wrong?"

Did he really call so seldom that she was surprised to hear from him?

"I'm just thinking about you, that's all. Biscuit and I want to take you to that new Thai restaurant up in Russell Gap."

"Why, Robert. That would be lovely. When?"

"Tonight? Pick you up about 6:30."

"Wonderful, dear. Thank you for thinking of me."

Zapota's name on the form recalled him to his purpose. He said goodbye to his mother, made a quick note on a yellow sticky pad—*call B /Thai*—she might still be sleeping—and went back to the report. The line for *Employment* contained a penciled question mark. Had Reebok forgotten to ask? He reached for the phone, but heard his deputy's distinctive footsteps approaching. Bob set down the phone and lowered his gaze to the paper. "Yes, Garner," he said without looking up, "did you forget something?" He raised his head in time to see the look of awestruck hero-worship in the deputy's eyes.

"How did you do that, Sir? How did you know it was me?"

"All part of the job." It was obvious the deputy thought Bob had worked some sort of magic, summoning his name from the ether. He relented. "Footsteps, Garner. Footsteps."

"Oh." Reebok looked crestfallen only for a moment. Then he brightened with, "I'll start practicing that right away, Sir. Footstep identification."

"Why did you come back?"

"Oh yes, Sir. I thought that, since I had the time, I'd head up to Happy Acres and fill in some other details. Mrs. Zapota might have remembered something else."

"What line of work was he in? You didn't say anything about that."

"She was pretty vague, Sir. I think she'd be more likely to tell me if I'm there in person. I can coax it out of her."

"Your report says the mother thought Charles might have ridden with his father. That means the father knows where he works. Ask him."

"I already did, Sir. I called him at work. He said he always just let Charles off at the corner of Hickok and Manning. Charles apparently walked from there."

Bob thumbed the outer edge of his mustache. "Find out as much as you can about what he does—and why nobody else seems to have missed him."

Reebok straightened his shoulders, seeming to go from perfectly-erect to more-than-perfectly-erect. "Yes, Sir."

Bob tapped the top of his pen against the report in time with Reebok's receding footsteps. Nothing to be done with it until the deputy reported back. He turned to the more mundane business of the day, although he kept returning to the question of Biscuit's attacker.

Reebok was back within half an hour. "No answer at the door, Sir, and no neighbors home, either."

"I'll try her later this morning," Bob said.

"No need for that, Sir. I left a note on her door with my home number so she could call me."

"Sleep, Garner?"

"Don't need much, Sir. I'll be fine."

~~~~~

~BISCUIT McKEE~

Glaze called me at around 9:30, just before Marmalade and I left for the library. I could hear voices in the background. Office sounds.

She didn't even say hello or how are you. "Would you like to take a walk tonight?"

"Is this in addition to our Saturday walk or instead of it?"

"In addition," she said. After a moment's pause she added, "I think."

"There's decisiveness for you."

"Well, can you?"

I thought for a moment. Bob had called me just a few minutes before. He wanted to take his mother and me out for Thai food. We usually went out for dinner on Friday nights. Always before it had been to Tom's restaurant, but that was closed for remodeling. Thai sounded good. I wondered why he'd decided to include his mother. "Rebecca Jo likes to be home before eight-thirty," I told Glaze. "Do you ..." Surely two of us together should be safe. "Do you mind a late walk?"

"Not a problem. I'll be on your doorstep at nine."

I gathered up a couple of books I needed to return and opened the front door. After maybe half a minute I closed it and went to the phone. "Sadie," I said when she answered, "do you think you and Esther would mind if I didn't come in to work today? I don't quite feel up to it."

"Now don't you worry one bit. Esther and Rebecca Jo and I were all three planning to be there. You just take good care of yourself."

After a few more such reassurances from her and a guarantee on my part that I'd be there tomorrow morning, Sadie said good bye with a cheery word of encouragement. I sat down at the table and put my face in my hands.

She called back around noon and told me, "I'll pick you up tomorrow morning."

"It's only three blocks, Sadie."

"That doesn't matter. You've been through a lot. And then I'm going to drive you down to Sharon's for your pedicure at lunchtime. I just made an appointment for myself. The girls said they could handle everything here without us. Rebecca Jo wants to know if you need to cancel the dinner tonight?"

"No," I said. I'd be safe with Bob. "No. I should be fine by then."

"Okay, I'll tell her. Bye, now. I'll be there at 9:30 tomorrow."

I knew Sadie preferred driving, but I liked walking. Around Martinsville I hardly ever drove. I looked at the trees out behind my backyard fence. It would be perfectly safe. I'd never known of anyone to walk through those woods, anyone except Bob and me.

I tried. I stood up and even opened the door. But those hands that had pushed me into the terror of the water had left hand prints that all the water in the world couldn't wash away. I locked the door and scooped Marmalade into my

FRAN STEWART

arms, feeling like a prisoner in my own home. Her scratchy little tongue licked away my tears.

CHAPTER 5
Friday noon to 10:30 p.m.

~REEBOK GARNER~

Mrs. Zapota apologized when she called Reebok. "I had to go out for some groceries, but now I'm home to stay."

Reebok stifled a yawn. "I'll be right there, ma'am."

He ran a comb through his tousled hair. It hadn't been a long enough nap, but he'd just have to make the best of it. A missing person case was more important than sleep. It wouldn't do to look like he'd just woken up.

Should he shave? He peered in the mirror, fingering his chin. There was hardly anything there to feel, much less remove. He saved a lot of time by not having to shave often, but there were times when he wished he could grow a full bristly mustache like the Chief had.

He straightened his collar and gave his badge a quick shine. No sense looking untidy on an important visit like this. It wouldn't be respectful to the frantic woman. The Chief was probably right; her son had just gone out of town without telling her. Young men did that, he thought, ignoring the fact that the young man in question was more than a decade older than Reebok.

~~~~~

~REEBOK GARNER~

Reebok moved his notebook away from the investigative nose of the biggest cat he'd ever seen. Its plumed tail twitched, and the monster planted its front feet on Reebok's thigh. The couch, covered in a bright blue and red quilt, wasn't big enough for the two of them, Reebok decided. He took a firmer grip on his notepad.

"Could you be a little more specific, Mrs. Zapota?"

"Specific?" All Mrs. Zapota's weight had settled between her waist and her hips. Her narrow shoulders seemed oddly out of place, and the helmet-shaped pouf of grizzled hair over a stringy neck made her look like a triangle on stilts, flying a steel-colored balloon.

Reebok pulled his notebook closer to his chest. The cat leaned farther onto his lap.

The triangle smiled indulgently. "Don't let Venus worry you. She's the sweetest cat I've ever had."

"I'm sure she is, but—"

"She's part Maine Coon cat."

And part mountain lion, he thought.

"That's why she's so big. She's more curious about everything than any of my other cats."

"Is that why she just took my pen?"

"I'm sure she'll give it back." She patted her ample lap, setting the folds of skin on her neck to wobbling. "Come on, Venus, sweetie. Give mommy the pen."

The cat flipped the pen, batted it, and sent it skittering toward the kitchen. Mrs. Zapota opened a drawer in the end table and handed a pencil to Reebok. "Sometimes it takes her awhile to get tired of whatever she's playing with."

"Yes, ma'am. Could we get on with the questions now? Are there any friends of his that you could contact? Maybe he's visiting somebody."

"I know, Deputy. You mentioned that when I called you this morning, but we have a very small family, and I don't know any of his friends. He's always been quite private about such matters."

"Could you call—"

"I did. I called my sister and my husband's sister, too, and Charles' cousin Horace, but they don't know anything. They promised to let me know right away if they heard

VIOLET AS AN AMETHYST

from him."

"Any girlfriends you know of?"

"He's never brought anybody home for dinner." She smoothed out the wrinkles on her lap. "I did wonder if he'd met someone. He's been out a lot of evenings for the last few months."

There's the answer, Reebok thought. He's gone off on a jaunt with a lady friend. Still, he should have called his mother so she wouldn't worry so much. "What sort of job does he have?"

"Well, now, you're going to think I'm silly, but I don't rightly know just where Charles worked. When he came home to help us with the house, he said he'd found a good job in Russell Gap. It must have been something creative. He was very creative." Her left hand fluttered up to her lips. "I mean, he *is* creative. He *is*. Just like his cousin was, my sister's daughter, before she... before she left." She folded her surprisingly youthful hands on her lap. "I know you think I'm being overly concerned, Deputy, but we lost our niece last summer, and I just don't think I can go through all that again."

Reebok never knew quite what to say when confronted with such open anguish. Platitudes. That's all he had to offer. "I'm sorry for your loss, ma'am. We'll do our best to find your son."

"When I think he could be lying injured somewhere, I could just—" She bent and scooped up the cat. It let out a startled squawk, but settled quickly, its haunches lapping generously over both sides of Mrs. Zapota's comfortable-looking lap. That was one monster cat.

He had to get back on track. "Surely someone from his workplace called when he didn't show up for work."

Mrs. Zapota shook her head, and Reebok was reminded of an old farm mule his uncle used to have. "Nobody has called," she said. Her full lips, out of place in her thin face,

- 73 -

compressed. "I would have told you if anyone had."

"I'm sure you would, ma'am.

"When I went for groceries today, that's the only time I've been away from the phone since we realized he was missing. One of us has always been here, usually me, since my husband works up the valley. Do you think maybe he tried to call me, and I wasn't here? What if he called and I didn't answer?"

Reebok made soothing sounds, trying to quell her rising panic. "Let's try to get some good information, ma'am. Could you tell me what sort of work your son was qualified to do? Maybe that would help."

"I told you he's creative. He loves to paint. He was getting ready to sell some of his paintings to a big gallery in Atlanta. He told me he's already had several meetings about it with the gallery representative." She nudged the cat off her lap and gestured toward a door. "I'll show you his room. It's full of his art work. Watch your step. Those stairs are a bit tricky with that turn at the bottom. Venus, don't you get underfoot, now."

Reebok waited for the cat to precede him down the rather narrow stairway. Talk about footstep identification. He'd have no trouble at all telling this one. Ker-thunk, ker-thunk. Cats were supposed to be quiet, he thought. Like Marmalade. Sometimes the Chief brought Marmalade to work with him. She could jump up on the desk with hardly a sound. This cat, though... Reebok paused and listened to the footsteps Venus made. Pawstep identification. He didn't think they taught that at the FBI Academy.

He wondered where his pen had ended up.

"Charles had his own outside entrance at the back—the house is built on a hill, you see. But he could join us for dinner just by coming up these stairs." She gazed back upwards as if she expected her son to materialize at the top.

Mrs. Zapota squeezed to the left of Reebok. She opened the door at the bottom, and Venus stepped through, tail waving. "Isn't this the most amazing art you've ever seen?" The pride in her voice was palpable.

"It's amazing, all right. Would you mind if I looked around a bit to see if I could find some clues as to where he might be?"

Mrs. Zapota's lips went from Pillsbury Doughboy to Wicked Witch. "He's very particular about his things. He's told me never to touch anything in here."

"I'll be very careful not to disturb his work, ma'am. If anything has happened to him, we need to find out all we can right away."

Once he'd convinced her to leave him alone and to take the cat with her, Reebok closed the door, drew on the gloves he'd placed in his pants pocket, and wished he had a camera with him. The Chief was never going to believe this.

~~~~~

~BOB SHEFFIELD~

"I've never seen anything like it, Sir. It's just one big room. The whole basement floor, with a little bathroom off to the side and a narrow bed jammed over along one side. There's a door onto a cement patio out back. Every wall surface is covered with paintings, painted right on the wall." Reebok paused, and Bob could practically hear his brain gears turning. "It looks like the man has painted everything he's ever seen. People, animals, cars, houses. Places I could recognize. Mrs. Masters' house—"

"Sadie's place?" Bob pulled open his bottom drawer and took out his jar of honey and a butter knife. Doc Nathan had shown him an article about how local honey could help relieve allergies. Or maybe even cure them. That was what he wanted. And Biscuit was trying to get him away from using plastic.

"Yes, Sir. And I recognized the library and the grocery store. There was a pencil sketch of your house, tacked up on the wall like he hadn't quite decided where to put it. The others were painted in full color. The Old Church and St. Theresa's. He even showed that garden plot Father Ames is always working in. And the signboard outside the Old Church with a Bible verse on it. The bed and breakfast place had that pretty Japanese maple right in front and Miss Tarkington was painted standing next to it. She looked right pretty. And there was the gas station, with Carl standing next to it. The Town Gazebo, too, with a crowd of people in front and the band playing. It looked like the Independence Day concert. All the flags."

Bob held up a hand to stem the flow and opened a package of crackers. "Everything you've mentioned is in Martinsville. Did he include anything from other towns?" He slathered honey on the first cracker and stuffed the whole thing in his mouth.

Reebok's face went still as he thought. "I don't think so, Sir. Except for a big outline of the US of A next to the outside door, only it looked sort of lopsided. And a big plantation house around the bathroom door. It had a horse."

"The bathroom had a horse?"

"The fancy house painted on Charles Zapota's wall. There was a horse tied up to a hitching post. And some people. In front of the house. Two men with a woman in between them. The woman's holding something that looks like a jack in the box. It has a crank on the—"

"Garner."

"Yes, Sir?"

"We're getting off track here." Bob wiped his nose.

This allergy, or whatever it was, was a pain. That magazine had better be right about the value of local honey. "What else was in the room? Any clues as to where he worked or what could have happened to him?"

"Nothing, Sir. Other than the walls and the art supplies, and all the racks of canvases, it was the most boring room I've ever seen. It looked like a cheap hotel room right before the maid service had a chance to clean it up. There was shaving gear and a toothbrush, things like that, in the bathroom. Nothing in the bedside table. No notes or writing materials. Nothing written down. Nothing to speak of on or in the desk." He reached into his uniform jacket and removed a notebook. "The list is here, Sir."

Alarm clock, painting supplies (39 brushes, 78 tubes of color, 16 pencils, two complete sets of colored pencils, charcoals, pastels, 14 sketch pads), 143 canvases, and clothing ...

Everything was listed, from the number of undershorts to the brand of shoes. "Quite a complete list, Garner."

"Thank you, Sir."

"You've even listed each wall picture you could identify."

"Yes, Sir. The list isn't complete, though, because some of the sketches are quite small. And some of the people I couldn't identify. That final page lists what's on all the canvases and everything I could recognize on the sketch pads."

Bob twisted his chair around so he could look out the window at the gazebo in the town square. "Did you find out where he worked?"

"In Russell Gap, Sir. Near the intersection of Hickok and Manning."

Bob turned his head and scrutinized his deputy. "We already knew that."

"Doing something creative, Sir."

"Very big help that is. Why don't you call the station in Russell Gap and see if they've had anyone *creative* reported missing?"

His sarcasm was wasted. "Yes Sir. Right away, Sir." Reebok reached for the phone. Within moments he was speaking to one of his counterparts up the valley.

Bob could tell he wasn't getting anything positive.

Reebok ended the call and turned to Bob, shaking his head. "Nothing, Sir. The only missing person they have is that woman who disappeared last year. They found her abandoned car just out of town, with her purse and sunglasses on the front seat. The car wouldn't start, so they think she might have been abducted when someone stopped to pick her up."

"I remember that case," Bob said. "Nothing ever came of it?"

"No, Sir. She's still listed as missing. No recent missing men, though." Reebok shook his head again.

Bob shook his own head. We must look like a couple of bobble-heads, he thought. Bewildered bobble-heads. He sniffed and pulled out a handkerchief. Damn allergies.

"I'll call the other towns, too, Sir. Just to be sure."

~~~~~

~BISCUIT McKEE~

My sister, who was usually late for everything, knocked right at nine. I waved at her through the lace curtains and detoured into the living room to kiss Bob. After my brush with that murderous maniac—that was how I thought of him—I'd sworn I would never again leave without a kiss.

"Thanks for dinner, honey. It was delicious."

"Yes. It was."

"Your mom really liked the Pad Kraprao."

"So did I."

"I'm not much for basil, but I'm glad I took a taste of yours." We'd already said all of this during the meal and on the drive home. This was just an excuse to keep my hand on my husband's shoulder for a bit longer. "My Sweet Lime Curry was delicious."

He knew non-conversation when he heard it. "Enjoy your walk, Woman," he told me and turned back to his book.

I turned toward my cat.

Excuse me? You are my person. I am the one who chose you.

"Marmy? Do you want to come along with Aunt Glaze and me?"

Yes, thank you.

I held open the door, and she scooted out to the front sidewalk, purring all the way. She headed downhill, so Glaze and I followed along to Second Street and around to the town square. We sat in the gazebo for awhile. Talked about birdfeeders and Maddy's unsuccessful publishing attempts and a pair of shoes Glaze had seen that might go with the dress she planned to wear Saturday night for the dance. "I was going to wear my spike heels, but I think I'd rather have comfortable feet while I'm dancing."

"Uh-huh. I know exactly what you mean."

She raised her feet and twirled her ankles around. "I'm going with Tom," she added.

As if that were a surprise. Who else would she go with? I told her about Charles, the missing man. "I'm going to tell everybody at the Beauty Shop tomorrow and ask them to spread the word."

"What does he look like?"

"Brownish hair, hazel eyes, 36 years old, five foot ten, medium build."

Glaze shook her head. "With that kind of description,

he'd blend right in to any crowd."

Eventually Marmalade meowed at us, so we meandered through the park up to Third Street and turned right. As we crossed Juniper, the street before Beechnut, I said, "Glaze? All this stuff you've been talking about is very interesting, but it's not why you asked me to go on a walk with you."

Before she could answer me, a faint woof sounded ahead of us. I spotted a dog—at least I thought from the woof that it was a dog, although the form on the sidewalk halfway down the block looked more like a gargoyle on sentry duty with pointy ears sticking up, and a froth of curly hair backlit by the moon. "That *is* a dog, isn't it?"

Of course it is a dog.

Glaze slowed to a standstill and studied the animal ahead of us. "It's not any of the dogs I know."

I'm not afraid of dogs, and fortunately there's no rabies in Keagan County, but I do think it's important to use caution around an unknown canine, especially when we couldn't see it all that well. The moon, just two days past the full, lighted our path, but the dog's face was in shadow. "Let's cross to the other side, just in case." I nudged her to the left.

"Okay," she said. "Bye, dog."

The dog stood up and swished its fat, feathery tail. I grabbed my sister's hand and we scooted faster than we should have toward the far side. You're not supposed to run. That makes dogs want to chase you. But the dog stayed where it was until we'd moved halfway up the block, directly across the street from it.

"Go home, dog," Glaze said.

At the sound of her voice, it bounded across the street and sat in front of us, brushing the sidewalk with a tail as bushy as a feather duster. I looked around for Marmalade. She'd disappeared somewhere.

I am under the bushes. I plan to stay here until the

dog is gone.

We moved around it. It followed. Each time we stopped, it sat.

At the corner, we paused. The dog looked up expectantly and pranced a bit on its rather fuzzy feet. "We don't have any food," I said, although I'm not sure why I thought it would understand me. Maybe because Marmalade often seems to know what I'm talking about.

I am a cat. That is a dog. There is a difference. I always understand you.

I hugged Glaze, called for Marmalade, and headed down the hill, half expecting the dog to follow me, but I didn't hear any more toenail clickety sounds. Marmalade still hadn't appeared. I turned to see Glaze pointing her finger at the dog.

"Stay," she said in a surprisingly firm voice. She waved at me and started up Beechnut. The dog, I noticed, stayed put. I love coincidences.

The evening was perfectly clear, not a breath of wind at all. I could hear Glaze's receding footsteps. "Glaze," I called.

"Yeah?"

"I'll see you tomorrow morning for our regular walk."

"You're waking up the neighborhood to tell me that?"

I could see the unmistakable ghostly gray-blue TV flicker from Matthew's front window. "Nobody's asleep yet," I said.

She swept her arm toward the dark bulk of Paul Welsh's house across the street from me. Even in the bright moonlight, it was a puddle of darkness.

"Paul's out of town on business," I said.

"So go ahead and shout some more." The dog still sat at the corner.

"All right," I shouted. I saw Matthew's curtain twitch, but that didn't deter me. "And tomorrow morning you're going to tell me whatever it is that's bothering you, okay?"

"Okay!" my sister hollered back at me, and the dog bolted up the street toward her. "Good grief, dog," I heard her say. "Go home."

The dog fell into step beside her, its tail waving jauntily. Marmalade joined me then, and we hurried the remaining half block. I'd like to say I enjoyed the moonlight, but without Glaze beside me I felt naked ...

You are dressed.

... vulnerable, and so alone.

I am with you.

I kept looking behind me, listening for footsteps ...

There is no one here besides us.

... but the only sound was Marmalade's rumbly purr.

Five Things for which I am Grateful:
1. Being alive
2. Phones
3. Yummy food
4. Dogs that don't bite
5. Bob and Glaze and Marmy

>   *I am grateful for*
>   *sunshine on the kitchen floor*
>   *my feather toy*
>   *a bed all to myself when Widelap and Softfoot*
>   *are gone*
>   *dogs that don't chase me*
>   *Widelap and Softfoot sharing my bed at night*

DAY THREE
SATURDAY

CHAPTER 6
8 a.m. to 1 p.m.

~BISCUIT McKEE~

I STEPPED INTO MY SHOES. THROUGH THE LACE curtain on the front door, I could see Glaze waiting for me out by the mailbox. That dog we'd found sniffed around in the middle of the daylilies. Those plants were strong enough to stand up to a Mac truck. I doubted one 30-pound dog would hurt them. I reached for the handle—I like door handles so much better than door knobs—but Bob waylaid my mad dash. Delightfully, I must admit. "What," I asked, "did you do that for?"

"Can't I kiss my wife if I want to?"

I didn't have an answer other than a breathless *yes*.

He chuckled and walked with me as far as the mailbox. "Morning, Glaze." He scratched the dog's head briefly. The dog shivered ecstatically, licked its tongue in and out repeatedly, and let out a grumbly little sound that made me laugh. Bob smiled down at it. "When did you get the dog?"

"It's not my dog," Glaze said. The dog turned to look at her.

Bob headed up the hill. Over his shoulder he called, "Enjoy your walk." Why on earth was he wearing that old pair of stained khakis? Even for work clothes, they were disgraceful.

"For somebody who ties that many flies," Glaze said, "he sure doesn't fish much."

Saturday mornings usually found Bob in the shed at his old house on the corner of Fourth Street and Upper Sweetgum, the house Glaze and Madeleine Ames, the sister of the town priest, rented from us now. Their lease specified that Bob would have access to the shed at all times. It was a crooked little building—designed that way deliberately, I was sure—and I'd dressed it up with flowering vines that attracted hummingbirds all summer long.

"He's headed to Sadie's this morning," I told her, although I still couldn't understand his disreputable clothes.

"Oh? Why?" A slight breeze lifted a strand of her hair, and she brushed it out of the way.

"Sadie called last night and asked him to stop by."

"Probably needs something heavy lifted."

A faint smell, almost like rotten meat, wafted across the sidewalk.

I smell it, too.

It smelled like a Dracunculus vulgaris, better known as the Voodoo Lily.

It is not a voo doolilie.

That plant had the most vile-smelling blossoms, which was why I never wanted it in my yard. I glanced toward Matthew's house. He wouldn't have planted any, would he? Of course not. Matthew's idea of landscaping was mowing his grass every couple of days. I took another sniff, and wished I hadn't. Maybe our septic tank was backing up.

Glaze gave a sniff, too, but didn't say anything. Our toilets were flushing just fine, but maybe I should have the septic tank company come out for a look. No. My poor yard had been dug up not too long ago, and it was only now recovering. I sincerely hoped it was a voodoo lily I was smelling. That would be a lot cheaper than a septic tank overhaul.

I told you, it is not a voo doolilie and it is not your sep ick tank.

The dog veered toward the side of our house, but Glaze called it back. "Stay out of Biscuit's flower beds," she said. It always amazes me that people think their animals understand English, although I had to admit that

Marmalade sometimes acted as if she understood me.
That does not even deserve a comment.

When Glaze headed up the hill, I matched my steps to hers. It looked like we'd be going counterclockwise around the town this morning. Didn't matter to me which way we went, as long as we ended up at the Delicious, a local landmark. Margo and Hans had given the deli their last name when they opened it, but nobody ever called it the DeliSchuss. Marmalade led the way, and the dog followed along behind Glaze, punctuating our footsteps with its toenail clicks. Little tufts of whitish fur sprouted from between its toes, making a whimsical counterpoint to the honey-brown fur. "Bob's been a big help to Sadie," I said. "I think she misses Wallace a lot more than she lets on."

Glaze paced half a block before she replied. "Bob must miss him, too."

"Yeah. He has lots of stories about Wallace—fishing with him, learning to whittle, watching him tend his beehives, charting all the species of trees in the Old Woods. Wallace was quite a treasure."

"Why couldn't our grandpa have been like him," she said.

It didn't sound like a question, so I murmured something indistinct and kept walking. There wasn't any answer to that anyway. I decided to give her another block or two before insisting that she tell me what was up.

We walked all the way to Willow Street before she said anything.

"I'm up against a problem," she said.

Yes! She was thinking of accepting Tom's proposal. "Uh-huh," I said in as encouraging a way as possible.

"I've been offered... something... and I don't know whether or not to accept it."

Do you love him, I thought, but I didn't say that. "So, how will you decide?"

"That's just it. I don't know how. I don't think I'm qualified."

"Not qualified?"

"I've never done anything like this before."

Well, sister dear, none of us had the first time around. Just jump in with both feet. "Why don't you make two lists," I suggested, "one with all the reasons to say yes and one with reasons to say no. Then see how the two columns balance." It seemed a cold-hearted way to approach marriage, but then again, too many people had no idea what they were getting into. Marriage wasn't just a matter of setting up house together. It was hard enough... well, I didn't want to go there. But really, come to think of it, what would my list-for-marrying-Bob have been? One—I respect him. Two—I love him. Three—I enjoy being with him. Four—I'm encouraged and challenged by him. Hmm. Love was number two. Odd. Maybe respect was more important, though. Love could always grow when respect was there. But without respect, love would be extremely difficult.

"... think about it some more."

I jumped back into the conversation. "That's a good idea." I hoped that made sense, because I had no idea what she'd said.

She and the dog made an abrupt u-turn. "You're right," she said. "See you."

I watched them walk away. She'd probably given me a very good reason for leaving our walk. I wondered what it was.

You were listening to yourself and not to her.

Marmalade and I headed back home to wait the forty-five minutes before Sadie picked me up. Good. I'd have time to start a crock pot of soup. Only once or twice did I look over my shoulder before we made it in the front door.

~~~~~

~BISCUIT McKEE~

Sharon waved the blow dryer and sent Ida's hair flying sideways, like a hurricane coming off the land instead of off the ocean. "Yep. I swear he is the handsomest man I've seen in this valley in a long time."

Pumpkin rubbed the hot soapy water up over my ankles in a gentle massage. I'd give her about three hours to stop that. It was so comforting to have warm feet. I'd spent the last thirty-three hours feeling cold, but who was counting? I was, that's who. Every hour I was alive now seemed precious, and well worth counting. Even now, except for my feet, I felt cold, and goose bumps tingled under my long-sleeved shirt. Out of habit I glanced at my watch. I had plenty of time to get back to the library. I loved having a long lunch time on Saturdays, something I wouldn't ever have been able to do without my Petunias. Of course, this particular Saturday nobody had expected me to show up for work, not even Sadie. She'd told me when I slid into the front seat of her yellow Chevy that she'd fully expected me to cancel. "You're supposed to be recuperating!"

I knew quite well, too, that even if I never again darkened the library door, my Petunias—what I called my three elderly but energetic volunteers, Sadie Masters, Esther Anderson, and my mother-in-law Rebecca Jo Sheffield—could run the place without me.

It wasn't just a little guilt about this extra-long lunch hour that bothered me. I'd been a bit nervous about facing Sharon this morning. I knew Carl had suffered a heart attack, but I also couldn't rid myself of the knowledge that I'd suspected him, all because of his awful aftershave. I wondered how tolerant Sharon would be if she'd known I'd practically accused her husband of trying to kill me.

I hadn't accused him. Not really. It was just that horrible smell.

But it couldn't be Carl. He was fairly obnoxious, but Sharon loved him. At least, I thought she did. So he couldn't be all bad. And he had no reason to kill me.

I'd never shown any outright antagonism toward him, not that I knew of, but I hadn't tried to hide my dislike of him either.

Of course, if he were the one who'd pushed me from the dock—I shuddered—then no wonder I didn't like him.

I glanced sideways at Sharon.

She saw me and turned off the blow dryer. "You doing okay, Biscuit? You look a little pale."

"Of course she's pale," Pumpkin said. "Her feet are like ice." She looked up at me. "Don't you worry, Biscuit. I'll get your tootsies warmed up in a jiffy."

Tootsies? Pumpkin was younger than any of my three children, but she sounded like someone from the nineteen-fifties.

Sharon turned back to Ida's hair. "Well, I still say we could use more good-looking men like that around here."

Darn it! I'd tuned out again.

"Where'd he come from?" Pumpkin asked, and I shifted my attention back to the conversation.

"Lordy, who cares, since he's here for awhile." Sharon smoothed Ida's hair back down the right direction.

Dee piped up from under her towel before I had a chance to say anything. "How would you know he's staying?"

"Easy. He's rented a room at the Rooster and Biscuit. He asked Brighton and Ellen about renting a room from them for a month, but it was already taken, so he had to go to the Rooster."

The Rooster and Biscuit was a B&B place halfway between Martinsville and Braetonburg. How would Sharon know who was staying there?

Pumpkin stopped rubbing my feet. "You mean the

room I gave up?"

Pumpkin had just recently moved into the herb shop, soon after Annie McGill died. I still half expected to see Annie, with her long red braid dangling over her shoulder, every time I walked into the store, but I supposed I'd get used to her being gone. I'd first met Pumpkin when Sharon hired her to do the manicures, but Pumpkin was as much of a health nut as Annie had ever been. I felt faintly guilty thinking that about Annie, so I shifted mental gears. Pumpkin had spent most of her non-working hours at the herb shop, and Annie had taught her quite a bit about the business.

Annie hadn't had much family, so it had seemed natural for Pumpkin to step into Annie's shoes, so to speak. Pumpkin had hired one of the local teens to tend the shop so she could still work at Sharon's from ten to two on Saturdays. Nobody knew Pumpkin's last name, if she even had one, but she was as friendly as a puppy, and smart as the dickens when it came to running that shop. I sure bought a lot there, which may have been one reason she'd already turned a profit, if what Glaze told me was right.

Where *was* Glaze, come to think of it? I had just assumed she'd be here the way she always was. We'd set up our appointments at the same time. "Didn't Glaze have her usual appointment today, Pumpkin?"

"Her pedicure? No, she called a little while ago to reschedule."

Well, phooey. She was still worried about something, probably about whether to marry Tom. Why wouldn't she confide in me in plain words? Why all this pussyfooting around? Didn't she trust me? Just last month, I'd thought she was dead. And then two days ago I'd almost died. It still gave me the creeps to think about that. When you almost lose somebody, you begin to think from a different perspective. Glaze and Bob had stayed at my bedside while I recovered from the hypothermia. Still, this morning when we'd taken our usual Saturday walk, she not only hadn't cleared up the mystery of why she'd wanted to talk to me Friday night, she also hadn't said anything about cancelling her pedicure. But she *had* cut the walk short. Of course, maybe she told me all that while I was off thinking about why I married Bob.

I stretched my back and wiggled my toes, luxuriating in the waves of warmth traveling from my feet upwards. Pumpkin smiled up at me.

I tuned back in to the conversation. Sharon was in full oratory style. "I'm not normally someone who gets her head turned. No, I'm not. But this fella looks so much like Clark Gable, except for his hair color, I could just fall into his arms if he'd have me. Yep. He even has one of those kiss-me-quick-and-don't-tell mustaches."

Kiss me quick? Where'd she get that one?

"He looks as sweet," Sharon went on, "as pineapple sherbet."

Ida let out a snort. "What on earth is that supposed to mean?"

"Well." Sharon had to think a moment. "I don't suppose I've thought about pineapple sherbet since my second daughter was born. Yep. I craved the stuff the whole time I was pregnant."

Dee looked confused. "And this has *what* to do with Clark Gable?"

"Oh, I don't know. I just think he looks ..." she giggled, "yummy!"

Come now, I thought. How could anybody be that attractive? Sadie, who was flipping through a magazine, set it aside. She looked as baffled as I felt. "Does anybody know his name?"

"Well ..." Sharon flipped her blond curls back from

her wide forehead. "His name, you won't believe this, but it's Red Butler."

Ida turned around and got a blow dryer blast in the face. "Rhett Butler? Like in *Gone with the Wind*?"

"No, not Rhett. It's Red. R-E-D. He's got dark red hair, you see. And that little Clark Gable mustache of his is sort of auburn."

"I remember a guy who looked like that." Ida held up a hand and fended off the blow dryer. "He came in the grocery store looking for Melissa four or five months ago."

"So?" Sharon eased the blow dryer back into position.

Ida took on the tone of a doomsday forecaster. "He didn't know her name."

"What did you do?"

"Well what do you think? I sent him packing. Haven't seen him since, either." She leaned forward and nodded in apparent satisfaction. "He didn't tell me his name, though, but it must be the same guy. I wonder if he's one of the Surreytown Butlers? There's a whole passel of them up at that end of the valley."

Ida always amazed me with her genealogical lore. "Is there any family in the valley you don't know, Ida?"

She grinned and settled back into the chair so Sharon had to rearrange the cherry-colored plastic cape again. "Guess I know most of those Butlers," Ida said, "but this Red Butler is a new one. I would have recalled a name like his. Do you know him, Sadie?"

Sadie, whose hair was finished but who was waiting for me, didn't even have to think about it. "In all my eighty-plus years I can guarantee you I've never come across a name like that, certainly not since *Gone with the Wind* came out in 1936."

"Nobody would name a kid Red," Dee said. "It must be a nickname. His real name is probably something awful."

Sharon gave a finishing flourish to Ida's hair, whipped off the cape, and handed her a big beauty shop mirror. I wish I had one that size. Ida nodded and hauled herself out of the chair. Turning to Dee, Sharon removed the damp towel. "Probably not an awful name, just a boring one." She picked up a new comb. "Yep. Like Gerald."

"Arthur," Pumpkin offered. "No boy would want to be called *Arthur*." She wrapped one of my feet in a warm towel and rubbed my instep gently. My wonderful husband had gifted me on my birthday with coupons for pedicures—every other Saturday for a whole year—for me and Glaze both. I'd wondered where he'd found a chunk of cash for such a generous gift, until Pumpkin let it slip that he paid once a month, in advance, tip included.

"No," Dee said. "It's probably either really ordinary, like *John*, or really stupid." She squinted her slanted, cat-like eyes. "Like *Carruthers*," she finally announced.

"That's a last name," I said, "not a first name."

"All the more reason," she said with a casual disregard for logic, "for him to go for a nickname, then."

I guess she had a point, but I didn't think anyone would saddle a child with a name like Carruthers Butler. "Billy Bob," I said. Here in Georgia, a lot of names were doubled. And apparently you got extra points for alliteration. Dee was Diane Marie, for instance—no extra points for her—and had been called that for thirty-some-odd years until she divorced my no-good brother-in-law and changed her first name.

Sharon nodded. "If he was Billy Bob Butler," she stressed the Bs, "no wonder he wants to be called Red."

"But what's he here for?" Pumpkin persisted as she took up my other foot.

"Something about building or architecture," Sharon said. "I'm not sure exactly what."

Dee grimaced. "Oh lordy, I hope he's not here to add

VIOLET AS AN AMETHYST

more of those monstrosities north of town."

"Now, Dee, you know a lot of those people are really nice." Sharon rested her hand—the one that wasn't waving the scissors around—on Dee's shoulder. "Didn't they start that quilting group and name it after Annie?"

Nobody had a reply to Sharon's comment. Annie McGill had been dead for a month, but the rawness of grief still pulled at me and, I looked around the Beauty Shop, apparently it still sat heavy on everyone else's shoulders. A veil of sadness wrapped itself around the room, and the only sound was the snip, snip, snip of Sharon's scissors. Dee's wet blond split ends dropped onto the linoleum and lay there like daddy-long-legs after a long cold winter. Red and his unknown purpose in Martinsville faded into the sunshine yellow walls.

A missing person probably wasn't the best antidote to sadness, but I motioned to get everyone's attention. "Bob told me there's a missing person. He wants to spread the word in case anybody's seen him."

Pumpkin stopped massaging my foot. "Who is it?"

"His name is Charles Zapota. He's 36, medium build, with brown hair and hazel eyes."

Pumpkin moaned. "How is that supposed to help? It would fit just about anybody."

"That's what Glaze said last night when I told her," I said.

"I don't know him," Sadie said, "but the name sounds familiar."

"He lives in Happy Acres with his parents," I added.

"Thirty-six and still living at home?" Ida's eyebrows rose higher than usual.

"Not *still*. He's come home to help his parents with some remodeling and repairs."

Ida snorted. "Mostly repairs, I'd bet, if it's Not-So-Happy Acres we're talking about. Those shoddy houses were thrown up to line the builder's pockets."

Dee interrupted, before Ida could go off on a tangent. "Zapota? There was a woman by that name at the funeral. One of those quilters from north of town. We stood next to each other. She introduced herself, but then she left right after the burial."

"Did she say anything about a family?"

"Not exactly." Her upper teeth left their imprint on her lower lip. "She said no mother should ever have to lose a child, no matter how old." Dee rubbed her forehead, as if she had a headache coming on. "I had the feeling she knew what she was talking about."

I thought about my three, all grown up now. I couldn't imagine losing any of them. Oh, there had been times, those sullen teenage years, when I could have gleefully flushed them down the toilet, but then Sol, their father, my first husband, died, and we were all so busy dealing with that tragedy, that we seemed to rally together, and all the petty stuff either went away or was hidden.

"Now I remember where I heard that name," Sadie said. "Remember a year or two ago when that young woman from Russell Gap disappeared? Mrs. Zapota was her aunt, I think. Hair like a big fat Brillo pad?"

"Right," said Dee. "That's her."

Sadie nodded. "I saw her on the news asking for help in finding—what was the niece's name? Kate! That was it."

"Did they?" Dee asked. "Find her, I mean?"

Sadie's corrugated forehead wrinkled even more. "Not that I ever heard." Another pall settled into the room, and the yellow walls didn't seem quite so bright.

"I remember now," Sharon said. "Red's here to plan the remodeling for Tom's restaurant."

Then we had to dissect Tom for switching his fancy upscale restaurant into a vocational cooking school. We'd still be able to eat there once he re-opened, but the menu was going from French to Southern.

"There's nothing quite like fried chicken," Sharon asserted.

Ida made a sound like a strangling sow—not that I knew what that sounds like, but she sounded like that was what she would have sounded like if she... my syntax was getting all mixed up. "I can fry my own chicken," Ida said. "When I go out to eat, I want to have something I can't make in my own kitchen. Not that we go out that often, Ralph being something of a skinflint, bless his heart."

Bless his heart. That strictly Southern euphemism that means anything from *rats* to *doggone him* to *wait till I get my hands on him.* Or her, as the case may be.

The bell over the door tinkled and Clark Gable walked in. "Ladies," he said with just the suggestion of a courtly bow, ignoring the collective gasp from every female throat, including mine.

Sharon fluttered away from Dee's trim. "Can I help you?"

He smiled. "Are you Mrs. Armitage?"

"Call me Sharon. Everybody does." I'd swear she batted her eyelashes at him.

"I'm so sorry to interrupt you, but I just stopped by the gas station to see about an oil change, and no one was there."

Sharon turned to the wall clock. "Ronnie's probably just zipped up to the Delicious for a bite of lunch. He should be right back."

Red had the most unusual off-white buttons on the sleeve of his tan sport coat. They looked hand crafted. Each one was slightly irregular in shape. I leaned closer to see them and picked up the most delightful scent. It was a citrusy aftershave, very light, very... well, I might as well admit it, very appealing. He drummed his hand against his leg. I'm probably the only one who noticed the movement since he was standing right beside Pumpkin, and her eyes were glued—I hate to be trite, but they were—on his face.

"I thought the owner's name was Carl," he said.

"Oh, yes. That's my husband, but he's been in the hospital since Thursday. They've said they'll release him Monday and he'll probably be back at work by Thursday or Friday, as long as he takes it easy. But Ronnie's real good. He's our head mechanic."

Other than Carl, he was the only mechanic, but I could see why Sharon might not want to say that.

Red gave her that funny little half bow. "I apologize again for having interrupted your work. Ladies." He nodded all around.

Sadie spoke up. "We're having a ballroom dance gala tonight at the library. We'd be delighted if you could come."

"What a kind invitation, Mrs ..." He waited for her name.

"Masters. Sadie Masters," she said. "Seven o'clock."

"Thank you. I'll be there."

He left to the sound of thunderous silence, followed by excited giggles from most of the women and harrumphs from Ida. "Quit your twittering, all of you. You sound like Maggie's hens."

~~~~~

~HENRY PURSEY~

The bell above the deli's front door tinkled brightly. Reverend Henry Pursey, already halfway through his first cup of coffee, raised his hand in greeting as Father John Ames threaded his way between the crowded tables. Henry enjoyed their Saturday morning talks. As Martinsville's only two religious leaders—he hated that term—it had been natural for them to gravitate into a friendship. Each one seemed to understand what the other was up against. For the most part. But Henry was married, and Father John, naturally, was not.

Father John slipped into the booth and turned his coffee cup upright. "Morning, Henry."

"Your four o'clock showed up right on time this morning."

"For a change?" Father John shoved his coffee cup closer to the edge of the table. "What is this, the first time this week she's been on time?" His smile was a little forced, Henry thought.

Ariel filled the priest's coffee cup, topped off Henry's, and plopped five more little creamers in front of Henry. "You fellas need anything else?"

"No," said Father John.

"Yes," said Henry at the same time, and ordered a full breakfast. "I've been spending a lot of my paycheck here the last month." He fiddled with the stand-up placard announcing a Ballroom Dancing Extravaganza. After sitting here for two months, this particular advertisement had begun to look a little ragged. "You going to this?"

"Yeah. My sister railroaded me into taking her."

"I guess I'll have to show up, too."

"Irene back yet?"

"Sure is. She's busy unpacking." His grin was somewhat sheepish. "She told me to get out of her way."

"Have I mentioned I'm glad I'm a priest?"

"Not since last week, and you don't have to mention it now, either." Henry moved the dance announcement out of the way. "How's the garden coming along?"

"You must have seen it. You walked right past it," he checked his watch and did a quick calculation, "six and a half hours ago."

"Yes, but it was dark."

Father John nodded to two women who greeted him as they slid into the next booth. "I can't keep up with the tomatoes," he said with a certain air of pride, "and my squash vines are going to take over. They'll be across the sidewalk if I'm not careful."

"Good as last year?"

"Better. Last year I was awfully late getting started. It was midsummer, and I only had that one little patch."

Henry snickered. "You keep planting things, you're not going to have a church lawn."

"Don't need one. I'm sharing vegetables with most of my parishioners. I think they like tomatoes better than Bermuda grass."

"At least it keeps you from having to mow so much." Henry was doubly grateful for Roger, who kept the lawn of the Old Church immaculately groomed.

He pulled back as the young waitress set two plates in front of him.

"Thank you, Ariel."

"Sure thing, Rev. Need anything else?"

"No. I'm fine."

Father John pointed to his coffee cup and smiled. Ariel winked at him and flounced off.

They watched her, looked sheepishly at each other, and resumed their conversation. "Did you ever find out who did that planting for you last year?"

"I always kind of thought it was you."

"Not me," Henry said. "I saw the guy, though. I was coming out of the chapel one night and there was this fella raking over the ground. Remember, you'd left those tomato plants and the broccoli sitting there in their plastic pots?"

"Yeah." Father John grimaced. "I don't know why I ever thought I should double-dig the whole garden patch. That was one devil of a job."

"What's a double-dig?"

"That's when you dig way down and mix in a lot of soil amendments, like compost and stuff. That way the dirt's loose. It's especially good for root crops like carrots and potatoes."

"And turnips?" Henry was particularly fond of turnips, but Irene hardly ever bought any.

"And turnips. You can have some if you want when they're ready. I'll even let you dig them up yourself."

Henry looked at him. "You pulling a Tom Sawyer on me? Getting me to do all the work?"

"Would I do that?"

"Yeah. You would."

"So, who was the guy?"

"What guy?"

"The one who planted my tomato patch. And the broccoli."

"No idea," Henry said. "I introduced myself, but all he said was that his name was Joe."

"I don't have any Joes in my congregation."

"I wondered at the time if he made it up. He kind of hesitated before he said it, like he had to think up a name first. He must have known you. I asked him how he could see what he was doing in the dark and he said he was doing it at night because he liked leaving the good padre a surprise present."

Father John raised his eyebrows. "Good padre?"

"That's what he said."

"Well, it was a good present, all right, and quite a surprise. I have never been so sore as I was with all that shoveling. All I wanted was to take a hot shower and crash. I sure was pleased to see those tomatoes planted when I walked outside the next morning."

"Looked like you got a pretty good crop, too."

"The best thing was that I didn't have to do any digging

this year."

They sat in companionable silence for a few minutes. Henry took another bite and said, "You heard about what happened to Biscuit?"

"Yeah. It's hard to believe what this town is coming to."

"I heard the ambulance leaving with her. It was right at the end of my shift Thursday morning."

"And you didn't know who to pray for, did you?"

"Not then. At least she made it okay."

Father John drained his coffee cup. "I had a parishioner at my first church who was robbed on the street late one night. She told me it was months before she could even step outside her front door."

Henry stabbed his fork in the air. "Not Biscuit. She's pretty tough."

"Uh-huh," Father John said, and slid out of the booth. "You might want to ask her."

~~~~~

~BISCUIT McKEE~

Once my feet were dry, Pumpkin presented me with a selection of her environment-friendly nail polishes. "What are you in the mood for today, Biscuit? Here's this nice *Amazing Amethyst*."

Sadie set down her magazine. "That's the same color as Melissa's engagement ring, wouldn't you say?"

"I thought amethysts were purple," Dee said.

"Not necessarily." Ida plopped herself down in the chair next to mine. "They come in all shades from deep royal to a light violet. Like that." She pointed at the little bottle Pumpkin held.

Several more of the women had comments about

Melissa's ring. I was glad Ida kept quiet about her theory that Melissa's amethyst was fake.

Pumpkin tapped the tray to get my attention. "Biscuit? Would you rather have *Passion Pink*? Or maybe *Blue Lagoon*?"

I cringed. "Don't mention anything having to do with water," I said. "I've had enough to last a lifetime."

Pumpkin stuffed the obnoxiously blue polish out of sight in a small drawer. I pushed a day-glo orange to the back of the tray. "You don't like the *Marigold*," Pumpkin said unnecessarily, and removed it. "That *Fire on the Mountain* would look luscious," she said as my hand hovered over a brilliant red.

"No, I need something gentler than that."

"What color is your dress tonight?"

"Navy," I told her, "but nobody's going to see my toes. I'm wearing comfortable shoes."

Pumpkin looked horrified. "Then we'll have to do your fingernails, too."

Oh, what the heck. "Sure," I said, but then I remembered my ride. "Do I have time to get my nails done, too, Sadie?"

She peered at her watch. "I'll need to leave pretty soon, but I bet anybody here would give you a ride." She looked around for confirmation.

"Why on earth do you need a ride?" Dee sounded thoroughly confused. "I thought you preferred walking."

"I do, I do. It's just that," I could not make myself admit to so much fear, "Sadie offered me a ride this morning, and I took her up on it. It gave us a chance to chat."

That seemed to satisfy everyone except for Ida, who muttered something about "all four blocks," but I ignored her.

"How about *Hollyhock Garden*?" Pumpkin pushed a bottle of polish to the front. "This one's real nice."

"I never saw a hollyhock that color." Ida said. She looked over the tray and pointed to a bottle that matched the fuchsia in the hanging basket outside my front door. "That one'll brighten your day."

I tipped the bottle to look at the name. Dusky it wasn't. The color fairly shouted at me. Oh, why not? "Sure," I said. "*Dusky Violet* for me."

Ida started to make some wisecrack about *Violent Violet,* but stopped when Sharon raised her voice a bit. "I saw Susan walking down First Street this morning."

Nobody had to ask which Susan she was talking about. Susan, with her knee-length raven hair and prickly attitude had breezed into Martinsville a month ago and declared that she was here to reconnect with her father. Only she had neglected to say just who her father was. She even stood up in church one day and told us all she was giving him thirty days and then she'd tell everyone his identity.

I had tried very hard not to suspect Bob, but her hair was black like his. And he was the right age to have a daughter in her twenties. As the town cop, there were a lot of things he didn't discuss about his job, but you'd think if he'd just happened to father a child he would have mentioned it, especially after Susan's ultimatum in church.

And I wasn't the only one. I'd seen Ida squinting speculatively at Ralph. With his slightly stooped posture, he always looked faintly guilty. Or maybe he just had indigestion.

Sharon wondered about Carl, too. Maybe not so much now, what with his having had a heart attack, but I'd seen her giving him that look a woman has when she's not 100 per cent sure of her man.

The only ones who weren't worried about Susan were Pumpkin—she wasn't married—and Dee. She'd divorced Barkley. So she could relax because Susan had said, "I'm giving him one month to tell his wife."

Susan hadn't stuck around for the speculations, though. A few days after her declaration, she just up and left. Moved out of that Rooster and Biscuit bed and breakfast place where she'd been staying. One day she was here. The next day she wasn't. I can't say we were sad to see her go. We'd all been in such a shock over Annie's death that Susan's leaving barely sent a ripple through our community.

But now, just about 30 days later, if she was back in town, she'd be stirring things up again. When would I ever get up enough nerve to talk to Bob about it? If I asked him, it would sound like an accusation. But if I didn't, and he *was* the father, would I find out about it when the rest of the town did? Surely not. He wouldn't do that to me. Would he?

Speculation blossomed on the perm fumes, and we examined Susan as thoroughly as we'd dealt with Tom and his vocational cooking school. We didn't have a clue what she was up to, but lack of knowledge has never been an impediment to juicy gossip.

Then the conversation veered around to why I'd been pushed into the river. Bob and Reebok hadn't found a thing. No suspicious personages. No vindictive people out to get me, not that I knew of, that is. No match on the license plate. I couldn't figure that one out. All license plates were in some sort of nationwide system, weren't they? Well, maybe statewide. I'd have to ask. Since then, nothing more had happened. I was just as happy to forget the whole thing, except that sometimes, more often than I'd like to admit, I felt eyes on me, the sensation of a hand creeping up to shoulder level, ready to slam into me. I shook myself to banish the image, and heard the last part of Ida's sentence. Something about "... persons unknown creating havoc in a quiet community."

"You've been watching too much TV, Ida," I said.

"There's probably a logical explanation."

"For being pushed into the water? There's nothing logical about that. And," she wagged her finger at me, "what were you doing on the dock at that time of night anyway." An accusation more than a question.

"Marmy woke me up, and I couldn't get back to sleep. So I pulled on some warm clothes and took a walk. It was that simple."

"Simple is not the word. Not when somebody tried to kill you."

I opened my mouth for a retort, but then couldn't think of what to say, so I closed it.

Dee spoke up. "I bet you were about to see something that somebody didn't want you to see, and you got pushed into the river to keep from seeing it. Maybe somebody was getting murdered or something, and—"

Ida's dry voice cut Dee off. "Haven't heard of any dead bodies lying around, have you?"

Sharon broke into their squabble. "Did you hear Irene's back in town? Yep. She came driving up about two hours ago. I flagged her car down to welcome her back."

"She's been gone a long time," Pumpkin said, and swiped a brush of brilliant polish on my big toe.

Ida looked down at her hands and started rubbing them as if she were Lady Macbeth wiping away imaginary blood. Before I could ask her what was wrong, she said, "She left right after the funeral." Nobody had to ask which funeral she was talking about. Annie's was the only funeral that had mattered lately.

"Yes, poor thing," Sharon said. "I wonder how Irene's sister is doing?"

I wondered why Irene hadn't given us any warning before she left town. It wasn't like her. She was a fairly self-contained woman; I'd always liked her a great deal; but like the wives of most ministers, she maintained a certain distance from the parishioners. She certainly wasn't one to come to a gossip fest at Sharon's Beauty Shop every Saturday. Still, you'd think she would have mentioned something to somebody. But no, the day after the funeral she'd simply driven out of town. Dee saw her turn up the road toward Braetonburg, and nobody had seen her since then. The next Sunday Henry announced from the pulpit that she'd gone to Ohio for an extended visit with her sister. He sounded worried, so we all knew right away that Irene's sister must have taken a turn for the worse. Henry preached on one of the beatitudes, *blessed are the merciful,* and asked us all to pray for Irene and her entire family. "The sister—what's her name?"

"Deborah," Sadie said. "I hate to miss the rest of this conversation, but I have to get going. I told Melissa I'd stop by for a few minutes." She patted her hair, paid Sharon, waved to me, and twinkled out the door. I hoped I had her energy when I was that age.

"Deborah must be better, then," I said, "if Irene's back home."

"Either she's better, or she's dead," said Dee in a voice of doom.

"Holly's coming home, too," Sharon added, using the back of her wrist to push an errant blond curl off her forehead. "Yep. Today."

What was Holly doing home from college? Or had she graduated already? With my kids all grown and my grandchildren not yet in school, I'd lost my awareness of school vacation schedules. And I couldn't recall receiving a graduation announcement. Then again, I couldn't *not* recall one. Was this just my normal inability to remember things that didn't seem important, or was I still fuzzy from the hypothermia? I didn't think those effects were long-lasting ...

"Irene told me Holly would arrive tonight. Yep, just in

time for the dance."

"I can't believe she'd want to go to a waltz night," I said. "Do young people even learn how to dance nowadays? I mean, *real* dancing?"

Ida stopped massaging her hands long enough to comment. "Sadie said she's learning how to do some of these newfangled dances."

"Why would Holly need to learn them? I thought kids just absorbed that way of hopping around, the way we did with the Twist."

"You're dating yourself, Biscuit," Ida said. "But no, Sadie's the one doing the learning. She told me she's taking private lessons from Miss Mary."

"Surely she's not going to let the musicians play anything other than waltzes and fox trots tonight. This is a *ballroom* dance evening." I had visions of my lovely outfit getting all whompy-jawed with fast dancing.

Ida shrugged. "You know Sadie. Anything's liable to come out of her."

She was right. Much to my chagrin, I'd discounted eighty-something-year-old Sadie when I first moved to Martinsville. It was true that she couldn't drive worth a darn, she always wore yellow, and sometimes she called Marmalade by other food-related names, like *Peaches* or *Jelly*. Still, she'd started taking tap dance lessons the same time I had, she was a whiz at playing the harmonica, and she'd turned into a role model that I respected highly. Her memory had been better lately, too, since she'd started eating more cinnamon—or maybe it was sage—and a bunch of other herbs and spices Annie McGill had told her about. Predictable, she wasn't, but definitely interesting.

Finally, toes and fingers all aglitter in *Dusky Violet*, I checked my watch once more and decided I had more than enough time to detour to Melissa's on the way to the library, so I could return a book of hers I'd borrowed, and by golly, I was going to walk there on my own. It was full daylight. I was perfectly safe.

~~~~~

~GLAZE McKEE~

She hated having to reschedule her pedicure. That was such a fun luxury every other Saturday, but Glaze needed to do some serious thinking. Why had she been so adamant about not telling Biscuit what was going on? They usually shared *everything*.

Biscuit would understand; Glaze was sure she would. But Biscuit would also have an opinion, whether or not she voiced it. If Biscuit was in favor of this, then would Glaze just go along with it, assuming that it was the right thing to do because her big sister said so? No. She wasn't that childish.

But if Biscuit frowned or humphed or shook her head, or even simply seemed less than enthusiastic, then wouldn't Glaze feel she had to turn this down?

She knew if she sat with her feet in Pumpkin's basin of hot water, she'd have been so relaxed, she would have told Biscuit—and everybody else in town considering how the gossip grapevine sprouted around here. This was one decision she wanted to make all by herself, without anybody else's input. She'd have her answer ready in a couple of days. Time enough to tell Biscuit then.

~~~~~

~BISCUIT McKEE~

I was out of breath when I reached Azalea House. Marmalade sat on the front porch grooming herself. I glanced behind me and bent to scratch the back of her head. "Were you waiting for me, Marmy?"

No. I just visited GoodCook for a snack.

I never—well seldom—feel funny talking to my cat. She always seems to answer me with that rumbly little purr. Melissa stood at her sink; I could see her through the kitchen window, so I tapped on the glass and she motioned me inside. I held the door for Marmalade, but she turned her head away, licked her paw, and drew it over the side of her face. Cats are so cute when they do that.

It is important to stay clean.

"I guess Marmalade doesn't like your cooking anymore," I said.

"You're wrong. She just finished." She held up the small bowl she was washing. "Chicken," she added, although I knew from past discussions that chicken was Marmy's usual fare at Melissa's. Sadie always fed her cream; Glaze and Madeleine always had catnip for her. Tom brought her leftover salmon from his restaurant. About all I ever fed her was cat food. Why on earth did that cat put up with me?

That cat? Excuse me?

I heard a yelp from the window. Marmalade had placed her front paws on the edge of the low windowsill. Maybe she was fooled by the bird in the stained glass panel hanging in the window. Or maybe she'd seen her own reflection.

Mouse droppings!

"She's not getting a cold, is she?" Melissa waved a hand at Marmalade.

"No. I've never known her to be sick. She makes that sound quite often. Sounds like she's sneezing, but I don't think it's a true sneeze."

"Want some tea? The kettle's on. Just needs to heat a bit longer."

"Thought you'd never ask." I pulled her paperback out

of my bag and held it up. She nodded toward the small desk in the corner, and I found a bare spot where I could set the book. It looked like she was getting behind in her paperwork. I knew it wasn't any business of mine, but I did wonder if that boyfriend of hers was entirely good for her. I was more than a dozen years older than Melissa—fifty to her thirty-seven—and here I was worrying about her like her mother. I shut my mouth tight without commenting on Chad's negative influence. Maybe she needed love more than a tidy desk. I turned up the gas flame beneath the kettle. She kept her special Chai tea in the pantry. "Join me?"

"Sure, but I won't have time to sit with you. I have some guests checking out in an hour and a single woman coming in this afternoon. She's staying only the one night. Then two more are coming in tomorrow sometime after noon."

"Keep right on with your cooking, but don't stop talking. Those guests—anybody I know?" She so often had repeat guests, this wasn't an idle question. I'd met many of her regulars.

"You know Dave and Carole. They're paying extra for dinner each day. So is the single woman. At this rate, I should start a restaurant. I still have this loaf of bread to bake." She slipped off her engagement ring and set it on a special ring-holder beside her sink. "Thank goodness I did all my grocery shopping this morning."

"Don't let me slow you down." I dropped a tea ball into her favorite mug and picked the one with the boats on it for myself. No, not that one. Boats reminded me of water. I switched to the mug with the leafy vine pattern. Out of curiosity I turned it over. Right. It was one my mom had made.

Melissa laughed—I loved how she so often chuckled for no apparent reason, just her inner happiness bubbling up—and measured flour into her big stainless steel mixing bowl. "Grab a doughnut. Made them for breakfast this morning."

Melissa's bed and breakfast specialized in the most scrumptious morning meals imaginable. Once somebody stayed at Azalea House they tended to come back on a regular basis. She never did any advertising, but always seemed to have just the right number of guests, although it sounded like she was over-extended at the moment.

"Dave and Carole?" I knew the names but couldn't place them.

"You remember them. The Pontiacs. They're Maggie's in-laws."

"Ahh," I said when my brain chimed in. "Here for the new grandbaby?"

Melissa frowned and held her hand out just below waist level. "He's not a baby."

"I know that. Grand*child* then." Maggie and her husband Norm lived one block up Beechnut Lane from me. They'd started the process of adopting little Willie whose mother died in a car wreck last month. There was no known father. "Surely the adoption can't be finalized already?"

"Heavens no. They're still just fostering him. But next week's his 4th birthday."

"Willie's?" What a dumb question. What other child were we talking about? Why do we pad conversations with meaningless comments and questions like that?

She nodded and turned away from her flour mixture to pick up the pan of buttermilk heating on the range. "Irish soda bread," she said, and started mixing with a big bamboo spoon. According to Melissa, bamboo didn't absorb oils and odors the way wood did. "When they made the reservation, Carol asked me to bake Willie a birthday cake with a big 4 on top."

"Why don't they stay with Maggie and Norm? That big old house has plenty of room."

"Sure does. But with Doodle-Doo raising the sun every morning, and those chickens cackling all day long …" she paused, apparently considering the menagerie on Beechnut Lane. Because of the rather erratic placement of streets in this town, Maggie and Norm's spread took up one of the biggest blocks in Martinsville. Pasture, small barn, a moveable chicken coop, tool sheds, and a rambling old farm house. They had a huge spring-fed pond. It drained into the creek behind my house. The creeks were all funneled under the streets. I loved the sound of the water as it gurgled along.

"And the goats," Melissa went on, "keep bleating or whatever goats do, and then on top of that, Norm's two sisters are coming with all their assorted children. Let's just say Carole and Dave want a place where they can avoid the ruckus."

"The whole group is staying at Maggie's?"

Melissa nodded, a little grimly I thought.

"Then no wonder the parents want to stay here." Azalea House was a haven of comfort. And quiet. If I hadn't married Bob, I'd probably still be living here. I added hazelnut creamer to my tea, inhaled the luscious aroma, and took a sip. "I'm really sorry I couldn't have you and Chad to dinner Thursday night."

Melissa gave me one of her looks. "Do you honestly think I'd expect you to serve us dinner after you spent the night in a waterlogged tree and almost died?"

She had a point. "We'd still like to meet him. You'll be at the dance tonight, won't you?"

"Probably not." She tossed her head to flip an errant curl out of her eyes. When that didn't work, she swiped at it with her wrist. That curly brown mop of hers was cute, but it desperately needed a trim. What a shame she'd been too busy to schedule with Sharon this morning. It would have been nice to have her in on the conversation.

"You can't miss the dance. I want to meet this mystery guy of yours."

"Biscuit, I just remembered I have to run to the grocery store while this bread's rising. And don't you need to get to the library?"

"What's wrong, Melissa?" I know a made-up excuse when I hear one.

"Nothing. Nothing much. I just really do have a lot to finish before that new guest arrives." She poured her tea down the sink. She hadn't taken even one sip.

"Fine," I said, and took a quick last bite of doughnut. "I'll see you soon?"

She didn't answer, so I let myself out. I looked behind myself only twice as I walked the half block to the library. I was getting better, but there still was that feeling that I had a target painted between my shoulder blades.

CHAPTER 7
Saturday 2:00 to 6:00p.m.

~REEBOK GARNER~

REEBOK WAS SUPPOSED TO BE SLEEPING. HE WORKED nights, after all. But he lay, pajama clad, on his narrow bed worrying instead. Even though the town was quiet, that didn't mean they could do without full-time protection. If they'd had more people on staff, maybe they could have found the man who'd pushed the Chief's wife into the river. Reebok felt bad about that. He should have been able to solve the case.

He turned over onto his side. What case? There wasn't a case. No evidence, no suspicions, no suspects. He hadn't even known anything was wrong until the Chief called him and said his wife had gone out for a walk half an hour before, wasn't back yet, and her cat was going crazy. Reebok had barely been able to hear the Chief with all those screeches in the background. They'd combed the town for hours looking for her. He'd never seen the Chief so out of control.

When the 911 center called, the Chief had torn out of the station. Reebok had thought for sure she was dead. Hypothermia wasn't anything to fool around with. Maybe she wouldn't have been pushed into the water if there'd been another officer on patrol that night.

He closed his eyes with grim determination, but M-L-X-1-0-6-6 floated behind his eyelids. Too bad that license plate hadn't panned out. She'd probably mistaken one of the letters, or reversed two of the numbers. It was hard to see anything clearly in the dark. And under the trees, at that. He wanted like everything to catch the bastard who'd hurt her. He was here to protect these fine people. If anything did happen, he was ready, on duty or off, but it sure would help if they'd get the numbers right when reporting a plate.

When Mrs. Zapota phoned him, he was already too awake to resent being called out again.

"I don't know if this will help, Deputy." Mrs. Zapota twisted what looked like a checkbook, as if she could wring her son's presence out of it. "I found it under the couch."

Along with Reebok's pen, maybe? No. That was too much to hope for. He said a noncommittal "Yes?"

"It has some teeth marks on it, so there's a chance my little Venus had something to do with its being under there."

Little Venus? There wasn't anything little about that tugboat.

She held it out to him. "I've looked through it. He was always private about his money, but I thought maybe you might find something, some clue to where he might be."

"Thank you, ma'am. I'll look through it and get it back to you as soon as I can."

Mrs. Zapota leaned down and stroked Venus. "You see, Deputy, there's an entry in there that I don't understand. He wrote a rather sizable check made out to Cash on Wednesday, the last day I saw him."

~~~~~

My Gratitude List for Saturday (written just before dinner because I may be too tired after the dance tonight)

    1. Melissa, even though she's upset with me for some reason

    2. Bob, who is STILL at work – something about a checkbook. I hope he makes it home in time for the dance. And I absolutely refuse to step on his feet tonight. Is there a goddess of the dance I should pray to?

VIOLET AS AN AMETHYST

3. Warm sweaters when I need them. I wish I could find Bob's sweatshirt. I like wearing it. Hope I didn't leave it at the clinic.

4. Sharon and Pumpkin and ~~all~~ the women in town (most of them).

5. This dear town, where I can walk anywhere I need to, although I still can't walk by myself at night. I get a creepy feeling right in the middle of my back, from my neck down to my waist. Do I need to see a shrink?

> *I am grateful for*
> *Widelap*
> *GoodCook and the chicken she gives me*
> *the butterflies above the flowers*
> *this puddle of sunshine*
> *the breeze that cools me when I walk for a*
> *long time*

~~~~~

~BOB SHEFFIELD~

"You're right," Bob said, thumbing through the checkbook Reebok had brought back from Mrs. Zapota's. "Two big checks for exactly the same amount, written about four weeks apart. It looks like this deposit on Tuesday was a transfer from a savings account, just enough to cover the second check."

"That makes sense, Sir. SV TRNS." He spelled it out. "But why make the checks out to cash? That's a lot of money to carry around."

"Your guess, as they say." Bob rapped his closed fist against his mustache three or four times. It sure would be nice if folks would write little notes about what they intended. Too much to ask, he supposed. "He was paying somebody off. Must have been. Cash, that much cash, means it was under the table."

"I asked his mother if he'd made any large purchases recently, but she said no."

CHAPTER 8
Saturday 6:30 p.m. to 10:00 p.m.

~BISCUIT McKEE~

I CLIPPED ON MY MOTHER-OF-PEARL EARRINGS and took a moment as I was doing it to admire my husband as he buttoned his dress shirt. Ordinarily I wasn't one to enjoy dances, but the library was the right place for one, as we had proved a year or so after I arrived in Martinsville when we held a town Halloween party there. Two months ago my Petunias, my three elderly and absolutely indispensable library volunteers, had talked me into a ballroom dance. The reason? Well, there wasn't one, and they'd finally just said they wanted to do it and who cared why. Far be it from me to stand in their way.

There had been some concern when Annie was killed halfway into the planning process. We'd sat down at the library one afternoon shortly after the funeral and discussed whether it would be wrong to have a dance so soon after Annie's death. And we decided the dance would be a great time to unveil the life quilt Annie had made, starting when she was just a little girl. She'd made one square each month for years. The quilt used to drape over a rocking chair in her store, but I'd asked if we could hang it in the library. Not that there was anyone to stop me. It seemed like the whole town was Annie's family.

So the Petunias and I had decided to go ahead with the dance. They had boundless energy, knew everybody in town, and exuded enthusiasm from their pores. Also, I imagined their recent discovery of a new high-class consignment shop in Garner Creek—and the resulting long gowns they'd all purchased—had something to do with their plans.

Sadie's gown was yellow, of course, a diaphanous,

swirly skirt over a sedate satin lining. Rebecca had chosen a violet number with a veil-like cape that hung from her shoulders almost to the floor. With her gray hair piled up, she would look downright regal. And Esther showed me a white gown with trim that matched her deep blue eyes. It reminded me of the outfit Vera Miles wore in *White Christmas*—only Vera's was trimmed in red, wasn't it?—when she and Danny Kaye tap-danced their way along the pier outside that supper club where the two sisters almost got arrested and—well, you know what I'm talking about—only Esther's gown was floor length and built to accommodate a figure that resembled a fire hydrant.

"I don't see why I have to wear this getup," Bob complained as he slipped two old-fashioned cotton handkerchiefs into his pants pocket. "The floor will probably be so crowded we won't do any dancing at all."

"How diplomatic of you." I laughed at his startled expression. "If I promise not to step on your feet, will you ask me to waltz at least one time?" Bob was a wonderful dancer. His grade school had started his dancing education in gym class, but Rebecca Jo thought he needed more polish and, despite his protests and those of his father, she'd insisted on ballroom dance lessons. By the time he no longer needed lessons, he didn't mind them, as they ensured that the girls at the high school dances all vied for his attention. How he'd ended up with me, I'd never know. "I'm glad we didn't have dancing at our wedding reception," I said. "Otherwise you might have scurried off into the sunset."

He smoothed down his mustache—the one I'd talked him into growing—and stepped across the bedroom to encircle me in his white-shirted arms. "Just think of all the fun I would have missed," he said and probably would have continued in that vein except that Marmalade bounded from the bed onto his shoulder.

I like our fun times. You could get down my feather toy.

How she did that without digging in her claws, I had no idea, but I was very glad she had such a good sense of balance. She reached out one dainty paw and brushed my nose.

I have told you before that I am a cat. Of course I have good balance.

Bob and I laughed at the way she rumbled ...

Mouse droppings!

... and at the funny little squeak she let out. He lifted her down to the bed and turned to pick up his cufflinks. "Can you help me put these on, Woman?"

"Sure," I said, "if you'll fasten my buttons."

Fur is much easier.

We might have found ourselves sidetracked again, except that Marmy let out another comment—at least it sounded like one—so we finished our dressing and headed downstairs. At the last minute I remembered the bowl of cheese straws, my contribution to the potluck snack table.

"Watch the house for us, Marmalade," Bob said as he closed the door, and she purred in return.

Of course. I will watch from the soft bed upstairs.

The weather was lovely, that balmy sort of evening that graces northeastern Georgia often enough in the spring, and this particular valley well into the summer. Too bad Bob was still all stuffed up, although it probably kept him from smelling that nasty plant odor borne on the gentle evening breeze. We strolled up the sidewalk arm in arm. For once my dressy shoes were comfortable—low-heeled, wide-toed, dark blue, and well-hidden by my long navy skirt. The matching knee-length vest flowed over an ice-blue silk blouse with wide sleeves and a jewel neckline. I'd put my hair up in what I hoped would remain a French twist. And my fingernails fairly glowed. I felt thoroughly elegant. Bob's appreciative glances helped, even though they were spaced between his sneezes.

I'm afraid I inspected every single white car parked beside the street. There were a lot of them, including my son's car—one of the very few I could recognize, but only because his left fender was an obnoxious shade of orange. He'd bought the car very used and very cheap. If he ever replaced the orange with a white fender, I'd never recognize it. Scott had been dating Pumpkin for some months and, quite naturally, had very little time for his mother. He'd come to the clinic with Mom and Auntie Blue, but we hadn't talked much then. I was looking forward to seeing him again.

Just about everybody in town must have driven to the dance, and there weren't any parking spaces to speak of. I wondered if Tom's restaurant parking lot was full. It was a block and a half away, but I'd be willing to bet a lot of husbands dropped their wives off in their tottery high heels at the library door and went to park their cars at Tom's.

I tried to be inconspicuous, but Bob picked up on what I was doing. "I haven't seen your license plate on any of these cars," he said.

"Neither have I. Not a ten-sixty-six anywhere."

He patted my hand in reassurance.

I squeezed his arm closer to my side as we approached Dogwood. "I think I need to apologize to you."

"Apology accepted."

"Aren't you going to ask me what for?"

"I figure you'll tell me, Woman."

"I'm pretty sure I left your sweatshirt—the one I borrowed—at the Montrose Clinic. I can't find it anywhere. Glaze did a couple of loads of laundry when she was staying with me on Thursday, but I asked her where it was and she didn't remember washing it."

He stopped walking and turned toward me. "You didn't leave it. We had to get the wet clothes off you and start warming you up in the ambulance. Your limbs were so stiff, I had to cut everything off."

"Including your sweatshirt?"

"Uh-huh."

"I'm so sorry, honey. That was your favorite one."

He laid a restraining finger on my lips. "I'd rather have you than that sweatshirt any day. Dr. Prescott told me that one of the things that contributed to your survival was the thick layers you had on. They helped trap at least some body heat."

He bent to kiss the end of my nose, but had to turn away at the last moment to sneeze.

"You're still stuffy," I said.

"Sadie told me this morning that local bee pollen was even better than honey for eliminating allergies if I eat it every day. She gave me some to taste. It's surprisingly sweet."

"Bee pollen?"

He nodded. "Wallace had twenty hives."

"Really? It never looked like that many."

"That's because he placed them in blocks of four, each hive facing a different direction. He used to have 200 of them when he was younger. Kept them in orchards all up and down the valley, but he gradually turned them over to other beekeepers, except for the twenty in his yard."

"He was awfully frail the last few years," I said. "How did he care for them?"

"Two people from the Keagan County Beekeepers Club have maintained them ever since Wallace had his second stroke. One of them was there this morning. He let me watch him work the hives. That's why I went up to Sadie's."

"Why did you have to wear those disreputable

chinos?"

"Bees get nervous around dark colors, and working the hives can be a sticky business with all that propolis. The chinos were the only crummy light-colored pants I could find."

They were crummy all right, but I supposed the bees wouldn't mind.

"The beekeeper invited me to the club meetings. He said they'd be harvesting the honey starting next week if the weather holds, and I could help. Sadie said she'd bring a few jars to the library for you and the others."

"Yes?" I wondered where this talk was heading.

"Sadie said it would be easy for me to get my own bee pollen if—"

His voice trailed off as he got that pinched-nose vibration that means a sneeze is on its way. I waited for the explosion. "Let me guess, Sadie wants, bless you, wants you to take the hives. Bless you again."

"Only half of them – thank you – the ones that aren't yellow. Roger's going to take those. He'll leave them in her backyard, but he'll be the beekeeper." He put away his handkerchief.

Visions of tall sky blue, white, and mint green boxes marching across my backyard filled my imagination for a moment or two. "Where will we put them all?"

"It's not like they take up a lot of room. We'll put three in the west corner, three in the east corner—"

"And four in the middle," I finished. "Well, the aerial antics should be fun to watch. Do you think Marmalade will mind them?"

"She'll learn soon enough to stay away from them."

My poor garden. It had taken quite a hit awhile back when the remains of those traveling salesmen were found. The garden hadn't been the same since. "I guess we could use the pollination."

Bob hugged my arm closer to his side. "Wallace had duplicates of most of the equipment. Roger and I can divvy it up next week. All I have to do is haul the storage boxes down from Sadie's attic."

"So it's a done deal?"

He placed his large, comforting hand over mine. "Don't worry. You'll love them."

I paused next to the library's white picket fence. "Do I get to wear one of those white suits with the screened hat?"

He bent and planted a kiss on the end of my nose, this time without sneezing. "I told Sadie I'd pick them up tomorrow night. You're not supposed to move hives until after dark."

I'd heard a special documentary about honey bees on Public Radio recently, so I knew honey bees foraged up to five miles from their hives. "Won't they just fly back to Sadie's yard?"

"Not if I pile some brush in front of the hives so the bees get confused the moment they fly out of the hives into our yard. The brush will force them to reorient on the new location."

"Speaking of orienting," I nodded toward the library, "we need to find our way there or the dance will be over before we show up."

He kissed my nose one more time. "Hmm," he said. "Are you sure you want to go to the dance?"

"We have to. I brought cheese straws."

We weren't the first ones to arrive. Sadie's yellow Chevy was parked out front as usual, with Margaret and Sam's classy Duesenberg right behind it. Seven o'clock seemed awfully early to be starting a dance, but when I thought about the respective ages of the ones who had organized it, I decided there was some reason.

"Looks like Glaze is here already," Bob said. "She and

Tom must have walked." He gestured to the honey-brown dog sitting beside one of the stone lions.

"It's not her dog," I said loyally. "She's trying to get rid of it."

He squeezed my arm closer to his side. "That's what you think, Woman," and patted the dog as we passed it, receiving one of its happy guttural whimpers in return.

Esther stood just inside the heavy oak doors. I've always loved this old building, and I had to admit that, impressive as it was, my Petunias had dressed it up even more. "Esther, it's lovely! How did you get all this done in so short a time?" The library had closed only two hours ago.

"It was nothing," she said. "We corralled some of the youngsters into helping out."

The "youngsters" turned out to be the knitting circle that Esther and Rebecca Jo belonged to. Many of them were in their sixties. "Well, you obviously put a lot of effort into it."

Enormous bows in shades of purple, from the lightest lavender to the most intense fuchsia, even brighter than my nail polish, adorned the railing of the grand old staircase. The musicians had their stands set up above the dancers, on the first landing. There was a bow on the community bulletin board—it was conspicuously free of any dog notice from Glaze. She could have brought one along with her, I thought, and pinned it up on her way in. The long refreshment tables off to our right sported swags of greens and purples, with gold rosettes. Had this come out of the library budget? As if she'd read my mind, Esther assured me, "Margaret said she would pay for the decorations and the musicians." Her middle-aged son, I noticed, was the one playing the accordion while one of her granddaughters chimed in on the saxophone.

Esther glanced over her shoulder, as if she were on a

secret mission, and leaned close to me. "I already filled out the checks," she whispered. "They're upstairs. All you have to do is sign them. Margaret said she'd have a manager soon who would give us the money to cover the checks."

Thinking of my limited budget, I said, "I hope this new manager hurries." We had enough money in the account to pay the checks, but I'd rather see library money going to buy books.

"Margaret said it'll be public knowledge by next week." In a louder voice she added, "We're going to make this a yearly event, so we can use the bows over and over again."

"I'll have to thank her."

"No, don't say anything." She looked across the room to where Margaret and Sam stood talking to Rebecca Jo. "She likes to keep her money out of the limelight, you know."

I did know. Margaret had quietly funded many improvements for the town, but I doubted that most residents knew where the fire trucks and the day care center had come from, to say nothing of the repairs to the gazebo in the park. Or, if they knew, they didn't talk about it.

"Well, dear, we're using the money wisely." She patted the covered bowl I held. "Are these your wonderful chocolate chip cookies? I can't wait to have one."

"Sorry, Esther. I brought cheese straws this time."

"Oh." For some unfathomable reason she looked relieved. I was miffed for a moment. I thought she liked my cookies. She rallied her face and pointed us graciously toward the refreshment area. I counted no fewer than six trays of chocolate chip cookies. No wonder Esther had been relieved. I triumphantly placed my cheese straws amongst them, like a pork chop in the middle of a kosher picnic. The big donations jar had a purple ribbon on it. I could see more bills than change. That was good. The punch on the next table was purple. Grape juice? Chosen to match the décor, perhaps?

Bob turned aside to greet Ralph Peterson. I didn't see his wife, but I spotted Maggie Pontiac and wondered how she and Norm could have possibly torn themselves away from Willie. When I thought of him, that sweet little boy, the term "limpet" came to mind, the way he clung to them. Or was I thinking of a barnacle? What was a limpet anyway? Where was a dictionary when I needed one? Bob was still talking with Ralph, so I headed toward the reference area, dodging around a couple doing an enthusiastic polka that took me back to my childhood. All the band members, except for Esther's granddaughter, were old enough to have learned their style from Lawrence Welk. I stopped when Maggie called my name and waved me over. The limpets would have to wait.

"That dress looks gorgeous on you," I told her as we got close enough to speak over the sound of the band. Thank goodness they weren't too loud. "I'm used to you in jeans and a tee-shirt."

"Oh, come on, Biscuit. I clean up pretty well on Sundays, don't I?"

"Yes. But you always look more comfortable in jeans."

"That's because I *am* more comfortable in jeans."

"Aren't we all?" I usually preferred a long denim skirt. Unless I was going to be weeding the garden. I was way behind on my weeding. First it was all that rain and then... and then I didn't want to be outside by myself. That was ridiculous. I couldn't quit living. I was going to have to schedule some—

"Biscuit?" Maggie had that raised eyebrow look that said she knew I'd been wool-gathering.

"How much did I miss?"

"Only a paragraph or two, including my compliments

on your classy outfit."

It's so nice to have friends who put up with me. I looked around. "Where's Norm?"

"He's home with Willie." Before I could ask the why-come-to-a-dance-without-your-husband question, Maggie swept her hand around like Cinderella's godmother. Bibbidi-bobbidi-boo. "I went to all this trouble, to say nothing of the expense, to find the perfect dress. There was no way I wasn't going to wear it. The last time I had a new gown was my high school senior prom, and that was …" Her mouth turned down as she calculated. "Seventeen years ago? Good grief. How did I get to be mid-thirty?"

"I had my thirtieth reunion two years ago. Don't go telling me you think you're old."

"You're right. Thirty-five isn't old. It's just that it got here sooner than I expected it to."

I laughed. "I know what you mean. But you were talking about Willie."

"Oh, yeah. My in-laws aren't arriving until tomorrow and we couldn't find anybody—anybody I thought Willie would trust—to stay with him." She waved her arm again. "Everybody's here."

"Bob will dance with you. I'm sure you're less likely to step on his feet than I am."

"No. That's okay. Thanks, but I want to leave pretty soon anyway."

"You'll miss the unveiling of the Annie McGill Quilt if you leave before 8:30."

"Yes, but I was on the committee to hang it." She turned slightly to look up at the large white sheet that covered the quilt. "It's going to look spectacular there. Still, I have some more papers I have to fill out."

"The adoption?"

She grimaced.

"How's the process going?"

Her grimace turned to grump. "Don't ask. It's slow as you-know-what in you-know-when. I swear we've handed over every bit of paper we've ever generated. We've had interview after interview. And now we have to go through another round again next month plus two home visits—one of them will be a surprise. With my luck they'll show up on the worst day possible."

"I'm really sorry, Maggie." It was one thing to read stories of the anguish delayed adoption proceedings could cause. It was quite another thing to witness it first-hand, although I had to admit it hadn't really been all that long. She and Norm were just anxious to make it official, but Willie sure looked like he already belonged with them. "I wish I could do something to help."

"You already did. You wrote that nice recommendation letter."

She twisted her neck around, and I thought she looked rather like a friendly version of Vampirah.

"What are you grinning at?" she asked.

"Oh, nothing." She would never understand a Vampirah comment. "I was just thinking what good parents you and Norm will be. You already are." She turned toward the door, but I put out a hand to stop her. "I meant to ask you, could Bob and I stop by tomorrow after church and pick up two half-gallons of milk?"

"Sure thing. The girls are producing it as fast as I can bottle it up. Just give us time to gather Willie from Sunday School. Then come on over."

"We'll walk slow," I promised. "It'll be good to see Willie again. Is he ..." I paused. I didn't want to sound too nosy. "Is he talking at all now?"

Maggie's smile flattened. "I don't know what to do except just to keep loving him. The only thing he says is 'where mommy?' and sometimes he asks about somebody named Gail."

"Gail? Gail who?"

"Beats me. I don't know anybody by that name. Every time we ask him who she is, he doesn't want to talk about it. Usually he just wants to brush my hair, and believe me, that makes quite a mess."

"I remember my Sally doing that when she was about Willie's age. Funny how kids are fascinated with hair."

"I'm gonna take off, Biscuit. Everybody's seen my gorgeous dress, so now I can go put my jeans back on and prop up my feet."

"You'll be the envy of every woman here who's wearing three-inch heels."

She laughed and waved goodbye.

The dance progressed nicely until 7:43 – I know the time because I'd just glanced at the big clock above the children's section. Bob and I had almost finished one whole waltz without my stepping on his feet even once, when the woman next to me stopped in her tracks, almost upsetting her partner. I—doggone it—kicked Bob's shoe unintentionally. That didn't count as stepping on his feet, did it? Gradually the stillness spread as one couple after another connected with the lack of movement next to them, and the whole floor, from the old rolltop desk to the checkout counter, past the reference shelves, and all the way back to the carpeted children's section came to a standstill, everyone looking toward the massive oak doors, where a tuxedo-clad Red Butler stood, not oblivious to his impact, but seeming not to pay it any mind. He studied our faces deliberately, and I felt myself flushing, probably as bright a red as his cummerbund, when he looked in my direction, but his gaze wandered on until it came to rest on Sadie. She looked like a little honey bee in her bright yellow. I did wonder if she wore her yellow tennis shoes underneath the chiffon. If so, the laces would probably be coming untied as usual.

Red's passage through the crowd up to her side reminded me of another such passage, like the parting of the Red Sea, when lava-haired Easton had moved through the same crowd of people on Halloween, the night Sam, Bob's friend from childhood, was killed. Maybe it was just because of all that red hair. The two of them, Red and Easton both, could have been hatched in a volcano.

I didn't even have to strain to hear what he said. His voice floated out to fill the room, even above the gentle strains of the music. "Miss Sadie, thank you so much for inviting me. I apologize for being late, but I was unavoidably detained." He not only looked like Gable, he sounded like him, as if a script-writer had known Red could pull off that stilted line.

Sadie didn't seem to notice anything amiss. "You're here now. That's all that counts. Come meet everybody."

"I'd be delighted."

Sadie reached up to take his arm, ready to pull him along with her, but that turned out to be unnecessary. People started moving past the two of them as if there were a formal receiving line. Sadie duly introduced people. Red shook every man's hand, and kissed the hands of the older women. I wondered briefly why Bob never kissed my hand. Wait. Bob *had* kissed my hand. In the clinic. As I was waking up. He'd kissed my hand, but I hadn't really been aware of it, so it didn't count.

With each of the younger women, Red grasped her hand and held it for a moment while he placed his left hand on top. Bob and I stood back and watched. Everybody, well, every female, felt treasured in those brief moments – I could see it on their faces. His act was as phony as a wooden nickel, but I couldn't wait to get my hand kissed. This time I'd be able to see it coming.

The men, though... I looked up at Bob to gauge his reaction. His arm around my waist tightened a fraction.

"What do you think, Woman," he whispered, "should we go meet His Highness?"

"His Honor?" I played along.

"His Eminence?"

"His Majesty?"

Bob shook his head, tugged me toward the fast-dwindling line, and I thought I heard him say, "Fathead." Glaze and Tom, I noticed, stood back near the reference books in a private conversation. Something about the way they were posed, something indefinable, excluded everybody else. Even Red. I saw him look in their direction, twice, in between the kisses and handshakes he was doling out. As far as I could tell, Glaze was the only woman in the room who hadn't even looked at Red.

Just before we reached our goal, Easton Hastings stepped right in front of me and kissed Sadie on the cheek. "You have to introduce me," she purred in that gravelly voice that always seemed to issue from bedroom thoughts. She'd redeemed herself somewhat in the past year—I think Sadie'd had a great deal to do with that—but she still left the ladies of Martinsville a wee bit anxious. She turned her purr on Red and stepped closer to him than was absolutely necessary. Brazen hussy, breaking into the line in front of me like that. Her waist-length fiery-orange hair floated around her and brushed the front of his tux. In the interest of perfect truth, I must say her hair clashed with his scarlet cummerbund. Humph. She had no sense of boundaries whatsoever. Every woman in the library held her breath. "Welcome to Martinsville," she said after Sadie finished the introduction. "We'd just love to make you feel right at home here."

"I already do feel at home." Red accepted her outstretched hand. She didn't have to stretch it very far. If he'd been sitting down, she would have been in his lap. "Quite at home," he said, and brushed his mustache over her hand before bestowing on it a gentle kiss.

I thought it would tickle, but Easton simply glowed, as if she needed anything to make her more attractive than she already was. I will say I gloated somewhat over the fact that so far Red had kissed the hands of only the *older* women. Easton would have a cow if she thought she'd been grouped with us old farts.

"Red," Sadie interrupted, "I'd like you to meet our librarian and her husband."

I held out my hand with a tingle of excitement. "Biscuit McKee," I said. "Welcome to Martinsville."

Red clasped my hand, but before he could raise it to his lips, Bob reached around me. "Bob Sheffield," he said. His long arm pushed mine down inexorably away from the upcoming kiss, forcing Red to let go. "I head the Martinsville Police Force."

I could hear the capital letters ring. Bob was one of the most self-effacing men I'd ever known. What on earth had come over him? Why even ask? I knew. I could smell the increase in testosterone as the two men sized each other up.

Their hands, grasped in a handshake that had gone on longer than necessary, quivered a bit, as if each were trying to outgrip the other. I could see the button on the front of Red's tux begin to vibrate. Unusual button it was, too, irregularly shaped and very shiny, like the ones I'd seen on his blazer at the Beauty Shop, only this one was dark and had one long red hair tangled about it. Easton had left her mark.

"How much longer will you be in town?" Bob's tone was fairly mild, but conversations stopped around us.

Red was saved from replying when Sadie moved between the two of them and forced the wrestling match to end. She called out, "Henry! Irene! How nice of you to come!"

Heads swiveled to the door, where our preacher stood with his wife. Irene sailed into the room ahead of him and greeted Sadie, then turned to Rebecca Jo, as staunchly elegant in her violet gown as I had assumed she would be. "I'm so glad I could make it. The library is lovely tonight." She stepped back and looked Rebecca Jo over. "And so are you. What a striking cape. It's almost like a veil, isn't it? You look positively regal." Rebecca Jo beamed. What woman doesn't love sincere flattery? She *did* look stunning. "This dance should be a yearly event," Irene added.

I turned back to Bob, who stared at Red's retreating back. I raised my hand to brush away a hair that tickled my chin, and I caught just a hint of Red's spicy aftershave—different than the one I'm smelled on him this morning at the Beauty Shop, and both of them much nicer than Carl's.

Now, why did I have to go and think about Carl and his aftershave? The library melted away, replaced by the moonlight shining on the surge of the river, the vibration of those pounding feet on the dock, and the impact as I was hurled toward the water.

Just before I hit, a tenor sax led off with a haunting melody. Wouldn't you know it? They were playing "Moon River." I pulled myself together just in time. Roger Johnson stood in front of me, asking me for a dance. Now there was a young man with promise. He had founded a garbage removal company in his early twenties, not that he was much older than that now. Before he'd come up with the garbage hauling idea, we all had to drive our own garbage up to the county dump outside of Russell Gap—quite a lot of gas wasted on those trips.

Roger had a monopoly on the garbage business in this town because he was the only person who wanted to tackle the convoluted streets and strangely-angled corners that effectively prohibited the big commercial garbage trucks from fitting in or turning around once they got here. Even the orders for Ralph and Ida's grocery store had to be transferred from 18-wheelers in Garner Creek, a town which had grown up on flatter land and had room for wider streets, onto smaller trucks for the trip down the valley. Ralph's brother owned the transfer trucks that made the twice-weekly trip, Mondays and Thursdays. No wonder our groceries were so expensive. And no wonder Roger's garbage trucks were so small. I'd heard him quip that he couldn't fit our long town name on his little trucks. Hence the name Mville Garbage, with not even enough room for an apostrophe after the M.

I asked him once why he didn't call his company Mville Trucking. "Because I haul garbage," was his most sensible answer. "You trash it; we stash it," he'd gone on to say. "You break it; we take it. You junk it; we plunk it. You throw it; we stow it. You dispose—off it goes." Despite all his goofing around, he was probably making a well-deserved fortune. In his younger years he used to make midnight sorties to paint our mailbox various ghastly shades of whatever paint he happened to find. I'd much rather have him hauling our trash than trashing our mailbox.

"I like this melody," he said, bringing me back to awareness of the world around me. He hummed a few bars of "Moon River," but seemed to think better of it, which was just as well. He could write the most beautiful music, but he couldn't, as my dad often said, carry a tune in a bucket with a lid on it.

His waltzing was wonderful, though. Much better than mine. I stepped on his feet two or three times in the first minute or so, but he simply laughed and put me at ease. He'd been so sad at Annie McGill's funeral; I was glad to see him bouncing back.

After the waltz ended, and before the next piece started, I asked him for some punch, and he dutifully headed off to the refreshment table, where I saw him speak to Pumpkin. My son Scott put a proprietary arm around her shoulder. What was it with all this male territoriality? Did a dance elicit the ownership hormones? I glided over that way. To tell the truth, I tromped over there, but in my more than vivid imagination, I walked with the grace of Cinderella at the ball, before she turned into a rag bag.

"Thank you, Roger," I said, taking the punch and nodding to Glaze and Tom as they approached. They were holding hands, I was happy to see. "Purple punch hits the spot. I love your dress, Pumpkin. Where did you get it?" Scott rolled his eyes, and Roger stepped aside to talk with Tom. The two of them wandered toward the front door. I should get a medal for defusing awkward situations. Bibbidi-bobbidi-boo.

"I made it," she said with well-deserved pride, and we chatted about techniques for hemming silk. Glaze held up her end of this conversation better than I, because she was the one who'd developed real sewing skills after a few disastrous aprons and pillows in school home economics classes. I stepped back so I could look at Pumpkin's toes. *Fire on the Mountain,* I guessed, with little white daisies painted in the center of each red toenail.

Glaze stopped in the middle of a sentence and looked over my shoulder. I half turned and almost collided with Red's fancy button. Easton's inadvertent souvenir hair was gone. My goodness, but he was tall.

"Are you ladies enjoying the dance?" The question sounded like it was addressed to all of us, but the only one he looked at was Glaze.

"Yes," I said, "we're having a lovely time."

He extended a hand toward Glaze. "I don't believe we've met."

Tom reached around her—where had he come from?—and took Red's hand in a peremptory shake. "Hello, Red.

This is Glaze. She's my date for the evening." He put a slight emphasis on *my*.

"Red, I hope you got your car taken care of," I said as Bob walked up beside me. The testosterone crowd zeroing in on their prey, marking their territory.

"Ah. No." Red shook his head. "Not yet. I decided to wait until I had more time."

"Let's dance," Tom said, taking Glaze by the hand. He looked over his shoulder at Red. "I'll see you Monday morning. Seven-thirty," and he twirled Glaze onto the dance floor.

Conversation around us stilled, and I looked up to see what had grabbed everyone's attention. The mysterious Susan, looking like some sort of Greek goddess, paused just inside the front door. Her waterfall of black hair cascaded down her back, well below her knees. A wispy shawl, light and airy, in an electric shade of violet, draped over her arm. I had the rather ungenerous thought—I admit it—that her shawl matched the bow on the bulletin board. The white of her gown set off the olive tone of her shoulders, one of which was becomingly bared. I couldn't see where Bob was, but the mouths of most of the other men went unbecomingly slack.

Red started to move toward her, but stopped when Roger stepped forward and offered Susan his arm. Where on earth did the town garbage man develop such suave self-assurance? It seemed only a year ago that he'd been a gawky young man with very little purpose in life. He led her past the check-out desk as the music swelled. I didn't know the difference between a tango and a foxtrot, or any of those others, but it was something with a gentle swing. Maybe it was a cha-cha, or a rumba. Glaze and Tom certainly did it justice. Gradually the other couples joined in. Conversations around the perimeter of the dance floor resumed, and all seemed to be well. Until one of the heavy

VIOLET AS AN AMETHYST

oak doors slammed open with a speed I'd never imagined it could attain, knocking my town bulletin board off the wall, where it landed bow-side down. The violin screeched, and the musicians halted in the middle of a measure. Several of the women around me did the same. Screeched, that is.

Irene and Henry's daughter, Holly, stood there with clenched fists. She looked like a cartoon figure depicting anger, and I could easily imagine steam rising from her ears and black clouds of fury pulsating around her. "You!" I couldn't tell who she was pointing at, but I stepped backward, as if I'd been shoved. "You!" she cried again and stabbed a finger toward the middle of the dance floor. "How dare you come here to ruin my life?" Dancers moved out of the line of fire. All except two of them. Irene started toward the door. "Don't do this," Irene commanded in a steely voice I'd never heard from her before. "You promised to behave yourself." She might as well have been talking to one of my limpets.

Susan stood perfectly still, but I could see a heavy pulse throbbing just below her jaw line, disconcertingly similar to the vein that throbbed in that exact place when Bob was upset. So, was she Bob's daughter?

Holly sprinted around her mother's outstretched hands and, before anyone could think to intervene, slammed into Susan, screaming and spitting and flailing. Susan hit the floor with a resounding crack, but rolled like a gymnast. A trail of blood spread across her arm, but whether it was from her impact with the floor or from Holly's fingernails, I couldn't tell. Susan ended up on Holly's stomach but Holly bucked like a crazed bronco. Nobody should treat such a pretty dress like that. Her gyrations sent Susan flying into one of the refreshment tables. The punch bowl tilted. Rebecca Jo grabbed at it and slowed its momentum, but not soon enough to prevent the cascade that, almost in slow motion, poured over Susan. Within seconds, people responded. Reverend Pursey grabbed his daughter by the shoulders, Bob pushed his way through the crowd, and Roger pulled Susan to her feet.

Susan's dress, soaked with the spilled punch, was in a shambles, the fabric shredded at the one and only shoulder seam. She pulled her wet hair around to cover herself, with more dignity than I would have been able to summon under similar circumstances. Roger whipped off his blazer and wrapped it around her, right over the punch and the blood. That was going to be a challenge for a dry-cleaner.

"I think we need to leave, Holly," the Reverend said.

"No! We need to get this straightened out once and for all." Holly seemed to have lost not only one of her shoes, but her sanity as well.

"Not here, not now."

Holly pulled herself from his grasp. "Why not?" Her volume was more suited to a gymnasium than a library. "You don't want to be embarrassed? You should have thought of that twenty-four years ago."

Henry dropped his eyes, straightened his shoulders, and looked up at Irene. "I wasn't yet married to your mother when it happened," he said. "I told you that. My only mistake was in not telling her right away, as soon as I found out."

Irene stepped forward, closer to Henry, Holly's shoe in her hand. "You're going to need to rewrite your sermon for tomorrow, Henry. I dare say the church will be packed." She handed Holly the shoe, took her by the hand, and steered her, like a recalcitrant two-year-old, across the floor and out of the library.

Henry tried on several expressions, none of which seemed to suit him. He stepped to his right, picked up Susan's shawl, and handed it to her without making eye contact. I noted how closely the shawl matched the punch Susan wore.

"Thank you," she said. "Dad," she added.

The dance was over. Once Henry was out the door, we stood there waiting to see what Susan would do. Nathan Young, the town doctor, stepped over to her. His high tenor voice carried easily through the room. "Why don't you come over to my office with me and we'll see about that arm?" Polly Lattimore, his nurse, joined them. Her husband looked like he considered scooping Susan up into his arms, but Polly gave him a look, and he trailed along behind them, pulling the door closed as he left. Roger opened it and followed them, and I was fairly sure it wasn't because he wanted his blazer back.

Three seconds of silence before the place erupted. There was going to be gossip enough for five years. I felt weary of it. Glad to know Bob wasn't Susan's father. Cheap for rejoicing in someone else's pain. All that time I'd wasted suspecting Bob, and there was nothing to it. But still, the town minister?

I skirted the puddle and picked up the now empty but blessedly unbroken punchbowl. Bob took it from me and headed up the main staircase, threading his way through the musicians and the music stands, to the kitchen in the library office. Men were already righting the downed table. At the other table, I gathered the three empty cookie platters—the rest were still practically untouched—and gloated quietly that my cheese straws had all been eaten.

As I turned to my right on the stair landing, I looked back toward the still-covered quilt. The official unveiling would have to wait. Maybe we could have another dance. I shuddered. Maybe not. Sadie, Rebecca Jo, and Esther stood beneath it distributing leftover cookies. Red accepted a bag from Sadie and walked out the front door. Poor Roger wouldn't get any. Skinny as he was, he could probably use some.

I knew the floor would be mopped up and the table

would be cleared of everything, including the bows and the tablecloth, before I was back downstairs. The exodus began as a trickle, but quickly became a torrent. I could just imagine the phone calls that would start at daybreak the next morning.

The musicians seemed happy to take their leave when I handed them their checks a few minutes later. Full pay for half a night's work.

~~~~~

~NATHAN YOUNG~

Nathan unlocked the front door of his office and stepped into the dark waiting room. Susan waited with Polly until he'd switched on some lights. "This is Rimski," Nathan said.

Rimski KorsaCat, named for the composer whose music he seemed to love, swished his fat gray and white tail and sat in front of Susan. She eyed him warily. So she's not a cat-lover, Nathan thought. One mark against her. But then he gave himself a mental yank. He was a doctor. He was professional. He would not pass judgment. Even if she was disrupting Henry and Irene's life like this. All right, so he *was* being judgmental. He moved behind the counter and lifted a white coat from the rack.

Polly raised her eyebrows at him and he swung his head slightly to his right. The motion conveyed his intent as clearly as if he had spoken. Polly nodded, picked up her lab coat and some paperwork as she passed the counter, and guided Susan around Rimski and down the hall to the first little examining room. Polly's sky blue ball gown rustled gently and her heels clicked on the shiny bright floor. Susan's wet gown, on the other hand, clung noiselessly to her legs below the dark gray of Roger's jacket.

Nathan supposed most men would find that alluring, but, unimpressed by feminine wiles, he merely assumed it would be uncomfortable.

Every few feet a drip of purple punch splashed onto the pristine cleanliness of the hallway. Nathan noted the way Polly's husband craned his neck to follow Susan's progress. But then Polly's husband saw Polly's employer watching him. He dropped his eyes.

Nathan stifled a laugh.

The front door opened and Roger Johnson walked in, nodded to Nathan, and took a seat on the far side of the room. "Mr. Lattimore," he murmured, nodding toward Polly's husband.

Nathan smiled. He thought Roger was a fine young man. It looked like Roger was totally smitten.

Nathan dodged the wet spots as he walked down the hall and paused outside the door.

Susan sat on the examining table. The crinkly white paper turned a purply-gray in a soggy ring around the pile of equally soggy hair that lay, like an abandoned puppy, in a pile behind her. Nathan wondered how much all that hair weighed. She must have two strong SCMs, he thought, recalling a medical school lecture about those ropy neck muscles.

Polly efficiently filled out a patient history, asked about allergies, previous medical conditions, all those questions patients so often found intrusive or bothersome, but that Nathan knew were vital. Susan faced away from the door, apparently unaware that the doctor was listening in.

Polly queried Susan about allergies, broken bones, surgeries. "And when was your last tetanus shot?"

Susan shook her head. "When I was a kid, I guess."

"We'll have to give you one, once we get your arm cleaned and bandaged. I'll let Dr. Nathan know." Polly pulled out some instruments. Temp, pulse rate, blood pressure. She noted them on the chart.

Nathan rolled his shoulders and consciously dropped onto the floor every bit of resentment he'd felt about the way this Susan had treated Henry and Irene. He could pick up those resentments later if he felt the need to, but for now she was his patient and she deserved the best he had to offer. He walked in as Polly tucked the blood pressure cuff into the chrome basket on the wall.

He took the chart Polly offered him and did a double-take on Susan's last name. From all the gossip he'd heard, he supposed he and Polly were the only people in town to know it, and Henry, too, of course. Mustn't forget him. Polly had a look of studied nonchalance. With such an unpronounceable name, maybe Susan had come to town to see if she could adopt Henry's last name.

Nonsense, he thought as he washed his hands at the small sink. His first college roommate had come from Wales, with as difficult a name as could be, but the fellow had been almost belligerent in his defense of the grand history behind that name. Nathan supposed Susan might be just as proud of hers, although he'd bet she'd had a hard time learning to spell it in Kindergarten.

Before he even touched Susan's arm, he asked, "Any pain?"

"Of course not. I simply love walking around with my arm ripped open by a psycho."

Sarcasm doesn't become you, Nathan thought, but he answered mildly enough. "I should have asked how much pain on a scale of one to ten." He raised his eyebrows waiting for her to answer.

"Seven." She reached up to touch her shoulder, but Nathan put up a hand to forestall her.

"We need to get that cleaned first," he said. Polly rolled up a little table covered with what he'd need to do the job. "Thank you," he told her and slipped his hands into the gloves Polly had readied for him. He'd known some doctors who never thanked their staff, but Nathan was well aware that a large part of his acceptance by Martinsville townsfolk was due to Polly Lattimore.

She'd come to his office the very first day he'd opened his doors, and had sat there half the day, watching what he did and how he did it. Before she left the office that afternoon, she'd informed him that she was ready to start working for him. "Making your own appointments looks unprofessional," she'd said. "I'll be here first thing in the morning."

She'd gone on to tell him she'd graduated from nursing school but hadn't found work. So," she said before he could take a breath to say he'd be happy to think about it, "I'll serve as your nurse and I'll handle the desk for you. You'll have to pay me, but I'll start with a fairly small salary. As your practice grows—and I'm going to make sure it does—you can pay me more."

Nathan hadn't known that first day what a gem she was, but his practice had bloomed far beyond the fact that he was the only doctor in town. He knew quite well that many people in town might not accept having a single, gay man as their medical provider. He knew there would be hurdles he'd have to jump. But Polly had simply started calling people, knocking down those hurdles left and right. Nathan could still hear her gentle badgering on those phone calls. "You know you haven't had a real checkup in years," she'd say to an unsuspecting friend. "I'm working here, and I'd love to see you when you come for your appointment. Would tomorrow morning work, or would you rather have an afternoon slot?"

Now, with the ease of people who work well together, Nathan reached for the tweezers Polly held out. "There's some debris stuck in here," he explained to Susan. "I need to get your arm thoroughly cleaned before the bandage

FRAN STEWART

goes on. You may even need a stitch or two. Then we'll have to give you a tetanus shot. It wouldn't do to risk lockjaw."

"Will I catch anything from..." she gestured toward her shoulder. Nathan couldn't tell whether she was indicating the wound or—he hated this—was she pointing to his own hands and, by extension, his lifestyle?

Polly answered before he could think of what to say. "Dr. Young is well-respected in this town. He's sewn up more cuts than you can imagine. Don't you worry. You'll be just fine."

Nathan noticed a slight tightening around Polly's eyes that nobody else would have noticed. So she'd heard Susan's implied criticism as well.

"How long until it heals?" Susan asked.

"That will depend a lot on you," Nathan said. "What you eat and how much you exercise will determine how fast this heals." He picked out one more fairly large flake of debris—no telling what it was—and began, with Polly's assistance, to irrigate the two deep parallel cuts.

As he worked, he could sense the small jerks and twitches running up her arm, up her whole body.

"Eight," Susan said. "The pain is up to eight."

"He's almost done," Polly murmured. "You've been very brave to sit there so quietly. It will just be another minute or so and he'll be finished."

Nathan almost curled his lip. Polly sounded like Mr. Rogers talking to a pre-school child. Susan was bound to take umbrage at that.

"He'd better be. I'm not paying for this if it's not done right."

Why, Nathan thought, would anyone antagonize a nearby person who had sharp implements in his hand? You'd think she'd wait until he'd finished.

Susan remained fairly quiet as Nathan sewed up the deepest parts of the cuts with four small stitches. Only once did she ask, querulously, how much longer this was going to take. Polly soothed her again, and Nathan made a conscious decision not to slow down. Childish retaliation, he thought, had no place in a medical practice.

He tied off the last suture and, again with Polly's help, bandaged Susan's arm quickly and efficiently. He gave her the care instructions that were standard for anyone with this type of injury, told her the nurse would give her that shot now, and slipped gratefully from the room. He didn't think he'd ever get used to people who didn't say thank you for common courtesies.

The moment Nathan walked into the waiting room, Roger jumped to his feet. "Will she be okay?"

Nathan found himself soothing Roger's ruffled feathers the same way Polly had soothed Susan's, although he hadn't finished his sentence when Susan walked back into the waiting room and Roger turned away from Nathan.

"I left my purse in my car," Susan told Polly.

"You can come by on Monday."

"Come to think of it, though, why don't you bill my father?"

Polly didn't miss a beat, but Nathan saw her nostrils flare. "That's between you and your...between you and Reverend Pursey. I'll see you Monday morning. The office opens at seven."

Roger ushered Susan out, as if it were the most natural thing in the world that he should be there to help her. Polly closed the door behind them, pulled off the white coat that covered her dress, and brushed her hand across her husband's shoulders. "Thanks for waiting for me, honey. Just let me clean up back there and I'll be ready to go."

"No," Nathan said. "You go on. I'll clean up."

"You sure?"

"Yeah. Take off. You've got a ways to drive, but I don't have so far to go." He gestured toward the ceiling; his living quarters were above the office. "I'll see you Monday morning."

Polly rubbed the back of her neck. "Do you know what caused those cuts?"

Nathan shrugged. "Probably a couple of loose nails in the floorboards."

Polly's top teeth worried at her lower lip. Her husband spoke up for the first time. "Not those floors. They're tongue and groove, and they're in beautiful shape. No way there'd be a nail sticking up."

"You know what I think?" Polly said. "I think our dear little Miss Holly filed her fingernails to a point."

Nathan shuddered. What was there to say to that?

He locked the door behind them and walked back down the hall. All those resentments he'd left piled up on the floor had melted away. But there was another pile forming with Holly's name on it.

~~~~~

~BISCUIT McKEE~

"Bob," I said once we'd taken off our shoes and greeted Marmalade ...

No. You greeted me before you took off your shoes, which is as it should be.

"... did you have any idea?"

He didn't pretend that he didn't know what I was talking about. "No, I didn't see it coming, but I've been busy enough not to spend much time worrying about it. I figured it would sort itself out in the end."

"Poor Holly. It must be really hard on her. When do you suppose she found out?"

"Probably as soon as she got home and saw her mother."

I'd flat forgotten about Irene. "So that's why she left. It had nothing to do with her sister being sick."

"It would have been a convenient coincidence if her sister had had a relapse right then."

"But you don't believe in coincidences." He'd told me that often enough in the past.

"You're right," he said. "Maybe she just needed some time to think."

"It sure took her long enough. She's been gone a whole month. Do you think she's forgiven him?"

"If she doesn't leave or kick him out, then I'd say so. Maybe they'll tell us all the details in church tomorrow." He held out his arm and I tried to unthread the cufflinks.

"Whoever invented these goldurn things ought to be shot," I muttered.

"They were invented at a time," Bob went into his historian mode, "when people with money—the only ones who could afford cufflinks—had body servants whose job it was to wrestle with all the inconvenient marks of status."

"Such as cufflinks?"

"Yes, ma'am. And the ladies had maids to undo those confounded buttons that went all the way down their backs."

I turned my back to him and, I admit, wiggled a bit. "Since I don't have a lady's maid, will you do the honors, sir?"

Sometime later, just before sinking into complete unconsciousness, I remembered the way Red Butler had kissed Easton's hand.

"Bob?"

"Hm?" He sounded drowsy, but not completely out of it.

"Don't you think that mustache-brushing routine would tickle?"

He wrapped one arm more firmly around me and

scooted closer until my back nestled against him. "I'd have no way of knowing, Woman. I don't intend to let him kiss my hand."

It didn't answer my question, but then again, who cared?

DAY
FOUR
SUNDAY

CHAPTER 9
10:45 a.m. to 1:30 p.m.

~BISCUIT McKEE~

BOB AND I SLIPPED INTO OUR USUAL PEW amazed to find it still available in the unusually crowded sanctuary. Amazing what it took to get a crowd at church. Ida picked up her purse and sweater as I climbed over people's legs. "Thanks for saving our place," I whispered. I nodded to Maddy, patted Glaze's shoulder, and said hello to Tom as I sat down. They always sat right in front of Bob and me, usually with Melissa, but she hadn't been to church in weeks. Probably off with her mysterious man.

There was room for two people beside Sadie. Maybe we should have sat there. But no. I could see two bulletins on the pew. Placeholders, apparently. I wiggled my fingers at Sadie and she waved back. Maggie, sitting with Norm on the other side of Sadie, looked back in my direction and made the universal milking gesture. I held up my thumb. Dr. Nathan, sitting across the aisle in the fourth row, right behind Sadie, turned and smiled at me. He was such a sweet man. He held my gaze for longer than usual, almost as if he wanted to ask me something.

It looked like everybody in town was here, except for a few diehard Catholics. Father John would have a sparse crowd this morning. Maybe a few people hadn't heard about the to-do last night. Ha! The way the grapevine worked around here, those few would have to be dead not to know what was going on.

"If I don't learn all the gritty details from Henry," Ida leaned closer to my left ear, "I'm going to be sorely disappointed." Staunch Catholic that she was, she still managed to show up at the Old Church on Sundays whenever something big was brewing, not just today but several times in the past. Henry had taken great pains to point her out each time, and Ida usually managed to turn it into an advertisement for the grocery store. She poked me in the ribs. "Look, there she is."

As if I couldn't see. Irene, who always sat on the front row where she could offer quiet encouragement to Henry during his sermons, nodding when he made a point, as if the rest of us might miss it, slipped in beside Sadie on the third row, leaving the aisle space empty.

"Uh-oh," Ida said. "That doesn't bode well for Henry." Apparently the rest of the congregation thought so too, for a quiet but powerful surge of whisperings passed across the pews. Bob, sitting on my right, said nothing, but I saw him fold and refold the church bulletin. Across the aisle, Sadie reached over and patted Irene's hand.

The wheezy old organ, played by the equally wheezy organist, wound up the prelude and launched into a hymn. "I come to the garden alone" we all sang, and hardly missed a phrase when Susan paced down the aisle and paused next to her—her what? There didn't seem to be a name for Irene's relationship to Susan. Irene kept singing and didn't budge an inch. No wonder Henry had preached all these sermons about forgiveness, but it looked like his wife hadn't forgiven anybody. Of course, she hadn't heard any of those sermons. She'd been in Ohio. Maybe he should have mailed her copies.

Susan, wearing a lilac-colored sleeveless summer dress, marched to the front pew, her bandaged arm starkly white against her olive skin. Her waterfall of hair swung gently to her knees. I wondered how long it had taken her to get the purple punch out of it, and how long to dry it. Thank goodness this was such a familiar hymn. I didn't miss more than a word or two as I watched. Susan stood quietly just beyond Irene's usual place until the hymn ended. Then, before she sat, she slipped her left hand around the back of her neck and pulled her hair to the front of her shoulder. I wondered what she was going to do with it—pile it in her lap? Let it hang to the floor? I couldn't tell for sure, but it looked like she arranged it on her lap.

As I turned to check my seat—why do I always do that? Look first, as if the pew had moved while I was standing. Why don't I just sit without looking? At any rate, as I turned I saw Red sitting in the back row. Ida poked me again. I needed to talk to her about the sharpness of her elbow. Then I followed her gaze. Henry stood at the pulpit watching his daughter Holly stomp down the aisle. How could anyone make that much noise on carpet?

She slowed as she came abreast of the third row and laid a hand on the back of the pew. Nathan, sitting right behind Irene, leaned forward and seemed to inspect Holly's hand. He grimaced and shook his head. I wondered why. Irene patted the place beside her, but Holly's eyes were trained on a different target. She kept walking, right to the front pew, where she glared at Susan and plopped herself down two places away from this young woman who was, apparently, her father's first, and heretofore unrecognized, daughter.

Irene placed her hand over her eyes for a moment, shook her head as if to ask, "Why me? Why now? Why this?" She nodded to Sadie, stood, and moved to the front, where she sat between Holly and Susan. Then all three of them looked at Henry.

"Talk about being in the doghouse," Ida said in that voice that carried more than she thought it did.

Henry passed his hand across his face, unconsciously mirroring Irene's earlier gesture. "Do you sell those doghouses at your store, Ida?" he asked. "I could use three of them."

"Don't have 'em on hand, Henry, but I can get them here on the Thursday shipment."

Irene's shoulders hunched up, as if she were crossing her arms. Bad body language. It meant she was shutting him out. Everybody else relaxed a bit, though, and we went through the announcements and readings and another hymn without pause, just waiting for the sermon.

After the service, the three women scooted out the side entrance, Irene holding onto both of them as if they were a couple of misbehaving toddlers in a grocery store. I was pretty sure she was shepherding both girls up to the parsonage. Bet that would be an interesting lunch. At least Irene was doing something instead of just letting Susan--or Holly--call the shots. I did wonder, though, where Henry would fit in when the commotion had finally died down.

The unusually subdued congregation filed past Henry at the front door without saying much of anything. The men seemed afraid to shake his hand, and many of the women marched straight out past him.

Red stood off to one side with his arms crossed over his navy suit jacket. I wondered what sort of scent he was wearing today. One woman, whose name I didn't know, passed close by him and turned her head slightly. I could see her take a surreptitious sniff. Red glanced at her as if he were quite aware of what she was doing, and his lip curled ever so slightly.

I heard a slight chuckle behind me and turned to see Dr. Nathan watching Red the same way I was. We shared one of those looks that said we each knew what the other was thinking. Bob was talking with Maddy, paying no attention to me whatsoever. He'd missed the show.

"How are you doing, Biscuit?" Nathan made it sound like more than a casual greeting.

"Just fine, Nathan." That Georgia non-comment. "Just fine."

"Um-hm. You're welcome to come by the office

sometime in the next couple of days."

I looked at him in some confusion. "Oh! You mean ..." I glanced around and lowered my voice. I didn't like calling attention to what had happened. "No, I'm not cold anymore. I've completely recovered from that."

He made a point of looking at the sweater I had on. Most of the other women were in sleeveless summer outfits. "Um-hm," he repeated. "I've got some time on Tuesday around one o'clock if you just need to talk."

Tears welled up inside and I coughed to cover my discomfort.

"Just keep it in mind," he said and turned aside to say something to Ida. She looked at me pointedly before she answered him, and I was afraid she'd heard what Doc had said to me.

Up ahead of us Sadie murmured a few words and Henry nodded back at her. This was good. Henry wasn't a complete pariah. Why did we expect our preachers to be without fault? Glaze and Tom reached Henry and paused there for a moment. Red took a step forward. I hoped he wasn't going to cut in front of me. I couldn't hear what Glaze said, but Henry's reply was enthusiastic. "Glaze McKee," he said, "you have just brightened my day considerably."

Maddy thanked Henry "for a good service," and then my sweet Bob grabbed Henry's shoulder in a firm grip. "Fine sermon, Henry," he said. "Takes guts to own up to a problem so publicly."

Henry's rueful smile hovered for a moment and then faded. "It was already quite public, thanks to my... to the show my daughters--both of them--put on at the dance." He gestured to the spot where Irene had always stood beside him after each service. "Looks like my apologies haven't been enough, though."

With an assurance I didn't completely own, I shook my head. "Don't you worry, Henry. Irene just needs to be sure Holly's okay. She probably wanted to keep both of those girls away from the crowd." As I said it, it began to make sense. "They'll all come around in no time." I came close to commenting on Susan's lack of manners—what a childish, melodramatic way to have introduced herself to a new family—but chose not to say it. Holly's actions, too, were reprehensible. Henry already knew that *both* his daughters had some growing up to do. He didn't need comments from me.

Henry cleared his throat. "I've been meaning to ask, Biscuit, are you doing okay? I know that—"

Before he could talk about my river trauma, I interrupted. I did not want to discuss it in public. "I'm fine, Henry. Just fine."

He looked as if he didn't know whether to believe me.

I excused myself as graciously as I could and we headed toward Maggie's.

Marmalade met us at the corner. "Bob? Why do you think Marmy never goes with us to church? I'm surprised she doesn't curl up on the carpet during the service."

I do not go to that singing building. It is not interesting, and the music maker hurts my ears.

Bob reached for my hand. "She was there the only day that mattered."

That was different. I had things to say that were important.

The sweetest vision of Marmy walking down the aisle on our wedding day brightened my rather gloomy mood. "Remember how she yowled through a lot of the ceremony?"

Excuse me?

"She wasn't yowling," my loyal, cat-loving husband said. "She was singing."

Marmalade preceded us up Maggie's walkway, but her

tail was twitching instead of doing its usual graceful wave.

That is because you do not listen to me.

We called through the screen door, and Maggie motioned us in. Willie waved his blanket at us. He'd latched onto that blanket when Maggie took it to him in the hospital, and I didn't think he'd let go of it since then. Maggie didn't seem concerned. As long as he needed it, she was happy to let him have it. Poor little guy, he'd been completely unconscious when rescuers pulled him from the car seat where he'd been strapped in for at least two days. It's a wonder he hadn't died.

I shivered from the remembered cold embrace of that tree on the river, and felt a sudden empathy for Willie. I knew quite a bit about what he'd gone through. But I hadn't had the dead body of my mother next to me. No wonder he didn't talk much.

"Want to visit the babies?" Maggie held her arms out to Willie. He nodded enthusiastically, although the nod might have been merely the result of his hopping up and down. He reminded me of that bouncy dog Glaze had found. Willie may not have spoken much since his mom died, but he got his point across. "They've grown a lot." Maggie beamed as if the knobby-kneed little critters were her very own. Well, in a way they were.

Bob liked them as much as I did. This was the second batch of goat babies I'd helped deliver. The first came from Joy, Moonbeam's sister, and they were cuter than I could imagine, both of them popping out and standing almost within minutes. Not that I was much help. I hadn't done a thing except lean against the barn wall in the middle of the night and watch. But I had my own maternal pride in those two and in the irrepressible triplets that Moonbeam had produced just a few weeks ago.

We trooped out the back door.

"Don't worry," Maggie told me as I paused a few feet

into her farmyard. "Elmyra's with the rest of the flock on the other side of the house." She knew I had a running feud with Vampirah, her lead hen. Well, maybe not a feud. A feud would suggest that I'd stood up to that bird in the past. Truth was, her black-hooded head scared me witless. That peculiar arrangement of dark feathers called to mind every scary story I'd ever read or dreamed. And when she spread those wings of hers, I could feel the bite marks on my neck—

"Biscuit? Are you coming?" Maggie looked at me with pity. With one more glance around the yard, I straightened my shoulders, caught up with Bob, and strode toward the barn.

Bob and I, still in our Sunday clothes, stayed outside the sturdy fence. It had to be sturdy, Maggie had told me, because goats will chew on anything. Heavy wooden posts and rails were lined with staunch metal screening, durable, and almost as heavy as the chain link fence surrounding our backyard.

Marmalade ducked through a small hole under the gate and skirted the goats, prancing right up to her friend Fergus, the Great Pyrenees watchdog. She was about the same length as one of the dog's enormous front legs. They touched noses. That business completed, Fergus turned his attention back to the kids chasing his wagging tail. They'd already grown so much. One of the babies, the little brown-spotted male, hopped right over Marmalade, and she took off running.

I am simply removing myself from possible danger.

Willie thought that was pretty funny. His giggle was infectious.

Marmy stopped abruptly and shook her front paw. It looked like she might have stepped on something sharp. Was she hurt?

Fresh goat poop.

She changed course and walked back toward us. She wasn't limping, so I breathed easier, but every few steps she shook her leg. I'd have to take a look at that.

Bob turned around and leaned back against the fence. "When is your company invading?"

Maggie laughed. "One set of them this afternoon. Norm's older sister. I wish those nieces and nephews of mine weren't such a terror. You'd better get your milk and run; they'll be here any minute. The others have quite a ways to drive, so they won't roll in until tonight."

"Dave and Carole are coming, too, aren't they?"

Maggie nodded and nuzzled Willie's neck, making him chuckle. "They're pulling in late tonight. They said they'd go directly to Azalea House and we'll see them in the morning."

They went on talking, but I was more interested in Moonbeam, who sidled toward the fence. I knew what she had in mind. I'd been the recipient of some of her ministrations several times, until I learned not to put my back against the fence. If goats could whistle, Little Miss Innocent here would have had quite a tune going. She paused right behind Bob, raised her front legs, and in one fell swoop, perched them on the top rail of the fence and nibbled at the back of Bob's collar. He whooped, causing Willie to clutch Maggie until she cooed at him and told him Moonbeam was playing with Mr. Bob. All I did was laugh.

We paid for our gallon of goat milk, hugged Maggie, and said good bye to Willie, who clung to her leg like a barnacle. Limpet? I'd forgotten to look that up. On the way home, when I scooped up Marmalade to look at her leg, it seemed to be fine.

Of course it is fine. I cleaned it.

CHAPTER 10
Sunday 1:30 p.m. to 9 p.m.

~BISCUIT McKEE~

I LOVED OUR HOUSE. AN OLD BUILDING, LIKE most of the Martinsville homes, it always reminded me of a grandmother's welcoming arms. The eyebrow windows in the third-floor attic needed a good washing, but I wasn't about to try that. Way too dangerous. They still let in enough daylight. Every time I went up those attic stairs, I was surprised with how light and sunny the room was, despite the fact that it was filled with every bit of detritus imaginable, from hobby horses to dusty old trunks, left there by numberless generations of Beechnut Lane residents. I knew I was going to have to do something about it someday, but so far, someday had never come.

Marmalade bounded up the front stairs and pawed at the door.

"She must be hungry," Bob said in that nasal twang of someone still fighting a cold, and he pushed the door wide open to let our little family inside. Marmalade headed straight to the kitchen, but when we followed her, she hadn't stopped at her food bowl. Instead, she pawed at the back door. Bob looked at me over the rim of his glasses. "She doesn't like the cat door I put in for her?"

"Nonsense," I said, "she uses it all the time. What's wrong, Marmy?"

Come outside with me.

Bob leaned against the counter. "She was acting like this about five o'clock this morning," he said.

At five o'clock I'd still been sleeping. "What did she do?"

I asked him to go outside with me.

"Just pawed at the door. I finally opened it and scooted

her out, but she was back inside a minute later."

"Cats," I said. "I'll never understand her."

That is because you do not listen.

He eyed Marmalade. "Ever notice how she sounds like she's carrying on a conversation with us?"

His words came out like *eber* and *souds* and *cahbersashuh*. "Aren't you getting better, Bob?" I reached for his forehead. "You sound even stuffier."

"Just these damn allergies. I feel great, but I can't breathe, and can't smell a thing."

"I don't think you have a temp, but you need some hot tea. I'll put the kettle on."

"Spare me your rabbit brews, Woman. I want coffee." He sliced off a good sized chunk of my homemade dill bread and slathered it with honey.

I eyed him the same way he'd eyed Marmy. He didn't have a fever, but he looked miserable. I picked up the coffee pot. "At least be glad you can't smell the voodoo lily."

"The what?"

It is not a voo doolilie.

"Oh, somebody—hush, Marmalade—planted a rather odiferous ornamental. Hopefully it'll finish blooming soon."

This would be a good time to take a walk out behind the fence.

"Glad I'm missing it." He reached down and ran a calming hand along Marmy's back.

After his second cup of coffee, he pulled out his sticky notes again.

"I've run every combination I can think of. M-X-L, L-M-X, and mixed the numbers around."

He still was hard to understand. *Cahbinazhun* and *nuhburz*.

"I can't find anything in the system. Are you sure it was a Georgia plate?"

"Pretty sure. And I'm positive of the number. William the Conqueror and all that."

"Uh-huh."

"Okay," I admitted, "it might have been a different state, but the license plate was white, the same color as the car."

"You're sure it started with an M?"

"Well of course I am. One thousand—"

He held up his hand. "I know. You told me. One thousand sixty six."

He certainly was grumpy this afternoon.

~~~~~

~GLAZE McKEE~

The phone rang four times before Glaze reached it. She spoke quietly, listened, spoke again, and finally hung up.

"What was that all about?" Maddy asked. "You look like you've been hit with a baseball."

"No. No, I just... don't know quite... quite what to do."

"What? Tell Doctor Madeleine here. She can solve all your quandaries."

"Silly goose. That was Red Butler. He invited me to dinner."

"You gave him your phone number?"

"No, of course not. All he had to do was look it up. I'm in the book."

Maddy, who Glaze knew had grown up in Atlanta with its three-inch-thick phone books, rolled her eyes. "I've seen comic books thicker than the Martinsville phone book."

Glaze didn't deign to answer.

"When are you going out with him?"

"Friday night."

"What about Tom?"

Glaze ran her hands through her hair. "I... don't... I'm not... it's not like we're going steady."

Maddy scoffed. "You may not think so, my dear, but everybody else in town has you two practically married off. You never go out with anybody else."

"That's because... because nobody else has ever asked me."

"Really?" Maddy sounded incredulous. "Why not? I should think everybody would want to go out with you."

Glaze rubbed her eyes and left her hands cradling her face for a moment. Her next words sounded muffled, even to her. "Think about it, Maddy. Most of the men in this town are married. The others are—let's see." She raised her head and held up one finger. "Doctor Nathan is a very nice man, but he's gay." Another finger. "Paul Welsh is dating Judy Smith on the few occasions when his job lets him be in town long enough to see her." She raised a new finger with each name. "Melissa's guy is a mystery nobody's met, but he's off limits anyway because of that very impressive amethyst and diamond ring he gave her."

"It's fake, I'll bet."

"It's still a ring. And then there's Roger Johnson. He's twenty years my junior, and he's following that Susan person around like a lovesick puppy." She looked at her fingers and held up her thumb. "Wait! There's one more man. Your brother, but he's ..." and she paused for effect.

"He's a priest. I see what you mean." Maddy settled in her usual chair, tucking one leg underneath her. Her face brightened. "You forgot to mention Buddy Olsen."

Glaze just glared at her.

"But you really like Tom, don't you?"

Glaze sank onto her own chair. "My last boyfriend was a creep who beat me up, stalked me when I left him, and tried to have me kidnapped. He finally murdered...

murdered Annie." She finger-combed her silky hair and held it back away from her face. "Before that, before I was diagnosed as clinically depressed, I was under what my shrink called *foreign management*. I dated some, but nobody who was worth much. So much of my life back then was just a fog."

"But you're fine now." Maddy's face clouded. "As long as you take your medication."

"Yes. I'm fine. And I've been dating the only eligible man in town. And I have nothing much to compare him to. Nothing worth comparing, that is."

"I see what you mean."

"I don't want him to be my only choice." Glaze propped her elbows on the table and settled her face back into her hands. How could she have such good friends and be dating such a nice man and still feel so lonely?

~~~~~

~BISCUIT McKEE~

Around 5:00 p.m. I stepped out to the garden for some fresh tomatoes. Marmalade peeked up at me from where she lay in the catnip. I encouraged its growth because it helped to repel a number of nasty garden-devouring bugs.

I thought you kept it here for me.

Bob carried his coffee mug out and sat on the back porch steps. "I hope you don't have any heavy lifting for me to do, Woman," he said. "My nose is so stuffy it's given me a headache."

"You never get headaches." I popped a golden cherry tomato in my mouth. Nothing like it anywhere under the sun. I could eat every one of them. Why did I even bother bringing a basket out with me? I held my fingers up to my nose and inhaled that tomato leaf scent. It's impossible to describe. A little pungent, a little spicy, a little summery.

"Now I do."

Do what?

"Do what?"

"Get headaches."

"Isn't the honey working?" I handed him a couple of baby tomatoes. I knew that at one inch in diameter this variety is full-grown, but I couldn't help thinking of them as babies.

"Sadie said it'll be awhile before it takes effect. And I don't have any pollen yet."

I looked across the yard. "Those hives will really look pretty here. What time are you picking them up?"

He popped a tomato into his mouth. "These don't taste as good when my nose doesn't work." He sounded rueful indeed. "Roger said he and his dad would bring one of the garbage trucks tonight at about 9:30. That way we can move the hives all at once."

"You said you didn't want to do any heavy lifting. If that's the case, you picked a poor day to get those hives."

"Why do you think I invited Roger Junior and Senior to join in the fun?"

"You're a regular Tom Sawyer."

Who is he?

"Speaking of the hives," he set his coffee cup down, "do you want to help me gather some brush?"

I looked back at the woods. "We'll need a lot of it if we have to put it in front of all ten hives."

"Why do you think I invited you along, Woman?" But his eyes twinkled as he said it.

I scooted inside and set the basket of tomatoes by the sink—I'd rinse them later—and grabbed my heavy duty work gloves.

Bob was waiting for me at the back gate with his big pruning shears. I stepped under the overhanging branches of the old trees. I loved this place. I'd walked here so often, enjoying the peace that seemed to infuse the very air. These stately old trees filled almost the entire block we lived on, and I couldn't believe our good fortune in having found this place.

A small clearing in the center of the trees gave a purpose, a sense of direction to my steps whenever I wandered through the woods. We'd put a wooden bench there soon after we bought the house, and we would occasionally take our morning tea, or in Bob's case, coffee, out there. We hadn't been there lately, though, and the brush might be taking over. Good. We needed it for the bees.

I made up my mind. I wasn't going to be afraid to walk by myself anymore, at least not here.

"Let's cross the creek," I said. "There's bound to be a lot of brush in the clearing."

I led the way along the path to the creek, hoping the stepping-stones across it would be above water level. I caught a faint whiff of that stupid voodoo lily.

Look more carefully.

Marmalade meowed at me, and Bob grabbed my arm.

Oh my God. Oh my God.

We didn't gather any brush that evening, and Bob didn't get the hives moved. What was left of a body lay sprawled in a shallow hole on the other side of the little creek, half covered with dirt, as if someone had started burying it, but had been interrupted. It certainly wasn't a voodoo lily.

I told you it was not.

I gagged, and Bob sent me back to throw up well away from the crime scene. He was gone all night long.

~~~~~

FRAN STEWART

My Gratitude List for Sunday
 1. I cannot sit here and think about gratitude. I cannot. I cannot. I'm going to call Glaze.

I am grateful for
 Widelap
 that is enough

DAY FIVE
MONDAY

CHAPTER 11
6 a.m. to 4 p.m.

~REEBOK GARNER~

"Mrs. Zapota, this is Deputy Garner from the Martinsville Police Station ....No, ma'am, we haven't, not for sure... Yes, ma'am, the radio... Yes, ma'am. A body was found, and that's why I'm calling you. We need the name of your son's dentist... No, ma'am, you shouldn't come here. They've taken the body to the—to a place where it can be identified... I can't tell you that, ma'am. We can't even say yet if the body was male or female. We have to wait for the report from the medical examiner... Please, Mrs. Zapota, please stay home. Just give me the name of his dentist... Thank you. I'll let you know as soon as I have any information at all... Yes. I promise."

Reebok Garner sank into the desk chair and rested his face in his hands for a moment. Was he really cut out for this work? He could handle it when he just listened to lonely people who called in the middle of the night. He could check license plates to be sure the registrations were current and help find missing wallets, something he'd done for old Mr. Harper. But he couldn't calm a woman's fears. He couldn't find the man who'd tried to kill Miss Biscuit.

He knew this dead man had to be Charles Zapota. And Mrs. Zapota knew it as well, even though she wasn't ready to admit it. And there wasn't a thing he could do to help her.

He slammed his fist on the desk. What a waste of time sitting here. There *was* something he could do. He could go get those dental records.

~~~~~

~GLAZE McKEE~

Glaze pushed her left leg against the desk and spun her chair around for the twenty-seventh or twenty-eighth time. She'd lost count and was, if truth be told, too dizzy to keep going, but she couldn't figure out what else to do. She was so tired she was ready to drop. Biscuit had called her in a panic at dusk, and Glaze had spent most of the night with her, calling home once to tell Maddy not to worry about her. They'd slept a little bit, but Biscuit kept waking up, her eyes all wide and staring, and then running to the toilet to vomit up nothing.

"I just keep seeing him, over and over again," she'd said. "That's why somebody... pushed me in the water. He thought I'd seen him burying that... that body."

Glaze had almost called in sick this morning, but Biscuit insisted that she go to work. "I'll be okay. The sun's coming up." So Glaze had come home, followed by that dog. It must have slept on Biscuit's front porch. She'd avoided Maddy's questions other than to tell her the bare minimum—that Biscuit and Bob had found a body, that Biscuit was pretty upset about it. Then she'd showered, dressed, and now here she sat, twirling around in her chair.

She owed Margaret Casperson an answer—today—and that deadline wasn't going to go away. She'd already asked for two extensions, and Margaret had been patient. Until last week. "Come to dinner Monday night," Margaret had told her. It didn't sound like an invitation. It sounded like an ultimatum, but that was probably just her own feelings of incompetence erupting through. She still didn't feel qualified to decide who would get foundation money and who wouldn't. She didn't like the idea of making enemies by saying no to people. She had no clue how to set up the records she'd need in order to keep it all straight. Margaret had told her she could hire some staff. Right. She'd either have dozens of applicants, in which case she would have to say no to a lot of them, or nobody would want to work with her after that fool stunt she'd pulled running away last month. They probably all thought she was demented. Psycho.

"Hey, Glaze?" Madeleine's voice drifted up from the kitchen. "You ready yet?"

Car pool time. Talk about a dead end job. Of course, if she accepted Margaret's offer, she wouldn't have to car pool ever again. She was still in a daze over the figure Margaret had mentioned as a starting salary. And then there would be a substantial budget on top of that. Money to set up an office and hire some staff. That really scared her. She hadn't found the time to talk to Biscuit about it, either.

Well, she'd made the time with the walk Friday night, but she just couldn't talk about it. If she talked about it, that would make it real. And she couldn't have talked about it last night, not with Biscuit in such a state. Maybe if she'd discussed this job, it might have taken Biscuit's mind off that body, but then, in the future, every time either one of them thought about Glaze working for Margaret, they'd tie it to the horror of last night.

"Glaze!"

"I'm coming." She hauled herself out of the chair, grabbed a lipstick from the top of her dresser, and trudged down the stairs, wondering how she'd ever stay awake at work and where she'd find three or four people to hire—people she could enjoy working with.

Dee, who showed up early every weekday morning for their car-pooling, shoveled in one last bite of cinnamon roll and took a final slurp of coffee. "Love this breakfast café you two open up each morning."

"Yeah? You won't like it so much when your teeth start to rot out from all the sugar you eat before work." Maddy switched off the coffee pot.

"That's what you think. I've got a toothbrush in my locker at work." Dee stretched and grinned as Glaze hit the last step. "I wouldn't be tempted if you didn't buy these scrumptious rolls all the time, Ms. McKee." She turned back toward Madeleine, "or if you didn't make such good coffee, Ms. Ames. If my teeth rot, it's your fault."

Maddy stuck out her tongue. "Let's hit the road."

Glaze ran her hands through her silver hair, grateful that it always seemed to behave without having to fiddle with it—at least something was going right in her life—and grabbed her purse.

Dee paused, and the smile left her face. "I'm sorry about what Biscuit went through."

Glaze nodded dully. To think they'd even smelled it, and hadn't known what it was. Bob might have known, or at least might have checked it out, but his nose was so stuffy he hadn't smelled anything.

Dee reached for the door knob. "Did you know there's a dog on your porch? Cute little thing."

"Yeah." Maddy's eyes brightened. "I hope you don't know whose dog she is."

"It—she—sure seems to need some attention." She looked down at her black pants and brushed away some hair. "She bounced around a lot."

Glaze groaned. "She followed me home Friday night."

"Oh, the poor thing. Why didn't you bring her inside?"

"I wanted to," Maddy said, "but Glaze wouldn't let me." She turned to Glaze. "I was going to bring her in last night, but she followed you down to Biscuit's house."

"Madeleine Ames." Glaze used her sternest voice. "That dog doesn't belong to us. It needs to go home." She nudged Dee aside and peered out the window. It was the same dog. Still. After two and a half days. You'd think it would have been hungry. Its tongue—her tongue—was hanging out. Thirsty. She looked thirsty.

She stepped back to the counter and filled a cereal bowl with water. As soon as she placed it on the porch, the dog pounced, knocked over the bowl, and slurped at the spreading puddle.

"We have to leave." Dee tugged Glaze's arm.

"One minute." Glaze went back in the kitchen and pulled out the largest, heaviest bowl they had. "Don't get used to this," she told the dog as she set the water down beside the door. The dog took one slurp and followed Glaze to the car. "No, go home," she said, shushing it away. The dog scooted back to the steps. Glaze slipped into the back seat and the dog took a step toward the car. "Stay," she said to the dog, and "Let's get out of here," to Dee.

Maddy and Dee seemed to draw their conversational gambits from the environment. Heading down Upper Sweetgum and right onto Third Street, they talked about the dog, wondering where it had come from. "I think she's traveled a long way," Maddy said. "Her paws are kind of ragged-looking, as if she's been walking forever."

"Poor thing," Dee said. "Do you think she needs to see a vet?"

"We probably need to take her for a check-up at least." Maddy turned and squinted at Glaze. "If she stays around," she added when Glaze glared at her.

When Dee turned left onto Pine, the topic shifted to Maddy's brother, the priest. Father John Ames, tending the garden he was enlarging on the front lawn of the rectory, waved as they drove past. At the bottom of Pine, when Dee turned left onto First Street and headed up the valley out of town, Maddy cleared her throat and raised her voice over the sound of the car's acceleration. "What's Hank up to now, Glaze?"

"Old Horse-face? I don't know. With him it's always something." Glaze couldn't figure out her boss. He seemed convinced that everybody was out to get him and to steal his company secrets. They made gadgets, for heaven's sake, most of which were shipped directly across the parking lot to Wish-Fulfillment, the catalog company where Dee and Maddy worked, and from there were sent to anybody across the United States who ordered from their catalog. Occasionally Hank reserved a few cases and sent them off somewhere else. Glaze didn't know where and couldn't care less. Hank was paranoid. What sort of secrets could there be in how to attach a handle to a jack-in-the-box, or how to build a kazoo? The Ultimate. That's what Hank Celer called his kazoo design.

Lately he'd been on another security kick, insisting on a draconian quality-control regime for an upcoming item, a double-walled flower pot designed to be self-watering, with a built-in reservoir that needed filling only about once a week. The reservoir wasn't big enough, Hank complained. He wanted a one-month water supply for people who took long trips. His design department—two guys and one gal—had been close to mutiny as he rejected one proposal after another. One of the men—someone named Zip—had quit without notice last week. Glaze didn't blame him. She'd never met him, but everyone said he was a quiet guy, the kind who would wilt under Hank's ranting. They were all surprised he'd lasted as long as he had. And the next day the other two had quit, given their two week's notice, so now Hank wouldn't have anybody in design. Served him right.

Glaze, who hadn't been there all that long, was already fed up herself. She didn't see how the other employees stood it. Several of them had been with CelerInc for years. Just to get away from Hank's craziness was a good reason to accept Margaret's job offer. The funny thing was, she liked the people she worked with, other than Hank. Was that a good enough reason to risk going nuts on a daily basis?

"You okay?" Maddy turned around and leveled a stare at Glaze. "You're awfully quiet."

"I'm fine. Just have a lot to think about."

"You're not allowed to think. It's a Monday." Dee looked at Glaze in the rearview mirror. "Are you okay? You look awful."

"Thanks."

"No. You do. What's wrong?"

Glaze couldn't believe such a question. "You have to ask me what's wrong? After that body and everything?"

"What body? What are you talking about?"

"What do you mean what am I talking about? You said you were sorry about what Biscuit had to go through."

"Yeah, when she was pushed into the river."

"Oh. You haven't listened to the news this morning, have you?"

"Are you kidding? I had to wash my hair. Who has time for the news?"

"Biscuit found a dead body in her backyard last night. That's why she called me to go down there and stay with her."

"You saw a dead body? Who was it?"

"I didn't see it, and they don't know who it is. By the time I got there, there was quite a lot of activity. Crime scene tape across the back fence and all that stuff."

Maddy bounced a little in the passenger seat. "It's exciting!"

"Maddy!" Glaze yelled, making Dee swerve the car. "Do you have any idea what it's like to find a body?"

"Well, sure. I write about it all the time."

"That's not the same. It's one thing to read—or write—about a murder victim, but it's not the same as stumbling across a partly-decomposed—"

"That's enough!" Dee hollered. "I just ate breakfast."

"All you ate were cinnamon rolls," Maddy pointed out.

"And I don't want them all over the seat of my car." Dee glanced once more in the rearview mirror. "Is Biscuit okay?"

"Aside from no sleep? And countless trips to the bathroom to throw up? And a nagging feeling that this is somehow connected to why she got pushed in the river? And suddenly after fifty years of walking wherever she wanted to, whenever she wanted to, now she's afraid of the dark and afraid to be alone? Yeah, I guess she's okay."

"I'm sorry. I ..."

"No. I shouldn't have barked at you, Dee. Or at you either, Maddy. I guess I'm still feeling pretty raw."

Maddy reached between the front seats to touch Glaze on the knee. "You could cancel that dinner tonight and maybe get to bed early."

"No. That's one dinner I cannot cancel."

"I've got an idea," Dee said. "There's a sign outside the theater that says *Gone with the Wind* starts Wednesday. That would take our mind off everything. We could look forward to it for two whole days."

"We could play miniature golf up in Hastings," Maddy suggested. "Tomorrow after work."

We could curl up in a ball and sleep for a year, Glaze thought.

They batted ideas around for several miles until Dee pulled a quick left off Manning Street into the parking lot between Wish-Fulfillment and CelerInc. "Time for work, ladies. See you both at five."

~~~~~

~REEBOK GARNER~

They had the X-rays and dental records ready and waiting for Reebok. The X-rays were dated last July. "Mr. Zapota," the accompanying note said, "broke #30 five months ago. He now has a composite filling covering 2 surfaces mesial/occlusal."

Right. Reebok was glad there were dentists in the world, but he was equally glad he wasn't one of them. What was a mesial/occlusal anyway? It sounded like a disease. He hoped it wasn't catching. He'd worn gloves when they worked the crime scene, but you never could tell.

~~~~~

~BISCUIT McKEE~

How I managed to get to the library I'll never know. I guess I had this idea that work would take my mind off... off what I had found. How did Bob manage? Of course, he had something active to do. Maybe that helped. I didn't walk, though. Despite the perfectly lovely day, I got into my Buick, locked the doors, and parked right behind Sadie's yellow Chevy.

All three of my Petunias were there waiting for me. We had the schedule worked out so there were usually two of them plus me. I guess they thought I'd be a basket case. They were right. I wasn't worth much. Every time the door opened I started. Every time the phone rang I jumped. Finally they tried to talk me into going upstairs and hiding out in the third-floor office. When I balked at that, Rebecca Jo offered to come up with me "to help get some of those new books catalogued." I knew what she was doing. She thought I didn't want to be alone. She was right.

Before we headed up, Doctor Nathan walked in the

front door carrying an armload of books. He greeted us in his usual mild way and wandered over toward where I hovered on the stairs. He walked right past the book return bin and ignored it. "Biscuit," he said, "I wanted to talk with you."

"Here." Rebecca Jo held out her arms for the books. "I'll just take those out of your way and process them."

I had a feeling I knew what was coming.

"Don't look so wary," he said. "I'm not going to bite."

"Why are you here?" I couldn't believe I was being so ungracious. The man had my own best interest at heart. At least I moved down a few stairs until I was on the same level with him.

"Just wanted to be sure you were going to stop by tomorrow."

Before I could say no he reached out and touched my arm. "Biscuit, you've been through a lot. I'm not going to try to psychoanalyze you, but it might help if you can talk about it."

I looked at his kind face and felt my eyes tighten up. I blinked to keep back the tears.

"Tomorrow? One o'clock?" he asked.

I nodded and fled upstairs.

CHAPTER 12
Monday 5:30 p.m. to 6:45 p.m.

~GLAZE McKEE~

THE DOG WAS WAITING WHEN THEY GOT HOME, lying in front of the door, although she jumped up and bounded down the walkway as Glaze stepped out of Dee's car. Glaze patted her, just once. "Don't get used to this," she said and nudged her gently out of the way—she was pretty sure it was a her. Maddy said so. The door squeaked as usual, and the dog whined its squeaky little grumble, sounding almost like an echo.

Maddy remained for a moment on the porch. When she came in, she called out, "We're home."

Glaze rolled her eyes. "Like there's anybody here to greet us."

"The dog did," Maddy said, but Glaze ignored her. Glaze tossed the mail onto the kitchen table, skewing the lavender and white striped tablecloth in the process. An envelope skidded off the top of the stack and landed on Glaze's chair.

"Must be for you, since it headed to your chair like that." Maddy's grin was infectious, and Glaze felt her jaw relax a bit. She hadn't realized how tense she felt. Clenching her teeth couldn't be good for them. She needed to schedule a dental appointment. Drats. One more thing to do that would cost money.

She switched on the answering machine. Margaret's voice chided her. "I heard about that body in your sister's backyard. That's no excuse to miss dinner tonight. I'll see you at seven."

If she accepted Margaret's job offer, she wouldn't have to worry about paying a dentist. She glanced at her watch. A little more than an hour till she had to be there. An hour plus a few minutes to make up her mind. A bubble bath. That would help. Nonsense. She didn't like bubble baths. She only liked the *thought* of bubble baths. As soon as the bubbles melted down to a dingy film, she began obsessing about her skin absorbing dirty water, water she'd been sitting in, water that she'd scrubbed her feet in. Yuck. She should probably take a shower first, then wash the tub out, and *then* take a bubble bath. Too much work. And a colossal waste of water.

She plopped her purse on the counter by the door and retrieved the envelope from her chair. *Madeleine Ames,* it said. "Looks like it's from that agent."

Maddy squealed and grabbed. "Yes!" Her face paled. "What if it's a rejection? I made all the changes she asked for. I rewrote practically the whole book. But she only wanted to read the first three chapters this time. What if she didn't like the changes?"

"Don't go assuming anything. Just open it and find out."

Maddy slumped against the counter beside the fridge, winding her right leg around her left. "It might be good news," she said. "I need a sign." She slipped a finger beneath the flap and slid it toward the center. Blood welled from her knuckle. "Criminey crud buckets! A paper cut? Is that the kind of sign I get?"

"Chill out, Maddy. You know better than to open an envelope that way."

"Thanks for all the sympathy. Here I am, not knowing whether this letter holds an offer that will vault me into best seller stardom, or," and she put the back of her hand against her forehead in a pose worthy of a silent movie starlet, "it might hold dynamite to blow my dreams apart, and you lecture me about safety rules."

Drama queen. "You're not the only one who's up against a life-changing event."

VIOLET AS AN AMETHYST

Maddy glared at her. "What are you muttering about?"

A bark, a loud meow, and a distinct yelp sounded from outside the kitchen door. Glaze, happy for the distraction, slipped aside and opened it. Marmalade hissed. Glaze had never heard her do that before. The dog poked its nose in, and Glaze noticed several distinct scratches on its nose. That must have been the source of the yelp. That was too bad. The dog did have a cute little nose. Sort of pinkish, with a couple of dark brown freckles on it. And now those scratches, too. Still, it wasn't her dog, and it couldn't come inside. She blocked it with her knee. Marmalade hissed again and sidled inside. The dog backed up, and Glaze closed the door. "Hello, Marmalade. What brings you here?"

Hello, Smellsweet. Your dog barked at me. I had to correct her. She glided farther into the kitchen and turned left to rub her side along one of Madeleine's pretzel-twisted legs, meowing gently. *Hello Curlup. I have come for some catnip.* She headed for her own particular lower cabinet and pawed determinedly at the door.

Glaze waited for Maddy to oblige the cat, but Maddy stood frozen in place, ignoring the cat, inspecting the envelope as if it might contain a biohazard. Marmy meowed louder. "Maddy, can you get out the catnip?"

"Huh?"

"Forget it." Glaze circled the table and rummaged in the cabinet right next to Maddy. She tossed a soft fuzzy leaf-encrusted ball across the floor and smiled as Marmalade pounced on it. She really needed to take a shower soon, but this was more fun.

"I have to change the title," Maddy wailed.

"Why? I thought *A Slaying Song Tonight* was a great name."

"It's already taken. Somebody else wrote a book and

called it that."

If you'd written faster, you could have had it, Glaze thought. She was smart enough to keep her mouth shut on that idea. Maddy looked positively stricken as it was. Glaze tossed the catnip ball one more time. "Is that all they said?"

"No. She's willing to look at the whole manuscript."

"Maddy, that's great news."

"But what if she doesn't like it?"

Humans worry too much about everything.

Glaze chuckled at Marmalade's little squawk. "She'll love it. Didn't you hear Marmy tell you so?"

"She was probably asking you to open the door for her. Maybe we should put in one of those doors like Biscuit and Bob have, so she can come and go anytime she wants."

Glaze could imagine that dog getting its head stuck trying to crawl in through a cat door. "I don't think so." She reached out and turned on the radio. "Anyway, she's not our dog."

~~~~~

This is Radio Ralph Towers, your *Voice of the Valley* in Keagan County, with all the news worth listening to. The body ...

~~~~~

~MELISSA TARKINGTON~

Melissa turned off the radio the moment she heard Radio Ralph start his news report. She laid plates with a gold and brown leaf pattern on the table. That dead body was the last thing she wanted the Pontiacs to hear about during dinner. She slipped in a tape of soothing piano music and pushed PLAY. She glanced at the telephone. He'd been in Atlanta for a week. Well, really only five days, but it seemed like forever. She turned her hand to admire the twinkling amethyst, but the twinkle seemed lusterless. He hadn't called her.

~~~~~

... of a man, found last evening in a Martinsville backyard, has been positively identified, based on his dental records, according to Martinsville Police Chief Robert Sheffield, but the name is being withheld until relatives are notified. WRRT Radio will have an update for you as soon as information is available.

~~~~~

~BISCUIT McKEE~

I shivered, switched off the radio, and carried the crock pot of hot soup to the car. I'd already loaded a basket with plates, knives, spoons, bowls, and napkins, and a bag with two loaves of fresh bread and two sticks of butter. At this rate, there was no telling when Bob and Reebok would be free.

After I settled the crock pot into place, I ran back inside and grabbed the two extra loaves I'd baked. The fire station was in the same block as the police station, so I might as well make two trips at once.

Bob and Reebok were grateful for the food, but they didn't waste a lot of time thanking me. I gave Bob a quick hug and drove the half block up to the fire station, where five men sat around playing cards and watching TV. One of them was reading.

I held up the bread. "I wanted to thank you all for saving my life last week."

The one who was reading looked up when I spoke. I thought he blushed, but it might have been the shadows in that corner of the room. I knew the others, but I'd never met him. "These are fresh out of the oven," I told them. "Don't leave them in the bag too long, or they'll get soggy from the steam."

"Don't worry about that."

"They'll get eaten right now."

"Are these as good as those chocolate chip cookies you brought us a few weeks ago?"

"Haven't had homemade bread since I was at my grandma's house."

The fellow in the corner set down his book. "You goons wouldn't care to mention to her that you weren't the ones on duty when it happened, would you?"

"Aw, Cartwright, did you have to ruin it?"

Cartwright, whoever he was, shrugged. "Just wanted to keep the record straight."

I looked them over. "None of you?"

The tallest of the men, a guy named George, pointed to the three others standing nearby. "We're still the day shift. Except for him." He pointed to Cartwright, the reader. "He's night shift but he came in early today."

"Well," I said, "it looks like I'll just have to bake two more loaves in a few days and come by later in the evening. You're all welcome to this, as my way of thanking you for the work you do." George reached for the bag, but I held it away from him. "I'd like Cartwright to get the first slice." I smiled as I said it. Didn't want the day shift to be angry with me.

Cartwright stepped forward. "All I did was drive the ambulance, ma'am."

"You be sure and share it with your friends here," I

said. "There's no telling whether I might need *their* services some day."

"Hope you never do."

"We're here if you need us,"

"Happy to help out if we can."

"Glad you came out of it okay, Miss Biscuit."

I got all the way back to the house after delivering the food, when I remembered that I still hadn't talked to Melissa about whatever was bothering her. Something was wrong. She'd cut me off when I'd asked her about Chad on Saturday, she hadn't come to the dance, and she wasn't in church on Sunday. Well, she probably hadn't skipped church just to avoid me. But still, I hated to leave that unresolved whatever-it-was gaping between us.

"Where are you, Marmy?"

I am resting on the back of the couch.

"Want to take a walk?" She came, purring her little heart out, around the corner from the living room. I slipped on a sweater, unlocked the door, and opened it.

The cliffs that surround the south and west sides of town bring an early dusk as the sun sinks behind them. In the short time since I'd driven home from the station, the birds had stopped their twittering. My green Buick already looked slightly grayish as the light faded. I'd drive over to Melissa's. No need to walk. I turned and picked up my purse and my keys from the beautiful old drop leaf table in the entryway.

I made it one step onto the porch, but no farther. I could not make myself walk down my own front steps. The thought of walking, unprotected, out to the curb and turning my back to the hedges around Paul Welsh's house while I got into the car, brought goose bumps to my arms. The thought of coming back here after dark paralyzed me. The thought of those hands shoving me... I jumped back and slammed the door without looking. Thank goodness

Marmalade was still waiting inside.

Yes. I knew your heart did not want to go.

I threw my purse onto the table. It slid off and scattered keys, comb, wallet, and all that stupid junk I carried around all the time. Why did I need it all? Why couldn't I just get rid of everything that was in my way? Why couldn't I go outside? Why couldn't I scream and shake somebody and make this go away? I sank down onto my knees and picked up my lipstick. I hated lipstick. I threw it as hard as I could and felt only marginally better when the case cracked. I had never in my life been afraid to be alone. Never. Never until now. Never, until those hands... until they... until ...

I am here with you.

Marmalade pushed her way into my arms. I scooped her up and rocked and sobbed. She never once stopped purring.

CHAPTER 13
Monday 5 p.m. to 11 p.m.

~REEBOK GARNER~

IF HE COULD HAVE SQUIRMED OUT OF THIS, he would have. Dreading what he had to do, Reebok raised his hand to rap on the door, but Mrs. Zapota opened it first. "I saw you drive up," she said. "It's Charles, that body they talked about on the radio, isn't it?"

Reebok nodded. "I'm very sorry to have to tell you this, ma'am."

"He's been dead all along, hasn't he?" She stood as if planted in the middle of the doorway, as if she refused to invite death into her hall.

"We believe so, ma'am. The medical examiner said it appeared he died very quickly." There'd been a deep knife cut on a throat vertebrae, but Reebok wasn't planning on mentioning that unless she asked. She didn't.

"We'd like your husband to stop by and identify the personal effects." There wasn't much else left. "It's just a formality, since the dental records provided a positive identification."

"I'll do it. My husband has a heart condition. I don't think he should be the one to see the body."

"Uh, no, ma'am. Not the body. It's the personal effects—watch, wallet and such—that we'd like identified."

The liver spots on her corrugated skin were the only things that didn't lose color. Reebok put out a hand to steady her.

"Let me get my purse, Deputy. I'd like to get this over as quickly as possible."

"Do you want me to call your husband?"

"I'll let him know when you bring me back home. No need to worry him unnecessarily."

On the way up the valley, Mrs. Zapota was surprisingly calm, or so it seemed to Reebok. He didn't know what to say, so he didn't say anything.

She finally broke the silence. "You probably think I'm coldhearted not to be crying."

"Not at all, ma'am. People deal with news like this in all sorts of different ways." *As if I know what I'm talking about*, he thought. *I've never had to give anyone this sort of news before.*

"My sister's daughter, they live up in Russell Gap, I told you about her, my niece Katie?" Each phrase sounded like a question. Reebok wondered why. "She's been gone more than a year now, and we've never heard anything from her. We keep hoping she's still alive, but now, with Charles really truly ..." She took a long, deep breath and exhaled loudly. "With him truly gone, I wonder if there's any hope at all for her."

"There's ..." Reebok was going to say there's always hope, but that sounded hollow, and after this long, it probably wasn't true. "There's no time limit on missing person cases. I'm sure the police are still working on it." That sounded outrageous even to him. There was only so much evidence people could process, only so many questions officers could ask. After awhile, they'd give up or at least not pursue it actively. "They'll have kept the file open," he added.

Mrs. Zapota turned and looked at him. He could see her in his peripheral vision, but he didn't want to meet her eyes. What he'd said had sounded lame, even to him. She must have thought he was completely inadequate. He clenched his jaw and kept driving.

Afterwards, the drive back to her house was even worse. Mrs. Zapota took a pocket watch out of the bag they'd given her. "This belonged to his grandfather, my husband's father. See? His name is engraved on the back."

Reebok knew that. He'd seen the watch at the crime scene. They'd wondered at that first name, Horace, but it was so obviously an old watch, and so obviously an old-fashioned name, they were fairly sure the name on the watch didn't match the name of the victim. And it hadn't.

Mrs. Zapota wound the watch, shook it gently, and ran her finger around and around the dial. Reebok glanced over quickly to see what she was doing. It looked like she was following the second hand as it swept along.

The crying started slowly. At first there was just a gentle intake of breath and a sniff or two, but the sniffs increased in volume, until the tears flowed freely down her wrinkled face. Reebok wondered if he should stop the car at one of the scenic overlooks. No. Better to get her home as fast as he could.

"Why." It didn't sound like a question. More like an accusation. "Why—why—why," she wailed. "Why my son?" She rocked and rocked, clutching the watch to her breast, and Reebok could hear, between her sobs, the soft susurration of the seat belt as it unwound when she leaned forward and retracted when her body went back against the seat.

He pulled the car to a stop, finally, in front of her house and walked quickly around to help her out. "Do you want me to come in with you, ma'am? Maybe call someone for you?"

She held up one hand, the one that wasn't cradling the bag close. "No." She looked off to the left and gestured. "My neighbor will ..." Reebok turned to see a woman steaming down the walk from the house next door, her arms outstretched, her face full of an awareness of what must have happened.

Reebok stepped aside as she gathered Mrs. Zapota into her arms and led her up the front steps.

~~~~~

~GLAZE McKEE~

Glaze dragged her feet down Fourth Street, the same way she had the last time she'd been to Margaret and Sam's house for dinner. That was the evening Margaret had offered the job. She'd said she didn't like having to decide whether or not to fund the various projects people in Martinsville kept requesting money for. Some of them had been no-brainers. Margaret liked helping the library and the art center. She'd been more than willing to pay for a new fire station, a town ambulance, and a day-care center. But she didn't want to feel that every time people approached her, they were angling for money. She wanted to put Glaze in that position. Glaze wasn't related to everyone in town and hadn't grown up here either, so Margaret thought it would be easier for Glaze to say no to some of the harebrained ideas. Half of Glaze wanted to accept the job, but the other half of her was terrified.

She passed Sadie's house and noticed Marmalade sitting on the front porch, licking a paw and rubbing it over her face. That cat apparently had a regular route. She must have come directly from catnip-at-Glaze-and-Maddy's-house to cream-at-Sadie's.

I call her Looselaces.

Marmalade meowed at her, and Glaze raised her hand in greeting.

Then she went right back to ruminating about this job offer. She couldn't use the dead body in her sister's yard as an excuse. She would have to give Margaret an answer; she knew Margaret would push for one—but she still wasn't sure what that answer would be. Yes? No? Maybe?

The dog, which had followed her expectantly along the street, stopped to inspect a bush. Glaze kept walking, her mind not really on the dog, although she did, just for a moment, admire the fuzzy whitish tufts that poked whimsically from the front of each of the dog's feet. The dog was obviously a girl, with those swirly, curly whirls of honey-brown hair all over her back and feathering out from the back of each leg. She looked like she was dressed up to go out to dinner at a fancy restaurant.

Dinner. That thought brought Glaze back to where she was going. She sincerely hoped Sam and Margaret wouldn't want to talk about that dead man over dinner.

Sam must have been watching for her. Before she even knocked, he swung open the bright purple front door that Glaze could have sworn had been red the last time she was here. Margaret must have painted it recently. It matched a nearby hanging basket of flowers. Biscuit would know what kind they were. Biscuit had a basket just like this one.

Come in," Sam boomed. "Come in, and make yourself at home." He looked behind her. "Who's your friend?"

The dog, again. "She's not mine. She's just been following me around."

Sam gave her a knowing look, but Glaze chose to ignore it. She handed him her sweater—the evenings could get a bit chilly here in the foothills of the Appalachians, even now, in midsummer. He pointed down the hall as Margaret sang out, "Come on back here. I thought we'd eat in the kitchen. It's so much homier, don't you think?" Margaret was the same age as Glaze, or pretty close to it, but her hugs always felt like a grandmother's.

"I was sorry to hear about Biscuit," Margaret said. "How's she doing? That must have been quite a shock."

"Two shocks in one week," Sam said. "Don't forget how she got pushed in the river."

Margaret turned back to Glaze. "Do they think the two are connected?"

Glaze spread her hands. "There's no way to know, but Biscuit's still pretty shook up." She laid one hand on the gleaming counter. "I love this," she said. "Is it some sort of tile?"

"Oh, you know how to say the right thing. Sam made these counters himself. He started with heavy plywood and built it up with some sort of special paint and acrylic stuff."

"Epoxy," Sam corrected.

"Right.

Sam was quite a handyman and, from what Glaze had heard, an inventor as well. She knew he'd come up with towel warmers for the bathroom that were powered by the solar hot water system he'd adapted. The same system kept their floors warm in the winter. There was no telling what else he'd invented for Margaret's ease and pleasure. Some people, if they didn't know him well, might discount him as just an oddball who spent way too much time tinkering with the 1933 Duesenberg his wife had inherited, along with a major fortune, when she was a child. Glaze had thought that, too, before she'd gotten to know the depths of him. Glaze liked Sam tremendously. "I thought epoxy was some sort of glue," she said. "What does it do?"

"That's right. You can stick almost anything together with epoxy. It can turn something that's relatively fragile into something quite strong. That's why it's used in a lot of jewelry making." He grinned at Margaret and added, "Or so I've heard."

Glaze ran her hand along the counter. "This is the same stuff as in Margaret's jewelry?"

"Not really," Sam said. "What I used on the counter is a special paint that has an epoxy base."

"Yeah," Margaret put in. "We had to rent Melissa's suite while he was putting it in. The fumes were something awful."

Sam considered the counter for several seconds. "Worth all the bother?"

"Oh, you." She slapped playfully at his arm. "You know

I love it."

"Do you have to wear a gas mask while you're making your jewelry?"

Margaret looked startled at the question, but grinned when she realized Glaze was teasing her. "Sam came up with a special kind of filtering fan for my workshop." She fingered her left earring. "Don't know what I'd do without him, but don't tell him I told you that."

She grinned up at her husband and they exchanged one of those looks married people shared. Biscuit and Bob did that a lot, too. Glaze felt left out. To cover her discomfort she gestured at Margaret's earring and asked, "Is that a new design of yours? I don't think I've seen them before."

Margaret unclipped her earring and handed it to Glaze. "Never could wear those pierced things. They make my ears swell up."

Glaze inspected the earring. Concentric off-white rings alternated with ones of a brownish red. They were formed of meticulously placed seeds surrounding a small reddish-beige disk. "I recognize the two colors of millet," Glaze said, "but what's the seed in the center? I've never seen anything like that."

Margaret's normally placid face puckered up in glee. "It's a peanut. I had to slice it to form that little center disk." She touched her other ear. "Two little disks. Then I had to stain them so they'd match the red millet."

Sam guffawed. "You should have seen how many peanuts she went through before she got two cuts that worked."

Margaret batted his arm again. "Peanuts are crumbly. That's where the epoxy comes in. It makes all the seeds—and the peanut—as sturdy as can be, and it fills in all the empty spaces in between the seeds."

Glaze ran her thumb across the earring. "Is that why it's so smooth?"

Margaret nodded. "You can make jewelry out of anything. Anything at all."

Glaze looked more closely and turned the earring over. "What's the backing?"

Margaret chuckled. "Cardboard. I wouldn't be able to use it if it weren't for—"

"Epoxy!" Glaze and Sam called out at the same time, and all three of them laughed.

Glaze handed the earring back. "What makes it so shiny?"

"Epoxy!"

This was getting silly, Glaze thought, but it was more fun than she thought she'd ever have again, ever since last month when she'd quit taking her medications and had gone into such a tailspin of depression. And certainly she felt almost guilty laughing this much after what Biscuit had gone through. Glaze turned away from her hosts so they wouldn't see the cloud descending over her.

Margaret clipped the earring back on and turned toward the salad bowl by the sink. Sam motioned Glaze into the same chair she'd sat in last time she'd had dinner here. Glaze knew better than to offer to help. She could do that in Biscuit's kitchen because she knew where everything was, but not here. She wouldn't know where to start. She felt useless.

Sam opened a cabinet and pulled out big bowls and small plates. "Here." He handed them to Glaze and winked. "We always put our guests to work."

Margaret placed the salad and a basket of garlic bread on the table and sat to Glaze's left. Sam carried a big pot of stew to the table, ladled it into the blue-ringed white bowls as Glaze held them for him, and sat with a resounding sigh of satisfaction. "Dig in," he said. "The food's been blessed by the love of the people who grew it and the ones who prepared it."

VIOLET AS AN AMETHYST

Glaze wondered if he had a brother. That was ridiculous. She had a perfectly good man who was madly in love with her, who'd even asked her to marry him. She'd said no to Tom repeatedly, held him at arm's length, denied what she might feel for him. Maybe this new job would keep her busy enough that she wouldn't have to think about it. Maybe when she went out with Red, she'd get a better sense of perspective.

"Glaze?" Margaret looked mildly concerned. "Are you okay?"

Glaze shook her head. She wasn't okay. She wasn't confident that she could do this work. She wasn't sure this was the right decision for her. Still, there was that *something* inside her that wanted more than what she had. Not just the *more stuff* a higher salary would allow her to enjoy—nice furniture, eating out more often, maybe some lovely jewelry. Those were tempting, but she needed more challenge in her life, more of a feeling that she was doing something valuable. The kazoos and flower pots at CelerInc simply didn't hold her interest. The salary there, too, wasn't enough to let her relax in the knowledge that she could support herself. She was just squeaking by on what Hank paid her. And she never wanted to be in a position where she got married for economic security—or because she didn't know what else to do. If she had a job she loved, maybe it would be easier to love something, someone else, too. Before she could change her mind, she said, "I'll do it."

"Yippee!" Margaret pumped her arm in a thoroughly un-ladylike gesture. "I knew you would. But it's a real relief to hear you say it." She pushed the bread basket closer to Glaze. "Eat up, honey. We'll talk about the details later. Where are you going to put your office?"

"Whoa, there." Sam held up his hand like a traffic cop. "You said the details came *later*. Let her at least take a few bites before you grill her." He raised his glass. "Glaze, you're going to do just fine."

Glaze paused only a moment before lifting her glass to touch his and Margaret's.

After dinner, Sam blended up a milkshake for each of them, while Margaret laid out her plans. "You'll have a cash fund to begin with. We're going to have to get your signature card on the checkbook, so you can withdraw cash whenever you need it. We have a separate account that all of the ..." she groped for a word, "... the discretionary funds for the town go into. My financial outfit deposits a certain amount each month. It's based on a percentage of the income from the estate. I'll let them know that all the statements will go to you from now on, as soon as you sign the paperwork at the bank. But don't worry about that. The point is, you'll be able to start right away."

Sam placed their milkshakes on the coffee table and handed Glaze a hefty envelope. "Here's a thousand dollars to start you out with. I don't want you carrying this kind of cash around, so I'll deliver it to your house tomorrow, along with a fireproof safe you can keep it in. In fact, we just happen to have a safe right here."

He picked up a graceful table lamp with a light purple-toned Venetian glass shade and Margaret pulled a floor length tablecloth off what Glaze had assumed was a rather substantial end table. "Impressive, isn't it?"

Before Glaze could think of what to say, Sam suggested that she learn how to operate the lock. "Here's the combination, only I wrote the numbers in reverse order." He handed her a slip of paper. "Instead of starting with the number on the left, you start with the one on the right. Just to confuse somebody if they pick your pocket."

Glaze gulped. This was beginning to sound serious.

"Here," Sam said, "You try opening it. Start by twirling

the knob around two or three times to the right to clear it." He sat on the floor beside her and walked her through the steps. It was a lot like her high school locker—she'd hated high school and still had nightmares about it—only there were more numbers, one of which required her to spin the knob twice the first time, three times after another number, and the others only once. Once she'd mastered it, she put the money envelope inside and closed the door.

"Good job," Margaret said. "You're going to do so well. Now, I know you probably want to get home so you can get a good night's sleep ..."

As if I'll be able to sleep after this, Glaze thought.

"But before you go, we want you to have $250 in cash, in case you need it before your first paycheck. The thousand in the safe is for the fund. The two-fifty is an advance on your pay, so you can spend it any way you want."

"But I'll have to give my two-week notice at CelerInc."

Margaret flicked her fingers as if such a detail wouldn't matter at all. "So you'll have two paychecks. You're hired as of right now."

"Do you want me to sign something?"

"Oh heavens no." Margaret swept her hand back and forth, as if brushing away objections. "We know where to find you."

All Glaze could do was nod as she rose from the floor.

Sam looked up at Glaze as he pulled himself to his feet. "Any chance you could meet Margaret and me at the bank tomorrow during your lunch hour? Margaret will have to add your name to the account. Then you can sign the forms and we'll give you the checkbook. You'll be ready to go."

"Cash is easier, though," Margaret said, "which is why we gave you the thousand dollars. I never bothered much with writing checks if I could avoid it."

Glaze kept her mouth shut.

Sam raised his hand like an evangelist at a prayer meeting. "Glaze can do it any way she wants to, but we want her fully operational right from the start, don't we?"

"I suppose so."

He looked back at Glaze. "Can you leave your door unlocked tomorrow?"

"It's always unlocked."

"It's not fair to tempt people. If you're going to have a lot of money on hand, even if it's in a safe, you'll need to start locking your door. The safe is pretty heavy, but anybody my size with a hand truck could move it."

She blinked. "I'll take my key with me in the morning."

"Fine. I'll lock the door after me." He stood, and smiled at Margaret, as if something had been decided for sure. "Better yet, I'll get a dead bolt lock and install it for you."

"One for each door," Margaret said, "and three keys. One for you, one for Madeleine, and one extra." She patted Glaze on the shoulder. "Where do you want Sam to put the safe tomorrow?"

"The living room, I guess. Over against the wall where the mirror is."

"If you change your mind," Sam said, "or if you want to set up an office somewhere else, I'll be happy to move it for you. I'll have those keys for you tomorrow at the bank."

"Thank you." Glaze folded the paper around the crisp bills. She looked at Margaret on her left and Sam on her right. "You knew I'd say yes, didn't you?"

They chuckled in stereo.

~~~~~

~GLAZE McKEE~

On the walk home, she and the dog passed by the Old Woods,

a grove of old-growth trees that had stood there since the town was founded in 1745. Before that even. Tradition had it that Homer Martin's wife would never allow certain trees to be cut, even though the usual practice at the time was to clear-cut, so predators and enemies couldn't hide behind the trees and so fire wouldn't spread so easily. But Mary Frances Garner Martin didn't hold with the usual practices. She liked trees, or so the town legends stated. There were three such stands in Martinsville, one of which filled most of the block where Biscuit lived, where that body had been found, this one here above the Old Church cemetery, and the third down by the river. They were all called the Old Woods, so conversational reference to them had to rely on context.

Glaze slowed her pace. One particularly enormous tree along here always caught her eye. It leaned out over the street in a welcoming presence. Glaze paused beneath the heavily-flowered branches and took a deep breath. "I did it," she said and exhaled loudly. "I have a new job." Now she could quit CelerInc and wave goodbye to Horrible Hank. It was just her imagination, she knew, but the tree seemed to lean a bit closer as the dog pressed against her leg and stood with one paw on top of her left foot. She felt supported, somehow. She reached up on tiptoes, disturbing the dog in the process, and brushed one of the blossoms on the end of the bough. "I can do it." The tree believed her, or seemed to, and for just a moment Glaze believed herself.

She barely made it to Juniper before the doubts poured in. *Whatever have I gotten myself into?* Once she reached the barrel, she turned right on Beechnut Lane and headed for Biscuit's house, accompanied by the dog. She could see lights on downstairs.

A car moved slowly up the street, its headlights blinding her. Glaze instinctively reached out for the dog's collar, the obnoxiously grape-colored one Maddy had bought, with a matching grape-colored leash no less, although, come to think of it, Glaze had never seen a grape that color except in cartoons. The dog growled softly.

"Evening, Miss Glaze." Reebok's voice poured from the car window and Glaze relaxed. He probably had no idea how scary it was to be a woman walking alone after what had happened to Biscuit. The dog whimpered.

"You're out kind of late, aren't you?"

It didn't sound like nosiness. It sounded like concern. He must have been frantic when they couldn't find Biscuit. He'd certainly hovered over her hospital bed, like a St. Bernard on a mission. The only thing he was missing was fur. And a brandy keg around his neck.

"Just heading home now from Margaret and Sam's. I thought I'd stop in and see Biscuit."

He glanced at his watch. "If you need me to escort you home, you just call the station, you hear? The Chief is there now, and I'll be back there in about ten more minutes."

Reebok was so... so earnest, Glaze thought. She could hear the capital letter ring every time he spoke of Bob. "Thank you," she said, "but I should be fine."

"Of course, ma'am. You've got your dog with you." He waved and pulled on up the street.

"She's not my dog." But Reebok was too far away to hear her.

~~~~~

~BISCUIT McKEE~

Bob was still at the station, and I'd just finished a dish of ice cream, when Marmalade jumped off the windowsill and brushed by my ankles.

SmellSweet is coming to see us. That dog is with her, too.

She purred gently and headed toward the front door, so I followed, peeked through the lace curtains, and saw Glaze coming up the walk. I unlocked the door and opened it wide. She cocked her head at me. "What're you doing standing at the door? Waiting for me?"

"Marmy heard you coming," I said, and Glaze bent to scoop Marmalade into her arms. "I'm okay," I said. I didn't mention my earlier meltdown. "Thanks for checking on me, but I'll be all right tonight by myself."

"No," she said. "I wanted to talk with you about something,"

"That's no reason to go walking around in the middle of the night by yourself. You could have called."

"I'm okay," she said.

I spotted the dog sitting politely behind her. "Well, I guess it's okay. You're not alone."

"I'm not?" Glaze looked over her shoulder.

"The dog," I said. "You're not alone." When she still seemed confused, I added, "The dog is with you."

"She just follows me around. Stay," she said to the dog with quiet authority. The dog sank down and laid her head on her curiously tufted paws, one back leg skewed out in back of her. "I keep hoping she'll go home soon."

FreckleNose has adopted Smellsweet, but she does not know that yet.

"Following you. Right." Marmalade made some of her rumble noises. I hoped she wasn't afraid of the dog.

Of course I am not afraid. I have already taught her to respect me.

I grimaced apologetically at—I wish she had a name—and closed the door. I locked it, something I never used to do. "What's up?"

"Nothing much."

"It's almost ten o'clock, Glaze. You don't stop by unannounced at this hour of the night, especially after the kind of night we had yesterday, if there's nothing much going on. What's wrong?" I looked her over. She was still awfully thin, but she was gaining back some of the weight she'd lost last month. The worry line between her eyes was still there, but it didn't look too tight. Of course, I hadn't helped much, calling her in a panic the way I had last night and begging her to stay with me.

I was with you.

I read a poem once by Christina Rossetti. She wrote, "There is no friend like a sister, in calm or stormy weather." Glaze was like that to me, a friend, a confidant, someone I could depend on. I reached out and hugged her, squashing Marmalade between us in the process.

I do not mind.

"What was that for?"

"Just being sappy. Having a Rossetti moment."

Glaze looked at me like I'd finally gone absolutely barmy.

"Never mind me. Come on back for some ice cream, and you can tell me what's on your mind."

"No. No ice cream. I'm stuffed. I had dinner with Margaret and Sam."

She didn't say anything else, but led the way into the kitchen where she plopped down at the round table in the bay window. Marmy wiggled out of her arms and onto the wide windowsill. My two favorite females, I thought, both in their usual places.

Not quite. I am facing a different way than I usually do. There are no birds to watch, and you have closed the curtains.

Marmalade let out a funny little yawp. I wish I could tell what she was thinking. "You want some tea," I asked, "or lemonade?"

I do not need anything to drink, thank you.

"No, I'm fine. I just need to talk."

I sat across from her, moved the vase of purple cosmos out of the way, and leaned my elbows on the table. Momentarily picturing Grandma Martelson clenching her lips at my breach in etiquette, I almost moved my arms to a more ladylike position. Instead, I remembered that Grandma wasn't here to see me. I rested my chin on my hands. Tell me about Tom, I thought. "So, talk," I said.

"I have to quit my job."

That was the last thing I expected. "Why?"

By the time she'd explained it, I was practically cheering. I needed some good news like this. "Glaze, that's wonderful! Think of all the good you'll be able to do."

"But I don't know how to organize all this. I can't believe I said yes. I'm not even sure why I did. It just popped out. They gave me a thousand dollars—a thousand," she repeated with something like awe in her voice, "in cash, just to get started."

"You're not walking around town at night with that much money, are you?" Invisible hands reached for the middle of my back. "It's not worth the risk."

"No. Sam said he'd deliver it to the house tomorrow, along with a safe to keep it in. We're going to have to start locking the doors all the time. This means I really have to do something, and I don't know where to start."

"Oh, for heaven's sake. You don't need to know it all. With that budget Margaret's given you, you can hire somebody who does know." I slapped my hand down on the table. "Brain wave! How about Dee? She's one of the most organized people I know. She could keep track of every penny while you just say yes or no."

Glaze straightened her spine. She looked like one of those slow motion films of a flower emerging from the ground. "And Maddy could handle all the paperwork, couldn't she? The letters and such."

"Wait a minute! Is this what you've been in such a snit

about for the last couple of weeks?"

She nodded slowly. "Silly as it sounds, I thought if I ignored it, it might go away."

"Like that dog of yours," I said.

"She's not my ..." She bit at her lower lip, apparently deciding whether or not to address the dog issue. Apparently not. "The salary is astonishing," she said, quoting a figure that made me take a deep breath.

"Wow. That's great."

"You know that trip to Scotland you wanted us to go on? I'll be able to afford it now."

I rubbed the back of my left hand. It still felt chilly every once in awhile. "I think the next place I go will have to be sunny. I've had enough cold to last quite awhile."

"Oh, I'm sorry. I didn't think—"

"Not your fault. I just need some more time to get over this... this fear I have of being too cold to move. Or of someone running up in back of me."

She reached for my hand. "I didn't realize. I should have known."

"No reason why you would. This was certainly something I never expected." I moved the vase of flowers farther to one side. "Next trip we'll go to Mesa Verde. That should be warm enough. Now can we change the subject? Where will you set up your office?"

"Um, I don't know. I thought I'd start in the living room. Sam's going to put the safe there anyway."

Glaze and Madeleine's old house, for some inexplicable reason, had two front doors, right next to each other. One—the squeaky one everybody used—went into the kitchen. The other opened into a celery-colored living room that they never seemed to sit in. I could picture a big desk and some file cabinets. "Move out those two overstuffed couches," I said, "and get rid of the old knickknack shelf." That had come from Bob's great-grandmother years ago. It was one of those thoroughly impractical pieces of furniture that did no good to anyone unless they collected doodads. "You could paint it yellow and give it to Sadie for her salt and pepper shaker collection."

I was fast asleep when Bob came home. He slipped into bed and pulled me close against him. Something about the way he did it reminded me of the blanket I used to have when I was little. I slept with that raggedy old thing tucked close to me until I was—when had I finally given it up? I yawned, decided that it didn't matter, and pulled Bob's right arm closer around me. Better than my blankie any day.

~~~~~

I am grateful for
    Widelap, who fell asleep before she wrote her list
    Softfoot, who remembers to scratch me even
        when he is worried
    LooseLaces, who gives me cream when I visit her
    the catnip growing in the garden, and the catnip
        toys SmellSweet and CurlUp keep for me
    that dog, because she stayed out on the porch the
        whole time SmellSweet was here and did not
        bark even once

~~~~~

~REEBOK GARNER~

For a long time after the Chief left, Reebok sat and thought. Something about his brief conversation with Miss Glaze disturbed him, but he couldn't quite call it up, like there was something buried he had to find. She'd looked really worried when his headlights first picked her out. That was why he'd called out to her so quickly. He didn't want to frighten any woman, particularly a woman walking alone.

She hadn't really been alone, not with that dog at her side. The dog. The dog. There was something about that dog.

No. He couldn't figure out what it was he was supposed to remember. He pulled a legal pad out of the drawer. Maybe if I make a list, he thought, and started writing.

DAY
SIX
TUESDAY

CHAPTER 14
6 a.m. to 6 p.m.

~BISCUIT McKEE~

My Gratitude List for Monday (written Tuesday morning, because I forgot last night)
1. My "blankie with a mustache" – a week ago I would have written "hee-hee" after this line with numerous exclamation points. But I'm having a hard time being enthusiastic about anything. I needed Bob's closeness last night. I needed to forget myself and my fears. I love him dearly.
2. Glaze and her new job. And her new dog, too! I do wish she'd pick a name soon so I can stop calling her "dog."
3. Our round table in the kitchen. We have the most amazing conversations there.
4. Maddy and Dee, who are going to be wonderful supports for Glaze.
5. The cup of tea I plan to brew as soon as I get downstairs.

~~~~~

~GLAZE McKEE~

GLAZE COULD HEAR THEM ARGUING IN THE KITCHEN.

"You've got to stop using pastries and coffee as your breakfast, Dee. You need something good, like oatmeal or scrambled eggs."

"I already ate at home. Fried eggs, cheese grits, and bacon. Rebecca Jo always cooks a big breakfast, and now that I'm living with her, she cooks twice as much and expects me to eat with her."

Glaze imagined Dee polishing off the cinnamon roll. She didn't have to imagine her slurping the coffee. Even upstairs like this, she could hear it, probably Dee's second cup.

"Sounds like you're eating two breakfasts each morning," Maddy said. "Why aren't you fat?" Before Dee could answer, Maddy called up the stairs, "You ready to go, Glaze?"

"Coming!" Glaze scooped up her shoes, gave her comforter a quick pat, and headed for the stairs.

Dee dabbed at her chin with a napkin. "Morning," she said. "Your dog's still outside. But she's got a collar on. Are you feeding her?"

"No," Glaze said at the same time Maddy said, "Yes."

Glaze looked at her housemate. "What?"

Maddy hunched her shoulders. "I bought some dog food Saturday. And a water bowl. And the collar. And a leash." Her voice grew louder with each sentence. "I've been feeding her on the back porch. And a dog bed. It's purple, to match her collar."

Glaze drew in a breath, but Maddy held up a hand. "She was hungry. We can't let her starve. And anyway, maybe I want to keep her."

"She needs to go home," Glaze said. "I'm putting up a sign at the grocery store as soon as I can get there. In fact, I'm going to call Reebok right now and ask him to listen out for anyone who's missing a dog."

Before she could lift the phone, it rang. She tucked her shoes under her arm. "Hello?... Yes... Oh, Esther, is everything all right?... Good... Yes, but how did you know... She did? That was fast... Well, I don't quite have everything set yet... Oh, then why don't you just jot up a request? I'll need to see the receipts... You can leave it on the kitchen table, no, wait! The door's going to be locked, so leave it in the mailbox. Yes, I'll have it for you by... uh... better say

Wednesday evening ....Sure, you're welcome. Bye."

"Hold up a minute," Dee barked. "What was all that about?"

"Yeah," Maddy chimed in, "and why did you tell Esther we'd lock the door?"

"We don't have to lock it yet. I'll tell you all about it later. Would you both be willing to join me for a little meeting tonight?" Glaze swept her hand in an arc, indicating the cheery kitchen. "Right here."

Maddy looked at Dee. "She sounds awfully serious. You think we should humor her?"

"Only if we can stop at the Delicious on the way home for buffalo wings and some of their potato salad." Dee grinned and lowered her voice to a mock whisper. "And Glaze has to pay since it's her meeting!"

Glaze lifted her purse from the counter beside the door. "Okay, but we have to eat fast and have a quick meeting because we all have to get to our tap dance lesson. And I'll pay for dinner."

"Hold on," Dee said, "I was only kidding. Of course I'll come to your meeting. Do we get to know what it's about?"

"Nope, not yet." She opened the squeaky door. "And I wasn't kidding. I *will* pay for dinner."

Maddy pointed toward Glaze's bare feet. "Aren't you forgetting something?"

"Whoops!" Glaze dropped her shoes, but forgot to block the door. "Out," she said as the dog nosed its way into the kitchen. "Go home." The dog dropped to the floor and laid her head on her front paws, one back leg sticking awkwardly out to the side.

"See, she *is* home," Maddy crowed.

The dog stood up and leaned against Glaze's leg. "Why is she being nice to *you*?" Maddy said. "I'm the one who gave her food and water."

Glaze stood up a little straighter. "I gave her water."

"Yeah," Maddy said. "One measly bowl of water after she'd already been here two whole days."

The dog stepped away from Glaze and stretched her freckled nose up to Maddy's hand. "And I bought her a collar, too."

The dog licked Maddy's fingers and walked back to Glaze. She stuck her head under Glaze's hand and quivered, just asking for a scratch.

Dee let out a laugh that sounded rather like a yodel. "Do you get the feeling you two are not nearly as smart as the average dog? Arguing over nothing?"

"She's not average," Glaze said, stretching out her other hand to Maddy's shoulder. "She's ours." She looked down at the curly brown head. She didn't want a dog. She'd never had a dog. She didn't know what to do with a dog. But, for now, the dog could stay. Until they found her a real home.

~~~~~

~BISCUIT McKEE~

For a part time job, with the library open just four days a week, Monday, Wednesday, Friday, and Saturday, I sure did spend a lot of extra time here on my days off. Reading the shelves—making sure every book was in the right place—was easier when there weren't library patrons around asking questions. If I could just start at one end of a shelf and work my way right down it and on to the next, then I didn't lose track of where I was. It's amazing how often people put the books back in the wrong place. I wasn't so surprised at finding one of the CEM fiction books stuck in between the CEDs and the CEEs. At least those were in the same general shelf space. But I'd just located the HAR Connie had on reserve to the left of a DEL. Made no sense.

You are right. What you are thinking makes no sense.

Marmalade's little gurgle brightened me for a moment. Lucky cat. She didn't have to worry about stuff like misplaced books.

It is my job to catch the intruders, and I hear a bug under this bookcase.

Why didn't people pay attention to the labels? Last week I'd found Mary Roach's *Packing for Mars,* a book about space travel—real space travel, not science fiction—in with the biographies, and Elaine Morgan's anthropological study *The Descent of Woman* in the gardening section. It made me wonder if some patrons left their brains on the doorstep next to the stone lions when they entered the library.

The lions feel cool when I sit on them on a hot day.

In the fiction section, shelf reading left my brain free to wander as I scanned the three letters of the authors' last names. Easy to spot mistakes at the same time I was thinking.

Bob had me worried. He was working so many hours with this dead body. They knew who he was, and they also knew now for sure that the man had been murdered. Well, they'd known that from the moment I found the body. People don't bury themselves. Still it was amazing what autopsies could show—not that I wanted any of the details. My librarian's inquisitive mind only went so far. But there was something else niggling at Bob. He'd spent a lot of time stewing over it, even before the murder, but he wasn't sharing anything about it with me. Not that I blamed him. He was a cop. There was so much about his job that I didn't understand, and I made it a point never to prod him for answers. Well, almost never. I could tell, though, that Bob was having a hard time. But what was it about?

Three or four weeks ago, well before we found the body, Sharon had mentioned that she'd seen Bob's car in front of Bushy Bagot & Green. What was he doing there, she'd wanted to know, and her eyebrow had arched in a particularly nosy way. But I'd had no idea. They'd handled the closing on our house, but I couldn't think of any reason why Bob needed to see a lawyer. Was he in trouble? No. He would have told me. Sharon seemed to be reading something into the event, though.

I'd swear, the way gossip floated around this town, seeping into every crack and cranny, and most of it with no more foundation than air. Bob was just fine. We were just fine. And he'd tell me soon enough.

Marmalade pulled a newly-dead cockroach from under the edge of the bookcase. I sure was glad she was on patrol. I hadn't seen a mouse in more than a year, other than the one or two she'd left lying beside the checkout counter, like little fur-wrapped presents. I bent and stroked her back as she purred gently.

I am good at what I do.

Still, if Bob's meeting with the lawyer were some sort of casual visit (as if any visit to an attorney could be casual), Bob would have mentioned it. Mr. Bushy was our own personal lawyer, but I knew the firm handled the town's business, too. Maybe something was going on with the police department. Or, come to think of it, Bob had gone to see Margaret a couple of times last month. I knew that because I'd seen his car in her driveway. What could that mean? Well, for heaven's sakes Biscuit, here you go doing the same thing you're always railing against. I could just ask him what's up. And he'd either answer me or tell me that he couldn't.

I pulled a Donna Leon mystery out of the GABs and

tucked it under one arm. I'd shelve it properly when I got to the LEOs; like the stone lions outside the library, I thought, picturing an astrology chart I'd seen somewhere or other, with Leo the Lion poised over the August birthdays—or was it September?

What does that mean?

I stopped at the end of that shelf. The reading room, which used to be one of the multiple living rooms in this old mansion, housed fiction from the AAAs to the end of the Hs. I was close to the end, but my eyes were beginning to cross. Time for lunch. I'd brought a sandwich along with me so I wouldn't have to walk back home.

I plopped myself down at the checkout counter, ate quickly, and then was faced with having to decide whether to take Nathan up on his offer. It wasn't far. If I looked left out the front door of the library I could see Nathan's office across the street and down on the corner. It was daylight. I could do it. He was a nice man, a friend, but not a close friend. I could tell him without making him feel inadequate for not being able to fix it.

Wait, I thought. Where did that come from?

And then I knew. I sat back down at the checkout desk. Was I really upset with Bob for not having solved my problem, for not having caught whoever it was who'd pushed me in the water? If I were perfectly honest with myself, I'd have to say yes. I was upset. I was more than upset. Deep down inside I was angry with him. He was a cop. He was supposed to catch the bad guys.

We do not know who did it. Softfoot is angry, too.

Marmalade jumped onto the counter weaving back and forth in front of me. I stroked her back absentmindedly.

I loved Bob. I couldn't let him know how frightened I was, how angry I felt, because then he'd feel bad. He'd think I was blaming him. I was blaming him. If he'd caught the guy I wouldn't be so frightened. He already felt bad about not catching the guy. I knew that. I couldn't add to his distress. I hadn't even been able to tell Glaze or Melissa how I felt. I propped my elbows on the counter and covered my eyes. Marmalade licked the end of my nose.

GoodHands listens well.

Nathan was right. I needed to talk. I stood and shook the crumbs from my lap into the wastebasket. "Want to come with me, Marmy?"

Of course.

I crossed the street and saw Tom just coming out of his front door. He waved and I paused at the end of his walk. "Headed back to the restaurant? How's it going?"

He smiled. "Great! I'm really glad I hired Red to do the design work. He's given me some wonderful ideas."

"Oh? Like what?"

"I wasn't sure where I was going to put classroom space, but he's figured out a way to tuck them in by using part of the porch area."

Tom positively glowed with excitement. The building up on 3rd Street that housed his restaurant had started out as a sprawling house. He'd grown up there, come back to town from a successful restaurant career in New York after his parents moved into a retirement home, and turned the old house into Chef Tom's, known around here as CT's. Now it was shifting into a vocational school for at-risk teenagers, where they'd learn the restaurant business from a practical standpoint. His dream was to see his students work in family-style restaurants and, eventually, possibly, start their own restaurants. I wondered if he was taking on more than he could handle, but figured we'd all know soon enough.

"That sounds great, Tom. I'm glad you found someone who could help."

"He's charging me a minor fortune, but it's worth it.

I'll get more than my money's worth."

"Will he be here much longer?"

"Just this week full-time. After that he'll get the blueprints set. Once construction starts, he'll be checking in every few days until it's finished."

"Can't wait for the grand opening."

"You and Bob are first on the list for invites."

"Good," I said, although I thought it far more likely that Glaze was first on his list.

He checked his watch. "Gotta run. Told him I'd be there by now."

He took off at a brisk jog toward the corner and I followed at a much more leisurely pace.

"Nathan was wondering if you'd come," Polly said as I walked into the office. "He's upstairs at lunch. I'll buzz him down. Why don't you just take a seat?" She smiled over the counter. "Hello Marmalade."

Hello Helper.

Nathan lived over his office, the way Pumpkin lived above her herb shop. I debated telling Polly not to bother him. In fact, I started moving back toward the door, but stopped when Rimski KorsaCat, the office kitty, stepped into my path.

That is GrayGuy.

He'd grown a lot since I'd found him as a teeny kitten, and he'd taken on the job of official greeter for Nathan's medical practice. He always seemed to know when someone was hurting. In fact, Polly had told me that he completely ignored any healthy people who walked in, oozing out from under their attempted pats, in that special u-shaped sinuous move that only cats can make. Rimski moved a bit closer to me and put one gray paw up against my knee. I felt like I'd been branded. I looked over toward Polly and caught an unguarded look of pity before she turned quickly away.

Nathan walked in, glanced at Rimski, pursed his lips, and nodded. "Come on back, Biscuit. Marmalade's welcome, too."

Of course I am.

Both cats accompanied us into Nathan's study. Marmalade hopped onto the couch beside me and then onto my lap. Rimski curled up against my feet. Nathan took the chair opposite me and smiled at the cats. "Looks like you may not even need me with the feline crew at work."

It took me a few minutes to get started and a few careful questions from Nathan, but eventually I poured it out—my fear, my frustration, my anger.

"Nobody should have to live in constant fear," Nathan agreed. "For now, though, can you see the fear as something positive? Fear is designed to keep us from doing things that may hurt us. And that much is positive. You've learned, perhaps, to be more aware of your surroundings. That's a good thing."

He looked at me carefully, as if he thought I might bolt. I almost did. "I don't want this kind of fear," I said. "This is more than fear. It's terror. I'm tired of being scared all the time. I feel so... so violated."

He nodded and waited a moment before speaking. "I acknowledge that, Biscuit. What that man, whoever he was, what he did to you was wrong. And..." He paused and repeated that word. "And, your fears have grown all out of proportion to what happened."

"What do you..." I stopped myself. This was Nathan. He was one of the good guys.

He is GoodHands.

"I know you don't agree, and you think I don't know what you're going through. And in a sense you're right. The fears I've experienced are different than what you've faced."

His face clouded for an instant, and I wondered what he'd been subjected to. I'd probably never know.

"Can't you see," he went on, "that this unremitting fear is one of the ways in which he violated you? You can fight back by refusing to cave in to it."

"And just how do you suggest I do that?" My empathy of a few seconds ago evaporated. I hate it when I get sarcastic.

Rimski stood up and put both paws on my lap. Marmalade stretched her neck and licked his head.

"Acknowledging the fear is the first step. Talking about it helps. Have you told Bob?"

He watched me shake my head. He just sat there and waited for me to speak.

"If I tell him, he'll think I'm blaming him."

He waited another minute. By the time he spoke, I'd already come to the same conclusion. "Bob's a grown man," he said. "He loves you. He can take hearing the truth."

"You're probably right." I paused, wanting to say something but unsure of how to phrase it. Finally I just blurted out, "What you said about learning a lesson from the fear—that makes it sound like it's my fault this happened, so I could learn something from it." My anger grew with every phrase. "And let me tell you, Nathan Young, no matter how *aware of my surroundings* I was, I couldn't have stopped this from happening, and I can't be sure it will never happen again, not unless I hide in my house every night for the rest of my life."

Nathan could have retorted, and would probably have been justified in doing so, but he simply sat quietly as the echoes of my outburst reverberated around the room. A crystal bowl on a side table hummed in resonance.

"Nothing about this was your fault, Biscuit. Nothing," he repeated. "It is up to you, though, to decide whether to grow from such a horrible experience, or," he waved his hand around in an ever-decreasing spiral, "or to retreat from any enjoyment of life as a result of this man's actions."

I looked at his hand, now barely circling above his lap. Did I want my life to be circumscribed like that, diminished, restricted, hemmed in? "I'll talk to Bob," I said.

Rimski ushered Marmalade and me to the door, where he sat and curled his tail around his paws, so obviously waiting for the next patient that I had to chuckle. I reached down to pat him, but he wormed away from my hand. I looked up to see Polly nodding approvingly. "You must be better," she said.

"Yes." I did a quick mental inventory. "Yes, I am." Time to put all this behind me. I was going to go bake some bread.

~~~~~

~BISCUIT McKEE~

"Drats!" I closed the fridge. I was out of eggs. Well, not absolutely out. I had one, which was two fewer than I needed for the Challah loaves I intended to bake. Had I left my mind back on that Lone Tree, or was I just being normally absent-minded?

"Maggie," I said when she answered on the third ring, "could I pick up a dozen eggs?"

"Sure, come on up. The more the merrier. You want to collect them yourself?"

I could hear Vampirah cackling in the background, circling around, just waiting to impale me with her beak as I reached for one of her eggs.

"Don't worry," Maggie said when the silence went on too long. "I brought some in this morning. They're all brushed off and ready to go. You come on up."

The noise receded. It wasn't Vampirah I'd heard. It was Maggie's enthusiastic nieces and nephews. "Be there in a sec."

I grabbed a sweater. "Want to go with me, Marmalade?"

Certainly. I like visiting HenLady.

She purred sweetly and walked out the door ahead of me.

Maggie's house, normally a fairly welcoming environment, was just this side of sheer chaos. I peeked through the screen and Maggie waved me in. Marmalade turned around and walked away, back toward the street. I couldn't say I blamed her. Toys were scattered underfoot, children ran to and fro hollering, Willie huddled in Maggie's arms. He must have been totally overwhelmed, poor little guy.

He lifted his head as one of his cousins—well, they weren't officially his cousins yet, but would be as soon as the adoption papers went through—went tearing through the hall. "Boo!" Willie crowed and ducked his head back against Maggie's shoulder.

"Boo?" I couldn't believe it. "Did he just say boo?"

Maggie grinned. "It's like he's a different child." She set him down and he went running off after the other children. "He's been playing like this for hours. Every so often he comes and snuggles, but then he's off again as soon as one of the other children shows up."

"That's wonderful," I said. "Isn't it?"

She threw her hands in the air. "I think so, but it's going to take me awhile to get used to this." She led me into the teeming living room. "You remember Dave and Carole, and these are Norm's sisters, Natalie—we call her Nat, and Edith—we call her Ed."

Eed? Strange name, but I didn't say anything about

it. I nodded and smiled, and couldn't hear a thing over the uproar.

Maggie shooshed the older children outside. "And don't chase the chickens," she warned. She scooped up Willie whose eyes, I noticed, were decidedly droopy. "Time for a little quiet," she said and sank onto the couch beside one of her sisters-in-law. "Have a seat, Biscuit. Let's have some grown-up talk."

I chose the big blue wing-back chair. "It's good to see you again, Carole and Dave. Did you have a good trip?"

We chatted desultorily for a few minutes.

"Willie's birthday party is Wednesday at ten," Maggie said. "Just after nap time. You're welcome to come."

I thought for, oh, maybe two seconds. Did I want to listen to the cacophony, or would I rather avoid it? "Wednesday?" I shook my head. "I have to work."

Eed looked at a magazine, lost in her own world, and Nat thumbed through an old issue of the *Keagan County Record*. They were probably enjoying the respite from their children's noise. I'm not sure I'd want to talk either under those same circumstances.

Willie leaned away from Maggie to reach for his blanket. "Gale!" he said. "Gale!"

"Who?" Carole and Dave spoke at the same time.

"We have no idea," Maggie said. "He's been asking for somebody named G-a-i-l ever since he woke up in the hospital. Her and his m-o-m-m-y."

"And you don't know who she is?" Carole asked.

"I've certainly never known anybody by that name." Maggie looked inquiringly at me.

"Beats me. I don't know anyone named Gail."

"Gale!" Willie insisted and lunged from Maggie's arms to land on the paper Nat held. "Gale," he said, and pointed to a picture in the newspaper.

It was Annie McGill. The picture they'd printed along

with her obituary.

"That's Annie," Maggie told him.

"No. No. No. That Gale."

Maggie's eyes widened. "She was there. Before his mo—his m-o-m-m-y died. He must have met her."

"Maybe he's trying to say McGill," I suggested.

Willie looked around the room. "Where Gale? Brush hair."

Maggie bit her upper lip. "Gale is gone, Willie."

"Like mommy?"

Tears brimmed out of Maggie's eyes. "Yes, sweetheart. Like your mommy."

"Want Gale. Brush pretty hair." Willie hugged his blanket. "Want mommy."

It would have been just like Annie to let a small child brush her long hair. I said as much, but the thundering herd, as Maggie called them, chose that moment to reinvade the living room. Willie jumped off the couch and ran after them. We adults just sat there for a few moments.

"Do you want your eggs?" Maggie finally asked me.

~~~~~

~BISCUIT McKEE~

Bob, I am happy to report, still kisses me when he walks in the door, even in the middle of a murder investigation. I've known so many couples who seem to slide into a casual unawareness of each other, like two leaves drifting side by side down the same stream, but each caught in its own little current. Of course, Bob and I had our own currents, his at the police station, mine at the library; his in his fly-tying shed, mine at my tap dance lessons; his with Tom Parker, his friend from childhood, and mine with Melissa and Maddy and Glaze and Sadie, with Dee and Sharon and Ida, and even Pumpkin. Women, I would bet, have a lot more close connections than men do. Most women. Most men. But still Bob and I made a point of connecting with each other when we were together. Today that meant a real kiss when he trudged into the kitchen. He'd lost some weight in his face. His skin was drawn tight over his cheekbones. This look of exhaustion seemed to hang on Bob like a hand-me-down suit. Maybe it was his stuffy nose. Not being able to breathe easily could be tiring. And he had a murdered man on his hands and my unknown attacker. Those both had to be tearing at him. Had Bob been falling apart without my recognizing it?

He is in one piece.

I couldn't tell him. I couldn't add to his burden.

He kept his arms around me and leaned back a bit so he could look me in the eye. "Did you have a good day?" he asked, as if he really cared about the answer. Marmalade wove between our legs, purring loudly.

Yes, I had a very good day.

"I visited Maggie and cleared up a lot of messes at the library." I'd tell him about Willie and Annie later. Maybe I wouldn't mention Nathan. I picked a cat hair off his collar. And another one. They must have transferred from me to him. Oh well, what good was a house without cat hair? "I found a book Connie has had on reserve for two months. Couldn't locate it anywhere until today."

"Where was it?"

"Shelved in the wrong place in the reading room."

"Reading room." He chuckled and turned toward the stove. "That's what my dad called the bathroom when I was growing up."

"My dad called it his aerie."

Bob looked askance at me.

"You know? Like an eagle on a mountain top?"

He must have decided to ignore that. He lifted the lid

from the soup pot and sniffed with his eyes closed. "Split pea?"

What is a spit pee?

"Yes. Oh! You smelled it?"

He grinned and looked down at Marmalade, who pranced around squeaking.

Squeaking?

"Not exactly," he said. "I peeked before I closed my eyes."

At least he admitted it.

"This is a split pea type of day," he said.

What does that mean?

"Why so?"

"Everything I started seemed to fall apart. I need some comfort food, Woman."

I hugged him again. "You came to the right place for that. All I have to do is set the table."

His grumble seemed to start at his toes and surge its way upward. "I have seldom been so glad to leave the office. I only have an hour or so. I need to go back in."

"Did you get anywhere on the murder?" I didn't mention the target still on my back. I was feeling less angry all the time. It wasn't his fault.

He plucked two bowls from the drain board, filled them, and sat them across from each other on the round table in the bay window. That was cozier than the big table. "We know it probably happened Wednesday, so there's a good likelihood you saw something that threatened the guy who murdered Charles. That's why he pushed you in the river."

"But I didn't see anything."

"You didn't have to. It was enough if he *thought* you had. Are you sure there wasn't anybody on First Street when you got to the dock? Anything at all that might have been suspicious, other than the car?"

I set a braided Challah loaf, fresh from the oven half an hour ago and now cool enough to eat, on the big cutting board and added a serrated bread knife. I like to slice Challah loaves, but I knew Bob preferred to pull the bumpy segments apart. It didn't really matter to me. Two different currents, but at least we ate at the same table. "Not a thing," I said. "Nobody was there. The street was completely empty. Of course, I was running, so I guess I didn't look too carefully."

"Running? What do you mean?"

"Running. I ran down Pine Street all the way to the dock." I laid out the small bread plates.

"No you didn't. You said you stopped in back of that car."

"Well, not *all* the way. I started running from where the car was parked."

Bob stretched through a big yawn. "For right now and the next thirty minutes or so, I refuse to worry about Charles the Dead." He moved the butter crock and the jar of honey from the counter to the table and then, wonder of wonders, held my chair for me as I sat.

"What's that for?"

"Can't I be gallant if I want to?"

"In a restaurant, yes, but not at the kitchen table. It's out of character." I reached for the hand he'd placed on my shoulder. "What's going on, Bob? You've been worrying about something for an awfully long time, even before this... this mess happened. Does it have something to do with Mr. Bushy?"

He slowly pulled his chair out and leaned, straight-armed, on the back of it. "If this were two hundred years ago, Woman, they would have burned you at the stake. How do you know about that?"

"Clairvoyance," I said. "Witchcraft."

He raised one eyebrow and peered over his glasses,

which must be hard to do when you're still standing up and your peer-ee is sitting down. I wonder if that feeling of being inspected is what bugs experience under microscopes?

"Nosy neighbors," I said. "Sharon Armitage saw you there and asked me about it."

"I'm used to the gossip channel in this town, but Bushy, Bagot & Green, as you very well know, is a ways up the valley in Garner Creek."

"I know. And that's where a large number of our neighbors shop. If you wanted anonymity, you should have driven to Atlanta."

What is an ohnimidy?

He tackled the loaf with unnecessary ferocity, ripping off two of the braided segments at once. "It looks like someone's stealing town money. I'm trying to keep the investigation quiet, so I don't tip him off, whoever he is, before we can get a case put together."

"But you don't know who it is yet?"

He shook his head.

"Any ideas?"

"Hubbard or Carl would be the logical suspects."

That made sense—the town chair or the town treasurer. "You don't sound too sure."

Bob slathered butter on another slice, took a big bite, and leaned back. A few chews later he shook his head. "That's the problem; we won't know until Bushy does his magic, which shouldn't be too much longer. I gave him copies of the records almost a month ago. Reebok and I spent hours making copies after everyone went home for the night. I don't think anyone suspects anything."

"Could it be connected to the murder?"

"That's the problem—one of the problems. It's a possibility, but we can't find a link between Charles and Hubbard or between Charles and Carl."

His quandary didn't slow his appetite. After half a

bowl of soup, he added, "We need an expert. That's why I went to Bushy's."

"Why a lawyer? Don't you need an accountant?"

"Oh," Bob said. "Sometimes I forget you're a newcomer." I kicked half-heartedly at his shin under the table, but stubbed my toe on the table leg instead. Once I quit complaining, he went on. "Mr. Bushy's son is a CPA. He has his own firm in Russell Gap, but he comes down to Garner Creek and does work through the law firm, too." From his tone I could tell he expected me to be impressed.

"Does he look as much like a walrus as his father?"

What is a wall russ?

Mr. Bushy's mustache was mighty indeed, and I could easily picture a junior Bushy hunched over a pile of ledgers like a... no, wait a minute. It's not a walrus I was thinking of. It was an otter. A sea otter. The ones with the fuzzy little mustaches. They float in the kelp beds and ...

"...where you get that idea, but he's quite a competent accountant."

I pulled myself back from the Pacific Ocean. "I'm sure he is. What did Margaret say about it?" Before he could accuse me of witchery again, I said, "I saw your car in her driveway twice in the last month."

He muttered something about having no privacy in a small town. "Margaret, I'm sorry to say, is a big part of the problem. She hasn't kept a firm eye on the money she's turned over to the town. She swears she's giving lots of money, more than a thousand dollars a month, to the day care center for their nutrition program, but none of it seems to have shown up on the books. She never insisted on good bookkeeping, never even wrote receipts, just trusted that the money would go where she meant it to."

"I wonder what Glaze is going to do?"

She is going to keep that dog.

"Glaze? What's she got to do with this?"

"Oh, I forgot you didn't know. She stopped by last night before you got home. She's been offered a job managing all the funding requests for Margaret's money."

"But she..."

"I know, she doesn't have any sort of background for that kind of work, but Margaret and Sam both seem to think she can do it, and Glaze will have a big enough budget that she can hire Dee and Maddy to help set up an office and organize all the forms and such. This way Margaret won't be bothered with everyone trying to get a piece of her fortune."

Bob was quiet for a moment. "I don't think it's that," he said. "I think she's known for a long time that something was off. People have been imposing on her good nature, and I bet she just got tired of it and wanted someone more organized to make sure everything stayed proper."

"But why didn't she warn Glaze?"

Bob slurped the last of his soup, leaving a hint of pureed pea just below his mustache. "Your guess is as good as mine."

"Are you sure there's a problem?" I sopped up the last of my soup with the rest of my bread. "Could it just be a mistake?"

Bob rubbed his face with both hands and grimaced when he encountered left-behind soup. "I wanted it to be a mistake," he swiped his napkin to good effect, "but that money really is missing. We wouldn't have found out about this if it hadn't been for Willie."

Willie. That sweet little boy. When his mother died and he spent a long time in the intensive care unit, they'd found he was horribly undernourished. His mother's kitchen held the cheapest canned soups, bread, and peanut butter. The town day care center where he'd eaten two meals a day when his mother was working, hadn't fed him or the other children any kind of balanced diet.

Ironically, now that we knew there was a problem, and a committee had been formed to correct it, Willie wasn't going to need it. I could just picture him growing up with Maggie's goats and gardens and bee hives. And the chickens, too, even though I was scared of those creatures and had real reservations about Maggie's lead hen. Despite the chickens, though, I knew Maggie and Norm would be good parents. They were already being good parents.

"...did the best they could with the funds they received."

Whoops! I'd been off somewhere. No telling how much I'd missed. "The day care center?"

Bob inhaled rather loudly. He was used to my habit of mind-wandering, but he wasn't always happy with it.

To deflect some of his frustration and to prove that I'd been listening—sort of—I asked, "So it's not their fault?"

"Nice save, Woman." At least his laugh lines crinkled up when he said it. "No, I can't believe the day care center was stealing." He rubbed his mustache and tapped it with his index finger. "Bushy will find it," he said. "He has to."

"Nobody can cover financial shenanigans forever. All Bushy has to do is follow the money trail."

I follow mouse trails.

"What if there isn't a trail, though?"

"What do you mean?"

"Since Margaret just handed out money without receipts, there won't be an obvious trail."

All you have to do is smell and watch.

Marmy sounded like she was expressing my exasperation. "It's so obvious, Bob. Cancelled checks?"

"You're assuming she wrote checks. That would have been nice, but she usually just gave out cash. With the town, she wrote one big check each month and gave it to Carl. From what I can see, that part all seems to be accounted for, but I'm no CPA." He held up a hand to forestall my objection. "I think the problem is with that money she gave the day care center every month."

"Who got the money? I thought the director was a nice woman. At least she didn't seem like a crook when I met her."

"You think you can spot a crook that easily?"

"Don't change the subject. Margaret's not that stupid."

"I never said she was stupid, Woman. But she *is* gullible. She thinks anyone with a nice smile must be as honest as she is."

I was meticulous about money. I'd learned the value of good record keeping working with the women's investment club I started years ago. We'd done pretty well. Thank heavens I hadn't needed to live strictly on my librarian's salary. I didn't like the idea of starving. "Surely there are some records."

"All the more reason to think that Carl and Hubbard are being framed." He paused and took a deep breath. "Unless they themselves planned it to look like they're being framed."

"Bob," I said with more than a little impatience, "that sounds like something out of that old TV show about the double agent."

"I Led Three Lives," he said.

You what? I take back what I said before. I do not understand you two.

I laid a restraining hand on Marmy's head to quiet her yowling. "That's right. But Carl isn't that smart."

"Neither is Hubbard."

Poor dense Hubbard. Not exactly the star on the family tree. I was glad he'd lost that county election, because he was the last person we needed as a county commissioner. Unfortunately, that meant we were still stuck with him here in Martinsville, since the chairmanship of the town council had always moved from father to son in a direct line from Homer Martin, the town founder. There had never been a case of a daughter running the town. I thought about Clara Martin and the whey-faced son and ultra-shy daughter she and Hubbard had. Lord help us. If Hubbard hadn't run the town into the ground, his children certainly would. "Hmm," I said. That sounded neutral enough.

"I hope your sister knows enough to keep track of the money once she's handed it out."

Poor Glaze. I was pretty sure she didn't have a clue.

She doesn't need glue. She has a dog.

CHAPTER 15
Tuesday 5:30 p.m. to 11:30 p.m.

~GLAZE McKEE~

THEY MET AT THE CAR AFTER WORK, AS usual. Glaze had known they would bombard her with questions, and she wasn't disappointed. Maddy started the barrage. "I have just about been peeing my pants all day wanting to know what's going on with you. Why all the mystery? What's happening?"

Glaze unlocked the doors, but said nothing as Dee ran up with her mouth in overdrive. "You were a downright stinker to leave us like this all day long with not even a hint. What have you been up to? I would have thought you'd be announcing your engagement, except that phone call this morning wasn't Tom."

"Would you two relax? We've got some buffalo wings to pick up."

"And potato salad," Dee added. "I can't believe you're paying for it. Are you sure?"

Glaze nodded. They didn't have secrets from each other—well, not many. Dee and Maddy both worked for Wish-Fulfillment, a company just on the other side of the parking lot from CelerInc. All the employees called it Whiffle. One week, all the Whiffle paychecks had been addressed wrong, and everybody had somebody else's paycheck in their envelope. Naturally, everybody looked. And once Dee knew what Maddy made, Maddy thought it only right that she should know what Dee made, and then Glaze wanted in on the information, too.

Now, the only major secret was what Glaze had up her sleeve. No matter how much they badgered her, she kept mum. When she pulled up in front of the Delicious, she tried to keep them in the car. "I'll run in and get it. You two wait here."

"Not a chance," Dee said. "You may be up to something."

"You'll need help carrying the food," Maddy added.

The wings and potato salad weren't enough for Glaze. She browsed along the deli selections and pointed to the three bean salad. "Give me a pint of that. Anything else you want, Maddy? Dee?"

"No," Dee growled. "Would you pay for the food and let's get going?"

"And some of that nice garlic bread," Glaze added.

"There has to be a reason you're slowing us down," Maddy complained.

"And three cinnamon rolls, please."

Dee drummed her fingers on the display case. "You're just doing this to irritate us."

Glaze paid a mystified salesperson, removing the wad of crisp bills from her wallet and counting out carefully. She let her friends pick up all the bags as she tucked away the change with a smile.

All the way home—all four blocks of it—Dee harped at Glaze. "What's going on? This isn't fair!"

Maddy was the first one up the steps. She rubbed the dog's ears. "Want to come in?" She turned the knob, but bumped hard against the unmoving door. "Dag nab it! Why is this door locked?"

Glazed reached around her and inserted the key that Carl had brought her at lunchtime. Without saying a word, she walked through the kitchen, dumped her purse on the counter as she passed it, and peeked through the archway into the living room. The dog took a quick run around the room, sniffing absolutely everything.

Stepping back into the kitchen, Glaze pulled out plates while Maddy and Dee unloaded the deli bags. Nobody said anything as they washed hands, arranged food, sat down. The dog curled next to Glaze's feet.

Dee looked at Maddy. "Now?" they both said as if at a prearranged signal.

Glaze picked up a chicken wing, but stopped when Dee growled. "Oh, all right. I propped a note with my two week's notice on Hank's desk before I left today. He'll see it first thing tomorrow morning."

"You're quitting?" They sounded like an echo chamber.

She grinned wickedly. "So are you two, I hope."

By the time she'd explained, they were laughing and sharing hugs all around. Even the dog joined in the glee, bouncing from one woman to another and shivering with excitement.

~~~~~

~BISCUIT McKEE~

Tuesday evening, Marmalade and I scooted out the front door as soon as I saw Glaze, with her dog shadowing her footsteps, turn the corner beyond Matthew's house. She was only a few minutes late for a change. The dog pranced beside her. Glaze still thought she was going to give the dog away. When would she wake up?

She is awake.

Marmy dove into the daylilies that surrounded the mailbox. The morning glories painted on the post shimmered in the early evening light. "They're still beautiful, aren't they?" Glaze said as she came closer.

Yes. The yellow flowers are beautiful, and there are juicy bugs under the leaves.

The dog slowed when Marmalade made a noise from the middle of the daylily patch, and seemed to hang back. The scratches on her nose looked like they had healed, but she was still a bit wary of my cat.

"Yes," I said, "they're gorgeous, but I think the ones on the south side are beginning to fade a bit. The blue paint has lost some of its gleam. Maybe I should ask Ariel to spruce them up." She was the one who had painted them originally.

"You'd better not." When I lifted an eyebrow in query, Glaze said, "At least, not now. She was pouting on her front porch a few minutes ago. Looked like she was in a real snit. She didn't even nod when I walked by."

"What do you think could be wrong?"

"She's a teenager. Nothing has to be wrong for everything to feel like it's wrong."

A shadow crossed her face. She must have been thinking of her own chaotic teen years when she had floundered in a bipolar haze without the benefit of understanding what was happening to her. None of us had known what was wrong or how to help.

I reached out and touched her arm. "She'll make it through." Glaze didn't look convinced. I turned and headed down the street. Hoping to take her mind off Ariel, I asked, "Did you practice the new tap routine?"

"I tried to on Wednesday, but by the time I got back from work, I'd forgotten the order. There's a shuffle ball-change in there somewhere, but I didn't know where to put it."

"Good. I won't be the only one who's lost." As much as I enjoyed our weekly tap dance lesson, I tended to be one of the slower learners. Sadie kept telling me just to feel the flow. Ha! All I felt was *slow*.

I am fast.

Marmalade ran past us to the corner. The dog sprinted after her for a few steps, but then seemed to think better of it and dropped back to Glaze's side. I'd swear Marmalade looked both ways before she bounded across the street. Maybe that was just my hopeful thinking. There was so little traffic in Martinsville I didn't worry about her, but still, she *had* been struck by a car shortly after I moved here.

No, I was not. A badman pulled my leg and hurt me.

Up ahead, Marmalade stopped and looked back at us, as if to urge us on. "We still have plenty of time, Marmalade," I called to her.

Goat poop!

She snorted and sat down. "It looks like she's waiting for us," Glaze said.

"So, tell me about the new job. Have you made any major decisions in the last twenty hours?"

"I've already agreed to my first request."

"Good for you. Who's the lucky recipient?"

"Esther," she said, and then clamped her hand over her mouth. "I can't believe I told you. I think all of this is supposed to be confidential."

"Why? Is Esther planning to be a spy?" Esther was about as clandestine as a merry-go-round.

What does that mean? Who is Mary Gorown?

"No," Glaze said. We both stopped to look down at Marmalade, who had just yowled at something.

"I already know about the decorations," I admitted. "Esther told me at the dance that Margaret was getting a manager who would hand out the money."

"But the dance was Saturday. I didn't agree to take the job until yesterday."

"Guess Margaret had you pegged all along."

"Humph." She sounded so like our grandmother, I almost laughed.

"Well," she said, "for future reference, I think only I and my employees should know the details. And Margaret, of course. I'll give her a monthly report. Or maybe she'd want me to report on a weekly basis."

"Knowing Margaret, I'd say she opt for a yearly report.

From what Bob says, her lackadaisical attitude toward cash has created some problems."

"Like what?"

"Whoops!" Now I was the one to cover my mouth. "Not sure it's supposed to be common knowledge yet. Keep it quiet, will you?"

"You haven't told me anything."

"Speaking of employees—"

"You're trying to change the subject."

"Right. Speaking of employees, do I get to know who they are, or is that confidential, too?"

She poked me in the arm and the dog looked up a bit apprehensively. "Quit teasing me. You know quite well I hired Dee and Maddy. Dee told me I have to buy a receipt book tomorrow."

"That's perfect. You three are going to take over this town."

Take it where?

"You're right Marmy," Glaze said. "We need to get a move on or we'll be late."

Goat poop AND mouse droppings! Nobody listens to me.

As usual, Marmalade left us outside Miss Mary's Dance Studio. I knew she'd come back in time for the end of class. Mr. Snelling had mentioned once that she visited him in his frame shop up the street most Tuesday evenings. I wondered briefly what he fed her.

He saves me little bites of meat from his lunch. It is cold from the coldbox he has in the shop, but I do not mind. I breathe on it to warm it up.

Glaze didn't tell the dog to stay, but it looked like that was what she was planning to do, since she curled up in a fuzzy ball on the grass by the curb and tucked her nose underneath one paw.

Ida looked up from buckling her shoes. "How're you doing," she said, not really a question since she'd seen me not four hours ago at her grocery store. And, in Georgia, nobody except out-of-state folk expected a real—an honest—answer to those words. We all just followed the formula. *How-you?-fine-and-you?-fine.*

"Fine," I said, "And you?" The standard answer. I could say *I have three broken legs* and nobody would hear it. *I'm fine, too* they'd reply.

"I'm fine, too," Ida answered. "Glaze?"

"Just fine," my sister said, as Dee and Sadie walked in. Pumpkin moved over to make room on the bench. Melissa ducked through the door a minute or two later looking thoroughly frazzled. "Thought I'd be late," she said. "Had a cooking crisis."

I knew a made-up excuse when I heard one. She sounded as phony now as she had last Saturday when she'd ushered me out of Azalea House. I hadn't had a chance to confront her. Ordinarily I would have walked over there Saturday night, but that was the night of the dance. And then, what with finding that body on Sunday, there wasn't time that evening. And Monday night—I didn't want to think about how scared I'd been to step outside my front door.

Miss Mary stuck her head in the dressing room door with a chirrupy, "Glad you all made it! Let's go, ladies! Time to tap away!" She even looked like an exclamation point, with her thin body and round little feet.

After class, during which I hadn't huffed or puffed as much as usual—maybe I was getting better at this—we stepped out the door to find the dog still curled on the grass. Marmalade, however, instead of sitting there with her tail wrapped elegantly around her feet as she usually did, was stretched out on top of the dog, her orange fur complementing the golden honey color of the dog's coat. She often sprawled that same way on the back of the couch, with her legs dangling on either side.

I am not sprawling. I am relaxing. The dog is warmer than the grass.

"Come on, Gracie," Glaze said.

"You named her?"

Yes. Her name is FreckleNose.

Glaze shrugged. "It seemed like a good idea."

Marmalade stepped off Gracie and gave a quick rumble, almost as if she were granting permission for the dog to move.

FreckleNose is well-trained now.

We all trooped up to Azalea House for our Tuesday night gab session. Sadie drove, of course, and Dee went with her. The rest of us always walked. One or two of us generally brought snacks, and Melissa had an unending supply of tea—hot or cold—but we really went just for the talk.

I go for the chicken GoodCook gives me.

When we first left the studio, I was at the end of the somewhat straggly line, which made me a bit nervous. I walked faster and scooted in front of Ida and Maddy. "Why are you in such a hurry?" Ida asked.

Melissa answered for me. "She wants some of my coffee cake. And she's afraid the rest of us will eat it up first."

I settled into stride beside Pumpkin. Marmalade led the way, with the rest of us trailing along two-by-two, except for Connie and Glaze and bouncy little Gracie. Three by three.

Sadie honked as she passed us. We watched the receding taillights as she wound her way up the street. She'd never hit anybody, and I was pretty sure she'd never sideswiped a car, but most of us knew better than to get in her way. She was so short, she had to sit on a stack of pillows so she could see where she was going. Years ago Wallace had installed special pedal extensions so she could reach the brake and the gas. If the old Chevy wore out, I wondered what she'd do.

"Why does Miss Sadie always drive everywhere?" Pumpkin asked me. "I know she has enough energy to walk; look at how she dances circles around the rest of us in class."

"She sure does. The first few months of class she had to sit down occasionally, but now that we've been doing this for a couple of years, she's absolutely tireless."

"So, why the driving?"

"She told me once that she learned to drive the right way in 1955, I think it was. And she loved it so much, she just never wanted to stop."

"What do you mean 'drive the right way'?"

"When she was twelve, she took her father's Model T for a joy ride and got it all the way up to ten miles per hour before she ran it into a ditch. She broke her nose on the steering wheel."

"And never drove again until 1950?"

"Nineteen-fifty-five. Apparently not."

On Melissa's front porch, Glaze turned to the dog. "Gracie, stay," she said firmly, and the dog lay down beside the door. Marmalade walked past and flicked her tail across Gracie's nose. I'd swear it was deliberate.

Of course it was. I am reminding FreckleNose of the priorities.

We settled into our usual places. Thank goodness Melissa's kitchen table was so long. Of course, when her B&B was full, she needed all this room. She had individual tables for two in her dining room, which was where people like the Pontiacs ate their evening meals, but breakfasts were always a casual affair, none the less delicious for being served around this table.

Marmalade chewed daintily from a small dish of diced cooked chicken beside the sink, and Melissa started the pitcher of sweet tea around the table. Dee had brought her usual cinnamon rolls, but I'd had way too much sugar recently, so I grabbed some squares of fried cheese—Connie's contribution. I munched and waited to see what conversation would develop. Thank goodness Miss Mary, our tap dance instructor, hadn't been able to come along with us this evening. I wasn't in the mood to listen to her never-ending exclamations. I shouldn't be so hard on her, but she always seemed to try just a bit too hard to fit in. The rest of us could all relax with each other, but Miss Mary gave me the impression that she was constantly on the outside looking in. Of course, I'd never had a good conversation with her. Maybe I should try harder to get to know her. On the other hand, I thought, that would take way more effort than I was willing to give right at the moment. Ida, sitting beside me, wrung her hands again.

Dee must have noticed it as well. "What's wrong with your hands, Ida? You worried about something?"

"No, I'm not worried. I went to that new massage therapist up in Happy Acres, and she showed me how I could massage my own hands. It'll help my circulation."

Sadie looked at her own hands, knobby with arthritis. "She didn't tell me that, and I should think I'd have more circulation problems than you."

"Did you tell her you were having problems with your hands?"

"I'm not having problems." Sadie laughed. "I just have lots of knobs. And I'm a little creaky," she added.

Melissa reached across the table and wagged her finger at Sadie. "You're about as creaky as an eel the way you out-dance all of us in tap class."

Sadie beamed. "I always wanted to tap dance. Ginger Rogers with Fred Astaire, and Vera Miles in *White Christmas,* and Debbie Reynolds in *Singing in the Rain.* They were all my idea of beautiful. When you asked me if I wanted to join the class, Biscuit, I could have hugged you to pieces."

I looked around the table. I was fortunate indeed to have such a circle of friends. These weekly sessions were therapeutic in ways I'm not sure I could have believed until a month ago when Annie died. Since then, I'd come to appreciate the women in my life, knowing just how quickly, how easily, each one of them could slip away. The way I almost had in the river last Thursday morning.

"Biscuit?" Sadie shook my arm. "Why are you crying?"

"I... you... we ..."

"Anytime you're ready, you can finish one of those sentences." Ida's grim practicality cut through the pall I had inadvertently cast on the group.

"Yes, ma'am." I gave her a mock salute. "I was just feeling happy to have all of you here."

"All except Annie," Dee said, and the pall was right back in place. Annie McGill. How I missed her. Her death had been such a shock to the entire community. Just the week before she died, before she was killed, I'd taken her with me to the circus. That was the memory of her that I needed to hold in my thoughts, not the way she'd looked when I'd come upon her moments after she'd been shot in the back by that—

"Biscuit?" It was Sadie again. "We need to lighten up the mood around here."

Ida took her up on that suggestion. "So, Melissa, when do we get to meet this fiancé of yours?"

Melissa blushed, but it looked more like anger than embarrassment. "I wish I knew. He's not back from Atlanta yet."

"You'd better keep an eye on him," Dee said. "They start staying away on business and pretty soon ..." Her voice trailed off and she pointed to the bare fourth finger of her left hand.

Dee should know, I thought, with all the problems she'd had over that former husband of hers. He may be Bob's brother, but Barkley sure hadn't inherited the same fidelity genes Bob had.

"...'ve you been hiding him?" The last half of Ida's question brought me back to the conversation.

Melissa blushed again. "We've been, uh, busy." She looked quite becoming in bright pink.

"Too busy to introduce him to your friends?" Ida sounded skeptical indeed.

"What's wrong with him?" Dee wanted to know.

Connie waved her hand, swallowed a bite of cinnamon roll, and leered, "You mean, what's right with him, to keep you so... uh... busy."

Melissa had less patience than the rest of us with Connie's constant suggestiveness, but I thought it was a good question. He must be quite a guy, I thought, if Melissa can't even spare him for a quick introduction.

"I still think you need to keep an eye on him," Dee intoned.

Melissa took a breath, seeming to fuel herself for a retort, but Glaze, with her voice as liquid silver as her hair, spoke up. "I'm considering getting a tattoo. What do you think?"

"What?" Ida blurted.

"Where?" Connie's question, once again loaded with bedroom tones, was totally inappropriate, I thought, given my sister's inability to commit to a relationship.

"How big?" Sadie wanted to know.

Melissa, the practical one, shifted gears and measured

her words the same way she measured flour. "What would it cost?"

"Why?" I asked.

"Just for something new. Right here." Glaze indicated a place below her waist, to the left of her belly button. "I thought a butterfly would look real nice."

Ida hooted, "Yeah, who's going to see it there?"

Connie snickered.

I like butterflies. They dance across the yard. They play on the flowers and one even tickled my nose once.

I thought Ida had a point. Glaze wasn't exactly at the bare midriff age.

"It's just for me. Just ..." She paused to pat Marmalade, who had jumped noisily into her lap. "... just some decoration. I need a change."

Dee pointed a finger at her. "Don't you have enough change—?"

Maddy was talking before Dee finished her sentence. "Tell them! Tell them!" She sounded almost like Miss Mary.

Everyone bombarded Glaze with demands to know what was going on. When she explained about the new jobs all three of them would have, the group seemed to heave a collective sigh of relief.

Sadie patted Glaze on the shoulder. "You're going to do a great job, all three of you."

Ida nodded. "Poor Margaret's been overwhelmed for years. This will be a big help."

"Yeah," Connie said. "Poor Margaret. All that money must be quite a burden."

Ida opened her mouth, but it was Sadie who broke the stunned silence. "You're fairly new to town, Connie, so I'm sure you don't realize how well-respected Margaret is. With all her money, she and Sam could have any sort of lifestyle they wanted, anywhere in the world, but they've chosen to stay here and help the town. She's the one who bought the ambulance, and that money of hers pays the crew."

For once Connie seemed at a loss. "I... I didn't know that."

"Of course you didn't," Ida said, "but your brother wouldn't have that job of his if it weren't for Margaret."

I looked inquiringly at Ida.

"The new ambulance driver is Connie's brother, Dave."

"Oh." Cartwright, I thought. The guy who was reading at the fire station.

Ida wasn't through with Connie yet. "Margaret never flaunts her money," she said.

"So," Connie drew out that syllable to three times its usual length. "She pays for things that will benefit the town?" She looked at Glaze the way a baby panther must look at a fat mouse. I could see she was up to something. No telling what sort of project Glaze would be getting a request for. Maybe blown glass toilet paper holders for the town hall bathrooms? Connie's glass blowing, from what I'd seen of it, ran from downright beautiful to downright bizarre.

"You know," Pumpkin said, "this new job will be like all three of you coming out of your chrysalis."

Maddy thrust her fists up into the air. "Yes! We're the Butterfly Brigade!"

"Yeah," Dee said, "we could all three get butterfly tattoos."

Pumpkin reached for the fried cheese squares. "I think it would look nice. What colors do you want?"

"Blue and green," Dee said.

"No," Maddy said. "Red and orange."

Glaze shrugged. "Maybe purple squiggles all over the wings?"

Sadie leaned back in her chair, lifted her left ankle across her right knee, and pointed. "You just wait a few years, girl, and you'll have the prettiest purple squiggles you can imagine. See? Mine run from lavender to royal purple," she trailed her finger along the side of her ankle, "with a hint of fuchsia, and even some violet. It's a real work of art."

All of us—those of a certain age, that is—nodded knowingly. Spider veins decorated most of us. They bloomed on my ankles the day I turned fifty, or so it seemed.

"And we don't even have to pay for them," Sadie added.

Ida raised an imperious hand. "Now you just wait a minute, Sadie. All those years I've spent standing on my feet on those hard floors in the grocery store? Ha! I sure as heck paid for mine."

I pointed to one of Sadie's spider veins. "That one matches my toenail polish."

"*Dusky Violet.*" Pumpkin spoke with an air of authority.

"No," Ida said. "Varicose Vein Violet."

Pumpkin heaved a big sigh. "I don't think that color would sell."

My Gratitude List for Tuesday
1. The women in the tap class. We have so much fun together.
2. Glaze and Maddy and Dee. I wonder if they'll really get a tattoo?
3. Bob. I hope he solves the town money problem quickly. I hope he finds that maniac even faster.
4. Nathan
5. Gracie, who made a couch for Marmy

I am grateful for
a soft dog
my special door
birds at the feeder
bugs under the flowers
chicken from GoodCook

DAY SEVEN
WEDNESDAY

CHAPTER 16
8 a.m. to 5:45 p.m.

~BOB SHEFFIELD~

"Margaret," Bob said into the phone almost before she'd finished saying hello, "could I stop by in a few minutes? I have some more questions about the money that's missing."

Reebok raised his eyebrows but refrained from commenting until the phone was back in place. "What about the Bushy report, Sir?" He laid one hand on the tidy multi-paged packet they'd received this morning. "They couldn't find anything."

Bob stood and reflexively checked his pocket for his keys. "They couldn't find a paper trail because there wasn't one. Margaret's been giving extra money to the day care center every month for the past year. Cash, of course. I don't think that woman knows what a checkbook is."

"But, Sir? The report says the day care center's books balance perfectly. They have receipts for everything."

Bob stomped out, calling over his shoulder, "Go home, Garner. Get some sleep."

"Yes, Sir." But the phone rang, and Bob closed the door on a cheery, "What can I do for you, Mr. Harper?"

Margaret ushered him into their brightly lit living room. Mirror-lined solar tubes, which Sam had once explained were threaded from the roof down between the upstairs walls, flooded the lower floor with daylight. "Have a seat. Sam's not here, but I should be able to answer your questions."

"Mr. Bushy Junior couldn't find anything wrong with the records from the day care center."

"That's good. I'm so glad there's nothing wrong."

"No, it's not good. There also is no record of any extra cash contributions coming in from you and no record of any money spent on better quality food."

"I don't understand." Her normally cheery face clouded. "They said they needed it."

"Who said?"

"The person I talked to."

"Someone called each month?"

"Oh no. I think they only called two times. I'm sure they gave me their name, but I didn't catch it. The first time was when they requested the money, and then the second time we just set up a regular monthly schedule."

"What sort of voice did she have?" Bob knew the director of the daycare center had one of those fake-sounding voices, very high-pitched.

Margaret looked nonplussed. "It wasn't a she. It was a man. He sounded kind of vague, if I remember correctly."

"Vague?"

"You know. Sort of fuzzy. But it may have just been a bad connection."

"Both times?"

She cocked her head to one side, looking very much like one of the cardinals on Biscuit's birdfeeder. "I do think you're right. Both times."

"Did you mail him the cash each month?"

"Robert Sheffield, I know better than to send cash through the mail. No, Carl always picked it up."

Bob knew only one Carl in town. "Carl Armitage?"

"Well, of course. I'm not sure I would have trusted anybody else. I write a check every month for the town expenses, and he always picks it up, so I just gave him the cash at the same time." Her face brightened and she reached toward the end table for the phone. "He missed his usual time this month because he was in the hospital, but he's home now. I called Sharon for a hair appointment a few minutes before you got here. She said he left this morning when she did and went in to the station. Silly man. I hope he takes it slow. I'll call and ask him who he gave the money to."

Bob stretched a hand out to stop her. "That's okay, Margaret. Don't you worry about it. I'm headed down toward the gas station anyway in a little bit. I'll ask him."

"Ronnie, is Carl around?"

Ron pulled his head out of the engine of an ancient Chevy. "He's up to the field. Said he'd be back in an hour. Wanted to look over his crop." He ran a hand lovingly along the front fender. "They don't make 'em like this anymore. Fifty-seven was the best year ever."

"I agree." Bob touched the black tail fin almost reverently. "Is his hour almost up, or should I head up the cliff?"

"Yeah, you'd better. He left about forty-five minutes ago." He wiped sweat from his forehead. "His one-hour breaks usually turn into two or three."

Bob wondered if Carl would even be in business if it weren't for Ronnie. Ronnie could repair anything. He ought to have his own shop. "Thanks. See you."

~~~~~

~BISCUIT McKEE~

Maggie carried the birthday cake to the table and set it in front of a wide-eyed Willie. "Blow out the candles, Willie." He'd apparently never seen candles before coming to live with her and Norm. They'd practiced blowing them out for the past five days, just so he wouldn't be scared on his birthday.

He'd had several days to get used to his new grandparents. Thank goodness they hadn't pushed him. She smiled across the table at her mother-in-law, and Carole smiled back.

One of Natalie's brood demanded cake, now. Another seconded the request. Norm held up his hand for silence. "We'll wait for Willie. He has to blow out the candles."

"Blow! Blow! Blow!" The chant increased in volume. Willie held up his hand, and Maggie could see that it was in conscious imitation of Norm's earlier movement. She just about choked up. This would be—was—their son. Willie took a deep breath, stopped, looked around. "Where Gale?" he asked.

"Remember, sweetie, I told you. Gail is gone."

"Like mommy."

"Yes, dear."

Willie thought for a moment, watching his new family around him. Then he blew out all four candles, one at a time, to the sound of much cheering.

~~~~~

~BOB SHEFFIELD~

Bob parked at the graveled turn-off at the top of Beechnut Lane and headed up the wooded path. He always loved this walk, although the lack of a real road up to the top of the cliff was inconvenient sometimes. He took a deep breath, admiring the crenellated land formations that had prevented anyone from clearing this stretch of land. They could farm all they wanted to up on the flat plain above the town—they had to bring in their equipment from a county road way to the west—but Bob, for one, was glad they couldn't touch this part.

As he trudged up the final incline, he saw the tractor

parked just to the right of the trail, almost on top on the growing kenaf. Its tall, bamboo-like stalks were topped, almost decorated, with bright yellow flowers. Carl, a baseball hat covering his bald spot, sat behind the wheel reading a magazine. So much for inspecting his crop.

"Carl," Bob called, and watched in some amazement as Carl whipped the magazine out of sight onto the floor and vaulted down from the high seat. With that much bulk, and having just had a heart attack, Bob would have thought such an athletic feat impossible.

He reached out his hand. "Bob, what can I do for you?"

Bob took it and held on longer than Carl expected. "Ronnie told me you were up here—" he scanned the field and settled his gaze on the silent tractor—"working."

Carl pulled his hand away and shifted uneasily. "Just having a little break. I'm supposed to be taking it easy, and I'll have to work late at the theater. *Gone with the Wind* opens tonight."

Bob took a casual step back, out of range of the virulent aftershave. "I'd like to hear about your heart attack, Carl."

"Why? You planning on having one yourself?" Carl chuckled at his own little joke, but Bob didn't join in the hilarity.

"Just want to hear what happened."

"A quarter to three or so and I'm flat on the floor beside the bed. That's all. They told me this was just a minor attack, but I've never felt so much pain." Carl rubbed his hand up and down his left arm and across his chest.

"And before that?"

"I was fine, maybe a little restless."

"Just lying in bed?"

Carl looked at Bob and frowned. "No. I got up just around two to get some air."

"Take a little walk, did you?"

"Yeah." Carl cleared his throat. "About as far as the front porch. Then I was so out of breath I had to sit on the swing for awhile."

"And then?"

"Then back up to bed and WHAM! Sharon was so scared I thought she'd kill me for frightening her like that."

Bob wanted to believe him, but it seemed too tidy, too convenient. And there was still the matter of the missing money. "Would you like to tell me why you've been stealing from Margaret?"

"I... I don't know what you're talking about. Why would I steal from Margaret? She's a great person. Where'd you get an idea like that?" Bob let him run on for awhile until Carl said, "Did she tell you?"

"Tell me what?"

"Did she lie about me?"

Bob let that one pass. "How did you disguise your voice those two times you called her? Handkerchief over the mouthpiece, maybe?"

Carl batted at a stone with his left foot. "One of Sharon's scarves," he finally admitted.

"Why, Carl?"

"Say, do I need a lawyer here or something?"

"No need for that, Carl. This is just a friendly discussion. All I want to know for now is why you did it."

"I needed it." He clamped his mouth shut. Bob could almost see the wheels turning under the rim of the baseball hat. "For a friend," Carl added.

"Mind if I ask who that friend was?"

"Can't tell you, and you can't force it out of me. It's private."

"If you'd been using your own money, I might go along with your reasoning. But you've been using Margaret's money."

"She can afford it. A thousand a month is nothing to her. She *gave* it to me."

"No, Carl. It was more than a thousand, and she gave it to the day care center. That's where she thought it was going."

"You can't prove anything. There's nothing in writing."

Bob looked Carl up and down, slowly, deliberately. "Let's think about this. Imagine a courtroom. We put you on the stand. And then we put Margaret on the stand." He smiled. "She's about as believable a person as a jury could want, now isn't she?"

"I want a lawyer," Carl said, and he walked past Bob toward the head of the path.

Bob waited until Carl was out of sight between the trees. He didn't touch the tractor, just looked at the magazine that lay on the floor between wads of used tissues. He sighed. About what he would have expected of someone like Carl.

~~~~~

~BOB SHEFFIELD~

Back at Margaret's, Bob ran into opposition. When he reported his conversation with Carl, Margaret proved singularly stubborn. "I will not press charges," she said. "If he's been helping out a friend, then I don't mind giving him the money."

"But you have no way of knowing who the money is going to."

"I don't care. Carl is a very nice man. He and Sharon have those lovely girls, and I will not do anything to bring shame on that family."

Bob clenched his teeth. "He's the one who's brought shame on his family by steal—" She shook her head and he revised his sentence. "... by taking money from you under false pretenses."

"I told you I don't care about that. I will not have him arrested. I will not get involved in a court case. I can afford it; I'm richer than anybody in this valley." She pushed the cuticle back on one of her nails. "I just wished he'd asked me right out. I would have given it to him."

"Margaret, what happens when the next person comes along and asks you for money? Are you going to end up supporting everybody in the valley?"

She pinned him with a glare. "First of all, I could afford it if I wanted to. But I don't want to. Secondly, I've hired your sister-in-law to field all these requests from now on, so I won't have to worry about it."

The front door opened. "I'm home." Sam's booming bass filled the room.

"Hello, darling," Margaret called. She looked at Bob pointedly. "Bob was just leaving."

Bob left.

~~~~~

~GLAZE McKEE~

"Esther! Come on in. We're all ready for you." Glaze motioned toward the kitchen table where Dee and Maddy stood behind their chairs. "We don't have the office set up yet, but this should do fine."

Esther fluttered over to the nearest chair. "I can't tell you how excited I am about the three of you working together. Sadie told me all about it at the library today."

"We knew the word would spread fast." Maddy straightened a small stack of paper in front of her. "That's why we've tried to get as organized as possible."

Glaze stretched out her hand. "Did you bring the

receipts?"

"Yes, I did. Ribbons, bows, tablecloths, swags, and musicians." She pulled two paper-clipped packets out of her capacious purse. "These I paid for myself," she handed over one set of slips, "and these, the musicians, we wrote checks to from the library account." She patted her ample bosom. "I have to thank you from my heart for seeing about this right away. As soon as we finish here, I'm going to run the check right back to the library and give it to Biscuit. She's been awfully worried lately. I hope this will help."

Glaze wasn't so sure a check would help dispel her sister's anguish. She changed the subject.

It didn't take long for Glaze to call out all the items, for Maddy to write them down and total the two columns, for Dee to place an acceptance form in front of Esther. "We'll need your signature here," she pointed, "as soon as Glaze finishes writing those two checks."

CHAPTER 17
Wednesday 6 p.m. to 11:45 p.m.

~BISCUIT McKEE~

I SHOULD HAVE KNOWN BETTER THAN TO DRIVE that far in my present state of mind. We closed the library at six, and since Bob was working late again and it wasn't dark yet, I dropped some dinner off for him and Reebok. He was in a tizzy about Margaret, but said he couldn't talk about it yet.

When I walked in my front door, the first thing I saw was that check from Glaze sitting on the drop leaf table. Well, it was from Margaret, really, but it had Glaze's signature on it. The checks to the musicians wouldn't bounce, but I'd feel better with this buffer back in the library account. I looked through the lace curtains on the front door. Still light enough for a quick trip up the valley. Why didn't we have a bank here in Martinsville?

As long as I was out, I might as well visit Auntie Blue. Maybe she could help me make some sense of this.

When I called to see if I could stop by for a quick visit, Auntie Blue had just come in from one of her interminable swim sessions in her backyard pool—she could swim laps faster than I could catalog a book. My mother's older sister was a favorite of mine. She could brighten up anyone's day. She was named Beulah at birth, but when I was a toddler I called her Blue, and the name had stuck.

I put Marmalade in her carrier and headed up the valley.

I was sure I could make it back home before dark.

It is not far, and I want to see WaterWoman. She feeds me tuna.

I'm so glad Marmy never seems to mind her carrier. I sure appreciate her company.

You talk to me all the time when I am in this box. I do not mind it.

"I haven't seen her in weeks," I told Marmalade as I drove along, "other than while I was at the clinic, and I don't think that counts exactly because I wasn't making much sense."

I did not see her. Softfoot did not take me to that place.

Marmalade grumbled softly. At least it sounded like a grumble.

As I placed the envelope in the night deposit slot, I remembered that the bank had installed an ATM just outside Ralph and Ida's grocery store a few months ago. I could have saved myself a trip.

Still, it would be good to see Auntie Blue.

My mom was just getting out of her car in Auntie Blue's wide driveway. "Bisque," she said, stepping around her car and extending her arms for a hug. Her favorite red, orange, and yellow caftan fluttered around her. "Blue called me. It's so good to see you up and moving around." She gripped my shoulders with her strong potter's hands. "You must be feeling better. You look wonderful."

You can't see my fear, I thought. You can't see how much of a box I'm in. "I'm doing great, Mom. I'm glad Auntie Blue invited you."

"You two get in here right now," Auntie Blue boomed from her front door. "I got coffee cake ready, and your Uncle Mark threatened to eat it all."

Mom winked at me. My uncle and aunt were the perfect example of Jack Sprat and his wife. Auntie relished all the desserts and Uncle Mark was built like a chopstick. He loved to eat, but nothing sugary for him.

He'd gone for a walk, anyway, so we three women had

the kitchen all to ourselves.

"I can't stay long," I told them. "Just a quick cup of tea, and then Marmalade and I need to get home."

Auntie Blue moved her mug aside and pinned me with an unrelenting stare. "You afraid to be out at night by yourself?"

She is not by herself. I am with her.

She glanced over at Marmalade eating a little dish of tuna and purring mightily, with a few of her usual cat noises added in, but then turned back to me, expecting a real answer, not some vague platitude.

I looked toward my mom for support, but she was watching me as intently as Auntie Blue was.

"I... I'm not exactly afraid."

"Not exactly?"

"It's just that I keep imagining things. Like noises and movement and... and hands... reaching... reaching out to shove me." I stuttered to a stop.

Mom touched my right shoulder and Auntie Blue grabbed my left arm. "It's understandable," Mom said.

Auntie Blue swung her head from her sister's hand to her own. "Sometimes hands that reach out are good for you."

"I know that, but your hands aren't around all the time." I pulled back away from them, and turned my mug—one that had come from my mother's pottery—around and around. "I can't spend my life being chaperoned like a two-year-old who's afraid of the dark."

"Maybe you could get a dog," my mom said.

Excuse me?

Marmalade let out an ungodly squawk that sounded so much like an objection, we had to laugh. I love coincidences.

Goat poop!

At least they stopped badgering me.

At 8:00, Marmalade and I headed back home. "Don't worry about me." I told them through my rolled down window. "I just don't want to be out after dark." I looked at my hands gripping the wheel in the violet midsummer twilight and tried to relax them.

Mom looked at me with—well—it was pity, pure and simple. "Are you sure you're going to be all right, Bisque?"

I am with her.

I could tell she wasn't talking about the drive home. "Don't worry, Mom." She leaned in to kiss me, and I started the car.

"Call us when you get there."

Auntie Blue waved, and mom blew a kiss.

I like WaterWoman and Sunset Lady.

Fortunately, when my left front tire blew out, I was coming up on one of those scenic river overlooks. Pop-whoosh. And the sudden jerking of the wheel to the left. Nobody was in the oncoming lane, thank goodness, and I could safely ease over into the gravel parking area.

"I'll have this done in a jiffy. You wait here, Marmy."

I am in this box. I cannot go anywhere.

I knew enough to block the rear wheels, and it didn't take me any time at all to get out the spare tire and line up the jack under the Buick. The day I got my driver's license when I was sixteen, my father took me out to the driveway and made me change all four tires, one at a time. I'd take one off and put it right back on. Let the car down. Move the jack and do it all over again. I never forgot that lesson.

But this time I was defeated. Some Neanderthal must have used maximum pressure putting on the lug nuts when I'd bought my new tires only a few months ago. I couldn't budge a one of them. I wasn't quite at the profanity stage yet, but I was very close when a car pulled up in front of

VIOLET AS AN AMETHYST

me. It was way too dark by that time, and I jumped to my feet, blinded by the headlights, holding the tire iron up before me.

"It's okay, lady. I didn't mean to scare you." The deep voice had a gentle tone, but I kept the tire iron ready. "It looks like you need some help." An enormous young man stepped into the light, his hands spread open in a decidedly non-threatening manner. "My great-grandma's with me," he said, and I heard a car door open.

"Hugh, come help me get out of here. The door's too heavy for me to push all the way open on this hill." She sounded more irritated with herself than with her grandson or his car. He hurried around to the passenger side, and a moment later they reappeared.

"It's a good thing we were out tonight visiting Hugh's mother. You can put down that gol-durn weapon, young woman. We're not going to hurt you." I must have looked rather sheepish, because she laughed at me. "It's good for a woman alone to be careful, but you're just fine now. My Hugh can change that tire for you."

"I know perfectly well how to change a tire." I was trying not to sound too defensive. After all, they hadn't been obliged to stop. "I just couldn't get off the lugs nuts."

"I'd imagine not, with that iron," the grandma said. "Crummy design." Hugh walked to the back of their car and came back with a rather hefty x-shaped tool. When he turned, so his face was illuminated by the headlights, I could see what a handsome young man he was. I wondered idly if he had a girlfriend. If Melissa's mystery man never came back, maybe she'd consider this fellow. What a ridiculous idea. He couldn't be more than twenty. I shook my head to clear it.

"Four different sizes of lug wrench in one," he said, and showed me how each arm of the X had a hexagonal end. "You can get just about any lug nut off with this—

just have to choose the right size." He checked the wheel blocks for stability and then demonstrated the x-shaped tool, loosening all but one of the nuts. He handed me the x-wrench, or whatever it was called. "Try this last one, ma'am. You'll see how easy it is."

I was skeptical, but I slipped the socket over the lug nut. The two side arms of the tire wrench stuck out, making it easy for me to push down on the left one and pull up on the right one. The mechanical advantage was amazing. After only a small struggle, the lug nut turned, and I let out a whoop of joy. "Where can I buy one of these?"

"Any old car supply store, ma'am. There's one in Hastings." His great-grandmother and I chatted amiably while he jacked up the car and changed the tire.

"Looks like you ran over this," he said and held out a vicious-looking screw.

Oh, honestly, I thought. That was paranoid. It was only a screw. Nothing vicious about it. "Thank you," I said when he stood up. "Did you say your name was Hugh?"

"That's right, ma'am." He let the car down, removed the jack, and placed it in my trunk along with the flat.

"And thank you, too, Ms ..." I let the syllable hang there for a moment.

"It's Przybylski," she said, "but you can call me Cornelia."

She couldn't figure out why I threw my arms around her, until I thanked them both for saving my life.

"I thought she looked familiar," she said to Hugh.

He scuffed the dirt with the edge of his work boot. He had that look of an embarrassed ten-year-old about him. "Grana's the one to thank the most. She's the one held the boat steady against that current. Not an easy task."

"I don't imagine yours was any too easy, either."

His eyes twinkled in the light from the headlamps. "No, ma'am, it wasn't. You'd wedged yourself in there so tight I thought I was going to have to saw off a branch to get you out. Wouldn't want to do that to a live tree."

"I hope the tree makes it. Surely all that water over its roots couldn't be good for it."

Cornelia hooted. "Hugh and I boated up there yesterday to check on it. Now that the water's gone down, the tree looks just fine."

After a few more hugs and reciprocal invitations to visit, I slid behind the wheel and locked my door. Before I could pull away, Hugh reappeared at my window, holding my tire iron. "Don't forget this, ma'am."

"That wimpy thing?" I rolled down my window. "I'm going to get myself a real one!"

He laughed and handed it to me. "Is that a kitty in the cage?"

I do not like to be called a kitty, but you sound kind.

I set the tire iron on the floor in front of the passenger seat and lifted the carrier so Hugh could see inside. "This is Marmalade."

"She sure does purr nice, doesn't she?"

Thank you.

He backed up a step. "I'll let you get on your way."

"Thank you again, Hugh."

"Not a problem. You take care."

I rolled up the window and turned gratefully for home. Once I arrived, I had to sit a few minutes, talking myself into getting out of the car and walking up to my own porch.

I do not mind waiting.

This was ridiculous. I felt like a basket case. I took a deep breath and tried to remember what Nathan had told me. That helped. I wasn't going to let the bad guy win. I picked up the carrier and caught a whiff of tuna breath.

It was delicious.

Luckily I remembered to call Auntie Blue so she

wouldn't worry about me.

~~~~~

My Gratitude List for Wednesday
1. The Prrzzlbykzzski's (???) of course. What a stunningly gorgeous and absolutely charming young man. That Red is awfully good-looking, too, but he somehow acts as if he knows he is. I doubt young Hugh ever gives it a thought. And I hope I have as much gumption as Cornelia when I'm her age.
2. My wonderful old car. She's always been so dependable.
3. My dad, for having taught me how to change a tire.
4. Humph (to quote Glaze) I'm not including the mechanic who installed those new tires. He needs to go on one of those forgiveness lists Henry's always preaching about. But I'm glad about my new tires.
5. Good grief, Biscuit, this is turning into a diary instead of a gratitude list. So – I'm grateful for Auntie Blue and Mom and Marmalade.

I am grateful for
this quiet time of night
the sounds of those cricket bugs. It is almost like
　purring
people who scratch my ears in the library
Widelap, who takes me with her
SunsetLady and WaterWoman and tuna

    I tucked my journal into the drawer of the bedside table and turned out the light. Marmalade settled down across my knees. Bob was already asleep, but he instinctively reached out and tucked me close to his chest. Sleep eluded me, though. Another round of that revolving door started, pulling my thoughts in one direction and then shooting them out in another.

What door? What are you talking about?

Marmalade's purr sounded like a freight train in the quiet room. "Bob," I finally said, "are you asleep?"

Yes. He is.

He didn't say *not anymore*, but I could hear him thinking it. "What's wrong," he mumbled, but it sounded like he didn't want an answer.

I couldn't let him get away with going back to sleep. "Bob." I spoke a little louder. "I'm angry."

"Huh?" He wasn't awake yet.

"At you." There. I'd said it.

"What did I do?"

"It's what you didn't do."

"Uh-huh." He had that *whatever you say, honey* tone to his voice.

I pulled away from him and turned onto my other side so I was facing him. Marmalade shifted with me and moved up between us. "Wake up and listen to me, Bob. I have to say this, and you have to listen."

That woke him up. "What's wrong?"

"I've been scared out of my wits for the last week, and you're not helping at all."

It seemed to take him a moment to register what I'd said. "I'm looking for the guy, Bisque. I just haven't found him yet. I'm trying to solve a murder, too."

"Quit being logical. I'm trying to tell you it's your fault."

He pulled himself to a sitting position, switched on the light, and ran both of his palms along his jaw line. I could hear the rasp, rasp, rasp of his beard stubble. "My fault." He waited. "How?"

At least he wasn't arguing with me. "I didn't want to tell you because I don't really blame you, but I really do, and I can't sleep anymore and I can't take a walk by myself without looking behind me." The words kept rushing out, like the sea breaching a levee. "I invited you to go along with me and you said you'd rather sleep and if you hadn't been sleeping, you would have stopped him before he could do this to me and I hate feeling this way, but you're supposed to protect me and you didn't."

His mouth was hanging slightly open. He'd been nodding, not as if he agreed with me, but as if he were pacing my frantic words. "You wanted me to go with you?"

I sniffed. "Uh-huh."

"And I didn't?"

"Unh-unh."

His face took on that, that *look*. The one that said *Ohmigosh I didn't know*. The one that said *I'm sorry*. The one that said *This hurts me*. He reached out ever so gently and brushed the tears off my cheek.

"I, Robert, joyfully take you, Bisque, to be my lawful wedded wife." Marmalade squeezed out of the way as Bob gathered me into his arms and kept reciting our marriage vow. "I promise to laugh with you each day and love you to the best of my ability. I promise that if anything unlike love comes between us, I will seek the Higher Path of greatest good for both of us, the path of compassion and communication. I promise to be worthy of your trust." He reached for my left hand and lifted it to his face. "As a symbol of my vow, I give you this ring, round as the circle of time, and never-ending." He kissed the palm of my hand. "I betrayed your trust," he said.

Of course, when he put it that way, I could see how senseless it had been to resent him. "I know I'm being ridiculous," I said, but he shook his head.

"No, you're not. That's how you felt. I'm sorry." He said it so simply. And that was all I needed to hear.

DAY EIGHT
THURSDAY

CHAPTER 18
10:30 a.m. to 10 p.m.

~BISCUIT McKEE~

I CAN GO YEARS WITHOUT THINKING OF SOMETHING, but as soon as it comes into my consciousness, I begin to see references to whatever-it-is all over the place, like when I decided to buy the Park Avenue, and all of a sudden there were green Buicks everywhere; or when I learned I was expecting my first child, and pregnant women started popping out of the woodwork. Or so it seemed.

So, naturally, when I commented on Pumpkin's necklace Thursday afternoon at *Healthy Self*, I must have been responding to some sort of bone-magnet.

"Thank you," she said, and nodded to Melissa, who'd just walked in. She cupped her hands under the necklace and held it away from her chest. "I made it myself from turkey bones."

Melissa was as startled as I was. "Turkey bones? You're kidding, right?"

"No, really." Pumpkin lifted the macramé loop over her head and held it out to Melissa, who cringed a bit.

I stepped forward, fascinated by the small disks. They looked familiar somehow. "Is that a thigh bone?" I asked.

Pumpkin grinned. "Wing bone. The thigh bones on a turkey are way too big. It took me quite awhile to figure out how to use this so it wouldn't look tacky."

Melissa raised her eyebrow. I jumped into the moment of silence. "How did you get them so shiny?"

"I polished them with fine sandpaper and coated them with clear nail polish." She waved her hand toward the rack of the environmentally-safe nail care products that contained no tolu-something-or-other. I could never remember that long name. "I had to use epoxy, too, even though I don't like to use such strong chemicals."

"What's the epoxy for?" Melissa asked.

"It strengthens the ends of the bone. Otherwise they might break off."

For somebody who didn't want to touch the necklace, Melissa seemed ghoulishly interested. "Matching earrings, too?"

"Yes. From the same bird."

They looked familiar, too, but I couldn't place them. "Have I seen these before?"

"Possibly," she said. "I wear them once in awhile."

Melissa finally relented and reached out a finger to the large central bone, anchored on each end with silk macramé cord. "Where'd you get the turkey?"

I knew Pumpkin was into saving the world through green living, but wasn't sure whether or not she was a vegetarian.

"My brother." I didn't know she had a brother. "He's a medical student, and he dissected the turkey before Mom cooked it for Thanksgiving dinner last year. Bones that have been cooked are brittle. That's why you should never feed cooked chicken or turkey bones to a dog."

"Must have been a challenge," I said, "to cook a turkey with all the bones gone."

"It did look pretty limp," she admitted.

"No drumsticks?" Melissa made it sound like a class-one disaster.

"No. But he left in the rib cage so there was room for the stuffing. It wasn't a total flop."

Melissa snickered and I had to school my face.

Pumpkin, unaware of her pun, eyed her necklace critically before slipping it back on. "I really could have used some ribs."

Melissa snorted, and turned it into a cough. "No," she said, "that would have made the necklace hang too long."

Pumpkin looked at me as if for a second opinion, but I was saved by the entrance of three women. I knew they were from Happy Acres, but I couldn't remember their names, even though they all had library cards. I was going to have to work on that.

Who on earth would name a development Happy Acres? It sounded... I groped for the right word... *puerile*. A much better word than *childish*, I thought. Happy Acres was stuck out there on the side of the valley like a ship stranded in the ocean with no ship-to-shore contact. Oh, nonsense, I told myself. They were here, weren't they? And they came to the library regularly. What more contact did they need? And they had that look of good friends who rest easy with each other. I added my greetings to Pumpkin's.

They said a pleasant hello, and Pumpkin wandered away from us to answer their questions.

Melissa and I fiddled around the shop awhile longer. I gathered herbal teas, handmade soap, and a bar of shampoo. Melissa filled her basket with vitamins and supplements.

"Why do you need all that? You're as healthy as can be."

She leveled a steely glance at me. "I'm healthy because I take all of these."

I didn't want to argue with her, but I didn't see any need to swallow supplements all day long myself. It was something we'd have to agree to disagree on, I supposed.

"Those earrings of Pumpkin's," she leaned close to me to whisper, "aren't they gross?"

"I don't think so. What's wrong with them?"

"They're made out of bone. Little cross-sections."

Her words conjured up an unpleasant image of a tiny power saw cutting tiny slices off of tiny ...

"... how she can stand it."

"Uh. Me either," I said, hoping that would make sense.

Apparently it did, because Melissa nodded in satisfaction.

"We missed you at the dance," I told her.

She set her basket beside the old-fashioned cash register. "I didn't need to be there, not really."

"You sound like you don't know for sure."

She twisted the mother-of-pearl pendant on her necklace. "Sadie told me she'd invited Red."

I knew a story-in-the-making when I heard one. "Red?"

She walked a few paces before replying, and even then, it wasn't really an answer. "Let's stop by the Delicious. I need to be sitting down for this."

Ariel smiled at us as the bell tinkled overhead. "Your booth's open," she said. "Head on back. I'll be right there. The usual?"

I nodded, but Melissa paused. "No. Bring me hot chocolate, like Biscuit's."

"A Crock o' Choc?" Ariel's eyes crinkled up. She loved that name I'd invented last winter.

I glanced at the community bulletin board. No FOUND DOG notice. Glaze had sworn she was going to spread them all over town. Ha! Fat chance of that, especially now that Gracie had a name. I followed Melissa back to the booth.

We sat for a few minutes, not speaking, until Ariel delivered the soup crocks filled with their rich hot chocolate, topped with whipped cream and a drizzle of the darkest yummiest chocolate syrup imaginable.

Ariel turned to leave, and I prompted Melissa. "Red?"

She fiddled with her necklace again. "Chad's father's sister is Red's mother," she said.

I tuned out trying to picture that relationship. If Chad's father's sister—that would be his aunt—

Melissa helped me out. "They're first cousins. Chad told me he used to live with Red. They shared a house up the valley for awhile until Red apparently stopped paying the rent. They were evicted and Chad ended up going back to live with his parents. But that's only temporary." She stopped and lifted her crock but didn't do anything except hold it. "Don't look so shocked. Chad's not a deadbeat."

"I'm not shocked." I reached out and touched her forearm lightly. "I'm just surprised because Red looked so... so prosperous at the dance."

Her face contorted. "He's a no-good, lazy... he's taken so much advantage of Chad it's practically criminal."

"Why does Chad put up with him?"

"He has this thing about *family*." Her tone made it sound like a swear word. "And I think he's somewhat in awe of Red's abilities as an architect. He showed me a magazine article about some restaurants Red designed."

"Have you known Chad for very long?"

"About five months."

That's not long enough, I thought, but I kept my mouth shut. Something in my face must have given me away, though, because she jumped to her own defense. "You don't know what it's like, Biscuit. I knew almost from the first time I met him that we were right for each other."

I waited for her to expand on that, but she just took a long sip of chocolate. I pointed to her upper lip, and she licked off the whipped cream mustache. "Thanks."

"That's what friends are for."

"I'd been planning to tell you about Chad, but there just never seemed to be a chance. We went out most evenings, and I didn't want to talk about him at the Tuesday night gatherings."

I was surprised that nobody in this gossip-minded town had seen a car in front of her house. If they had, they certainly would have talked about it. "Where did you meet him?"

She chuckled, and her eyes lit up. "In the grocery store. He wandered down the aisle looking kind of lost, so I asked him if I could help him. He assumed I worked there. Said he was looking for an avocado, but hadn't much hope of finding such a vegetable in this small a town."

"I thought avocado was a fruit."

"Whatever." She flicked her fingers in dismissal. "At any rate, I showed him the produce aisle and left."

"When did you tell him you didn't work there?"

"I didn't. He came in the next day looking for me, described me very well, so that Ida knew who he was talking about. She's the one who set him straight, but she wouldn't give him my name or my phone number."

"I thought that was Red," I said.

"What?"

"Ida told us she'd sent some guy packing when he came looking for you in the grocery store. She said he looked just like Clark Gable."

"Chad told me they look a lot alike, but Red is quite a bit taller than Chad. They're cousins."

"Yes. You told me."

She lapsed into silence, and I spent a minute or so watching her sip her chocolate.

"So, what happened?"

"He found me. I'd driven up to Hastings to get my teeth cleaned, and he was there the same time I was. He'd broken a tooth on a popcorn kernel. We got to talking, and you know there's that yummy restaurant just up the block from the dentist, so he asked me to dinner, and... and he swept me off my feet." A blush crept its way from her neck to her chin and on upwards. She looked up at me and quickly lowered her eyes. "So to speak," she added.

Hmm. Well, that part wasn't any of my business. So to speak. "Yes?" I said, as neutrally as I could.

"I'm really not sure why I agreed to marry him. I always thought a long engagement was a good idea. But when he asked me," she held up her ring finger, "I just said yes."

"It would have been nice if you'd let me know you were dating somebody."

"I don't know why we've kept it such a secret. I'm so sorry I didn't tell you, but we just enjoy our time together so much, I don't think about much else. It seems like all day long I'm either working or getting ready to go out with him. And then later on, it's too late to call."

Right.

She plowed on, as if she had to convince me. "We always have such exciting times together. He takes me off on jaunts around the valley and down to the city. He has so much energy, but he can be happy just passing the time, too, just sitting on a park bench. He can draw anything without even thinking about it. You should see him sketch people as they pass by, and he doesn't make fun of them either. They're portraits, not caricatures." She was quiet for a long time before she added, "We laugh so much together."

It's a good thing that Crock o' Choc was as big as it was. She needed a lot of sipping in between sentences. To get her talking again, I asked, "Where does he work?"

"The same place Glaze does." The slight furrow between her eyes deepened. "He's been gone a week now, and he hasn't called me even once."

I pushed a package of Kleenex across the table.

"Thanks," she said. "I'm such a fool about him. But why hasn't he called me?"

"Everybody has a story like that, of a guy who gets cold feet. If he's gone, maybe you should just be glad you didn't marry the fellow. That way, you didn't lose as much as you might have."

"Shut up, Biscuit. I know you're trying to make me

feel better, but you're only making it worse." She fingered her ring. In this light it looked garish. "I know what you're thinking," she said. "The ring's a fake."

"I wasn't thinking that." Ida thought it was fake, but I wasn't going to tell that to Melissa.

"I'm pretty sure it's cubic zirconium, even that so-called amethyst in the middle." She rubbed her ring finger again. "You know, Chad was so happy about it. He told me a friend of his had given him a really good deal. I don't think he even suspects he was cheated. But I'll never tell him about the ring. It's not important."

"I hope he never gets another good deal from that friend of his."

She laughed. "I'm not going to worry about it. All I want to do is marry Chad and be Melissa Zapota. He said he can commute from *Azalea*—What?"

I gripped her arm. "Melissa! What did you call him?"

"Chad?"

"No! His last name!"

"Zapota. His first name was Charles, but he said nobody but his mother ever called him that."

"Charles Zapota. Haven't you been listening to the radio?"

"Not if I can help it."

"That body, the one we found in the backyard. That was—" I stopped. I couldn't tell her this way. Not here. Not so abruptly.

"Oh my God. You don't mean—" Her face went all wobbly, like a puppet with no hand inside it. "No. It can't... Oh my God." People at other tables were looking at us. "My God, no."

I coaxed her out of the booth. "Let's get you home." Ariel held the door open and we passed out of the Delicious into a day that was far too bright.

~~~~~

~BISCUIT McKEE~

Melissa had to talk with Bob and Reebok, of course. I put it off as long as I could. I got her to bed with an ice bag on her head and stayed with her until her breathing slowed. She needed the rest. I didn't want to leave her alone, but I had to call Bob, so I breathed a soft "I'll be right back," quietly, just in case she was asleep behind those tear-swollen eyelids. I tiptoed to the kitchen.

Bob insisted I bring her in to the station. I insisted he wait an hour and then come to Azalea House. I won.

He and Reebok were as gentle as they could be, but they had to ask if she knew anyone who wanted to murder her fiancé. They coaxed the story of her five-week love affair out of her, and Bob showed remarkable patience with her frequent bouts of howling distress. "I don't even have a picture of him," she wailed at one point, slamming her fist against the couch where she sat. "He hated cameras."

I found it hard to believe how she'd managed to keep Azalea House running, considering all the time she'd spent with Chad, but even more so, why hadn't anyone in this gossipy town seen him, seen his car, seen the two of them together? Bob must have wondered the same thing and he asked her.

She seemed intent on watching the floor. "I have a very private backyard. There are hedges all around it and a parking area off to one side. Chad always parked back there beside my car. You can see how private this apartment of mine is, tucked like this at the back of Azalea House. I keep this one for me so I can get away from my guests when I need to. We came and went through the back door, and I usually drove my car so he'd be free to sketch."

She twisted her ring around and around her finger. "He was going to move into Azalea House as soon as we were married. He hadn't told his parents yet. He said he had some things he had to clear up first."

"What did he mean by that?" Bob's question was gentle, but I could hear his cop instinct sharpen.

"I don't know. He was... I couldn't always... There was ..." She needed a Crock o' Choc, I thought, to cover all these false starts. Eventually she took a deep breath and plowed on. "He liked to be private. He was a very private person." She must have sensed Bob's skepticism. "Not secretive," she insisted. "Just private."

"So you don't know what he was clearing up?"

"No." She thought a moment. "I think it might have had something to do with this meeting he went to."

"You don't know where that was?"

She shook her head. "No. He called me on Wednesday morning and said that ..." Her voice took on a questioning note. "He told me he'd learned something at CelerInc that he had to deal with." Bob shifted in his chair. "No," she said, "he didn't tell me what it was." She swallowed with obvious effort, as if something had stuck in her throat. "That was when he told me he might be gone a few days."

"Did he say anything else? Any little detail, even if it doesn't seem important."

Her face went blank, the way of people who are truly lost in thought. "He said something about a jigsaw puzzle. Almost having the last piece."

Reebok had sat quietly to one side, taking notes, throughout the entire interview. When they finally rose to leave, he handed her a slip of paper. "It's Mrs. Zapota's address and phone number," he said. "I think she'd like to know she would have had a daughter as nice as you."

Melissa sank back down on her couch and buried her face in her hands.

Reebok headed down the walk, but Bob lingered at the door. Now was not the time for me to launch myself into my husband's arms, much as I wanted to. Instead, we both reached out a hand at the same time, two magnets, each responding to the other's pole. "Bisque," he whispered, "be careful."

I closed the door and turned back to my friend.

I am grateful for
Widelap, who cannot write her list tonight

DAY NINE
FRIDAY

CHAPTER 19
8 a.m. to 6:30 p.m.

~BISCUIT McKEE~

"WILL YOU COME WITH ME," SHE HAD SAID, and it wasn't even a question, and of course I had to say yes. I spent the night with her Thursday night, and woke on Friday to a day as rainy as her mood. My mood wasn't great, either. I wanted to go home and get into some clean clothes.

Melissa called Mrs. Zapota to ask if we could stop by. There was no answer. She kept calling, every hour or so until mid-afternoon. I needed to get home. I had things to do, like changing into clean underwear, but each time I mentioned leaving she held me back with my own words. "You promised to go with me," she said.

Finally, after yet one more phone call unanswered, Melissa stood and pulled two raincoats off her coat rack. "She's home. I know she's home. Chad always said his mother was happiest right at home. She's just not answering the phone."

I wondered if home might be a very painful place for her to be just now, but held my tongue on that conjecture.

Melissa rang the bell. A curtain stirred in the window to our left, and a monstrous cat peered out at us, as if to ask why we were disturbing its owner. Or maybe it just wondered why we'd woken it from its nap. I couldn't tell if it was male or female. Part whale, I thought, and part panther, except for the fuzzy mottled gray coat.

A face appeared above the cat, and Melissa raised her hand. If my son had just been killed, I'm not sure I would have opened my door to two total strangers, but Mrs. Zapota was apparently more trusting than I. She invited us in and hung our raincoats from a multi-pegged coat rack beside the door, then headed straight to the kitchen. "Would you like some tea?" It didn't sound like a question.

"No, please," Melissa said, following her. "We don't need anything."

Mrs. Zapota turned in the narrow hallway. "Maybe you don't, young woman, but I do." She settled us at her kitchen table, warning us to keep our voices down. "Mr. Zapota is resting. He hasn't had much energy since we... since we found out."

"I'm sorry I didn't come sooner," Melissa said. "I didn't know ..."

"That's all right, dear. I haven't wanted any casual visitors, but you're very welcome here. I recognized you right away from some of the pictures Charles drew."

"Pictures?"

Mrs. Zapota smoothed the fabric of her dress over her lap. "He drew that ring, too. I should have known, I suppose, but he never told us anything about you."

Melissa looked stricken. "We never meant to hurt you. We were planning ..." Mrs. Zapota continued to inspect her lap, and Melissa turned her panic-filled face to me. I was no help. I had no idea how she could get around this. Melissa swallowed. "We were planning a surprise dinner. We were going to tell you then."

"Oh?" Chad's mother raised her head. "When?"

"Last... last Thursday."

"But that's my quilting group. Every Thursday. Charles knew that."

Melissa blanched. I could tell she'd just picked that day out of the ether. "He... he wanted you to have the good news so you could tell all your friends."

"Well, isn't that thoughtful. He's such a dear."

They talked together and cried together, held hands and hugged. Mrs. Zapota patted Melissa's curly mop of hair, and Melissa laid her arm around Mrs. Zapota's narrow shoulders. I was entirely superfluous. Only the enormous feline seemed to be aware of my presence. She poked her nose in my purse. I reached down, ostensibly to pet her, but truthfully to push her away. She wouldn't budge. She was probably named *Tank*, or *Gibraltar*. Something immovable.

I lifted my purse, but one heavy paw, tangled in the strap, hung on with extended claws. "Come on," I coaxed, "give me my purse."

I'm used to Marmalade. She's curious, she's inventive, but she's always willing to see my side of the story, or so it seems. This cat, on the other hand, was determined to get inside my bag regardless of my wishes. She wasn't at all cooperative. I tugged one more time and the cat objected audibly.

"Venus," Mrs. Zapota said, patting her lap. "Leave the nice lady alone." It was obvious she'd forgotten my name. She bent to one side to peer under the table. "Let go of her bag."

Venus looked at her mistress, looked up at me, dove headfirst into my purse and snatched my silver pen, one Bob had given me. I scooped that cat up and grabbed my pen so fast she hardly even had time to squawk. "Sorry, Venus. You can't have that."

From the astonished look on Mrs. Zapota's face, I gathered that I was perhaps the only person who had ever challenged the cat's supremacy.

I set Venus down, gently, and she licked her paw, as if I didn't exist. After that, I held my purse on my lap.

Eventually Mrs. Zapota asked Melissa, "Would you like to see my son's artwork?" She said it almost shyly, but brightened at the look of intense interest on Melissa's face.

We walked down a narrow stairway, preceded by

Venus, into a cacophony of art. Melissa was entranced. I was overwhelmed.

"Oh, Biscuit, look!" and half a minute later, "Oh, look here!" She pointed to a pencil sketch of my house. "He drew that when I drove him past your house." She must have sensed my indignation because she added, "It was one of those days I knew you weren't there, so we couldn't have gone in to meet you." She pointed at the miniscule date sketched beneath his name, as if to prove her point. "But he loved your house, especially the funny little eyebrow windows just below the roofline." I inspected the drawing, taped to the wall as if he'd been trying to decide where to put it in all that chaos. He'd drawn it—I couldn't quite put my finger on it, but it seemed like it was *loving*, like the way I always pictured it—welcoming. Melissa was right. He really liked my house.

Another foot or so farther along, Melissa peered more closely at a miniature scene. "Here's the Old Church, with its little signboard out front. It even says, *Thou shalt not kill.*" She looked up at me. "I don't remember that as a sermon topic, do you?"

"I think that commandment is the shortest one." The tiny signboard couldn't have measured more than two inches square. "I doubt *Remember the Sabbath Day to Keep it Holy* would have fit in such a small space."

"Yes, but it's so detailed, don't you think? He was an amazing artist."

From somewhere off to our left Mrs. Zapota crooned her approval of Melissa's comment. She stood in front of an out-of-kilter map of the United States. I couldn't place what exactly was wrong about it. I'd have to look more closely. I started in that direction, but Melissa's quiet intensity pulled me back to her side.

"Biscuit, look here." As if I could miss it. The town gazebo, bedecked with flags, was shown full of the town band, complete with brassy trumpets, trombones pointed almost skyward, and even a tiny silver piccolo. Little music notes spread over the crowd, wafting their way toward the Town Hall, where my Bob had his office. One little note, bent in the middle, seemed to be knocking at the door under the "Police" sign. Cute.

"He saw so much," Melissa said. "We could look at something and I'd see the broad outlines, but he picked out the tiniest details." She pointed to a recumbent form just under the overhanging branches on the edge of the painted woods. "Look. Somebody's taking a nap in the middle of the band concert."

There weren't that many trees so close to the town park, but I didn't mention that because Melissa teared up again and turned away to blow her nose. I looked closer. That woman lying there wasn't asleep. And the red white and blue she wore wasn't patriotic. It was a blue and white dress spattered with what looked disconcertingly like blood.

"I don't understand this one," Mrs. Zapota said, and I heard a strain in her voice, as if it hurt her to question her son's artistic abilities. She pointed up to the map and I saw what had bothered me. The entire northeast was oversized, each state outlined in vivid oranges, greens, reds. New York, the entire state, overshadowed the rest of the region, and the huge swath of the Adirondacks, mile after mile of mountains and woods, took up most of the state. I looked closer. Another figure, with a similar red-splotched shirt, was drawn in meticulous detail, lying beside a highway that wound along the edge of the National Forest. A tiny blue car zoomed along the road, little cartoon-like puff marks showing its speed, its orange and black license plate a blur.

"I don't either," Melissa said, "but look, here's Carl Armitage." She turned to Mrs. Zapota. "He owns the gas station in town. See, here it is," and she leaned down a bit to indicate Carl's station, firmly planted on First Street in Martinsville, directly below the body on the Adirondack highway.

"What do you think all these dollar signs are for?" Mrs. Zapota traced a line of crosshatched S's that floated, rather like the musical notes, from Carl's shoulder off toward the plantation house a little farther down at the end of the room.

Melissa waved her hand in dismissal. "Carl comes from New Jersey. Everybody in town used to rib him about being from the mafia." She edged to her left, obviously losing interest in Carl. "Nobody much thinks about that nowadays. He and Sharon are pretty firmly entrenched here. And he certainly doesn't look like a mafia type. Look, Biscuit!"

Something about the way she said it, told me that this was what she'd been aiming for all along, from the moment we'd entered the room. Melissa reached up to touch the face of one of the men painted there. An enormous Tara, complete with tall white columns, adorned that wall. The door to Chad's bathroom formed the front door of Scarlett O'Hara's mansion from *Gone with the Wind*. The door was slightly ajar. I could see a sink and the edge of a tub. In front of Tara stood three people, two men and a woman; four people really, because you had to count the figure of Melissa who stood beside a smaller Azalea House, but with her right arm linked through the left arm of one of the two men.

The man on the right, the one connected to Melissa, was Chad; I could tell it from the way Melissa looked at him, from the way her fingertips lingered over his cheek. "We laughed about what it would have been like to have a house that looked like Tara," she said. "It looks like he painted one for us." I held my breath, expecting a new spate of tears, but Melissa just went on talking about the details. "This horse. I bet it's the one he told me he rode when he was out West a few years ago."

It looked to me like the horse's face was a caricature of a person, but it wasn't anybody I recognized. Whoever it was, it was drooling a little bit.

"He worked on a ranch for awhile, and Daisy here," she touched the horse's alert-looking ears, "was his favorite."

"I didn't know that," Mrs. Zapota said. "He never told us much about his travels, even though he called home once a week."

"I wish I could have known him then."

The figure of Melissa on the wall wore an enormous ring, glittering with diamond-shaped points of light, like something straight out of a Disney movie. Her curly hair framed a face that Chad had obviously drawn with a lot more love than he'd used to draw anybody else on that wall. I wondered if Melissa could sense that.

The Chad on the wall held a flower pot. Incongruous indeed, but Melissa didn't seem to think there was anything strange about it. "He designed it," she told us. "He was very proud of his design, although his boss kept asking him to change it. He told me last Tuesday, the last ..." she swallowed and went on, "the last time I saw him, that he was going back to work after he left me. He said he had come up with one more idea he wanted to try out. I'd forgotten that until just now, seeing him here with that silly, wonderful pot."

"You knew where he worked?" Mrs. Zapota touched Melissa's shoulder.

"Yes. A little manufacturing plant in Russell Gap. He designed products for them. He didn't like his boss very well. He called him Horse Face, but he enjoyed the work."

"That nice young deputy was wondering where he worked, if that might have had something to do with why he disappeared."

Melissa shrugged. "I shouldn't think so. They make kazoos and flower pots, for heaven's sake."

I'd held my peace long enough. "I recognize Red on the left, but who's the woman standing between them?"

"That's Kate, my dear sweet niece." Mrs. Zapota pulled a handkerchief from her pocket. "She disappeared two years ago, on the Fourth of July. She was on her way to one of the town festivals, probably Hastings or Martinsville, when her car broke down and she simply disappeared. She was such a lovely girl. Charles painted her just like she was, except for those bones." She pointed to the skeletal hand her son had painted. "I don't know why he'd paint something silly like this. She was beautiful, wasn't she? We've... never... given up hope," she said in a voice that reflected nothing but hopelessness, almost as if she were trying to convince herself. "Isn't that ribbon around her neck pretty? She was so full of life, so bright."

"Why is she holding a music box?" I pointed to the ornate contraption in her hands. A little crank stood out from one side of it, painted in cunning detail. The box looked like it was leaking around the crank.

"I don't know." She screwed her rather puffy lips up in a little pout. "It's something she designed at work. A place called Celery or something like that."

"CelerInc." Melissa's voice was flat. "She worked at CelerInc, too? That's where Chad worked."

"Melissa." I pulled her to one side. "We have to go. Now."

~~~~~
### ~BOB SHEFFIELD~

Bob took his flashlight with him to the Zapota's house. From what Biscuit had told him, he'd need to see every

# VIOLET AS AN AMETHYST

little detail. Reebok hovered behind him, still apologizing. "I didn't see anything like what Miss Biscuit described, Sir."

You were too busy counting shoes and paintbrushes, Bob thought. No need to say that now. He'd have a little talk with this deputy of his later, when they weren't standing on the grieving mother's front doorstep.

Bob steeled himself for what he was sure she would say—*you need a search warrant before I'll let you in the house*. Instead, she opened her front door and invited them in. "Of course you can, Officer. I'm glad you're interested in my son's work." She led them down a staircase and left them there. "If, as you say, this can help you find out who... who did... who hurt ..." she straightened her spine, "who killed my boy, then you go right ahead and look all you want to."

Biscuit had given him a fairly complete description of everything she'd seen, but it didn't even come close to expressing the sheer sweep of this work. He started with the Independence Day concert in the park and the corpse in the blue and white dress lying nearby, close to the Old Church signboard with its injunction against murder.

Just to the right of the signboard was Charles' rendition of St. Theresa's. Reebok was right. Father John's garden patch was there. He must have just started planting, because there was a mound like the ones Biscuit piled up to plant her zucchini on, but Charles hadn't painted anything growing there yet.

Next he looked at the map, thought about the position of Carl below it, and the dead body—because that's what it was—lying broken beside a northern New York highway. He considered the line of dollar signs floating from Carl to Tara. Or was it the other way around? Were they headed from the three cousins toward Carl? He looked again at the New York body. A faint red line, almost invisible, linked it to the top of Carl's head. Biscuit hadn't mentioned that. He wondered if she'd even noticed it.

He looked at the red ribbon around Kate's neck. Biscuit was right. It wasn't a ribbon. He looked at the music box, and the trail of what looked like white sand leaking from the side, just below the crank. The white sand-like powder was leaking out of that horse's mouth, too, and he'd just bet the face on that horse was recognizable to someone. Kate's hand, the one holding the box, was just a skeleton. One of the bones looked like it had been neatly sliced into pieces, little disks, less than an inch in diameter, like a package of thick pepperoni in a grocery store.

"Garner. Look at this." He pointed to one of the windows on Tara, a window positioned directly above Gracie's head. "What do you see?"

"A window, Sir?"

"Look closer."

"There's a question mark in the glass, Sir. Like a reflection."

Bob looked more closely. He'd missed that. "What else do you see?"

"I don't know, Sir."

"Look at the window sill."

Reebok drew in a quick breath, not quite a gasp, but pretty close to it. "It's a knife, Sir."

"Now look at the woman. She's the one who's been missing for two years."

"She's really beautiful."

"Garner," Bob's tone held a warning, "what do you *see*?"

"She's all dressed up in that blue and white dress, with that pretty red ribbon around ..." His voice trailed off. "Oh."

That question mark in the window bothered Bob. Charles was obviously trying to tell them a story. Kate with her throat cut, a knife above her head. Why the question mark? Did Charles not know who the killer was? Did he not find out until that Wednesday night just before he was killed and half-buried in the Old Woods? Had he been looking for the answer? Was that why he was killed?

Bob looked back at the wall. Three people, three cousins. Two of them were dead. Was Red the next victim? Bob didn't particularly like the guy, but he certainly wouldn't wish him dead, with his throat cut like Kate and Charles. And why had Charles painted that sliced bone?

And Carl. How did he tie into this?

There was only one thing to do. Ask him.

~~~~~

~GLAZE McKEE~

Usually Glaze didn't have much of a problem deciding what to wear, but going out with Clark Gable's look-alike was a bit intimidating. Glaze ran her hands through her silver hair. Grandma McKee's hair, she thought. Could I pass as a white-haired Vivian Leigh? Not a chance. She grabbed her full-skirted navy shirtwaist—she rather liked the old-fashioned look of it, especially with these three-inch heels—and draped a paisley scarf, patterned in shades of light violet and dark blue, around her shoulders. Tom had a paisley tie that came close to matching it. She heard Red's car pull up outside. There was something wrong with the engine. It had a funny rattle. He really ought to get that checked out. She took one more look at herself, added a heavy silver chain necklace, checked her hem and the fall of the scarf. She was dressed up enough for dinner, but not too much. This was going to be a fun evening. It was.

She headed downstairs as Gracie began to bark. "Hush, Gracie. It's a friend." She could see him through the kitchen door, carrying flowers. Tom seldom brought her flowers, and when he did, it was usually just a single blossom. Or maybe a bouquet he'd gathered from the roadside. The dog kept barking, and Glaze laid a hand on her head. "Just hush now, Tom. I mean Gracie." To be on the safe side, she slipped her hand through the violet collar and unlocked the door. "Come on in. I don't know why Gracie is so noisy. She's usually quiet."

Red extended a hand, closed in a fist. "She just wants to meet me better." Gracie eyed him and took a tentative sniff. She stepped forward and slipped her head underneath his hand. "She's a beauty. And look at this. She wants a good scratch."

Glaze let go of the collar, but not before Red's hand lingered on hers. Gracie shivered in ecstasy—nothing like a good scratch—but Glaze stepped back, took the flowers, and went to pull out a big vase.

~~~~~

~BOB SHEFFIELD~

"You're working kind of late, aren't you, Carl? I thought you were supposed to be taking it easy."

Carl gave Bob a wary look and straightened his ball cap. "What's wrong with that? I got a right to work whenever I want to."

"Had a vacation lately, Carl?"

"No, not since... no, not recently."

Bob let his gaze wander around the gas station office. "Not since before you moved to Martinsville?"

"What is this? What do you want?"

"Just wondering if you'd like to tell me about what happened on that road in the Adirondacks."

Bob was afraid he'd gone too far. Carl went ashen and

sank onto the edge of the desk. "How did you... who told... did Red say ..." He pulled out his chair and dropped into it. "You haven't told Sharon, have you?"

"No, not yet. Why don't you just give me the details? Be sure I have the story straight."

Carl rubbed his chest.

Don't let him have another heart attack. Not now. Not yet. Bob slid a blue plastic chair forward.

"Sharon doesn't know about it. Red's the only one who knew. Sharon and I used to live in New Jersey." He looked at Bob. "You knew that. Well, we went camping one summer for a week. In the Adirondacks. We had one of those pull-behind trailers. Parked it in a KOA campground, and were having a great time. On the last day of our vacation, Sharon wanted some special brand of ice cream. They didn't have any in the little KOA store, so she asked me to drive to town. It was maybe twenty-five miles down the road. We'd gone through it on the way to the campground. They had a supermarket there, and Sharon—well, we didn't know it yet, but she was expecting, craving pineapple ice cream like nobody's business."

He paused. Bob didn't say a word.

"I left her and our daughter and drove... to get the ice cream. I had a little cooler in the back seat so it wouldn't melt on the way back." He ran his hand over his head, smoothing what little hair he had across his bald spot. "There was this hitchhiker, I guess that's what she was. I came around a bend too fast, and she was too close to the road, and I... and I... God, I didn't mean to hit her. I didn't. I've lived that horrible... every minute since then I've ..."

Bob just looked at him.

"There wasn't any other traffic. She was lying down in the ditch. I scooped up some ditch water to wash off the... the blood and stuff. It was on my fender. Then I drove back to the town and found one of those do-it-yourself car washes. Sharon was pretty upset that I'd taken so long to bring her the ice cream, but it hadn't melted. I... I couldn't say anything about... about what had happened."

Bob waited a moment. "Do you remember what day it was?"

Carl stared at him for quite awhile. "It's branded on my damn heart," he said. "I thought they'd see it when I had my attack." He gave Bob the date.

"So how did Red find out about it?"

Carl swore with more vehemence than originality. "I told him."

Bob just raised his eyebrows.

"I was drunk. A little more than a year ago Sharon and I had an argument. I was pissed off about something—looking back I can't even remember what it was, so it couldn't have been that important. But I went tearing out of the house and drove up to Surreytown, about as far away from this town as I could get without leaving the valley. There's a bar up there. I'd never been there, but I'd heard about it. I don't know how many hours I was there, but I ended up talking to a sympathetic ear. Or so I thought at the time."

"Red?"

Another round of swearing. "Red and another guy he had with him. They looked like brothers. I don't even remember what I told them, but a day or two later he called me at the gas station. Said he had a little business proposition he'd like to talk to me about. He said just enough that I got scared." He looked at Bob with open anguish in his face. "He knows Sharon's name and where she has her shop. I must have told him that, too. I agreed to meet him, up at that bar again. This time he was by himself. He told me he expected a certain amount each month, just so he'd be sure to keep his mouth shut about our little secret. That's what he called it. Our little secret."

"And where did you get the money?"

Carl snorted. Bob felt like a matador confronting a bull, whose neck muscles were already compromised by the barbs of the picadors. "You already know where," Carl said. "It's the money I got from Margaret. Every bit of it went into Red's greedy hands, every month. I was late this month. He called me. He said he knew I'd been in the hospital. He said Sharon had told him. When I asked her, she said he'd come into the shop. That scared me. I have until Monday to get him the money. Otherwise, he said he'd give her another visit. Sharon still doesn't know that I... I killed... some poor girl."

"Is that why you moved here? To get away from the Adirondacks?"

Carl's face looked sullen, defeated. "As far away as I could. Shoulda gone to California."

Bob pulled out a yellow pad of sticky notes. "Give me a few more specifics."

~~~~~

~REEBOK GARNER~

"What are you doing here, Sir? I thought you'd be at home."

"I've got a little project for you. Here's a date, a town name—it's in New York state—and a highway number. I want you to find out what you can about an accident, a hit and run, along the stretch of road north of that town. It may not have been discovered that day. Maybe a day later. Let me know as soon as you have some information."

"Yes, Sir." Reebok took the little note and stuck it next to the phone.

"I'll be at home until about seven. Then I have to drop by Sadie's. She needs me to carry some boxes down from

her attic."
 "Yes, Sir." He pulled out a legal pad so he'd have some room to write.

CHAPTER 20
Friday 7 p.m. to 9:30 p.m.

~GLAZE McKEE~

Red handed her into the car, and Glaze watched him as he strode around to the driver's side. A big man. Taller than Tom. Heavier through the shoulders. Or maybe it was just shoulder pads in his blazer. She'd never seen him when he wasn't dressed up.

"I know I invited you for Thai food." He settled behind the wheel and adjusted his seatbelt. "But would you rather have Chinese? Or Japanese?"

"You must have grown up in Asia, if those are the only choices."

"Not at all, Mademoiselle. Zere eez a lovely place for ze French cuisine just an hour from here. And if you're up for a drive of an hour and a half, we can have the best-a Italiano food in-a all of North-a Georgia. A small-a restauranté, known only to those-a with truly discriminating tastes." He kissed his fingers with a resounding smack.

His faux French and his Hollywood Italian were truly awful. Laughing, Glaze said, "Let's go with the first choice. How far is it to Thailand from here?"

"For you, my dear, it's just up the valley in Russell Gap." He jammed the shift lever into drive.

No wonder his engine sounds dicey, Glaze thought. "Do you prefer this automatic transmission, rather than a stick shift?"

Only a quick sideways glance betrayed his surprise. "That's a most unusual question for the beginning of a dinner date."

"I've always enjoyed a manual transmission, even after I broke my finger when my car was totaled a few years ago. There's no comparison."

"Ah," he said. "But shifting can be bothersome if you have to stop suddenly."

"I guess you're right, but my dad taught me that manuals required less fuel because they were so efficient."

"That may have been true way back when, but technology has advanced a great deal."

"I suppose." They lapsed into an uncomfortable silence. Tom was easy to be silent with. He never seemed to expect anything of her. He never expected her to be dumb and agree with everything he said, either. She looked at Red's hands, relaxed on the steering wheel. But they weren't relaxed. The more she watched, the more she could see the minor twitching of his fingers. Subtle, but faintly unsettling.

Nonsense. I'm being unfair to him, she thought. He's perfectly comfortable to be with. I need to stop comparing him to Tom. Tom has nothing to do with this. I've told him time and time again that I wasn't ready to marry anyone. And I can certainly go out with anybody I choose. Anytime I choose. She leaned back and watched the trees whiz by, aware all the time of Red's restless hands, drumming and twitching.

~~~~~

~GLAZE McKEE~

Dinner was simply lovely, and Red carried most of the conversation but didn't overpower her with his own stories. There was give and take to the talk, almost as easy as the way it was when she was with Tom.

"A few years ago," she said in answer to his question. "I came for my sister's wedding—she's the town librarian, and she married the town cop."

"Yes," he said. "I think I met them at the dance."

"They're quite a combination. I'd just lost my job in Philadelphia, and Martinsville seemed like a good place to start over again."

"Philadelphia. I love that city." He leaned back and took a long swallow of wine.

"Did you live there?"

"No." He set down the glass. "Just many happy visits. The Freedom Trail and all that."

If she'd thought first she wouldn't have challenged his inaccuracy. A first date probably wasn't the time to engage in debate. "You mean the Constitutional Walking Tour?"

"What?"

"The Freedom Trail is in Boston. Philadelphia has the Constitutional Walking Tour."

He gave her a look she couldn't decipher and drained his wine glass. "I've done them all. I love history, although the British saga is much more interesting than the American one. Some great role models if you read between the lines."

"I prefer American history. It seems more… relevant somehow."

He laughed deep in his throat. He's humoring me, Glaze thought. Tom never does that.

"But tell me more about you," he said. "Where do you work?"

Glaze lifted her own wineglass to cover a momentary unease. She didn't want to relate to a relative stranger how she'd be handling all those money decisions. And he *was* a stranger. She had to remember that. "I do office work," she said, "for a small manufacturing plant in Russell Gap."

He leaned forward, shrugged his shoulders, and sat back again. "Manufacturing?"

She nodded. "Just little stuff, music boxes, flower pots, things like that. The owner, Hank, he's my boss, is hard to understand. He goes off on these tirades every once in awhile." She shifted in her seat. "I won't be working at CelerInc much longer. I have a... much better deal coming up."

"Oh? Do you?"

"Yes. I do."

She was surprised that he didn't ask what it was. Instead he simply looked at her. Finally he nodded, twice. "I suppose everyone feels a need to move up the ladder." He pulled his right cuff down over his wrist.

What was he talking about? To break the silence, Glaze asked, "And what line of work are you in?"

"I'm an architect. I specialize in the food industry. I'm in Martinsville to work on a restaurant that's being remodeled to serve as a vocational cooking school." His voice carried just a hint of scorn.

Tom's restaurant. He was talking about Tom's place.

"Seems a bit pretentious," he said. "I can't imagine any student would want to spend two years in such a small town."

"I like Martinsville," Glaze said.

"Oh, I'm sure it's a nice place. It seems to be prosperous enough. I've thought about settling down, but travelling is so much in my blood, I'm not sure I'd be happy living in one place." He buttoned his jacket and then unbuttoned it. Glaze wished he'd quit fiddling like that. Tom never fiddled. "I'm a hands-on architect. I go where the jobs are."

Glaze drummed her fingers on the table. She never did that when she was with Tom. "I used to travel a lot, too, but I never enjoyed it that much."

"A homebody, are you?"

She didn't like his tone, the slight hint of a sneer on his handsome face. "Yes. I guess I am. I like home." She nodded once, to emphasize her point. "Now," she added.

Maybe he simply hadn't noticed her momentary discomfort, or maybe he didn't care, but he let her comment pass without notice. "Don't you ever travel anymore?"

"My sister was trying to talk me into going to Scotland with her, to look up some of our long-lost relatives, third- and fourth-cousins or some such. But after the dunking she got in the Metoochie on Wednesday night a week ago, she said she'd rather go somewhere warm."

"Dunking? What do you mean?"

"Somebody pushed her off the dock, and she almost drowned."

He shifted in his chair. "I heard someone *had* drowned in the river. They found her body washed down to Enders."

"Well, that wasn't Biscuit. I don't think they've identified that body yet." Glaze was still amazed, gratified, that her sister had survived. "Biscuit got stuck in a submerged pine tree. She climbed up above the water and hollered until somebody heard her. But by the time they got to her she had hypothermia so bad they had to practically thaw her out."

"That's terrible." Red's voice was almost liquid in its concern. "Does she know who pushed her in?"

"No. There's no reason why anyone would do that, she's such a great person. But her husband thinks she must have seen something. She just can't remember what. He's even talked about hypnosis."

Red waved the waiter over. "Do you want dessert, Glaze?"

She massaged her tummy. Her shirt-waist dress was decidedly tighter than it had been an hour or two ago. "No, I'm stuffed as it is." And those three-inch heels were killing her feet, but she wasn't going to mention that.

~~~~~

FRAN STEWART

~REEBOK GARNER~

"Sir? Sorry to bother you at home, but I finally got through to an officer in that New York town. He said he remembered it. A woman was hit by a car that day. Hit and run. They never did find out who did it."

"When did they discover the body?"

"When she walked into town that night. Best they could figure, she'd been unconscious for an hour or so. When she woke up, she had a broken arm, and blood all over her. Heavy bruises, too. She had first aid gear in her backpack. She wrapped her arm up and stumbled into town all on her own. All she could remember was that it was a blue car."

"Thanks, Garner. Good work."

"Is this important, Sir?"

Bob sighed. "Think about Charles Zapota's wall, and see if you can come up with any conclusions."

~~~~~

~BISCUIT McKEE~

Bob hung up the phone and turned to me with a look I couldn't place.

"Woman, I am constantly amazed at the depths of stupidity people exhibit for no reason whatsoever."

"There's always a reason. We just might not know what it is."

"I think you're right. I'm going to walk up to Sadie's to get all that extra beekeeping equipment down from her attic. I told her I'd be there by seven. Do you want to come along?"

Yes.

Marmalade meowed, and I agreed with her. "I think the cat and I will stay in. I want to put my feet up."

Goat poop!

"That's just as well. It may take me awhile."

Marmy surprised me by walking out the door with Bob. Deserted by my cat.

I like to go with Softfoot sometimes.

I locked the door behind them.

~~~~~

~GLAZE McKEE~

Red proffered his arm as they left the restaurant. It was most definitely done with a movie star sort of flair, but Glaze chuckled and wrapped her hand around his forearm. Tom usually just held her hand. Nothing as gallant as all this. Still, in these spike heels, she appreciated the steadying influence of a muscular arm. Very muscular. She could feel it ripple beneath the fabric.

The well-lit parking lot was still rather full. There'd been a steady stream of patrons the whole time they were eating, but it had never seemed rushed or crowded. She liked that sort of restaurant. This would be a good place to come back to. She wondered if Tom had ever eaten here.

Red had parked facing away from the building, one line over. There'd been nothing closer at the time, although now spaces were beginning to clear out. She paused behind his car. "What an interesting license plate. Roman numerals, isn't it?"

"Yes. I told you I was a history buff. William, Duke of Normandy, was quite a hero of mine ever since I first read about him. He accomplished so much and changed the course of history."

"My sister said he was a bastard in more ways than just the obvious one."

As he pulled out of the parking lot, Red turned and

smiled at Glaze. "Don't believe everything the history writers tell you." He gripped the wheel. "They don't like William because he was such a success."

Glaze thought about the story Biscuit had told her of how William the Conqueror had some of his enemies skinned alive. It didn't sit well on her full stomach.

"This is a lovely drive," she said. "And your car is so comfortable." She wouldn't mention how ragged the engine sounded.

"Ah, it is my pleasure to share it with you."

They talked as he drove toward Martinsville. As they passed through Garner Creek, Red brought up the topic of William of Normandy again.

Glaze didn't enjoy hearing about the battles, the defeat of Henry the Second. It sounded like slaughter to her. Tom liked fishing. "I'm confused," she said to turn the conversation away from the bloodbath. "You said your license plate has something to do with William the Conqueror?"

"The Norman Conquest." Glaze could hear the capital letters as he said it. "M-L-X-V-I. Those are the Roman numerals for 1066, a date burned into the memory of every student of history. The year William invaded England. The year he defeated England."

Glaze had a hard time swallowing. That was the other part of what Biscuit had told her in the hospital room. *M L X*, she'd said. *Ten-sixty-six.* Glaze and Bob and Reebok had all thought the license plate was M-L-X-1-0-6-6. No wonder there'd been no trace of it.

CHAPTER 21
Friday 9:30 p.m. to 10:15 p.m.

~BISCUIT McKEE~

I COULD SEE MADDY STANDING OUT BY THE MAILBOX, her left leg wrapped around her right one. Why she didn't fall over, I'd never know. The woman must have an incredible sense of balance. Gracie, on a leash, sniffed the daylilies, and Madeleine had that look of dog walkers everywhere that said, "You know dogs. They have to smell everything they see."

I'd forgotten to check the mail, so I stepped outside, looked around quickly, and called to her. "Nice evening, isn't it?" As I walked up, Gracie lifted her head and nuzzled my hand for a scratch. "Good dog," I said. "I'm glad you found Glaze."

"We decided we both sort of own her."

Maddy sounded a wee bit defensive, but I let it pass. That dog was Glaze's for certain. "So you're out for a walk?"

"I've been cooped up writing all evening long, and I had to get out."

"A new novel?"

"Don't I wish. No, Dee drove Rebecca Jo down to Atlanta yesterday for some exhibit at the High Museum. They stayed at that cute little hotel Dee loves, and they'll be home late tonight."

I couldn't see where this was headed. "So?"

"So Dee was going to help, but since she's gone I got stuck designing forms for people to fill out so they can apply for MM funds."

"MM?" I searched my stock of financial knowledge. "What's that?"

Maddy grinned. "Margaret Money, of course."

"Of course. Makes sense." I patted Gracie again. "Why didn't Glaze come with you?"

"She's out on a dinner date."

"She couldn't be. I saw Tom walk by maybe twenty minutes ago."

Maddy waved her hand dismissively. "She's not with Tom. She's with Red Butler."

"And didn't tell me about it? I'll get after her for this."

Maddy pushed her glasses higher on her nose. "They look so good together. He's so handsome, and she's so beautiful." She sounded somewhat wistful. "Gracie really liked him. Red scratched her head for a long time."

I had the feeling Gracie would like anyone who'd scratch her head. "Where are they going?"

"No idea. They sat in the car and talked for awhile before they drove off, so maybe they were deciding." She switched the leash to her right hand and uncurled her legs, wrapping them the other way. Why did she always have to act like a pretzel? "That white Lexus of his sure is fancy," she said.

"Is it? I don't think I've ever seen it." I paused in my scratching and Gracie whined for me to keep going.

"Oh, you'd know it if you had. Hard not to miss it. And that classy vanity plate, too. Roman numerals." She unwound her legs. "Let's go, Gracie. We need to get back before it's too dark."

I grabbed at her arm. "Roman numerals? Is that what you said?"

She didn't exactly shake my hand off, but she did step back a pace. "Yes. Roman numerals."

"Do you remember what number it was?"

She screwed her lips up in one of those how-dumb-do-you-think-I-am looks. "Of course I do. M-L-X-V-I. One thousand sixty-six. Anybody would remember it."

The Old Woods on the other side of our block. The car nestled in among the dark trees. That white car with that particular license plate. He'd probably just started covering the body in the hole he'd dug by the creek, and he'd seen me looking at his car. Me running down the street to the dock, hearing footsteps bouncing off the walls of the stores once I crossed the street. Only they were footsteps running behind me, but I hadn't known that.

"Are you sure you don't know where they're going?" My tone obviously startled her, and Gracie looked up at me, apparently surprised as well. "This is important, Maddy! Where are they?" I brushed my hair back impatiently and caught a whiff—it was from my hand—the aftershave I'd smelled just as I was pushed into the water. I bent and sniffed Gracie's head. Not strong, but definitely that musky scent. "Where'd they go?" I yelled.

"I don't... I don't ..." she was spluttering. I shook her arm. "Thai. They were going to that new Thai place. Why? What's going on?"

But she was asking my retreating back. I dashed into the house and phoned Sadie.

"Bob's up in the attic," she said.

"Tell him to call the station. I have to go." I hung up and dialed Reebok, wishing as the phone rang that I'd told Sadie how important it was.

When I got Reebok on the line I barked out the news to him. "I was right about that license plate," I added. "It was MLXVI."

"But, ma'am," he argued, "you said it was MLX-ten-sixty-six."

Oh for Criminey sakes, of all the stupid—I had no time to explain Roman numerals to him. "Just trust me. And tell Bob. He should be calling you any minute. I'm headed after Glaze."

He told me not to go. I'm sure that's what he was

saying when I hung up on him.

I grabbed my keys and ran to the Buick, not even bothering to look around me. Adrenaline. Anger. No room for fear. I wasn't going to let him hurt my sister. Maddy jumped in, Gracie along with her. She pushed Gracie beneath her feet and buckled her seatbelt as I peeled away from the curb, managed a quick three-point turn, and pelted down Beechnut.

"Where are we going? What's going on?"

It's hard to explain something that complicated and drive at the same time. I'd managed a fairly coherent story by the time we reached Braetonburg. As I slowed through the business district, Maddy urged me on. "Hurry! There's no telling what he'll do to her."

Gracie barked and tried to climb up on the seat. Maddy unclipped the leash and pushed her back down. "Hurry," she said again.

~~~~~

~REEBOK GARNER~

Georgia plate MLXVI, Reebok soon learned, was registered to a Horace Butler III.

Why did that name sound familiar? Reebok twiddled his thumbs for a moment. Horace. Unusual name for sure. The name that was engraved on the back of the pocket watch, given to Charles Zapota by his grandfather. Mrs. Zapota had said she'd checked with all her family, including Charles' cousin, Horace. She'd asked them all if they'd seen Charles, and they'd all said no. Someone named Horace—Horace the Third—had that license plate. Glaze was out to dinner with Horace. Glaze was in that car. Glaze? Reebok knew he was missing something here. He thought back to the last time he'd seen her, walking with that dog of hers. Glaze's dog. Something about her dog. Reebok had seen a dog that looked sort of like Glaze's dog that evening he'd driven out through Happy Acres. That cute little Chihuahua had bounced out in front of his car, followed by a brown dog that looked a lot like Glaze's dog. But what was it that he was supposed to remember?

Reebok sat forward at his desk and visualized that drive. He'd stopped quickly, waved at the dog owner who had shouted an apology. Then he'd taken a right turn into that cul-de-sac and, just before he pulled out of it, another car, a white car, had passed in front of him. About two houses farther on the white car had stopped to pick up a man standing on the curb. That was it! A car with a vanity plate. Nothing but letters. No numbers.

That car had stopped in front of Mrs. Zapota's house. Reebok hadn't known at the time that she lived there. But since he'd visited it, he was sure. He'd seen Red—Horace—with license plate MLXVI—pick up Charles the evening Charles was murdered.

The phone rang. "Chief?" Reebok said. "We have a problem here."

~~~~~

~BISCUIT McKEE~

I rounded a steep curve halfway between Hastings and Garner Creek.

"There they are," Maddy yelled and pointed up ahead where the road curved back to the right, following a bend in the river. All I saw was headlights preceding a white blur. "That's the car. I'm sure of it. I'd know that Lexus anywhere."

It looked like any other white car to me. I wish I'd had

the guts to skew my beautiful old Buick across the road and stop him in his tracks, but that would have put Maddy in the direct line of impact. It would have involved Glaze in a head-on collision. And it probably would have totaled my car. How could I think of my car when my sister was in danger? In the split second it took me to have all these thoughts, they zoomed past and disappeared around the bend.

"They're getting away! He's out of sight now. Hurry!"

Gracie added her comments from the floor.

I stomped on the brakes and did a highly illegal and exceedingly dangerous three-point turn. "Madeleine Ames, you're not helping me here. Quit yelling at me."

"I'm not yelling," she yelled. Gracie barked again. "Down," she yelled at the dog.

The road twisted so much, we kept losing sight of them. Just a whisper of headlights and occasional brake lights. A mile or so this side of Hastings, he disappeared. We went around a bend, and he was nowhere in sight, even though the road was blessedly straight for a long stretch there.

"Where'd he go?" Maddy threw up her hands, splay-fingered. "He wasn't that far ahead of us."

I slowed and—where had all this traffic come from?—waited for three cars to pass. Once the road was clear, I did another three-point turn and crept back toward Garner Creek. "Keep a look out," I told Maddy.

"You don't have to yell." She rolled her window all the way down and hung her head out so far I thought she'd be decapitated by the guardrail.

"They can't be on that side," I told her. "The river's on that side."

Gracie barked.

Maddy leaned close to me, peering over the steering wheel.

Trees towered over the road, in some places almost

joining branches with ones on the other side. Ordinarily I would have appreciated their graceful arches, but right now they were an impediment. Where was that car?

We got back to where we'd lost them the first time. Yet another turn-around, and back the way we'd just come. Maddy's head was out the window again.

"There!"

I braked hard, and a horn blared behind me. Someone zoomed into the left lane and passed me, honking repeatedly, one of those little pathetic-sounding honks, hardly loud enough for anybody to hear it. I backed up, praying I wouldn't be rear-ended by another car in a hurry. It was stupid to put a road this close to a curve with no warning signs.

The dirt lane Red had disappeared down wasn't by any means a proper road. It dipped abruptly, and my poor old Buick scraped her bottom repeatedly as we bounced along through gullies and between heavy brush. The only indication that Red's car had been here before us was a veil of dust hovering above the road and glimmering in my headlights.

"Turn off your lights! He'll see us coming!"

"Quit yelling at me. I want him to know we're coming."

"What if he kills her faster?"

I turned off the lights and crept along in the fitful moonlight.

When we saw headlights through the trees way up ahead and a little to our left, I turned off the dome light switch—see? I could think straight in a crisis. "Stay," Maddy told Gracie in a whisper.

Gracie whimpered. "Shh," we both said at the same time.

I eased the tire iron from underneath Gracie's legs

and opened my door quietly. I needn't have worried. Red's car was still running, and its engine sounded like it had a stutter—probably the only reason he hadn't heard my Buick. We crept forward and ducked behind the trunk of a big old tulip poplar tree.

"If you'd kept your mouth shut about the plate, I might never have known." Red sounded almost conversational. "But you also made the mistake of telling me about your sister. There's no way I'm going to let her get hypnotized."

Hypnotized? What was he talking about? His left hand pinned her by the throat to a giant tree. She kicked and thrashed, but his arm was far longer than hers. She tried to yell, but all that came out was a pathetic whimper. She tried to pull his hand away from her throat. He was slowly choking her, the bastard. "Nobody can hear you this far back from the road," he said, and pulled something from his pocket. He waved it in front of her face, and a wicked-looking blade sprang out. I'd seen switchblades in old movies, but never in real life.

"You can't horn in on my business," he said. "You with your 'better deal coming up.' You thought you could take over part of my territory. Or were you looking to stop me altogether? Not a chance. I'm going to kill you just like I did that other meddling female. And then I'm going to go find that nosy sister of yours."

Glaze had stopped kicking and made a strangled sound, like a cough gone awry. "You leave her alone." I could barely hear her, although her face showed the effort she was making. "She doesn't know anything."

"Ah, maybe she doesn't, but I'm not willing to take that risk. I have too much to lose."

"Yeah? Like what?" At least he'd eased up on her throat, but he hadn't withdrawn the knife. His headlights made it easy for me to see her blackened eye and the glinting reflection from the blade.

"I killed my cousin right here," he said. "I would have buried her here, too, but a car drove in looking for a place to picnic. Luckily I heard them coming and dumped her in the trunk. Stupid people."

"Where *did* you bury her?" Glaze sounded interested. I could tell she was talking only to keep him occupied, but I wanted to hear his answer.

He laughed, and for a moment he sounded so jolly, I almost smiled myself. "Nobody ever knew," he said. "That Catholic Church in Martinsville was putting in a garden. I'd seen it that afternoon, the priest getting all hot and sweaty trying to dig pretty deep. I just took Kate by there about three in the morning and buried her right in the vegetable patch." He laughed again. "The priest had left all his tools and a whole bunch of plants. I thought it was the least I could do, since he'd given me a burying ground, to plant his tomatoes for him."

"And no one ever guessed?"

"Never. And it was easy. I only had to dig down another foot or so. She didn't take up much room lying there all stretched out." He laughed out loud. "Some old geezer came out of the church just as I was finishing up. I thought I might have to take care of him, too, but he congratulated me on the fine job I was doing. Blessed me for being so kind to Father what's-his-name. So I decided to let him live. Anyway, I didn't feel like digging any more. Katie was enough for one night."

He waved the knife around in a circle. "Our parents brought us here on outings. We three cousins used to play in this clearing while they set up the picnic table." With a faint air of surprise, he looked around the bare clearing. Maddy pulled her head back out of sight, cracking my nose in the process. "I wonder what ever happened to that picnic table?" Red's voice was loud enough to cover my faint grunt of pain.

Glaze shifted her weight, and Red brought the knife back, closer to her throat. "Once Kate grew up, she wasn't fun anymore. She tried to come between me and Hank. Tried to stop the good deal we had going. It was bobble-head statues that time. Or was that when we were shipping the goods in those music boxes?" He shook his head. "My cousin. You'd think blood would be thicker than water, but she wouldn't listen."

I tensed my muscles, ready to charge, but Maddy laid a restraining hand on my arm. "He's got his knife against her throat," she whispered, no louder than a soft breath. "We don't dare startle him."

"And then, less than a year later, my one and only other cousin gets a job at the same place. And he finds out why those flower pots had to be bigger. Good old Charles. Or should I say Chad? That's what his friends called him. Not that I was a—" Glaze gasped, and he loosened his hold a bit. "What?"

"Chad?" Glaze moved her left hand slowly behind her. "You mean Melissa's fiancé?"

"Oh yes, her fiancé." He made the word sound like sewer sludge. "Did you like that ring he gave her? I sold it to him at a very good price, half down on delivery, in cash, of course, and the other half—poor boy—the day he died. Poor and stupid, too. He actually thought the stones were real."

Glaze raised her left foot slowly up behind her as he spoke. I could see what she was planning. The full skirt of her dress hid her movement. Those killer shoes of hers had three-inch spike heels. One would make a pretty good weapon, but there was no way she could get it off in time to hit him with it. He'd slice her throat first. Maddy must have had the same thought. She gripped my arm so hard I almost hit her.

"Yes," Red was still bragging, "he found the first stash,

saw us loading up those flower pots he'd designed—"

Glaze yelped. "You mean Zip?"

"Zip? I haven't heard that nickname since he was a little tyke. Zip Zapota. He used to run circles around all of us on the playground."

"You killed him?"

"Of course I did. He wanted to stop me; then he said he'd changed his mind, wanted in on the deal. I invited him out for a drive last Wednesday so we could talk in private. Told him I'd take him to meet our supplier, down in Atlanta. He was just trying to get more details before he turned me in. He didn't have a crooked bone in his body, the dumb schnook."

"And you dumped the body in back of my sister's house."

"Her house? Really? Didn't know that. I knew the body would decompose faster near the water. That creek's a nice hidden place. I thought about burying him in the church garden so he could have rested in peace with our cousin Katie." He waved the knife back in the general direction of Martinsville.

An unexpected breeze stirred the leaves above Glaze's head and blew her hair forward into her eyes. I know it was my imagination, but I thought I could smell fear on that breeze as it blew past my face and back down the lane behind me. Fear and my sister's vanilla perfume. I'd been straining to hear the conversation, but now Red's words seemed to carry to us easily. Or maybe he was just talking louder.

"Shall I kill you here by the tree? Or," he pointed the knife toward the far side of the clearing, "over there?"

"You mean I get a choice?" The shoe was in her hand. "Thanks a lot."

"Speaking of thanks, you forgot to thank me for dinner tonight. I don't like that sort of inconsiderate behavior."

Gracie bounded past me and hit Red full tilt at the same time Glaze lashed out at him with the shoe. He swore as he tried to keep his balance. The knife flashed in the headlights. Glaze screamed. As I ran toward Red, I saw a spray of blood arc across my sister's face. She collapsed and Red struggled to get Gracie loose from his arm. The knife slashed out again, and Gracie fell, whimpering.

Maddy and I were there before we even thought about it.

The crunch a tire iron makes when it hits a head is something I wouldn't ever forget.

DAY TEN
SATURDAY

CHAPTER 22
8:45 a.m.

~BISCUIT McKEE~

"We're going to have to engrave the McKee name on this particular bed," Dr. Prescott told me. "You and your sister seem to be making a habit of visiting us in dire circumstances. And," she waved her stethoscope like a laser pointer at the crowd surrounding the bed, "we'll need to enlarge the room as well." The word had spread as we'd sat through the night waiting for Glaze to get out of surgery. I'd called my mom and dad. Bob had called Tom and Nathan. Maddy called Dee and left a message. She'd gone to Atlanta with Rebecca Jo to visit the museums and apparently hadn't returned yet.

"Dr. Prescott," I said. "The man who attacked her, is he here as well?" He'd been transported in a second ambulance, right after they took Glaze out. He was guarded by two of the Hastings police officers who had reached us not three minutes before Bob got there.

Dr. Prescott shoved her hands in her pockets. "He's already been transferred to Emory. The helicopter came while I was stitching up Ms. Glaze here." What might have been the beginning of a smile touched her lips. "I'm told he was handcuffed to the stretcher."

"Will he live?" I didn't want him to. I wanted this valley to be rid of him forever. But the crunch of that tire iron and its vibration through my arm gave me waking nightmares. Who knew what would happen when I finally got a chance to go to sleep? At least I hadn't killed him, although I'd surprised myself with the surge of murderous intent that had fueled my swing.

"He'll live, most likely. He's definitely lost that eye." She pushed her thick glasses more firmly into place and looked at Glaze. "You've got amazing aim, my dear. The real question, though," and she turned back to me, "is whether he'll ever be able to feed or wipe himself. I rather doubt it from what I hear. That amount of brain injury is usually irreversible."

Bob's arm tightened around my waist, and I saw Tom increase his grip on Glaze. She looked up at him and gripped right back.

"What I want to know is whether Glaze will be all right?" Maddy hovered at Glaze's feet, rubbing the left one obsessively. The right foot was encased in plaster, the result of her sideways fall off one three-inch stiletto heel, trying to clobber Red with her shoe and at the same time avoid his knife.

I would bless Madeleine Ames forever. She had run all the way to the main road to flag down help while I was trying to stop the bleeding on my sister's face. The paisley scarf Glaze wore had come in handy. I knew I was supposed to use a sterile bandage—I took a Red Cross First Aid course—but sometimes you just have to improvise.

"Don't worry, Ms. Ames," Dr. Prescott said. "Glaze is made of tough stuff. As long as we can keep the incision from getting infected, she should be fine."

Red had fallen with one of his arms across Glaze's leg. When I'd shoved it away, my fingers had caught on one of those oddly familiar buttons. In the panic of the moment, I'd not paid much attention to it. Caring for Glaze had taken up all my attention. Now, though, now that she was safe, I knew why those small shiny disks on his blazers had looked familiar. I gasped. Pumpkin's turkey bone earrings. Kate's skeletal hand, the bones sliced into button-sized pieces. My God, what kind of monster was he?

Dr. Prescott tilted her head to one side and assessed my stricken look.

"Don't look so worried," she said. "I'm pretty good at

what I do. I got an A in sewing at medical school."

I couldn't tell her the real reason I was so upset. I'd tell Bob later when we were alone. The buttons, the bones, would need to be collected from all of Red's clothes and given to Kate's mother.

Dr. Prescott turned back to Glaze. "You're going to have quite a scar. We can talk about reconstructive surgery later. It's not my specialty, though. You'll have to go to Atlanta for it."

Indistinct mumbles came from the general direction of the honorary McKee hospital bed. "Gracie," Glaze said, although it sounded more like *Gay-zee*. "Is she okay?"

Dr. Prescott smiled. "She's doing great. This isn't a veterinary clinic, but the ambulance driver brought her along anyway after your sister told him what a brave dog she was. She needed a few stitches."

Glaze's eyes widened.

"Red tried to kill Gracie," I explained, "but all he did was rip open a large flap of skin." Her eyes widened. "If your dog hadn't attacked Red, he would have... he wouldn't have missed... you'd be ..."

Glaze raised a hand, the hand that wasn't linked to Tom, to her throat. "She's not..." she paused as if she were reconsidering. "She's such a good dog," she said.

"You're in pretty good shape for somebody with a bruised throat, two black eyes, a broken ankle, and twenty-three stitches down the side of her face," Dr. Prescott said.

Just beyond her shoulder, I could see the expression on my mother's face. I was glad Red wasn't still in the building. Mom looked positively homicidal.

The nurse who had been caring for Glaze stuck her head in the door. "Need another visitor?"

Gracie's toenails clicked against the floor as she limped toward the bed, growling in her unique, friendly dog monologue.

Glaze sighed in deep contentment. It must be hard to smile with half your face stitched up, I thought.

Tom stepped around the bed and lifted Gracie carefully, avoiding the shaved, bandaged area on her side. He placed her carefully across Glaze's upper legs, garnering a quick dog lick on his chin. A shiver of what looked like sheer joy passed over Gracie's whole body, and she nuzzled my sister's hand. Maddy reached out to stroke Gracie's back.

"Gracie can go home," Dr. Prescott said, "as long as she has somebody there to take care of her." Maddy nodded enthusiastically and raised her hand like a schoolgirl volunteering to answer a math question. Dr. Prescott ignored her and kept her eyes on Glaze. "I'm going to have you stick around here for a few days until we can be sure you're okay." She grinned. "I know you're looking forward to our soup through a straw."

Bob snickered and Glaze groaned.

"I'd... rather have... Tom's... fried chicken," Glaze said, and even though she could hardly move the left side of her face, the words were pretty understandable. So was the look she gave Tom. The two of them might have been the only ones in the room right then.

I reached out and brushed the silver strands off her forehead, trying to avoid the worst of the dark purple bruises Red had inflicted when she tried to get away from him. "You scared me, Sis," I said. "Again," I added, although I regretted that word as soon as I saw the shadow that passed across her swollen face. "Do you have any idea how frightened I was?"

She closed her eyes. "That," she said and paused a long time, as if she were trying to decide whether or not to speak aloud what she was thinking, "is un... undoubtedly... one of the dumb ..." and her words got more distinguishable the longer she spoke, "the dumbest things you've ever asked me."

I was saved from replying when Rebecca Jo hurried in, followed by Dee, who flung herself at the hospital bed, managing at the last moment to avoid slamming into Gracie. "Don't you ever scare me like that again, you hear me?"

"I told her the very same thing," I said, "and she grumped at me."

Glaze looked at me, shook her head, and started to giggle. When the giggle threatened to break forth into a belly laugh, she winced, pulled her hand away from Dee, and took a deep breath to calm herself.

"All right," I said. "I give up. What's so funny?"

"We should have figured it out right away."

I glanced over at Maddy, who splayed her fingers in the universal *I dunno* gesture. Dee shook her head. So did Mom, Dad, Nathan, Rebecca Jo, and Dr. Prescott, like a wave at a football game. Tom looked baffled. Bob just shrugged.

"It should have been obvious," Glaze said, the bandages muffling her words. "The Butler did it."

The End
Not quite

My Gratitude List

When the Atlanta area was inundated with flood waters in September of 2009, one particular car was swept off the road into a raging river. The Swift Water Rescue Team rescued the driver in slightly less than an hour, but by that time her core body temperature had dropped drastically. Although **Diana Farmer** was never in quite as bad a shape as Biscuit, Diana's experience and what I learned as I interviewed her caused a complete rewrite of the first scene. I'd started out having Biscuit stuck in the water all night long, not realizing she had to get out of the water in order to survive. Hence, the tree. Thank you, Diana, for keeping me from making a very big mistake.

Biscuit is afraid of chickens for a reason. I had a hair-raising experience with chickens when I was a child. If you'd like to read about it, you can check out my blog. It's on Day #288 – July 27, 2011. I finally decided to do something about that fear, and I visited **Julie Porath** at **Wholesome Country Farm** in Sugar Hill, Georgia, where she and her husband grow the best veggies and raise some of the nicest chickens I've ever met. Okay, so they're the **only** nice chickens I've ever met. Biscuit's still afraid of Vampirah, but thanks to Julie, I'm not.

A big thank you to my pre-readers, **Diana Alishouse** and **Millie Woollen.** They are so darned good at catching errors! And they tell me when they want more depth to a scene. Besides being my sister, **Diana Alishouse** is also the extraordinary artist who took my rather wordy directions and drew the two intelligible maps that grace the beginning pages of *Violet.* She serves, as well, as my main reference in the books where Glaze's depression acts up. Her book *Depression Visible: the Ragged Edge* helped me understand bipolar disorder, because it shows what depression feels like. If you or any of your friends, family, or colleagues seem to act like Glaze in *Blue as Blue Jeans* or in *Indigo as an Iris*, be sure to find a copy of Diana's book (www.DepressionVisible.com).

Some years ago, **Dr. Harry Gentry** in Suwanee, Georgia, repaired a tooth of mine I had broken eating popcorn. More recently, he helped me get the dentist part right in this book, so the medical examiner could identify the body. Dr. G. gave me the wording of the report about the popcorn-broken tooth. Have I given up popcorn yet? Well, no, but I'm more careful when I bite down on those kernels.

Clyde Woollen served as my boat advisor, so the Susie Q would be ship-shape.

Award-winning artist and photographer **Mikki Root Dillon** let me sit in her art studio and absorb the ambiance. She also let me count her brushes and tubes of paint. Just call me Reebok! I met Mikki when I joined the **Atlanta Branch** of the **National League of American Pen Women**, an organization of professional writers, artists, and musicians. The NLAPW was birthed in 1897, when a group of journalists were not allowed to join the National Press Club in Washington, D.C., because they were <gasp> females.

My father taught me to change a tire when I first learned how to drive, but I wasn't sure about which way a blown tire would cause the car to veer, so I asked **Dan Barber,** my trusty mechanic at **AutoStop** in Sugar Hill GA.

I must mention, too, an **anonymous man** attending the annual conference of the Georgia Council of Teachers of English in 2005. During my speech to the GCTE, I mentioned that I had titles for all my planned books in this series except for Violet. He called out from the back of the room, "How about *Violet as Varicose Veins*?" I, like Pumpkin, didn't think that title would sell, but it was too good not to use somewhere – hence, Glaze's mention of a tattoo and Sadie's response.

My editor, **Nanette Littlestone**, who has nurtured my vision ever since she edited *Yellow as Legal Pads,* took a rather shaky *Violet* and challenged me to explore what I was afraid to face. I'm glad she did.

A big thank-you to the wonderful folks at **Journey of a Dream Press** for helping Biscuit and Marmalade reach the world.

Finally, I truly appreciate all the emails (and even some handwritten notes!) I've received from readers over the past years. I'm delighted that Biscuit and her friends touch your hearts in a special way, and am gratified indeed that you take the time to tell me so.

Gracie

When I went looking for the perfect dog to adopt Glaze, I contacted the Walton Animal Guild in Loganville, Georgia, at the recommendation of a woman I met at the Lawrenceville Farmer's Market.

W.A.G. ran a fund-raising event where everyone who donated $10 was entered in a drawing. The winner got to have their dog in my next mystery. W.A.G. received donations from people who never would have heard of them otherwise, and I found the ideal dog for Glaze.

Interestingly enough, the winner, Carol Baum, volunteers occasionally at W.A.G., where dogs are rescued from the county pound and are placed in foster homes awaiting adoption.

Gracie showed up one day in 2008 outside a drugstore, where she sat and greeted everyone passing through the doors. When Carol and Ted Baum saw her, they knew there was something special about her. They took her to the animal shelter, to give her owners (whoever they might be) a chance to claim her, but when nobody came for her after a few days, Carol and Ted went right back to offer her a forever home.

Gracie was in pretty bad shape, but lots of good love (and veterinary care) brought her back to glowing good health. She fills their home with bouncy joy, and has great fun collecting stray socks.

Fran Stewart

Fran Stewart lives quietly and happily beside a creek on the back side of Hog Mountain, Georgia, where she shares her home with various rescued cats. She is a member of Sisters in Crime, the Atlanta Writers Club, and the National League of American Pen Women. She sings, works as a freelance editor specializing in doctoral dissertations, knits, plays the piano, volunteers at her grandchildren's school libraries, and manages quite well without a TV set.

Author's Note:

I feel it is part of my responsibility as a writer to give more than just a good story, so all of my books deal with specific social issues such as depression, ecological responsibility, and ethical treatment of animals. Some of my books focus on specific issues, such as suicide prevention (Green as a Garden Hose) or sexual abuse (Blue as Blue Jeans).

I include this resource list so you can find information or help for yourself or for your family, friends, or colleagues.

Resource List for the Biscuit McKee Mysteries

Depression
Depression and Bipolar Support Alliance
www.dbsalliance.org
1-800-826-3632
National Institutes of Mental Health (for a depression self-check list)
www.nimh.nih.gov
1-866-615-6464

Green Cemeteries
I highly recommend the book *Grave Matters: A Journey through the modern funeral industry to a natural way of burial* by Mark Harris ©2007
www.gravematters.us
www.memorialecosystems.com

Ecological Responsibility:
Mother Earth News
(the only magazine to which Fran subscribes)
www.motherearthnews.com
The Nature Conservancy
www.nature.org

Suicide Prevention
1-800-SUICIDE (1-800-784-2433) or
1-800-273-TALK (1-800-273-8255)
www.suicide.org
This website provides links to other suicide prevention sites.

> **Suicide is never the answer.**
> **Getting help is the answer.**

Childhood Sexual Abuse Prevention
Rape Abuse & Incest National Network (RAINN) is both a hotline and a referral service to direct you to an approved local resource.
1-800-656-HOPE (1-800-656-4673)
www.RAINN.org

Prevent Child Abuse America
1-800-CHILDREN (1-800-244-5373)
www.preventchildabuse.org

Animal Communication and Ethical Treatment of Animals
There are many fine organizations out there. These are two I regularly support through contributions. I donate a portion of all my book sales to these two organizations, as well as to libraries and local animal shelters wherever I sign books.
The Gorilla Foundation
www.koko.org
The Humane Society of the United States
www.hsus.org

American Red Cross Blood Donation
1-800-GIVELIFE (1-800-448-3543)
Please donate blood as often as possible.

Thank you for reading *Violet as an Amethyst* by renowned author, Fran Stewart. Journey of a Dream Press invites you to visit our website to see additional books by Fran as well as these other best-selling authors.

www.JourneyofaDream.com

Javier J. Farias
Spiritual Symbolism in the Wizard of Oz

Natala Orobello
Forbidden
Destined for Greatness

Diana Alishouse
Depression Visible: The Ragged Edge

Vada Carter
An Outside View

Marva Rogers Thomas and Lynnette Thomas Carodine
Growing Young: One Woman's Search for Health,
Inner Peace and Longevity

Made in the USA
Lexington, KY
08 December 2016